EXPECTANT AMISH WIDOWS
3 BOOKS-IN-1 (VOLUME 5)

AMISH WIDOW'S NEW HOPE: AMISH WIDOW'S STORY: AMISH WIDOW'S DECISION

SAMANTHA PRICE

D1712961

AMISH WIDOW'S NEW HOPE

EXPECTANT AMISH WIDOWS BOOK 13

CHAPTER 1

Judge not, and ye shall not be judged:
condemn not, and ye shall not be condemned:
forgive, and ye shall be forgiven:
Luke 6:37

ISLA ZOOK SAT down in the house of Mr. and Mrs. Miller. Instead of this day being her wedding to their youngest son, Benjamin, she was attending his funeral.

She'd agreed with Benjamin that returning to the Amish would be the best start to their married lives and the only way they wanted to raise their children, but Isla had one stipulation—that they have a "white wedding" first. The wedding she planned had cost them a small fortune. If she'd had an *Englisch* wedding, she told herself, she could go back to the Amish community without missing the *Englisch* lifestyle that she and Benjamin had lived the last eight years.

Out of guilt, Isla could barely look at Benjamin's parents. They knew it was she who wanted to marry before their return, and that meant Benjamin would've sold his motorbike earlier and he wouldn't have gone on that one last ride where he'd collided into a truck.

It was the delay in returning to the Amish that had killed Benjamin as much as the fatal accident. It was vanity and pride that had taken over her mind—wanting to dress up, be beautiful and be the center of attention on her one special day. Now she could only wonder whether God was punishing her.

The cold reality was that Benjamin lay dead in the closed casket before his baptism into the faith. Every time she glanced in his mother's direction she saw a downturned mouth and a mournful face, and Isla couldn't blame his mother for looking so distraught.

Isla sat quietly, with her parents to her right and two of her sisters on her left, while Benjamin's mother cried softly into a handkerchief. As more people came to her to pay their respects, Isla could barely speak to anyone. She couldn't stay any longer in the same room with Benjamin's body. Once full of life, it was now trapped within the confines of the coffin—his body not fit for the usual viewing that was favored in the Amish family home before burial.

Needing fresh air, Isla headed outside at a fast pace—too fast for well-wishers and fellow-mourners to stop her with their kind words from sympathetic lips.

With her head hung low, Isla headed to the first row of buggies. She was aware of someone running behind her, but her stomach was suddenly too nauseated for her to even look up.

"Are you okay?" It was the voice of one of her older sisters, Liz.

Isla's body convulsed and she was sick, hanging onto the rear wheel of a buggy. With all her energy gone, she slid onto the ground. Her sister crouched down beside her, stuffing a hand-kerchief into her hand.

"It's all my fault. We should've come back to the community months ago and then he'd still be here today."

"You can't say that for certain."

"If I hadn't been so selfish things would be different right now," Isla insisted, as she glanced over at Benjamin's parents' house. "I hate funerals."

"No one likes them."

"They know it's my fault."

"Who knows what?"

"Benjamin's family—well, at least his mother. They know it was me who delayed our coming back to the community."

"Benjamin had his choice; he could've come back at any time. You've both been gone for what was it? Eight years?"

Isla nodded, remembering how they'd left at eighteen as friends. It was only two years ago that the friendship had become a romantic relationship.

Liz and Isla looked around when they heard a buggy. It was Mr. Fuller, Isla realized, and next to him it looked like James Miller, one of Benjamin's older brothers.

"I didn't know he was coming back," Liz said, squinting at the buggy. "I think it's James." She stood up and looked down at Isla. "We should go back inside before they come looking for us."

"I can't do it." Isla dabbed at her mouth with the handkerchief and then her sister grabbed her by the arm and pulled her to her feet.

"Steady," said Liz.

"I'm not feeling well."

"Move over a little." Liz nudged Isla to one side and with her boot pushed dirt to cover the patch of sick.

While Isla was absentmindedly watching what Liz was doing, she became aware of someone walking over. It was James.

Without saying hello to the two of them he launched into a conversation. "I'm glad I've arrived, finally. The Greyhound was delayed several times and I didn't think I would get here before nightfall. Then I had a child behind me crying all the way." He frowned and shook his head. "It was dreadful."

Isla was strangely comforted by his talk of something other than how and why Benjamin had died. She hadn't seen James for years and it was nice to see someone who looked so similar to Benjamin. They were the only two Miller brothers who had inherited their father's dark coloring; their other four brothers had all taken after their mother's fair features.

"Listen to me complaining." He shook his head and looked at Isla. "I'm sorry for your loss, Isla."

Isla held the handkerchief tightly in her hand and looked down at the ground and nodded, too weak to say a word.

"Denke," Liz said for her. "Isla's not feeling well. She's glad you came such a long distance. It's good to see you again. We're sorry for your loss, too, James."

He nodded in appreciation, his eyes returning to Isla.

"Jah. I'm glad you could come," Isla said quietly.

"Would you be staying on here for awhile?" Liz asked.

"Maybe a week or two. I'll see how things go. I'm certainly not going to turn around and go back tomorrow. I have to recover from that nightmare of a coach ride." He gave Liz a wry little smile.

Isla vaguely remembered that Benjamin said James had gone north to start a community somewhere close to Canada.

"I have something to give you later today, Isla. Now, I should go and find my parents and let them know I'm here." He strode toward the house.

Isla studied the way he carried himself and the way he walked. "He looks so much like Benjamin," Isla said softly.

"They said he'd never be back," Liz said. "It's such a long trip."

"No one ever expected something like this to happen—for Benjamin to die so young."

Hundreds of people had come to the funeral, and they filled the Miller household to overflowing. Many were outside the house; even though it was large, it was too small for such a crowd.

"We should go back in, Isla."

"I can't." She held on to the end of a buggy. "You go back in."

Liz took her by the arm and started walking and Isla had no choice but to move with her.

When they neared the doorway of the house, they could go no further as people were filing outside. Isla took four steps backward knowing that Benjamin's mother and father would be next out the door. She wanted to do everything she could to avoid them.

Four men were now carrying the casket out of the house. Isla watched as the casket was placed in the back of the long buggy that had been made years ago for funerals. Everyone headed to their buggies in readiness to follow the funeral buggy in a long single-file procession to the graveyard.

Isla wanted this day to pass quickly. Each and every moment was a reminder of her decision that had delayed their return to the community.

Soon, Liz and Anna, who were her two local sisters, her three eldest sisters, who lived in their husbands' communities, all of their families, and her mother and father surrounded her.

"Are you okay, Aunt Isla?" the oldest of her nieces, seven-year-old Milly, said as she reached her arms around Isla's waist.

"I'm better with you close by, Milly."

Milly looked up at her, her face beaming. "I'll stay with you."

"Good."

Isla traveled in her parents' buggy along with Milly, who kept hold of her hand. Isla's four older sisters and her younger sister were all married and all had young children, so each family rode in its own buggy.

The next hour was a blur.

Isla stayed behind the crowd that gathered by the open grave. The bishop said a few words about life, death and the purpose of life.

The dreadful thing was that Benjamin was being buried before he'd been baptized into the Amish faith, which meant he wouldn't receive his full reward in heaven. Isla had to carry that guilt. She knew she'd feel even worse when she was baptized at the next Sunday meeting, without Benjamin.

Milly hung onto her hand the entire time, until her mother, Liz, called her away to travel back to the Miller's house with her own family. Liz and her husband, Peter, also had a five-year-old daughter.

Isla was walking back to the family buggy when her mother caught up with her. *"Mamm,* do we have to go back to the Millers'?"

"You know we do."

"Can't you take me home first?"

"Why? Aren't you well?" her mother asked.

"Nee."

Her mother narrowed her eyes. "You look okay. Can't you force yourself to go?"

"I could if I have to."

"Then you should."

Isla looked over and saw everyone was moving back to their buggies. It was a tradition to go back to the house of the family of the deceased and have something to eat.

When they pulled up at the Millers' *haus,* Isla told her mother and father she'd catch up with them in a minute. She just needed a moment to compose herself. Isla knew she was not going back into the Miller house today. When everyone else was in the house, Isla jumped down from the buggy and walked up and down in the fresh air, careful not to be seen. The last thing she wanted was for some busybody to persuade her to come inside.

She walked along the back of the row of buggies, shuffling her feet as she walked. The day was gray and cloudy, matching her gloomy mood. When she turned around to head back, James was striding toward her. He'd seen her.

"I said I had something to give you, and here it is." He handed Isla an envelope.

CHAPTER 2

Forbearing one another, and forgiving one another, if any man have a quarrel against any: even as Christ forgave you, so also do ye.
Colossians 3:13

ISLA'S FOREHEAD wrinkled as she wondered what it could be. She opened it to see an official document. Looking up at him in surprise, she asked, "What's this?"

"This is the deed to that *haus*. Benjamin's *haus*." He pointed to the small blue house to the left of him. "Benjamin would've wanted you to have it."

It was the house that they'd been going to live in on their return.

She handed the paper and envelope back to him. "We didn't get married."

"He left things for me to sort out. He'd arranged that many years ago. Today was to be your wedding day and you would've been married."

Isla nodded, needing no reminding of what day this was. It was a knife through her heart that the funeral was the same day as the *Englisch* wedding was to have been held. "You have it," she said thrusting the paper back at him.

"No." He held her hand gently and with his other hand, he closed her fingers around it. "It's yours. He would've wanted you to have it."

"Denke." She didn't want to make a fuss at the funeral. "I've come back now to the community. The bishop is baptizing me next week."

He smiled broadly. "I'm glad to hear it."

"I know some will say it's a little late."

"Don't let that worry you. Many people told me not to try to start a community. They said I'd fail. Now we've got ten families plus a few single men, and it's growing."

"That's good, and are you the bishop?"

He smiled. "No. The bishop is a man called Whylie Hesh."

"Oh. I don't know him."

"You wouldn't. He's never lived 'round these parts."

"What do you do there?" She imagined it would be a difficult life so far away from anyone he knew, and starting the community must've been hard.

"I have a farm I share with a few others."

Isla nodded remembering that she'd heard that sharing farms was something that many were doing. "It's a good idea," she said.

"And what about you? I'm sorry, I should know. But I didn't hear from Benjamin much. Probably only twice since he left."

"We were only together in the last two years, but we were always good friends before that." She grimaced wondering why she was telling him things he hadn't asked. He hadn't asked her how long she'd dated his brother. "I had a job at a child care center."

"Ah, you like children?"

"I do. Doesn't everyone?"

He smiled.

"Do you have *kinner*?" Isla couldn't remember if he was married, but assumed he was, given his age.

"*Nee*." He leaned in and whispered, "Between you and me, I'm hoping to find a young lady who'll agree to marry me on this visit and I'll take her home."

Isla nodded. "A whirlwind relationship. Well, I hope you find someone."

"Jah. There aren't many women where I come from."

Isla looked down at the document in her hands. Now her future looked different from the one she'd imagined. If she said yes to the house, she wouldn't be living with her parents.

"Do you want to see it?"

She looked up at James. "What's that?"

"The *haus.*"

"Oh, yes."

"Are you staying at your parents' *haus* now?"

She nodded.

"How about I collect you mid-morning? You and your parents, and I'll show you together."

"That's nice of you."

He laughed and she felt a little embarrassed. She sighed. If only she could've said goodbye to her love without all these people around—people, most of whom she hadn't seen in many years.

As though reading her mind, he said, "You can stay by me if you want to come inside."

She smiled up at him and gave a nod. *"Denke."* It was odd to hear herself speaking in Pennsylvania Dutch when she hadn't spoken it in so long. Her old life was gone now and she had to face life back in the community without Benjamin.

When they walked a few steps, she said, "I don't think I can go in. No, I can't."

"That's okay. No one's forcing you."

"There are just too many people—so many faces. I know I should probably be helping with the food and everything, but I can't."

"No one expects that. Your *mudder* is helping."

"Is she?"

He nodded.

Now Isla would have to get a ride home with one of her sisters. Her mother would most likely stay behind and help with the clean-up as well. "You go inside."

"*Nee*. It's too nice a day to be inside."

Isla looked up at the gray clouds. "It must be strange weather where you come from."

"It can be. I feel as though I never should've moved away," James said.

"Why? Because of Benjamin?"

"*Jah*. He mightn't have left the community if I'd stuck around."

Isla sighed. "Life's going to be so different without him. We saw each other every day for the past eight years. He was my best friend." She rapidly blinked back more tears.

"He was my only younger *bruder*. We got along the best since the others were a lot older than both of us. Benjamin was the only one I was allowed to boss around." He shrugged. "Who am I going to boss now?"

Isla gave a little laugh. "I'm sorry. I shouldn't laugh. I know he was very fond of you."

"We were close, but then he didn't need me when he found you."

"I'm sorry."

"He grew up and found you. It's a special thing to find someone you want to share your life with. He was blessed. I've never found that." He sighed.

As he looked into the distance, Isla didn't know whether he was saying all these things to make her feel better, or whether he was truly self-centered and didn't know it. Or perhaps she was the selfish one, since he'd lost his brother? Still, it was nice of him to keep her company and talk about Benjamin.

"He died instantly. He didn't suffer. That's what they told me."

"Denke for telling me. I was wondering that but didn't like to ask. I'd heard it happened quickly."

"He loved his motorbike. The man he sold it to was coming to collect it the next day and Benjamin took it for one last ride. My last words to him were, 'Be careful.' His last words to me were, 'I will.'" Isla sighed and looked down at the paper in her hands. "I can't take this, James." She held it out to him.

"It's yours. You can't give back a gift; it's very impolite."

I don't deserve it, she wanted to tell him.

"Benjamin would've insisted you have it and I'm not going to hear another word about you not wanting it. Do you want a cup of coffee or tea?"

She glanced over toward the crowded house and shook her head.

"I'll bring it out here for you. I'm not one for crowds, either."

"Okay, *denke.* Can you bring me a glass of soda?"

"Coming right up."

When he was gone, she looked over at the blue house, remembering... She hadn't let Benjamin go near it in the past few years through fear someone might talk him into going back to the community before she was ready. He'd wanted to fix it up and make it fit for them to move into, but she'd insisted on doing it afterward so all their money could go toward the wedding. What had seemed like something joyful that she was going to remember for a lifetime was now something vile. Benjamin had always gone along with whatever she'd wanted. He'd said it didn't matter that much to him, but now she wished he'd insisted.

19

CHAPTER 3

But I say unto you which hear, Love your enemies,
do good to them which hate you,
Luke 6:27

"Denke, for bringing me back," Isla said to Liz as she climbed down from Liz's buggy outside her parents' house.

"I'll come in and stay awhile."

"*Nee,* you get back to Peter and the *kinner* and your guests." Isla didn't want to keep Liz away from them on account of her, and they were hosting their eldest sister and her family for the night. "I need some time alone anyway." Their other sisters and their families were staying with friends, and all of them were leaving in the early morning to return to their homes.

The small family home hadn't changed since she'd been a child. Six children had been raised within its walls. She'd shared her bedroom with her five sisters and she'd been the second youngest and the only one to leave the community. Now she was back home for good, and she had to get used to how humbly and simply not only her parents lived, but the whole community. She hadn't known the difference until she'd lived outside of the Amish world.

She walked into the once-crowded bedroom that now held only one bed, used by the occasional guest. Isla sat down on the bed as memories of her childhood years came flooding back. With so many sisters, chores were never drudgery. They were just things that were done when necessary, like brushing one's hair or tying one's shoelaces. There was always more than one conversation going on at any given time, and sometimes three or four.

Her father had always laughed about being surrounded by women, complaining that even their dog and their cat were female. The girls always told their father that their two horses were males, and that he should be happy having so many women to fuss over him. He was pleased, of course, and he loved his family above everything else. He always said he put God first, and then family, and everything else was under that.

After suffering a stroke two years ago, her father had never been the same—he had trouble communicating. The messages from his brain were blocked when it came to speech. He knew what he wanted to say, and he could still speak in very short sentences, but it generally frustrated him when he couldn't form the syllables he was trying to form. And, of course, the frustration only made it worse.

As it would soon be dark, she lit the lamp beside her. She'd only been back in the community a week and already she felt the effects of everything being slow. It was as though time was creeping by. There were no cars whooshing by, no deadlines to meet, no noise of cell phones sounding, no music, and no TV blaring.

In a strange way, she felt close to Benjamin being back here, where they had both grown up.

Her thoughts turned to the small house they had intended to live in. It was nice of James to hand her the house papers, but she didn't know how she was going to live so close to Benjamin's parents. They acted like they harbored no grudge, but they had to know that she was the one who'd kept Benjamin away. She wiped another tear from her eye, wondering when she'd stop hurting.

Earlier that day, just before the beginning of the funeral, the bishop's wife, Hilda, had said she'd visit the next day and Isla was glad of that. Hilda was a kind woman and one who'd had her share of sorrow. Surely she could learn a thing or two from her about how to manage the heartache.

Isla flopped onto the bed and closed her eyes. When she opened her eyes again, it was pitch black outside. She headed to the living room to say goodnight to her parents. Her father was in the living room with a blanket over his knees, tired out from the day's activities, and her mother was rattling around in the kitchen. She sat beside her father and put her arm around him.

"Gut nacht, Dat."

He looked at her and smiled, giving her a nod. It was easier for him to use signs and gestures rather than making a frustrating attempt to speak. Seeing him like that pained her. She shouldn't have been away for so long. As a teenager, the outside world seemed exciting and bold, and it had been a bit of that for a few years, but nothing lasts forever and the world had pulled her and Benjamin away from God just like the bishop had warned.

Isla leaned over and kissed her father on the cheek. "I'll see what *Mamm's* doing in the kitchen."

He made a noise in the back of his throat as she walked across and into the kitchen.

"Hi, *Mamm*. What are you doing?"

Her mother spun around. "Your *vadder* likes a cup of hot chocolate before bed. He says the milk helps him to sleep. Do you want one?"

"Nee, denke." Isla hadn't told her mother about Benjamin's brother giving her the house yet. She'd leave it until morning because her parents thought she was there to stay and she didn't want to risk upsetting them tonight. But Benjamin's house was within walking distance, so she could still visit her parents every day.

The next morning when Isla woke, she was surprised she'd gotten as much sleep as she had. It was her best night's sleep since the accident. There was no clock in the bedroom to tell her what time it was. Never owning a wristwatch, she had become used to glancing at her cell phone, but that, along with all her other pieces of electronic technology, had been left behind. After she had dressed, she headed into the kitchen to see her mother looking out the window while tying her apron strings behind her back.

"Do you want a hand with that?"

"*Nee, denke.* I can do it." Her mother turned around and looked at her. "It's nice to have you home."

"It's good to be back."

"I'll get the eggs, and then I'll make you some breakfast."

"I can get the eggs."

"Okay. The basket's just by the door there."

As Isla bent down to get the basket, she asked, "Is *Dat* still asleep?"

"*Jah.* I normally wake him when breakfast is on the table if he hasn't gotten up on his own."

Isla made the familiar trek to the chicken house with visions of the childhood fun she and her sisters had had playing with the chickens. They were their pets. She walked into the coop and the door closed behind her. In her searching, she managed to find only six eggs, which weren't very many with three people now living in the house. She wondered how her mother and father were surviving now that her father could no longer work. When she got back into the house her mother was mixing flour into liquid in a big bowl.

"What are you doing, *Mamm*?"

"I'm baking bread."

"Why don't I do that, and you make the breakfast?"

"Very good. First I must put the coffee on for your *vadder*. He still likes a strong cup of *kaffe* first thing every morning."

This was Isla's fourth day back at the house and the first morning that she'd been out of bed this early. Her mother normally had to shake her awake because, since Benjamin's death, it was only in the early mornings that she'd managed to get a little sleep.

As her mother made coffee, Isla took over the bread making. Once it was the correct consistency, she sprinkled flour on a baking sheet and on her hands in readiness for the kneading process.

Just as her mother had taught her, using only her fingertips she lightly rolled the edges into the middle. *Edges into the middle.* Her mother's voice from long ago still rang in her head. While concentrating on the bread, life and all its problems were elsewhere. She was transported back to her childhood where her days were filled with the laughter of her sisters as they played and ran in the wide open fields under the summer sunshine. Those were carefree days and back then she'd never thought how things would turn out once she grew up. She placed the kneaded dough back into the large bowl to rise covering it with a clean tea towel.

"Did you buy your bread?"

Isla looked up at her mother. "*Jah.* Bread is so inexpensive it seemed a waste of time to bake it." She paused, and then blurted out, "How do you and *Dat* survive now that he's not working?"

Her mother looked up, a little startled at the question. "Your sisters and their husbands give us money each month to live on."

"And that's all you have?"

"That's all we need. *Gott* has provided."

Isla felt dreadful. She and Benjamin had been busy creating a life for themselves, totally unaware that her parents were living in this way. If any of her sisters had said anything to her or asked her to help, she would've contributed. She considered that fact another thing to add to the list of things of which she should be ashamed. It was just one more reason she and Benjamin should've returned to the community earlier.

"I'm sorry, *Mamm.* Someone should've said something. Benjamin and I would've helped, too."

"There was no need."

"I have some news to tell you and *Dat* over breakfast."

"What is it?" her mother asked.

"I'll wait to tell you both."

Her mother continued to set the table. "Is it good news? You're making me nervous."

"*Jah.* It's very good news. Well, it *could* be good news, but it's not bad news."

"We could do with some happiness around here."

"But it's something I'll need your advice about." Isla shaped the raised bread dough and filled the baking tins and put them near the warm stove to rise before baking.

When breakfast was on the table, Isla's father walked into the kitchen.

"Just in time. I was just about to fetch you."

He nodded to his wife, and then he nodded to Isla before he sat down. They closed their eyes and said the silent prayer of thanks for the food.

As soon as they opened their eyes, Isla's mother said to Isla's father, "Our *dochder* has something to tell us. Some good news."

He looked at her, nodded, and then looked expectantly at Isla.

"Benjamin's brother, James, said I should have his house. Benjamin's house, I mean. James gave me the deed and every-thing yesterday, and said he'd have it transferred to me. At first I said no, but then he told me that Benjamin would've wanted me to have it and he said he would not take no for an answer." She looked at her father. "It's the house right next to the Millers' house. The blue one."

Her father nodded, telling her he knew the one.

"It was the one we were going to live in when we returned," Isla added. "Do you think I should accept it?" She looked between her mother and her father.

"Take it," her father said in a low tone, surprising her with his emphatic speech instead of a nod.

"Your *vadder* is right. You don't say no to something that *Gott* has given you."

"Do you think that *Gott* has given it to me?"

"Of course. Every good and perfect gift comes from Him," her mother said.

"Okay. James is coming to get us at ten, no, at eleven I think it was. Would you both come and have a look at it with me?"

Her father nodded as her mother spoke for both of them, "We'd love to."

"*Denke.* I'm so glad it's close. Within walking distance, and I can walk that every day to come and see you." A good thing since she didn't yet have a buggy and didn't know when she would get one. Transport was the last thing on her mind right now.

Isla got up and checked the bread dough, saw that it had risen sufficiently, and put the pans into the oven to bake.

CHAPTER 4

Confess your faults one to another,
and pray one for another, that ye may be healed.
The effectual fervent prayer of a righteous man availeth much.
James 5:16

AFTER BREAKFAST, Isla helped her mother wash the dishes while her father went for a walk.

"Does he walk every morning?"

"*Jah*, the doctor said he should walk for twenty minutes every day and that is supposed to help him. If he didn't do that, he'd just be sitting in the chair all day."

"He seems to think it's a good idea that I take the *haus*." Isla took another wet plate from the drying rack and rubbed it with the tea towel.

"Of course, why would you even question it?"

"I guess I feel guilty for not coming back to the community earlier and that's the truth. I feel so selfish, *Mamm*."

Her mother looked down at the sudsy dishes in the sink. "What's done is done. We can't turn back the clock and do things different."

"I know that. I just have to become a better person from now on." The dishes were dry, and Isla began putting them away in the cupboard.

"You're changing your life when you get baptized on Sunday. You've arranged it with the bishop, haven't you?"

"*Jah*, we had a long talk the other day." Being baptized was something that she and Benjamin had planned to do together.

Her mother drained the water from the sink. "It'll take you some getting used to and you'll never forget about Benjamin, but things will get easier with time."

"That's what everyone keeps telling me. I just wish I could get rid of these feelings of guilt."

"Have you talked to the bishop about it?"

"*Nee*."

Her mother said, "Well you should."

"Okay. I suppose I will."

After Isla had helped her mother with the other morning chores, they were sitting down and sharing a pot of tea when they heard a buggy.

"That'll be James." Isla sprang to her feet and looked out the window to confirm that it was in fact James, climbing down from the buggy.

"Ask him if he wants a cup of tea first," her mother said.

Isla walked to the front door to meet him. "Good morning, James."

"*Guder mariye*. Are you all set to go?"

"*Jah*. My parents are coming too. Would you like to come in and have a cup of tea first? *Mamm* and I were just having one."

"*Denke*. That would be nice."

He walked in the door and looked over at her father who was sitting down on the couch. Her father pushed himself up and shook James' hand.

"Are you joining us in the kitchen for tea, *Dat?*"

Her father nodded and followed them into the kitchen.

Once they were seated, Isla poured a cup of tea for her father, and another for James.

"How are Abe and Mabel doing?" her mother asked James, referring to his parents.

"They seem to be okay. We have visitors at the *haus* who are staying awhile and that's taking their mind off things."

"Jah, there's nothing like keeping busy," Isla's mother said, while Isla's father quietly slurped his hot tea.

"Is it all right with your parents that I have the *haus*?" Isla asked.

"It was Benjamin's and now it's yours. That's the way it always would've been."

From his answer, Isla was none the wiser. His parents could very well be upset with having her living so close—a constant reminder of their son and their loss.

"As I said, I'll get the papers in order soon as I can, and it will be officially all yours."

"We can't thank you enough," her mother said.

Her father touched James on the arm, and nodded to let him know that he too appreciated the gesture.

Isla said to James, *"Dat* has had a stroke and it's affecting his speech. He talks, but it takes him a while to form the words."

"I hadn't heard that. I hope you get better soon, Mr. Zook."

"Mamm says he's gotten a little better," Isla said.

After they finished their tea, they set off in the buggy that James had borrowed from his family. A few minutes later they arrived at the house. Benjamin had bought it cheaply from one of his older brothers when he was in his early twenties and it had sat there unoccupied. Isla had never seen the inside. In the early days, Benjamin was always talking about going back and doing repairs so he could lease it, but he'd never gotten around to it.

As they approached the front door, James handed Isla the key. "Welcome to your new home."

She took the key from him. *"Denke."*

"I have no idea what state it's in inside. I haven't ever been in it," he said.

Isla placed the key in the lock, turned it and pushed the door open. She was the first to walk inside, and she was engulfed in warm stale air that smelled of dust. From what Benjamin had told her, there were three upstairs bedrooms, two living areas, a bathroom and a kitchen.

The first thing her mother said was, "I'll open some windows."

Isla's father quietly walked farther in to look around.

"This is lovely," Isla said.

"I guess it has potential. It needs a good clean up and lots of painting, and the floorboards need to be redone," James said.

Isla roughly added up cost estimates in her head. She had a few thousand in savings, and she would've had more if it weren't for the non-refundable wedding dress and the money she hadn't gotten back from the wedding venue. Pulling her mind away from things that couldn't be changed, she walked around the house studying every inch. She figured she could do most of the work herself—the painting, the cleaning—and she could learn how to do any other repairs. Maybe even the floors.

James put his hands on his hips and, looking around, he said, "It looks like I'll be staying on here longer than I planned."

"What do you mean?"

"I'm not going to leave here until you're settled in and comfortable here in this *haus.*"

When Isla opened her mouth to speak, he said, "That's the way Benjamin would've wanted things to be."

"Thank you, James. For allowing me to have this house."

"I'll head to the courthouse today, and I guess you'll have to sign some papers."

"Thank you, but please, I don't want you to delay going back home. I'll feel dreadful if you do." She figured he'd be missed in such a small community.

He leaned in close, and whispered, "It'll give me a chance to do that other thing we talked about." He gave her a wink and she smiled, remembering he'd mentioned he was there to find a wife.

She whispered back, "Then I'll take it upon myself to help you."

He drew back. "Will you?"

"Jah, I'd love to."

"Denke. I'll need all the help I can get. I haven't been blessed where the ladies are concerned."

"I don't think it will take too long," she said.

He shook his head. "I'll tell you right now that women don't seem to like me."

Isla held in a giggle. "Maybe you shouldn't tell too many people that, because then women will wonder why other women have passed you by."

He frowned. "That shouldn't make any difference."

"It could. You'll have to trust me and do what I say if I'm to help you."

"Okay. I suppose it can't hurt, because my do-it-myself success record is bad."

Isla shook her head, put her thumb and forefinger to the side of her lips and made the sign telling him to zip his lips.

He laughed. "You might regret saying you'll help me."

"You'll have to listen to exactly what I tell you to do and to say."

Her mother and father came back from looking in the bedrooms.

Her father nodded, his smile telling her he liked what he saw, and her mother said, "It's a very nice house."

They stepped out onto the porch and Isla locked the front door.

"*Mamm* and *Dat* have a spare table and chairs in the barn; you could put them on the porch here," James said.

"Oh no. That's okay. I'll get things in time."

"They won't mind. It's only sitting in the barn gathering dust."

"Okay. *Denke.* As long as they don't mind."

"We'll have the place decent in no time."

James took them back home.

"Will you come in for awhile again, James?" her mother asked.

"I'd love to."

He secured his horse and went into the house with them.

At the kitchen table, her father managed to ask James what he was doing with himself while he was back. James told him he was relaxing and visiting people, and then added he was also staying until Isla's house was comfortable and she was fully moved in. As if to say thank you, her father reached forward and held onto James' arm and gave an appreciative nod. James smiled at him and patted his hand.

Isla's parents had never had much and she could see how happy it made her father that she now had a house—no husband to take care of her, but at least she had somewhere to live. Isla knew that's what was uppermost in her father's mind.

Her father excused himself and signed that he was going to lie down. Isla's mother accompanied him, carrying another cup of tea for him and leaving Isla alone with James.

"I suppose you heard how he died?"

He nodded. "Jah, and you told me he didn't suffer."

"That's right. He was taking it for one last ride before the man who bought it came to collect it." Isla wasn't sure who knew what.

"You told me that earlier when you mentioned he hadn't suffered."

"I'm sorry." Isla shook her head. "I can't remember who has heard what. The police said he was speeding, and I guess he was. He liked to go fast."

Their eyes locked. "It was an accident, Isla."

"I know it was, but I can't help thinking if we had just come back to the community sooner, he'd be alive right now."

"Things turn out how they are meant to. It's not you delaying your return to the community that caused the accident. Many things had to take place for that accident to happen then and there. He had to have decided to leave on the bike at that very second, and to go at that speed, and to ride that route."

"I see what you saying. And my head knows you're right."

"Of course I am. You just have to concentrate on making a life for yourself now."

"Do you think your parents will ever be able to forgive me?"

He drew his dark eyebrows together. "They don't blame you for what's happened."

SAMANTHA PRICE

"Are you sure? Your *mudder* could barely look at me at the funeral."

"That might only be because you remind her of Benjamin. Trust me, she doesn't blame you at all; no one does. Accidents are a part of life. No one can see them coming and that's why they're called accidents. They're things we could prevent in hindsight if we only had the chance."

He smiled at her, but Isla couldn't bring herself to smile back.

Her mother came back into the room with a tray of empty tea cups. Isla jumped up. "*Mamm*, you should've called out for me to help you with this."

"I'm not too old to do these things. I had no idea so many cups were upstairs."

"I know you're not too old, but it doesn't hurt to have help every now and again, especially now that I'm here.

"*Jah*, Mrs. Zook, take advantage of her while she is here because soon she will be living in that new *haus* of hers. Well, it's not new, but soon it'll look as though it is."

Mrs. Zook giggled. "That's right, I should take advantage of her. It was nice to get help with the bread baking this morning. Since it's just Murray and me, I don't need to bake bread every day now. It's just two times a week instead of five like I did when all the girls lived here."

"That was some years ago," James said.

"Jah, they're all married now and have *kinner* of their own. Of course, not Isla."

Isla blocked out everything her mother said, her head full of other thoughts.

"Denke for the tea. I should go and make myself useful somewhere. That's right. I'm seeing about making your *haus* legal, Isla." He stood.

Isla stood as well. "Thank you again for seeing to it that I have the house. Are you sure that's truly alright with the rest of your family?"

"Of course. I keep telling you that. Why wouldn't it be?"

"I don't know, I just keep wondering. I don't want to take the *haus* unless it's fine by everyone."

"Trust me, it is."

She stood at the door with her mother and they watched him drive the buggy down the driveway and back to the road.

Her mother said, "I'm sure your *vadder* wishes he was young enough to help you get the place fixed."

"I know. If he could, he'd be there as much as possible, working on the place."

"I'm sure you'll have plenty of helpers anyway."

"I'm sure I will."

CHAPTER 5

But if ye forgive not men their trespasses,
neither will your Father forgive your trespasses.
Matthew 6:15

THE VERY NEXT morning Isla set off early with the key to her house firmly in her hand. In the other, she clutched a pen and a small pad of paper to make a list of what repairs needed to be done to the house.

She pushed everything out of her mind and concentrated on putting one foot in front of the other on the dirt road underneath her feet. The cool of the morning air blowing across her made her feel peaceful. Birds swooping and chirping overhead caused her to smile as she admired their carefree morning games. Breathing in deeply and appreciating the fresh air, she was glad to be home where she belonged.

She turned up the shared driveway and walked toward the two houses. About a hundred yards from the road, the driveway split into two. The right fork went to the Millers' house and the left went to the house that would soon be Isla's.

Once she got closer, she saw James on the porch arranging furniture.

"Hello," she called out.

He looked up, surprised to see her. *"Guder mariye.* You're out and about early."

"I thought I'd come to make a list of what has to be done. I didn't have a detailed enough look yesterday to do it from memory." She stepped up onto the porch and looked down at the two wooden chairs and the table. Yesterday he had offered furniture that had been in his parents' barn, and she had accepted mainly because it was hard to refuse James. "Are these the ones you were talking about? They look like they're new."

"These are new and they're my gift to you." His eyes flickered uncomfortably away from her.

Her best guess was that his parents had refused to allow her the use of the chairs and table they'd stored in the barn.

"Denke. That's so kind of you."

He tapped on the back of one of the chairs. "Have a seat. And, you're welcome."

She smiled and sat down, placing her things on the table.

"This is so comfortable."

He sat down next to her. "It is. I've already tested the chairs."

"All that's missing is a morning coffee," she said with a smile, enjoying the view of the fields.

He leaned forward. "I believe we have a freshly made pot of coffee at home. I could bring us back some."

She shook her head. "I've just had some at home."

"I don't think the house needs all that much work, and with your permission, I'll start on it today."

"*Nee.* Definitely not. You didn't come to Lancaster County to do anything of the kind."

"It's the least I can—"

She held up her hand. "Definitely not! I know how to clean and I know how to paint. And you've got better things to do with your time."

He pursed his lips, exaggerating the expression. "We shall see."

She laughed.

"It's nice to see you laugh again," he said.

She put her fingertips to her lips. "I never thought I would. I think that doing work on this house will take my mind off things. It'll be good for me to have something to think about."

"I'm glad."

"And then after that I'll get a job as a nanny. I guess that will be the easiest job for me to get, with all my child care experience."

"*Jah,* that'll be easy enough to do when you're ready for it.

"Yes."

"Why didn't you use your parents' buggy to drive over here rather than walk?"

"I could've, but walking clears my head."

"You will let me know if you need my help with anything, won't you?"

"I will. I tell you what. You can help me right now. Here." She passed the pen and paper to him. "I'll tell you what needs doing and you jot it on the paper."

He took them from her and then set them back down on the table. "For that, I'm going to need that second cup of coffee." He stood up and looked down at her. "What about you?"

"You're going to bring coffee back here?"

"That's the plan."

She smiled impishly. "If you're bringing one, I suppose you might as well bring two. Just black with a dash of milk and no sugar for me, please."

He grinned back. "Coming right up."

She sat on the porch of her new house and watched the man who would've been her brother-in-law stride across the lawn to his parents' home. He looked so much like Benjamin from behind that she could not take her eyes from him. James slipped into the back door of the house.

If only the Millers' house weren't so close. Maybe in time they might be able to forgive me, she thought.

In no time he was on his way back holding two cups of coffee.

Seeing that he was stepping cautiously, she said, "Careful, now. Don't spill a drop."

"Don't make me laugh," he called back. "If I spill any it'll be from yours."

He made it back without incident.

As he sat down, he explained, "The coffee was in the pot waiting. I hope it wasn't waiting for anyone in particular. Oh well, it's ours now." He took a sip.

"How many people are staying in the house at the moment?"

He shook his head. "I can barely count them all. There are the Eichers and the Fosters from Ohio, and Aunt Mary. Oh, and then there's me. The Eichers are heading off today and the Fosters are staying on for a few more days. I'm not sure what Aunt Mary is doing."

"Sounds like a full house."

"It's a little crowded."

"And do you like living by yourself back home?"

"I do. I've got a small house that I've added onto. At first it was just a box-shape, with a kitchen and a living area all in one, and my bed was in one corner with a screen around it. I've since added a bedroom and a bathroom, and then a little while later I built on a covered porch."

"It was good of you to come back for the funeral. I know it's a long way."

"When we were younger, Benjamin and I got along the best. I suppose that's because we were the two youngest ones in the family, but you already know all that. Anyway, I just needed to be here for me and for my parents, and maybe for you."

Isla nodded. She'd stayed in touch with her family more than Benjamin had stayed in contact with his.

Sipping her hot coffee, she looked over at James. "Mm. This coffee has a good flavor."

"I brought it with me."

"Don't tell me you grow coffee?"

He laughed. "No. Not a chance. I just know where to shop." He shook his head. "Coffee grows where it's warm. And I'm hopeless with growing things anyway, and I can't work out why. First my flowers started dying and I figured out that I wasn't watering them enough, so the next lot died from overwatering. They were covered in a white powdery substance and I figured it was mold, and the plants went spongy and rotted.

Isla smiled. "You grow flowers?"

"I was trying."

"What about vegetables?"

"They're a lot easier. They're like crops. I guess that goes with being a farmer, but flowers are tough to figure out. They're too delicate for me, apparently. The farm I have, that I was telling you about, is pesticide and chemical free. We're working to have a good balance within the environment."

"That sounds like the way to go. I think when people started using all these things there was no thought to how harmful they were. I'm glad we Amish have avoided them."

"I agree." She sighed. "Benjamin would never have thought of growing flowers."

"I'm not surprised. It makes me happy to see flowers. Now, if I had a *fraa* that would be her doing—to look after the flowers and to keep them alive."

"I'll do my best to find you one. The meeting's on this Sunday and I'll find a few candidates for you."

He gave a little laugh before he took another mouthful of coffee.

"Anything I should be aware of? Any specifications for your *fraa?*"

"A kind woman who'll be good company."

Isla nodded and smiled. It was a simple and plain request from a man who was humble. She hoped she could find him a truly goodhearted woman who would suit him well.

"I've never been in love," he blurted out.

His statement caught her off guard. She glanced over to see him staring into the distance.

49

"Well, there is nothing else like it in the world—knowing that God made you to be with that one person. I can't describe what it's like. When you're in love, you'll know it."

"I want to experience that." He took another sip of his coffee.

"Everyone should, but I truly don't think that many do. Benjamin and I used to talk about that. We knew how blessed we were to be in love and so suited. I'm sorry, I hope you don't mind talking about him," Isla said.

"It helps. I like to talk about him. Sometimes I still feel him around me. I don't know how that can be, but I'm not going to question my sanity." He chuckled. "Many might think that I should. Shall we go inside?" He looked into her mug. "You've hardly had any of your coffee."

"I've had enough. I've drunk half." She stood and pushed the paper and pen toward him before she took up the key and unlocked the door, ready to start the list.

At the Sunday meeting, Isla got baptized. She'd been gone a long time, but now she was officially home and had made her commitment to God in front of all in attendance. During the meal after the service, she had her sister Liz introduce her to people she hadn't met.

One woman who caught her attention was Sally, and she made inquiries and learned that her family had recently moved to the community.

When Liz walked toward her from talking with Sally, Isla asked about her. "How old do you think Sally is?"

"She's twenty two, I think. Why?"

She knew James was probably just under thirty. She wondered if a woman of twenty-two was too young for him. "I thought she was about the same age as me, that's all."

"She's not that much younger. She seems nice, as much as I've gotten to know her."

Isla nodded. And as they moved on to talk with others, Isla got the idea to invite people to her house once it was finished. She'd be sure to invite Sally and some other single women. Finding James a wife was the least she could do for him. She'd hurry with moving in so she could do that before it was time for him to go home.

CHAPTER 6

And when ye stand praying, forgive, if ye have ought against any:
that your Father also which is in heaven may forgive you your trespasses.
Matthew 11:25

ISLA WAS HEADING to the food table when she saw James nearby talking to a couple of men. He glanced over at her and left the men he was speaking with.

"I hope you're not gonna be mad with me," was the first thing he said to her.

She frowned at him. "Why? What have you done?"

"I've got a group of men lined up to work at your place on Friday and Saturday."

She raised her eyebrows, trying hard to look stern. "You have, have you?"

"*Jah.*" He looked a little worried.

"That's marvellous!"

"You're not mad?"

"*Nee.* Just teasing you a little. I'm pleased, because I'd like to move in as soon as possible. But I'll have to get supplies for them—paint, and the like."

He said, "I can take you to do that."

"You don't need to. I'll take my *vadder's* buggy."

"You'll be doing me a favor if you allow me to do it. It'll get me out from under my *mudder's* feet."

Isla gave a little giggle and looked over at the Fosters and his Aunt Mary sitting with James's mother. "I can see you still have visitors."

He whispered to her, "The time for visitors is over. I think they've moved in."

Isla laughed.

He added, "Don't tell anyone I said that."

"Well, okay, and I'll take you up on your offer as long as it's helping you out."

He nodded. "*Denke.* I'm grateful."

"How about tomorrow? Are you free?" she asked.

"I have all day at your disposal."

~

The next morning at Isla's house.

"He's certainly being helpful," Greta Zook said with a slight rise of her eyebrows when she learned that James was taking her daughter to buy paint.

"He's doing it for his *bruder,*" Isla told her mother.

"Are you certain that's the only reason?"

"Of course, *Mamm;* other than that he is just a nice person."

"Maybe," her mother said.

Isla sat down at the table. She thought it funny her mother thought James might be interested in her. Her mother was easy to read and that's what she'd meant by her little comments and the flicker of her eyebrows. Her mother had no idea that she'd offered to find James a wife, and Isla wasn't about to betray his confidence by telling anyone.

"Also I forgot to tell you that he's arranged for people to go to the house on Friday and Saturday to help fix the place up."

"That's good. You'll be in there in no time at all. There's not that much to do, aside from the floors, other than a good clean and painting. Your sisters and I could've helped you with that."

"I know. I'm looking forward to choosing the paint today."

"It's certainly made you seem a lot brighter than you have been."

Isla glanced at the basket on the sink and saw that her mother had already collected the eggs that morning. "Do you want me to get anything at the market while I'm in town?"

"How about something for dinner tonight—chicken?"

"Whatever you see that looks good. What would you like for breakfast?"

She placed her hand over her stomach. "I think I'll just have a bowl of cereal today thanks, *Mamm*." She rose to her feet. "I can get it myself."

"*Nee,* sit down. I'll get it for you. What are you looking like that for? Are you ill?"

"Just a little queasy."

Isla listened to her mother for the next fifteen minutes, telling her she was sick because she didn't eat enough. According to her mother, she was far too skinny.

Isla hurried out to meet James when she heard his buggy approaching the house. She was keen to get to the paint store and she knew if he made eye-contact with her mother, *Mamm* would invite him in for tea, James would accept, and that would be another two hours wasted.

When he stopped the buggy, she climbed in before he could get out.

"You look bright today," he said.

She looked over at him. "My *mudder* said the same thing."

"It must be true. I'm not the kind of man who gives empty compliments."

She gave a little laugh, not knowing whether he was serious or joking. He usually said the first thing that came into his mind, which wasn't always a good thing.

He turned the buggy around and started back down the driveway. Glancing over at her, he said, "You seem excited."

"I am."

"Have you given any thought to colors?"

She knew by 'colors' he meant the choices of cream, white or something else neutral, as the Amish never had bright color on their walls.

"I was thinking I would have one room green, one pink and then one room blue."

He continued to look ahead and then said, "It might give you a headache after awhile."

"I'm teasing you, James."

Glancing over at her, he smiled. "I didn't know. Totally missed it, didn't I?"

"You did," she said with a smile. "I want everything white."

"What? Every every room white?"

"*Jah.*"

"Don't you think that'll look unfinished—too much like an undercoat?"

"No, it shouldn't."

He shook his head. "I don't know about white."

"That's what I want. What color were you thinking?"

"Maybe a cream."

"I want it all white. I once leased an apartment and all the rooms were white. I found it refreshing and cheerful. And that's what I want my house to be like."

"White it is, then."

"What color is your house inside?"

"Most of the walls are a creamy shade, but I didn't put much thought into it. Do you want the outside of the house white as well?"

"I think it's fine as is for now. Maybe I'll paint it later."

"You're right. The best thing to do is get you into the house as quick as possible."

"What, so you can leave town?"

He glanced over at her. "I'm in no particular hurry. I was thinking for your sake to get you into your house." He smiled at her. "Were you teasing me again?"

She slowly nodded. He might have looked like Benjamin, but he was nothing like him. Although he clearly shared his quiet and caring nature with Benjamin–and that was one of the things she had loved about Benjamin.

~

On the way home from the paint shop with gallons of white paint, a car drove too close to the buggy. James had to swerve to one side. Once the car was in front of them, the driver sped off honking the horn.

James stared at Isla. "Are you okay?"

She doubled over, holding her stomach. "I need to get out."

"I can't stop here. I'll stop a little further up." When the buggy stopped, she jumped out and he followed her. "What's wrong?"

Isla was too sick to speak as she held her stomach. She walked up and down trying to relieve the nausea, and then she gave up the fight, leaned against a tree, and vomited.

He leaned down beside her. "What's happened? Are you hurt?"

"I'm okay." She was sick again.

"It's all my fault, I'm sorry I should've watched where I was going."

"It's not your fault. I was queasy this morning at breakfast."

"Perhaps I should take you to the doctor?" he suggested.

She shook her head. "*Nee,* I'm okay."

"Stay there; I'll get you some water." He went back to the buggy and then came back with a bottle of water.

"Rinse out and then take a couple of mouthfuls."

She did as he said and then he helped her to her feet and they walked back to the buggy.

"Please don't tell my parents I was sick. They'll make such a fuss and I'm alright, really I am."

"Are you sure?"

"*Jah.* I'm just rundown. I've been that way since the accident."

"That's perfectly understandable."

"Is the paint okay?"

"That's the least of our concerns." Once Isla was seated in the buggy, he checked on the paint. Thanks to his careful packing, the paint hadn't moved.

Isla suddenly remembered that Hilda, the bishop's wife, was visiting that afternoon, so she had to get back to her parents place before then.

CHAPTER 7

And be ye kind one to another, tenderhearted,
forgiving one another,
even as God for Christ's sake hath forgiven you.
Ephesians 4:32

IN TWO SHORT weeks the house had been thoroughly cleaned, the floorboards had been resurfaced, and the walls and ceilings were painted. As soon as the paint was dry, Isla had moved in. The house was now ready for her special dinner, and she'd invited several suitable women for James.

The dinner was at seven and Isla had James come beforehand so she could school him on what to say and what not to say. She'd gotten to know him well in the past weeks. He was a little stuffy and serious, so she'd told him he'd have to lighten up.

"And if someone says something odd, remember that they might be joking."

"Teasing me, like you do?"

"*Jah,* but not teasing in a horrible way. Teasing like 'having a laugh.'"

"I think I know what you mean."

"And please don't tell the women you never have success with women. That's the death knell for sure and for certain."

He nodded. "I haven't said that once since you told me not to."

"If they ask why you're not married, it's because you've never found the right woman. And that's the truth."

"What if I've found the one I like, and she's not interested in me?"

"That's a dreadful thing to say, it's just as bad if not worse. You can't say that. They don't want to hear that you liked some woman and she didn't like you back."

His lips turned upward, his eyes twinkled and then he chuckled.

"Oh, you find that funny, but you don't know when I'm joking or teasing you? You only laugh at what you say?"

"Who said I was joking?"

She shook her head. "You've got to take this more seriously, because I am."

"Okay. Why am I unmarried? Tell me one more time so I can get it right."

She sighed. "I hope this bad rehearsal means the performance will be good. You haven't found the right woman and that's all you need to say. After that, you keep your mouth closed. Zip it!"

"Okay. What else? There's such a lot to remember."

"Just be yourself and you'll be fine."

"Got it. Be myself, but don't say the things that my normal self would say." His mouth tilted upward and off to one side.

"That's right, because you want to present the best you. And let's face it, people don't want to consider what other people have passed over."

"*Denke* for helping me, Isla. I think I've got a real chance now."

"Me too." She passed him a bundle of knives and forks. "Can you set the table for me while I make the gravy?"

From her position at the stove, she could see him arranging each knife and fork precisely on the table. She hoped she could find him a wife; otherwise, left to his own devices, he might never find one.

She had invited three other young women besides Sally, the one she'd set her mind on for James, and she'd invited two other single men.

"Do you need any other help, Isla?" James asked.

"*Nee, denke.*"

"If you don't mind, I'll sit outside then so it doesn't look like you and I have been alone in the *haus.*"

"Okay." She'd forgotten about the Amish ways of abstaining from even the appearance of wrongdoing.

The guests all arrived at about the same time and Isla was pleased that Sally had come with one of the other young women and not with one of the young men. That would've been certain disaster.

Isla told everyone where they should sit, putting Sally next to James.

Throughout the dinner the conversation was lively, and one of the young men sitting next to Isla talked so much that she could scarcely concentrate on James to gauge his progress. Every time she looked over, James and Sally were talking, and she hoped he was not saying anything she'd told him was off limits.

When the dessert was over, Isla had everyone gather in the living room. She'd gotten her furniture out of storage, and it suited the house perfectly well. The two couches were charcoal in colour with white and charcoal cushions that went nicely with the white walls and the polished hardwood floors.

"I'll make some coffee, " Isla announced.

Sally sprang to her feet. "I'll help."

Once they were in the kitchen, Isla said, "What do you think of James?"

AMISH WIDOW'S NEW HOPE

"He's very nice."

"I think he likes you."

"Do you?" Sally asked.

"Jah. He'd make the best husband, I'm sure. You don't have a boyfriend, do you?"

"Nee, not really."

Isla put the coffee pot on the stove, wondering what Sally meant by that. Either she had one, or she didn't have one. "Well, if I were in the market for a husband, I'd snap him up."

Sally's eyes widened. "Would you really?"

"Jah. Why not? He's everything I want in a man. He's generous and caring, and he's tall and handsome, which doesn't hurt anything."

"Jah, he is handsome, in a way." Sally leaned closer, and whispered, "I don't mean to be rude, but he's kind of stuffy or something. He acts sort of like my *Dat."*

"I think he's just nervous around you."

"Do you think so?" Sally blinked rapidly.

"I do." Isla peeped around the corner of the kitchen and saw that James was now speaking with Jessica, and she seemed interested in what he was saying. "It seems you might have some competition, Sally."

Sally looked around the corner too. Isla could see that Sally was disturbed by him getting along with Jessica.

When the coffee was made, Sally went back into the room and made sure she talked to James once more. Things were going well and Isla couldn't wait to find out from James who he liked —Jessica, or Sally.

One by one the guests left and soon it was just her and James. She walked with him a little way outside as he made his way back to his parents' house.

Isla suddenly rushed back toward her house without a word. As she paced up and down willing herself not to be sick, she felt the same way she had at Benjamin's funeral. Waves of nausea came over her and she was sick in the seedlings she'd planted the day before. So much for her delicious dinner!

As she was down on her haunches, she heard James walking up behind her.

"Stay back. I've been sick," she ordered, her hand half covering her mouth.

"That's something I've seen before."

When she felt a little better, she asked, "Do you mean me at Benjamin's funeral?"

"That, and the day we went to get the paint. Can I get you something?"

"A cup of water please."

She wanted to get over everything and be a normal person, but it was hard. Now she had been sick without even thinking about Benjamin. In fact, the entire night had passed with him coming to mind only a couple of times.

James was back and he passed her a glass of water. "Here you go."

She took the glass from him and had couple of mouthfuls, and then he handed her some paper napkins and she wiped her mouth. He took the glass from her and she crumpled the napkins into her hand.

"Thank you. You're always coming to my rescue."

He chuckled. "You've done the same for me. You've done a fine job by finding me Sally."

She stood up. "Sally's the one you like?"

"She suits me just fine." His face beamed under the moonlight. "Are you feeling better now, Isla?"

"A little. The fresh air helps, I think."

He looked down at the seedlings. "It seems I'm not the only one who has a problem with growing flowers."

"Hopefully they'll survive," was all she could manage to say.

"I'll help you back inside." He held her arm and walked her back to the house.

As she stood in the doorway of her home, she turned to him. "I'm glad you like Sally. I thought she would be good for you as soon as I met her."

"Are you going to be okay?"

"I'll sleep it off. I should be fine in the morning."

"You could stay at our place. We've got spare rooms."

"Nee, denke. I'll be fine. I just need sleep."

Isla walked back inside her house. There was nothing more to do because her guests had helped her wash up, and they'd even washed up the after-dinner coffee mugs. All that was left to do was fall into bed.

Even though her stomach was still squirming, she was pleased that she'd been able to do something nice for James. She changed into her nightgown, took her prayer *kapp* off and slipped between the covers, too weak to brush out her still-braided hair.

CHAPTER 8

Let all your things be done with charity.
1 Corinthians 16:14

IT HAD ALREADY BECOME an early morning tradition that James would bring coffee to Isla's house and they would sit on the porch discussing life and love. The next morning was no different.

She sat on her porch and watching James walk carefully, bearing the usual two mugs of hot coffee, from his parents' house to hers.

He placed the mugs down and then sat next to her.

"Now tell me about Sally and what the two of you talked about," she said before a morning greeting.

"Firstly, are you feeling better?"

"A lot better thanks. All I needed was sleep. Now tell me about last night. I need all the details."

"I can't remember exactly. Sally and I talked about a lot of things. I kept silent about my lack of success with women."

That was something, at least. "Good."

"Things are looking up thanks to you, Isla."

"I didn't have anything to do with it. I just put the two of you in one room together."

"*Denke.* I'll have to call my first child Isla."

"You better hope your first child is a girl, then."

They both laughed.

Isla hoped Sally was feeling the same way about him. She was a good-looking woman and there were still a few single men in their mid-twenties in the community. The distance between the Eggleton community and this community might be a deterrent to Sally and her parents.

"Do you think she'd marry a man like me? Do I have a chance with Sally, Isla?"

Isla swallowed the mouthful of coffee she'd just taken. "Of course, James. Of course you do."

"Do you really think so?"

"I do." She took another sip of coffee and a sudden wave of nausea came over her. She held her mouth.

"What's wrong?"

She shook her head. "Sick again."

"It might be something you ate last night."

Without taking offense at his accidental insult about her cooking, she rushed toward the garden and was sick while holding on to the side of the house. After that, she leaned down and threw up once more.

"I'll get you some water." He disappeared into the house and came back out and kneeled beside her, offering her the water.

Before she could take it, she was sick yet again.

"I don't like this, Isla. You've been sick too much. Maybe you should go to the doctor," he said.

"I never get sick," she protested. "It's a bug or a virus, or something. It's probably just stress or something, because of Benjamin."

"It might be and it might not be, but there's only one way to find out. I'm taking you to the doctor."

"How about we wait for tomorrow and then I'll go if I'm not better?"

"I'm bringing the buggy around and I'm taking you to the doctor whether you want to go or not." He frowned at her and she felt like a small child.

Being too weak to argue, all she could do was nod.

Twenty minutes later, he had the buggy hitched and he knocked on her door. Isla was resting in the kitchen.

"Come on, are you ready to go? It's too late to back out now."

She walked out of the kitchen and saw him standing there. "I'm feeling a little better."

"You're not getting out of it even if I have to put you over my shoulder and carry you kicking and screaming."

She rolled her eyes, knowing it was no use protesting, and smiled weakly at that mental image.

He continued, "I've called the doctor and we have an appointment at nine thirty. If we leave right now, we'll be in the waiting room with ten minutes to spare. That'll give you a chance to calm yourself."

"Okay."

He reached out for her arm and walked her to the buggy.

As Isla waited with James beside her in the doctor's waiting room, she glanced at the posters on the wall and spotted one to do with pregnancy. She gulped. Could she be pregnant? She quickly looked away. No, it wasn't possible.

The doctor appeared, walked over, picked up a file and looked at the name tab. He called out her name. She stood, breathed deeply, exhaled and followed him back into the room. When she sat down, she told him what had happened with her fiancé and her symptoms.

"Is there a chance you might be pregnant?" he asked looking at her over the top of his gold-rimmed glasses.

That was something she didn't want to face. "I don't think so. I think it would just be nerves or something like that."

The doctor took her blood pressure, and then her temperature.

"We'll eliminate pregnancy first." He handed her a specimen jar, and slid open a wooden door to reveal a small toilet and wash-basin. "Half fill the jar and that's all we'll need."

She wasn't being asked, she was being told he was doing a preg-nancy test. "And I'll find out the results today?" she asked.

"It'll only take a few minutes."

Once she closed the door, she had a feeling the results would be positive. That would explain the random bouts of vomiting, and she also only just now realized she was late. She was almost too nervous to find out for sure. Would she want a baby—Benjamin's baby—with him gone? Then again, it would be her only chance of motherhood. She leaned against the basin and put her head against the mirror.

Closing her eyes, she imagined how she'd feel if the doctor told her the test was negative. She lifted her head and looked at her face in the mirror. She'd be a little disappointed. Next, she closed her eyes and imagined how she'd feel if it were positive. She'd be overwhelmed, but secretly pleased. That was her answer. She opened her eyes. Even though the road ahead might not be an easy one, she wanted to be pregnant.

She jumped when the doctor knocked on the door. "Are you okay in there?"

"Yes. I'll just be a moment."

When she opened the door, she handed the doctor the half full specimen jar.

The doctor called his nurse who took the jar away.

"We'll know in a few minutes. I'll take down a brief history while we're waiting, since you haven't been here for years according to our files. The doctor you used to see has retired."

The nurse came back several minutes later, and the doctor sprang to his feet and took a slip of paper from her. He unfolded the paper and his bushy eyebrows raised. He took off his glasses, and looked over at her. "Congratulations. You're one hundred percent pregnant."

CHAPTER 9

He that loveth not knoweth not God; for God is love.
1 John 4:8

"REALLY? I don't think it can be true. I mean, we both wanted to wait until we were married and we only just did it the one time."

"How many times did you think it would take?"

Isla frowned. "What do you mean?"

"It amazes me when people say they did it only once. I hear that a lot. One time is all it takes. There are no practice runs."

She was stunned. She was sure the doctor had a point with his rambling, but she wasn't certain what it was—she was in shock. This wasn't in her plans. Just six months ago she'd had her life planned. There was to be the white wedding, and then their return to the Amish, and then they'd start their family. Everything was happening upside down, and there was no Benjamin by her side. A tear trickled down her cheek.

"Shall I call someone for you?" he asked softly.

"I have no one to call. I have a friend who's driven me here."

"It'll be hard for you without the father of the child around. A sudden death of a loved one takes time to recover from. Have you considered attending a bereavement group? I can give you names of some good ones. There's one held in a community center nearby."

She shook her head. "Thank you, but I have the bishop and the community to help me get over the death of my fiancé. And, of course, my family."

He gave her some papers on some prenatal clinics. "These might come in handy."

She shook her head. "Thank you, Doctor, but there are two midwives in the community and I'll use one of them."

"Okay. Let me know if I can help you with anything. Anything at all." He smiled at her for the first time since she'd gotten there.

"Thank you, Doctor, I appreciate your help." She didn't have to ask how far along she was because she knew exactly. The baby had been conceived the very day before Benjamin was killed. A tear trickled down her cheek and the doctor saw it and passed her a box of tissues, compassion in his eyes.

She plucked out a tissue before she walked out to face Benjamin's brother. After she'd quickly wiped her eyes, she tucked the tissue into her clothing, took a deep breath and tried to put on a happy face so James wouldn't see how shocked she was.

It hadn't worked. Her face must've told the story. He jumped to his feet, rushed over and put his hand on her elbow.

"Are you okay?" he whispered.

"I just need to get out of here."

She fixed up the necessary paperwork and paid the bill, and then she walked out of the office with James' arm through hers.

As soon as they were down the front steps of the building, he stopped and looked at her. "Now tell me what's wrong."

She swallowed hard, wondering how she could tell him. She looked into his deep brown eyes and realized she'd also have to tell his parents. "I'm... I'm pregnant."

He stepped back a little and his eyes bugged wide open. "Is that for certain?"

"Yes. Can you just drive me home?"

"Of course."

She was silent for the first half of the trip until he said, "A child is always a blessing."

"I've been telling myself this is my only chance of motherhood. It is a blessing," she repeated to convince herself.

"You're still young, Isla, and you've got your whole life ahead of you. No one expects you to stay single forever just because Benjamin has died. You'll marry again and have more *kinner*. There's nothing surer."

She shook her head. "Don't talk about it. I don't want to be with anybody else."

"Well that's your choice. It's certainly not expected of you. In that case your *boppli* is even more of a blessing."

He was trying his best to make her feel better and she was grateful for it. "How are your parents going to take the news, do you think?" she asked.

"They'll be pleased that part of Benjamin will live on through your child. They'll be delighted and so will your parents."

She put a hand over her stomach; she hadn't even thought of telling her own parents. *What will* they *think?* she wondered as her eyes went wide. *What will everybody in the community think?*

"*Gott* is looking after you, Isla."

Was that right, or was having a child with no husband another burden she had to bear? As well as her own tears, she'd listen to the cries of her child who'd never know their father in this world.

"I guess it is a blessing, and deep down I think I'm happy, but right now it also feels like something else has been thrown at me. I don't think there is another unmarried mother in the community. Sure there are widows, but no one like me. I was never married to Benjamin."

"Maybe you were, though, Isla. In the sight of *Gott,* maybe you were."

"I suppose you think less of me now, James."

He glanced over at her. "Of course not! I don't. I know you. I've gotten to know you pretty well these past weeks and you're one of the nicest women I've ever known. It's no wonder my *bruder* fell in love with you."

Isla sniffed back tears. "I wouldn't blame you if you lost respect for me."

"It doesn't matter, Isla. You weren't in the community back then and you are now. We can't look back; we must always look forward. All your past sins and indiscretions are covered and no longer exist. Anyway, your *boppli* was conceived out of love."

"Thank you. That makes me feel better."

"It's a time for rejoicing."

She wiped her tears away. "Do you think so?"

"I'm going to be an *onkel* again."

"How many nieces and nephews do you have?"

He laughed. "I can't even count them, but there aren't enough of them. Each one is a precious gift."

When he saw her smile, he said, "There, that's better. Keep your face like that. This *boppli's* coming anyway, no matter what you think or say. Make the most of it and celebrate."

Isla wiped her eyes again. But... Benjamin wasn't there to share the news. "I know. You're right. I will be happy when I get over the shock of it all. That was the last thing I expected, but the doctor seemed to know. I started off telling him how Benjamin died several weeks ago, and he asked me if I could be... I didn't think it would happen." She wiped away the last tears, doing her best to focus on this as a blessing.

When they turned into the driveway, Isla was feeling a whole lot brighter. He stopped right outside her door. "I'll unhitch the buggy and come back to check on you."

"I'll be here. I'll make you a cup of hot tea to keep my mind occupied." She stepped down from the buggy.

CHAPTER 10

*Greater love hath no man than this that a man lay down his life for his friends.*John 15:13

NOTHING SEEMED REAL TO ISLA. Being in Benjamin's house without him, and now learning that she was having his baby. Her entire life had changed in the space of weeks.

How was she going to go through pregnancy and the birth and then raise a child, all without a husband?

With all of her sisters busy with their own children, and all but two of her sisters living a distance away, she was glad to have a ready friend next door in James.

She walked into the kitchen, filled the pot with water, lit the stove and set the pot on the burner. Just when she began laying out the cups and the saucers, she saw James making his way over. Before he got to the house, she saw him stop to look down the road. When Isla moved to the other window, she saw Sally heading toward James in a buggy.

Sally's coming to see James. What rotten timing.

Isla knew she should've been happy, but she needed James to herself right now. Then it dawned on her that Sally might've been coming to visit her.

She reached into the cupboard and pulled out an extra teacup and saucer before she headed to the door.

Isla saw James and Sally talking as they walked toward her. She opened her door wide and waved to Sally.

"Hello, Isla. I've come to see if you feel better today."

Isla recalled that she'd told Sally she was feeling a little unwell the night before, just before Sally had left. This wasn't the time to say anything about the pregnancy. "*Jah,* I'm fine *denke.* It might have been my own cooking that didn't agree with me. Come in, I've just made a pot of tea."

Sally and James both walked into the house.

"We can sit at the kitchen table," Isla said as she led the way.

Isla was thankful she had cookies and cake left over from the night before, and she placed them in the center of the table, and poured them each a cup of tea.

"I'm sorry, I feel like I've invited myself over when you might have come here, Sally, just to speak with Isla," James said.

"I was hoping to see you too," Sally said with a small embarrassed smile.

And then, just like that, Isla felt she was in the way, but she couldn't really excuse herself since they were in her house.

"How long have you been in the area, Sally?" Isla asked.

"We've been here about six months now."

"And do you like it here?" James asked.

"I do, but I liked where we were before that as well."

Isla thought she was giving him the hint that she wouldn't mind moving all the way up to his community.

"The other reason I came here was to invite you to my mother's house next Thursday, Isla, because we're all baking for the pie drive. It's on the following day, Friday."

"I'd love to." Isla knew that baking days were a good way to get to know everyone better, and she'd been gone for so long that, in addition to meeting the new women in the community, she needed to reconnect with those she'd known before.

"What is the pie drive supporting?" James asked.

Sally fluttered her eyelashes at him. "The local firefighters."

"That's a good cause. Any reason to make pies is a good reason," James said.

"You like pies, James?" Sally asked.

He laughed. "What man doesn't?"

"What is your favorite pie?"

"Apple pie. My mother used to make an apple pie every Saturday. She doesn't make them so much any more."

"I'll be sure to bake lots of apple pies," Sally said, smiling at James.

"Well, I might have to buy all of them from you."

Sally giggled and her cheeks turned scarlet.

Isla hid her annoyance at Sally's coy giggles and blushes. She wanted them to be a couple, but she didn't need to watch it play out in front of her. "Cookie anyone?" Isla pushed a plate of cookies toward them.

As James and Sally chatted, Isla munched on one cookie after another while wondering how she was going to support herself. With her savings, she had enough to live on for a few months and after that she had planned to get a job but now with the baby coming she would have to reassess her plans. The only sensible thing would be to get a job soon and work until the birth of the baby, or just a few weeks before.

"Don't you think so, Isla?" James asked.

She looked across at him. "I'm sorry, I was somewhere else for a moment. What was that?"

"James said that we should both go and visit him," Sally said.

She squinted at James. The invitation was obviously directed at Sally. Isla knew she wouldn't be going anywhere, not with the baby coming.

"I think that's a marvellous idea," Isla said. "We should do that."

"Is your *mudder* home, James?" Sally asked.

"*Jah,* she is. Do you want to stop in on her?"

"I might say hello to her before I leave, since she's right next door."

James turned to Isla. "Do you want to come too, Isla?"

She hadn't said two words to Benjamin and James' mother since the funeral. She shook her head. "You two go on ahead."

"*Denke* for the tea and cookies," Sally said as she rose to her feet.

"*Denke* for coming to visit me. It was lovely to see you again."

James stood as well. When they both walked out of the house, Isla put the empty dishes in the sink and filled it with water. She watched out the window as Sally and James walked to his parents' house.

They were an attractive couple and would have nice-looking children.

"And the child will have two parents," Isla said out loud.

After the sink was filled, Isla sat down to plan out the rest of her life. Soon, she'd have to announce to the world that she was having a baby. She wondered how hard it would be for her child to grow up never having a father around. What was done couldn't be undone.

The idea of telling people of her situation was daunting. She'd leave it a few months. There was no need to tell people too soon. Besides, she reminded herself, many people didn't announce their pregnancies until their second trimester.

"I'll have to tell *Mamm* and *Dat* first," she said out loud.

The easiest way to do that, she thought, would be to tell one of her sisters and have her sister come along when she broke the news. "I won't worry about that now."

Her first priority was to find employment, and the best person to approach about that was the bishop's wife, Hilda. Perhaps there was a family who needed extra help looking after their children while both parents worked. Or Hilda might have heard about an *Englisch* family who needed a nanny. The child care center she used to work at was too far away from where she now lived.

From what she'd heard from her sisters, their morning sickness had only lasted the first couple of months and if that's what had happened to her sisters, she hoped she would be the same.

 Tomorrow, she would borrow her parents' buggy and drive to Hilda's house.

Two hours later, Isla woke from dozing on the couch in the living room. She heard a buggy driving away from the house next door. She raised herself up so she could look out the window. It was Sally's buggy. Pleased that Sally must've gotten along well with James' mother, she settled back down and closed her eyes. It was always important to get along with someone's future mother-in-law, and she would've gotten along with her mother-in-law, too, if Benjamin hadn't died.

~

By the time morning came, Isla had planned everything before she'd even gotten out of bed. She would find a job, work for as long as she could and, as soon as her child was old enough, she could look after children in her own house. By doing so, she could be with her baby. As long as she got a job fairly soon, she didn't see why her plans wouldn't work.

Isla had a shower and dressed, all the while waiting for the dreaded morning sickness to return. There was no sickness, but then again, it didn't only affect her in the morning, it seemed to show up unexpectedly at different times throughout the day.

She brushed out her long hair that hung well below her shoulders. She'd had it cut short when she first left the Amish, and then had left it alone. Dividing it into two, she braided it tightly and then pinned it against her head before she popped the white prayer *kapp* over the top. Then she was ready to enjoy her early morning coffee with James.

To her surprise, James was already waiting when she opened the door.

"Oh, here you are already."

"*Jah,* here I am. I'm just escaping from my *mudder.*"

Isla sat down. " What's the matter?"

"All she talks about is Sally and how much she likes her."

"That fantastic!"

"It was fantastic yesterday, it was fantastic last night, but this morning... Not so much."

Isla giggled and when she saw no mugs on the table, she asked, "Does that mean I have to make the coffee this morning? It's not as nice as the coffee from your place."

"Two coffees coming up." He stood up and headed back to the house.

"I'll be waiting," she called after him, pleased that her plan with Sally and James was working out.

CHAPTER 11

And above all things have fervent charity among yourselves:
for charity shall cover the multitude of sins.
1 Peter 4:8

ISLA WAS a little sad at the thought of James having to leave eventually. If he married Sally and stayed here, they would become her very best friends.

In no time, he was coming back with two mugs of coffee. When he saw her watching, he laughed.

"Why are you laughing at me?" she asked.

"I was going to pretend to trip and fall over, but then I couldn't because I really would've spilled the coffee."

"That would've been a total disaster." She reached for her coffee. "I've come to enjoy our mornings together."

"And you living right here by the house has been a blessing. I can come visit you when life gets too hectic over there."

She took a small sip of the hot coffee.

"I know you said many weeks ago that you would stay here until I'm settled. I'm settled now. I don't want you changing your plans on account of me."

"You're hardly settled, Isla. You're even more unsettled now, since we had that recent news."

"Everything will work out fine. You should look after yourself for a change. Ask Sally to marry you and take her back with you."

He took off his hat and rubbed the side of his forehead. "Do you think she would accept a proposal at this early stage? We hardly know one another."

"That makes it more romantic."

"Do you think so?"

"Well, maybe. Do what feels right. I can tell you like her because I can see it on your face," she said.

"I didn't know I was that easy to read."

Isla nodded. "Most men are."

"Is that so?" He took a sip of his coffee and swallowed.

"No instruction manual needed."

He laughed as he placed his mug back down on the table. "Good thing I already swallowed! You're in a cheeky mood today, I can see that."

"I'm off to visit Hilda today."

"The bishop's wife, Hilda?"

"*Jah.* I'm going to ask her if she knows anybody who needs child care or a nanny."

"Isla, I don't think you should be working in your condition."

"I'm not sick, I'm just having a baby."

"All the same, you should take things easy."

"I will take things easy when I have enough money to support my child and myself." Her parents couldn't help her, and her sisters and their husbands were supporting her parents. She had to look after herself.

"I'll help you, Isla. I don't want you to work. Benjamin wouldn't have wanted that."

"That's a very kind offer, James. But you've got your own life and soon you'll have a family to worry about. And Benjamin is not here, but I am. I need to do what I have to do to support myself and my child."

"You don't have to put yourself under a burden."

"I'm not." Isla took another mouthful of coffee and then stared back at James because he was staring at her. "You can't talk me out of it. This is something I'm doing. If there was any risk to the baby I wouldn't do it, but I'm perfectly healthy."

"How about a compromise?"

"Now you're sounding more like an older brother than a friend. Not that I've ever had a brother, but I figure they're like a protective father only worse." He frowned at her and she laughed. "Okay. Let me hear it."

"Let me take you to Carmen first."

Carmen was the local midwife.

Isla pursed her lips. "And then if she says there's nothing wrong with me working, you'll be happy about that?"

"I will."

"Then will you stop nagging me?"

He nodded. "I'll stop nagging about that, but I might find something else to nag you about."

"I can believe that," she said.

"Just let me visit Hilda today and then I will call Carmen and make an appointment. I don't think Hilda will know about a job right away. I'm just asking her to let me know if she hears anything."

He nodded. "That sounds reasonable."

"Good."

"Now drink your coffee. Wait, should you be drinking coffee?"

"I don't see why not."

"That's something you should ask Carmen."

Isla thought for a moment. "I think I just can't drink alcohol; I think I'm fine with coffee."

"Nevertheless, I want you to ask Carmen that."

"Do you want me to write out a list of things I should ask her?"

He laughed. "I'm sorry. I'm just overprotective."

"I'm only teasing. It's nice that you care."

He frowned. "Of course I do."

"When are you seeing Sally next?"

He smiled. "Funny you should say that because I'm taking her on a picnic this afternoon."

"Good. Don't forget to be romantic because women like that."

"Romantic?" He scrunched his face. "What can I do that's romantic?"

"You could pick some wildflowers while you're on a walk and hand them to her."

"Aren't you forgetting I'm no good with flowers? They die whenever I'm near them."

"That's right. I totally forgot. Well, forget that idea."

"What else?"

Isla turned her gaze to the sky. "What about a kitten or a puppy?"

"You mean give her livestock?"

Isla laughed. "I didn't say give her a cow. A puppy or a kitten will remind her of you every time she looks at it."

"That's something I would never have thought of. Can you think of anything that doesn't require feeding or looking after? It might be hard to take back to Eggleton on the Greyhound, if she eventually agrees to marry me."

"Chocolate. Women love chocolate as long as they're not allergic."

"That's a good idea, but what if she's allergic?"

"It doesn't matter, she'll still like the chocolate and will probably eat it anyway and be sick for the next few days."

"Ah, I see. So I can't lose with chocolate even if she is allergic?"

"That's right."

"I'll take her to the chocolate shop and she can choose her own."

Isla shook her head. "*Nee!* That's not what you do."

He stared at her.

"You really haven't done this before, have you?"

He screwed up his face. "*Nee,* I've been too busy and as I said, there are no single women where I come from, only married ones. I'm grateful to you for giving me a few pointers."

"So, you haven't been rejected like you once told me you'd been?"

"When I was younger I was."

He opened his mouth to tell her about it and she put up her hand to stop him. "I don't need to know. Okay here's the thing about the gift. It's better if you choose the chocolates because it'll be a surprise."

"And women like surprises when it comes to presents?"

"*Jah,* they do."

"*Denke.* I'll head down to a chocolate shop before I collect her for the picnic."

"Very good."

"What flavor should I get? Dark chocolate, light chocolate, white chocolate? Hard center, or soft?"

Isla laughed. "You're on your own with that. Just get a pretty little box with a bow on it. It'll be the thought and the fact that it's chocolate that counts."

"You're a smart lady. Anything else I should know?"

"I can't think of anything. You'll be fine."

"I can drive you to Hilda's."

"Okay, thank you. What time are you leaving?"

"Since I have to buy chocolates first, I'll leave at eleven."

Isla smiled. "I'll be ready."

CHAPTER 12

Husbands, love your wives, even as Christ also loved the church,
and gave himself for it;
Ephesians 5:25

As Isla got ready to visit the bishop's wife, she prayed there would be a job that suited her, with a family she'd get along with. A job for six or seven months was exactly what she needed. And if she was working, it would help take her mind off herself—exactly what she needed.

At eleven o'clock, she waited on her porch. She would've gone to meet James but she was still keeping away from James' parents and their house as much as she could.

She walked out to meet him when his buggy came around the side of the house toward her.

When James stopped the buggy, he started to get out to help her. "I can manage," she said as she climbed up next to him.

"I hope you have a successful visit with Hilda," he said.

"And I hope the same for your picnic. Except that might mean you leave me, and I'll have to have coffee by myself every morning, and bad coffee at that."

James looked over at her. "Before I go, I'll get you a decent coffee machine."

She laughed. "That will solve half the problem."

"You might not be drinking coffee soon."

"It might not be a bad thing that you go back home soon. I'd forgotten how much you nag."

He frowned. "Someone has to look after you."

"I can look after myself."

"I hope you can, otherwise I'll worry about you when I'm away."

"I'll be fine."

"You should come and visit my *mudder* soon."

"I can't help thinking I'm the last person she wants to see."

"She'll be fine. She'll be pleased to hear about the *boppli* and she can be of help when the time comes."

"We'll have to see how things work out."

He pulled into the bishop's driveway.

"I hope she's home," Isla said.

"How are you getting back home?"

"I'll call one of my sisters to fetch me. Hilda and bishop John have a phone in their barn."

"Okay. I'll wait here, though, until you see if she's home."

"Thanks."

Isla knocked on the door and was pleased when Hilda answered it.

"Isla, come in."

Isla waved to James to let him know he could go. He gave her a wave and clicked his horse onward.

"Come in. I'll make us a pot of hot tea."

"Thank you."

Hilda turned around. "Oh, are you here to see me, or John?"

"I came to see you."

"Ah, good. I was hoping so."

Isla followed her through to the kitchen, where she was directed to sit in a chair at the table.

When she was seated, Hilda fussed around the kitchen making tea.

"I was wondering if you knew of anybody who might need some child care or a nanny."

"You're looking for a job?"

"*Jah,* I was working at a child care center before, and I've got all my qualifications for that."

"I did hear mention of a family that was after a nanny."

"Was it for a live-in nanny?"

"Did you want something live-in?"

"*Nee.* I'm living in the house next to the Millers."

"Oh, I know which *haus* you mean. This job is with an *Englisch* couple. I'm sure I heard about it from Molly Hershey." Hilda put the kettle onto the stove and sat down with Isla. "I'll see what I can find out and I'll stop by your *haus* and let you know."

"That would be *wunderbaar, denke.*"

"That's the least I could do. You're going to need some way to support yourself. Let us know if you need any financial help. We have a fund for people having trouble."

"*Jah.* I know. *Denke.* I should be fine. I'll find a job doing something even if it's not in child care."

"How are you coping? It can't be easy."

"I'm doing just fine, I suppose, under the circumstances. He's gone and he's not coming back."

"You'll never forget him. Did you know that John wasn't my first husband?"

Isla had heard but couldn't bring herself to admit it. *"Nee,* I never knew."

"Not many people do. I married Seth when I was seventeen and he died two months later. We only had weeks together. I still treasure those moments, and he's still alive in my heart. Now those memories are in the back of my mind, forty years and seven *kinner* later, but you don't forget when you love deeply."

"Do you mind me asking how he died?" She knew she'd lost her husband but had never known the details.

"He went swimming with his brothers. He dived into shallow water and broke his neck."

Isla could feel tears stinging behind her eyes as she felt the pain that Hilda must've felt. Then the tears started to trickle down her cheeks. She wiped them away with the back of her hand. "That's sad. I'm sorry for crying."

Hilda handed her a tissue. "Never be sorry for your emotions, dear."

Isla wiped her eyes with the tissue, now feeling a headache coming on. "It must've been hard for you with his sudden death."

"The same as it was for you, except you hadn't yet married. I'm not sure if that's better or worse."

"Me either." Isla shook her head. "I don't like it when people die."

"We can't escape it, dear. All we can do is appreciate those *Gott* has left with us here on earth, and look forward to someday rejoining those who've gone on before us."

"That's true. I'll remember that."

Hilda jumped up when she heard the water boiling.

Hilda was so nice that Isla considered telling her she was pregnant. She was sure she'd give her some good advice, but she couldn't tell Hilda yet when her parents and sisters didn't know.

"Thank you for telling me about your first husband. It makes me feel someone understands."

"I do understand. You can come and talk to me whenever you want. No matter what you're going through, there's always someone who's gone through it before. There's nothing new under the sun."

"I'll try to remember that, too."

"Well, hopefully, you'll have a job soon."

Isla nodded. "I hope so."

"Now would you like lemon tea or regular tea? Oh, I've got nettle as well."

"Nettle please."

When her visit with Hilda was over, she asked, "Can I use your phone to call my sister to come and fetch me?"

"Where are you going?"

"I'm just going home."

"I can take you home."

"*Nee*, I don't want to trouble you. Besides, I want to catch up with one of my sisters."

"Very well."

Hilda walked with her to the barn and waited while she made the call to her sister. Liz answered on the first ring, having just gone out to their barn to check the supply of chicken feed, and she agreed to come and get her. Liz's daughters were playing at a friend's place. This would be the perfect opportunity for her to have a good talk with Liz.

WHEN SHE WAS in Liz's buggy and they were headed down the drive from the bishop's house, Isla could hold it in no longer. "I'm pregnant."

Liz took her eyes off the road and stared at her with open mouth and eyes wide open. "You're *what?*"

"Pregnant."

She pulled the buggy to the side of the road and stopped.

"Keep driving. Hilda might be watching."

Liz clicked the horse on. "I'm in shock. How did this happen."

"The usual way."

"That's not what I meant."

"Well, it wasn't planned. It happened the day before he died and I guess no one would've ever known that we didn't wait until we were married if he hadn't died."

"That's no surprise. You came back to the community from living amongst the *Englisch*. Everyone assumed you might have been living together anyway."

"Did they?"

"*Jah.*"

"Well, we weren't."

"That doesn't matter. What matters is you're having a *boppli*. That's *wunderbaar*."

"Really? You really think it is?"

Her sister nodded.

"Well it's still quite early. You're the first person to know. Well, one of the first people to know."

"Who else knows?"

"The doctor for one. And me..." Isla quickly changed the subject, not wanting to let her know how close she'd become with James. "Should I tell *Mamm* and *Dat* now, or wait?"

"That's up to you."

Isla sighed. "I'm finding it increasingly hard to make up my mind about anything."

"That's the hormones for you." Her sister giggled.

"I guess I'll have to visit Carmen soon."

"You should."

"I've got a million questions to ask you about the birth. I'm scared."

"Carmen will help you with that. She always says to relax and go with the pain rather than fight against it. The more stiff your body is, the worse the pain is and it's harder for the baby."

Isla grimaced. "I'll worry about all of that later. Firstly, I have to get a job for few months, and I'll work up until the baby is born, so we'll have enough money to live off."

"Oh! Peter is looking for someone else to work in his furniture store. It's just three days a week, though."

Peter, Liz's husband, owned an Amish furniture store that was right by the farmers markets.

"Really? Do you think he'd consider me?"

"I'd say he would. I can drive you in there now to talk with him. I think he'd give you the job happily, especially since you're family."

"*Jah*, could we go in now? That would be wonderful! Thank you, Liz."

CHAPTER 13

Rejoicing in hope; patient in tribulation;
continuing instant in prayer
Romans 12:12

WHEN LIZ and Isla walked into the furniture store, the first person they saw was Peter's older brother, Daniel.

"Daniel owns half the store," Liz told Isla as they greeted Daniel.

Isla remembered seeing Daniel at the funeral. He was tall with dark hair, tanned skin and dark brown eyes.

"Is Peter in?" Liz asked Daniel.

"*Nee*. He's just gone to have a meeting with one of our suppliers."

"Oh," Liz grunted.

"Can I give him a message?" he asked.

"*Nee,* that's okay. Do you still have that job available in sales?"

"We do. We're holding interviews today and tomorrow."

"Isla's looking for work."

Daniel turned to Isla. "Have you done this kind of work before?"

"I've only done child care."

"Have you been involved in any kind of sales before?"

She thought back to her very first job. "I did about six months of phone sales. I'd forgotten that."

"Are you one of those annoying telemarketers?"

"Yes I was. But not anymore. Never again."

He laughed. "We get them all the time on the phone. I suppose that's a start." He studied her for a moment, before he said, "That must've been a hard job."

"It was. I got abused on a daily basis."

"You can hardly blame them," he said with a grin.

Isla shrugged and smiled, hoping the dreadful telemarketing experience might help her get this job. "I guess it's annoying to be called like that, unexpectedly. I tried not to let it bother me when people were rude."

"Do you know anything about our furniture?"

"I'm a fast learner."

He looked at Liz. "Peter and I do the interviews together and he'll be back in fifteen minutes. Is it possible for you to come back in, say, half an hour?"

Isla looked at her sister. She hoped Liz didn't have to collect her children any time soon. "Do you have the time to wait, please?"

"I do. I'm free until five."

Isla looked back at Daniel. "Thank you, that would be good. We'll be back in half an hour."

Liz and Isla walked out of the store. Isla had a good feeling about working there. She was sure she'd enjoy it. "Let's grab a bite to eat at the farmers market."

"That sounds good to me. Have you been eating more?"

"I haven't noticed that I have, but I've had a little bit of morning sickness."

"Just a little bit?"

"I've been sick a few times but not every single day."

"Hopefully it doesn't get worse."

"I'm praying that it doesn't."

"He likes you, I can tell," Liz said.

"Good, but isn't it up to Peter if I get the job?"

"I'm not talking about the job, silly."

She abruptly stopped walking and stared at her sister. "Oh, you mean he likes me in *that* way?"

"Yes."

"He's not married, then?"

"He's a widower. His wife died in childbirth, and the child died at the same time."

"Oh, that's awful. That's so sad."

"It happened several years ago." She pointed to a coffee shop. "Let's go in here."

When they were seated, Isla asked, "And Daniel has no other children?"

"*Nee.* Celia had already had two miscarriages."

"That's awful. I heard about Hilda's first husband today, and now I learn about Daniel and his wife and child. I don't feel so alone."

"You're never alone when you've got your family, either. None of us could ever work out why you left the community," Liz said.

"I think it was a big adventure, going out into the unknown. Being able to do anything and have anything. I had nothing to feel guilty about and I felt free."

"If it was that good why did you come back?"

"We decided to come back because we both knew it was the best place to raise a family and I guess if it's the best place to raise a family, it's probably the best place for the both of us to be." Her thoughts turned to the job. "I should tell Peter that I'll only be able to do the job for six months or five months."

"You can't do that. He'll want to know why, and you can't tell them yet since no one else knows."

"I have to say something. What if they want someone for two years; someone who is going to stay a long time?"

"Ask them that in the interview," Liz said.

Isla sat down in the interview room with her brother-in-law and Daniel.

Peter began, "We're looking for someone we can train, someone who can fill-in when people are sick or on holidays. To start with, it'll be full-time for two months during the training period. Then the person we employ will be on call."

"We'll call you when we need you," Daniel said.

"Does that sound like something that would suit?" Peter asked.

It sounded perfect to Isla. She could still come in after the baby was born and leave the baby with her mother or one of her sisters. That might even be better than running a child care business from her home after the birth of her child. "That sounds absolutely perfect for me. And I can learn really fast."

"Do you have your own transport?"

"I will have, soon."

"What about a telephone?"

"My *haus* is right by the Millers' barn, and I have permission to use their phone."

At the end of the interview, the brothers took a few minutes for private discussion, and decided to give her the job then and there.

CHAPTER 14

Now the God of hope fill you with all joy and peace in believing,
that ye may abound in hope,
through the power of the Holy Ghost.
Romans 15:13

ISLA STOOD and shook Daniel and Peter's hands once she learned they were giving her the job, and then she sent up a prayer of thanks before she went in search of her sister, Liz.

Liz was waiting by the front of the store. As soon as she saw Isla's face, she asked, "It went well?"

"I've got the job."

"That's fantastic! When do you start?"

"I start on Monday."

"I'm so happy for you. It's got to make you feel a lot better to have some money coming in."

"It does. I have some savings but that would've been gone soon and I don't know how much time I'm going to need to have off with the baby." She told Liz the hours she would be working, and that she would be a casual employee. "I'll have to buy a buggy."

"Nee, just use *Mamm* and *Dat's.* They rarely use it now and I can drive them wherever they need to go."

"That's a mile's walk. I don't know if I could do that once I get bigger."

"I mean you could keep your horse in the paddock by the house and the buggy in the Millers' barn."

She bit her lip. That would mean asking the Millers for permission. "Maybe. Right now all I can think about is the roasted peanuts I saw back at the markets."

Liz laughed. "Let's go find them."

Isla nestled into her couch with her bag of peanuts, wondering how James was doing on his picnic with Sally.

It wasn't until later when she was cooking dinner that she saw James' buggy driving past.

"It must've been some picnic," she murmured to herself, pleased her matchmaking seemed to be working out. She'd need to decide on something to occupy her time of an evening. Before she'd left the community, she used to sew with her mother and her sisters.

Perhaps she could sew some outfits for her baby, or maybe start on something simple like baby-sized sheets for a crib. There were so many things to think about with the baby coming along.

Her sisters had seen to it that she had plenty of clothing on her return to the community. They'd each given her dresses, *kapps,* capes and aprons. She hadn't had to sew any of them for herself and she'd been grateful for that.

The evenings on her own were slow. Isla decided to go to bed early, knowing when she woke, she'd hear all about James and Sally's picnic. Her mind drifted to the widower, Daniel. Would she end up marrying a man like him in a few years time? Since he'd known tragedy and grief, he'd be able to understand hers, but did two broken people make a whole? And, would a man be able to love a child who wasn't his, as much as he would've loved his own? Her future seemed muddy, and no scenario that ran through her mind worked out.

As much as she wanted her child to have a loving father, she couldn't see that as a reason for her marrying. She tossed and turned while trying to plan a good future for her child, and in the end she cried out to God. Isla told Him that none of her plans had come to fruition, and then she placed her life and her child's life in His hands. She would trust in Him for her own and her child's future.

It had been a hard thing to do, to give up control, but she knew it was the only way for her to move forward.

When Isla opened her door in the morning, she saw that James was already on his way over with their traditional two mugs of coffee.

"That's good timing," he called out.

She sat down and waited for him to walk the rest of the way.

"*Denke,*" she said as he placed a coffee down on the table. "I've got some news to tell you, but tell me yours first."

"What makes you think I have news?" he asked.

"I can tell you do and I've been waiting all yesterday afternoon and all this morning to find out what happened on your picnic with Sally."

He chuckled. "What happened between us is private."

"That's not fair. You can't say that to me. I was the one who put the two of you together. Just tell me a little bit?"

He raised the mug to his lips.

She pouted. "Did you get her chocolate candies like you were going to?"

"I did. And I have to thank you for that idea."

"Did she like it?"

"She did."

"And?"

"And what?"

Isla frowned at him. "That's not fair, James. I need to know what happened because if she's not going to work out for you, I'll need to find somebody else."

He chuckled. "I can't put a burden like that on your shoulders."

"It's not a burden, not at all. Enough about me, now. Tell me your news. You're not having twins, are you?"

"I wouldn't know. But that would be a shock. I got a job yesterday."

He leaned back. "Hilda knew someone?"

"Hilda? Oh, no. I'll have to tell her today that I found a job. It was my sister, Liz, who told me about it."

"What job is it?"

"In Peter's furniture store, selling furniture."

"Your *bruder*-in-law's furniture store?"

From the expression on his face, she couldn't tell if he was pleased or not "*Jah*. It's two months of full time for training, and then I'm going to be filling in for people who are taking time off, sick or on vacation." She was relieved when he smiled.

"That's perfect. That's just what you wanted."

"And I think I would be able to keep doing it after the baby is born."

He shook his head and his jaw stiffened. "I told you, you don't need to work. My family will always support you."

"I can't ask that or expect that." *Or rely on that,* she thought.

"The child is going to be my niece or nephew, so that makes me responsible."

It was nice and honorable and all that, but Isla didn't want to feel like she was infringing on anyone's life. Her baby was her responsibility. "I'm the one who is responsible, though, and I will provide the best I can. *Gott* will provide. He already has."

"There are different ways *Gott* provides. He could be providing for you through me."

"I want to be independent."

He laughed. "You're a modern thinking woman."

"I guess I am."

"Remember, I'll always be here if you ever need anything. All you have to do is ask. And I mean anything."

"Denke." Isla figured that the date with Sally must've gone extra well if he didn't want to talk about it.

"And I'm not forgetting you said you'd go to see Carmen soon," James added.

"I will. I haven't forgotten don't worry. But I'll need to tell my parents first."

"And you'll have to tell my parents, too."

Isla looked down. She didn't want to have to tell Benjamin and James' parents, since she hadn't even spoken to them in ages. It was awkward now. "I will."

"What's wrong?" he asked tipping his head to one side.

"I think you know. Your mother doesn't want to speak to me."

"You're going to have to tell her you're expecting eventually. She'll be pleased."

"She thinks I kept her son away, and I guess I did."

"Stop judging yourself. You didn't force him to get on that motorbike. That was his decision, wasn't it?"

Isla nodded.

"You worry too much about what other people are thinking."

"I guess I do. I was raised that way. To worry about what other people are thinking and what they might say about me." Isla put her mug down on the table and fiddled with the strings of her prayer *kapp* while James took another mouthful of coffee.

"Maybe you should dip your toe in the water first."

"What do you mean?"

"Come for dinner one night, or just call in and visit, and then when you've got the big news to tell her it won't be so daunting."

Isla nodded and wondered why it was up to her to reach out. Couldn't his mother be the first to do that since she was older? Mrs. Miller knew where she lived and she hadn't even called in yet to see what she'd done with the house. She was hurting too. "I might visit her today. Would that be okay?"

"I think you'd be surprised."

Isla sighed. "I guess you're right. I'll do it today."

"I'll make myself scarce for the rest of the day. You two should talk alone."

Isla took a deep breath and tried not to sigh, not wanting to let James know just how reluctant she really was to speak to his mother. "I'll make a cake and take it over."

"That's the way."

"What are you doing today?"

He chuckled. "I'm helping Sally's father with repairing his barn."

"Oh. You're making it a family thing?"

"I'm not trying to get into her father's good graces by helping him. He needed help and I offered. It'll give me something to do now that your place is done."

"I'm teasing. Will Sally be there?"

"I'm not sure. " He stood. "I'll let you know tomorrow morning."

"*Jah.* I'll be waiting for an update. Make sure you tell me, or I'll be cross. None of this keeping silent. I'm your confidante."

He took hold of the empty mugs and held her gaze. "When I come home late this afternoon, I'll be expecting to hear my *mudder* tell me you visited."

"I'm going to make the cake now and as soon as it's cooled, I'll take it over. Happy?"

He gave her a nod, and then strode toward his parents' house.

CHAPTER 15

And now abideth faith, hope,
charity, these three;
but the greatest of these is charity.
1 Corinthians 13:13

IT WAS AROUND one o'clock when the cake had cooled enough for her to top it with frosting. She hoped that James' mother liked chocolate cake. She hadn't even thought to ask James that question.

After she put the cake onto a plate, she took a deep breath and said a little prayer, and walked across to the house.

She stood at the door and knocked, waiting a full minute before the door opened slightly. Benjamin's mother, Mabel, stared back at her.

"I brought cake," Isla said.

"Come inside."

She walked in past the woman.

"*Denke,* Isla. The place is a bit untidy because our visitors have just left.*"* Mrs. Miller leaned in and said in a low voice. "Except for my *schweschder,* Mary, who could very well have moved in without letting us know. She's upstairs having a nap."

Isla giggled and immediately relaxed. "Did you know your other visitors well?"

"*Jah,* and we haven't seen them for a long time. Come through to the kitchen."

"It's chocolate cake." Isla said holding the cake out. It was obvious it was chocolate, but nerves were still rippling through her.

"Shall we have some?"

Isla nodded. *So far so good.*

"Would you like a cup of tea, or the coffee you're so fond of having in the morning?"

She knows about the early morning coffee sessions with James. "Whatever you're having will be fine."

Soon they were seated and Mrs. Miller had served her a cup of tea. Isla was quiet, wondering where the conversation would go.

Mrs. Miller said, "I don't know why you and Benjamin stayed away from the community for so long, and planned to come back only after you married. It doesn't make sense. Why wouldn't you come back and get married in the community?"

As much as she hated it, she had to tell the complete truth. "It was my fault. Benjamin wanted to come back and get married and have our wedding in the community. I wanted to have an *Englisch* wedding with the big white dress and a triple layer white cake, and have photographs so we'd always remember it. We had a big reception booked and had all our *Englisch* friends invited. We had white vintage cars to take us to the reception area from our wedding in the park under the trees." Isla sniffed back tears. The wedding she'd dreamed of had become her worst nightmare.

"I'm glad you told me. I can see it's hard for you. I know you're telling me the truth."

"I wouldn't tell you anything else. We both loved Benjamin; you as a *mudder* and me as a *fraa*."

She nodded. "We were both robbed. I'm sad that I didn't see much of him in the past few years since he left."

"I know, and I guess you blame me for that."

Mrs. Miller inhaled deeply. *"Nee.* He left because he wanted to. I know you only became close in the last couple of years. I don't blame you for keeping him away. He was an adult."

"Jah, we both were," Isla said hoping what she'd just said had made sense.

"I'm sorry I haven't said much to you since the funeral. Every time I see you, I'm reminded of Benjamin. I don't want to feel sad all the time. It's a sadness that won't leave like a long cold winter, and I don't know what to do. It follows me everywhere like a dark cloud."

She looked into Mrs. Miller's red-rimmed eyes. Losing a son must've been torture, and losing one before his baptism into the community had to be so much worse. "I can understand that. We should be friends. We both loved him so much."

"I'm glad you stopped by."

"Me too." Isla looked over at the untouched cake on Mrs. Miller's plate. "The cake's no good?"

"Ah, I haven't even tried it." She stuck her fork in and broke off a portion of cake with some frosting and popped it into her mouth and smiled. When she'd swallowed, she said, "It's very good."

Isla knew the cake wasn't really worthy of being described as good. The flavor was pretty good, but it hadn't risen very well. "I haven't made a cake for awhile."

After they chatted a while longer, Isla left the house feeling greatly relieved. She'd misjudged Mrs. Miller, and she was glad James had encouraged her to clear the air. Her mind then turned to James, who was helping Sally's father. James deserved happiness and Isla hoped God would reward him with a good wife.

"My mother told me the two of you had a nice talk yesterday." That was the first thing James said when he sat down with Isla on her porch the next morning. As usual, he placed two steaming mugs on the table between them.

"We did. I'm so glad I went over there. Now we really understand each other."

"I know it will be easier, now, when you tell her about the *boppli.*"

Isla looked into the distance.

"You're going to have to tell her." He slurped his coffee.

She whipped her head back and faced him. "I know I'm going to have to tell her, but..." She licked her lips. "I'm not looking forward to it. I wish I could just sleep through these next several months and then wake up when the baby's a few months old and everyone's gotten used to everything."

"You're going to have to put what everyone's going to think to one side. You're also going to have to put the sadness about my brother to one side while you concentrate on making a happy home for your *boppli.*"

Isla nodded.

"*Gott* has blessed you with a precious gift."

She looked into his eyes. "Everything makes sense when you say it, James. I know all of that in my head, but..."

"But nothing."

She nodded. "You're right."

"Of course, I am. It's just common sense. Now drink your tea. I brought you nettle tea today."

After she'd taken a sip of tea, she wondered what Benjamin would think of his big brother bossing her around. *He would find it funny.*

~

Isla was pleased to go to the pie-making day that Sally had invited her to. If James wasn't going to tell her what was happening between them, she was certain Sally would.

"I heard you and James went on a picnic, and James has been helping your *vadder* with his barn."

"*Jah,* we've seen a bit of one another."

"That's great."

Sally smiled. "He's a nice man."

"I knew you'd like him."

When Sally remained silent, Isla knew that was either because she was in love with him, or else she wasn't impressed. Either way, she had to know. "Do you think you'll see him again?"

She shook her head. "I don't think so. There's someone else I like."

This wasn't what Isla wanted to hear. *Who would be better than James?* she asked herself. Now she'd have to find someone else for James if she couldn't manage to talk Sally around.

"That's too bad. You don't think he might grow on you?"

"Nee. He spoke about you nearly the whole time."

"He spoke about me?" Isla asked, quite startled.

"Jah. Isla thinks this, Isla thinks that. Isla said this, Isla said that. I thought if I heard your name one more time I might scream."

Isla grimaced. "Sorry about that."

"It's not your fault the man's in love with you."

Isla laughed. *"Nee.* He's not in love with me. We're good friends, and that's all. Is that why you think he doesn't suit you?"

"No woman wants to hear about another woman when she's alone with a man."

"Some men have no idea how to behave around a woman. I think he did that because you make him nervous. We have coffee every morning and talk about our day and I guess I tend to talk about him to people as well. We're simply friends and nothing more."

"Is that it?"

"I've no interest in men now, and James only has eyes for you."

"Are you sure?"

Isla quickly searched her mind for what James had said about Sally and then she remembered that James had agreed that she would make him a fine wife. He had it in his mind to marry and return to Eggleton with her. "I'm sure. You'll have to forgive his inexperience with women. If he were experienced, he'd be married already."

Sally put her fingertips to her lips and giggled.

"Will you give him another chance?" Isla asked.

Sally nodded. "Okay. I will."

"Good." Inwardly, Isla gave a sigh of relief. Sally was James' best chance if he was to find a wife on this visit.

Chapter 16.

While the earth remaineth, seedtime and harvest,
and cold and heat, and summer and winter,
and day and night shall not cease.
Genesis 8:22

THE DAY after her first visit to Carmen, the Amish midwife, Isla broke the news to her parents. She wanted Liz to come with her, but Liz told her it was something she should do alone.

Her mother opened the door. "Is anything wrong?"

"*Nee.* I have some news for you and *Dat.*"

"*Dat's* in the kitchen."

She walked into the kitchen and sat down at the table with her father, and her mother sat down too.

"Isla has news for us, Murray."

Her father stared at her and waited.

Isla took a deep breath. "I'm having a *boppli.*"

"What?" her mother shrieked with her hands flying to her cheeks.

Isla nodded, trying to figure out if her mother was pleased or devastated. It could've gone either way.

"I can't believe this," her mother said, finally looking pleased.

Isla was relieved and turned to her father. His expression hadn't changed. "Did you hear what I said, *Dat?*"

He nodded.

"Are you happy?"

He looked over at his wife and Isla gathered from that, he'd be happy as long as his wife was happy.

"*Mamm,* what are you thinking?"

"This is... I don't know. You have no husband and... Are you having this *boppli* by yourself?"

"Well, that wasn't my choice. I would've had Benjamin here if he hadn't died."

Isla knew the doubts her mother was having. She'd gone through everything in her mind so many times. "I can't take back what has happened, *Mamm*. I was out of the community then, and now I'm back and this baby is coming whether people like that, or not. I can't worry about what other people say or think. I just have to concentrate on giving this baby the best life I can."

Her father reached out, grabbed her hand and squeezed it. When she looked up into his eyes, he gave her a nod. Apparently, he liked what she'd said. She looked again toward her mother. "You'll have another *grosskin,* isn't that what you want?"

"*Jah,* I will have another, and *jah,* I do want each one *Gott* sends. You just need to give me a moment to think about this. It's unexpected. Have you told Mabel and Abe Miller yet?"

Her mother's cheeks had turned bright red, which happened when she was upset about something. "*Nee,* I wanted to tell both of you first. Liz knows. I'll tell Benjamin's parents soon, and I'll have to tell the bishop."

"What about your new job? Are you still working there?"

"*Jah.* Liz said they won't mind since I'm not full time once I complete the training. I can tell them about the baby, now that you know."

CHAPTER 16

And let us not be weary in well doing:
for in due season we shall reap,
if we faint not.
Galatians 6:9

THE NEXT MORNING, as soon as James sat down on the porch beside her, he said, "We should get married, Isla."

Isla drew her eyebrows together. "To each other?"

"*Jah.* It makes sense."

"Makes sense? That's hardly a reason to marry."

"I didn't mean that exactly. I would like it very much if you and I got married. That way, I could always look after you and the baby and make sure you're safe."

"Thank you, that's so sweet, but what about Sally?"

"Sally and I aren't suited."

"I think she's trying. I mean, I still think you might be suited. You're spending a lot of time with each other."

"I haven't seen her for days now."

"Really? She told someone she was with you yesterday."

"There must've been some misunderstanding, because she wasn't with me. I was doing some work on fences here most of the day."

"You're thinking of me as an easy option. It would be easier to marry me because we get along so well. When really, you should be trying to do a better job with Sally. I saw her at the pie-making day yesterday and she said you talked about me the whole time when you were with her. The poor girl was probably bored out of her mind."

"I had to say something. She didn't speak at all. What else was I going to talk about? You're a fascinating person."

Isla wagged her finger. "Stop it. I know you're being sarcastic. You're always telling me what to do and now I'm going to tell you what to do. I'm giving you a dose of your own medicine."

He raised his eyebrows and a faint smile touched his lips. "I'm listening."

"You're going to see Sally today and ask her if she'll allow you to take her out again and give you another chance."

His hand went to his hat and he tipped it back slightly on his head and leaned back folding his arms over his chest. "You can't force love on someone."

"You said yourself she'd make a good wife."

"And she will, I suspect, but maybe not for me."

Isla's shoulders drooped. "Do you mean you don't like her now?"

"She's perfectly fine. She's too hard to get to know."

"Then, you'll have to work harder and stop talking about me. Find out what interests her and talk about that. Ask her questions about herself."

He huffed.

"I'm gonna find you a wife if it's the last thing I do."

"Everyone needs someone, Isla."

"That's right."

"Oh, you agree do you? What about you, then?"

Isla shook her head. "I've had my chance at love and that's enough to last me the rest of my days."

"And how old are you?"

"The same age as Benjamin was, twenty-six."

"So if you live to eighty-six, that's sixty years you'll live alone. I don't think you're being practical."

Isla frowned at him. "You're the one who said not to worry about what people think."

"That's right, but when I said that, I wasn't including myself. You'll marry in a few years, I know it."

"That's where you're wrong. I won't."

"Sixty years without sharing your life with someone is a long and lonely stretch."

"I've got my family, and I'll have my child." She put her hand over her belly.

He sighed. "You really think I should try again with Sally?"

"*Jah*, I do. She's a lovely girl, well, she's a woman."

Slowly, he nodded.

"How does it feel having someone boss you around?" Isla asked, smiling.

He laughed. "I don't like my own medicine at all."

"You and I give each other good advice."

"My advice to you is good, but your advice is still unknown. If Sally and I work out, then you can say you gave me good advice."

"You're so nit-picking and frustrating, James Miller."

"*Denke.*"

"That's far from a compliment."

He leaned forward and took his mug in his hands. "Why can't life be more simple, Isla?"

"Because it's meant to challenge and test us. *Gott* wants to see what we're made of. Anyway, how would your life be more simple?"

"Never mind."

"Tell me."

He chuckled. "I've got no complaints. It's an effort for me to talk to women, but if I don't, I know I'll be a bachelor forever. You're the only woman I've found who's easy to talk to."

"That's because we've got something in common."

"Good coffee?"

"That too, but I meant Benjamin."

He looked away. "*Jah,* we both loved him. That must be why I feel close to you. If Benjamin had lived you would've been my *schweschder*-in-law. Anyway, we've said all we can say."

"You told me not to go through all the ifs."

He held up both hands. "Guilty."

She folded her arms. "Are we agreed you're going to visit Sally today?"

"I will, and I'll ask her out somewhere and we'll talk about something other than you. Something she's interested in. If she's interested in anything."

"Of course she's got interests and it's up to you to ask the questions to find out about her. Get her talking."

He shook his head. "This dating business is tough."

"Not as tough as having a baby."

He chuckled. "You've got that right."

"Be thankful you're a male. Now, you want a *fraa,* so you'll have to put the work in to get yourself one. Crops don't grow by themselves, they need to be planted, watered, and all that. It's the same with relationships, they start with a seed and then—"

"I get the point." He stood up, leaned over and took hold of both mugs. *"Denke* for helping a sorry bachelor out."

"You're welcome."

CHAPTER 17

Thy faithfulness is unto all generations: thou hast established the earth,
and it abideth.
Psalm 119:90

THE NEXT MORNING, she was waiting, eager to get an update on his romance with Sally.

When James sat down on the porch chair grinning from ear-to-ear, she knew things had gone well with Sally.

He said, "You were right that I should give her a second chance."

A twinge of jealousy jolted through her body. She'd grown used to the attention he gave her and if he married that would disappear. "That's good. Tell me about it," she said pushing her emotions away.

"I sat down with Sally and her *mudder* for awhile and then I asked Sally if she wanted to have lunch with me. We went into town and had lunch at a nice restaurant."

"And did you ask her questions about herself?"

"I did and I found she does a lot of work for charity."

"That's right. She does the pie drives for the local firefighters. We found that out at the dinner I had here at the *haus*."

"I didn't remember that, but anyway, she's a very caring and unselfish woman."

Isla twirled a stray strand of hair around her finger. When she saw him looking at her strangely, she tucked the loose hair back under her *kapp*.

"Did you hear what I just said?" he asked.

"I did. That's great news."

"I think you were absolutely right in urging me to give her another chance."

"She'd be glad that you didn't talk about me at all throughout lunch."

"I didn't talk about you at all. You didn't even come into my mind."

That was news she didn't want to hear. "I'm glad things are working out for you."

"There's a long way to go yet."

"You can't be too fussy. No one is perfect."

"I have to have that feeling that the woman I choose is the one I'm meant to be with. I've seen people in the community with marriages that don't work out and they have to move away from each other and live separately. I don't want to live like that. I want someone who thinks the same way as I do about the important things in life, and has exactly the same values."

"Do you hear what you're saying? You do want someone to be perfect."

"That's not what I said."

"If you play back that little tape recorder in your head, you want someone to be perfect."

"No I don't. But I'm not going to marry just anybody."

"I know what you mean. I'm only teasing. It's good to be careful about who you marry, especially at your age."

"What do you mean, at my age? I'm only thirty-two."

He acted older. "Forget it. I'm still teasing."

"I don't know what's gotten into you lately." He shook his head and picked up his coffee and took a mouthful.

"Is this the same coffee as usual?" she asked, sniffing it.

"It is."

She pushed it away from her slightly. "It tastes different."

"It's just the same. Maybe your *boppli* doesn't like coffee."

"Maybe. Liz said I might lose the taste for it. It happened to her while she was pregnant, both times."

"Does that mean I have to start bringing you tea instead?"

"Peppermint would be nice next time, *denke*."

CHAPTER 18

Thou wilt shew me the path of life: in thy presence is fulness of joy; at thy
right hand there are pleasures for evermore.
Psalm 16:11

A WEEK LATER, James arrived at Isla's *haus* for their usual morning talk.

"Well, what's the news? Are you an engaged man yet?"

He chuckled. "Wait until I get there." He walked up the steps and placed the mugs on the table.

"What's happened? You've got a funny smile on your face. Are things going good with Sally?"

"Things are going splendidly. She's agreed to marry me."

"What?"

"That's right. We're going to get married."

Isla's fingertips flew to her throat. "What happened to making sure she was the right one and waiting and wanting her to be perfect, and all that?"

"I took your advice. You were right, what you said about me running out of time. I don't want to be too old when I have *kinner*. Sally is anxious to start a family as well, and she's looking forward to coming back to Eggleton with me."

"I'm so happy for you."

"I know it's all thanks to you, Isla. I never would've persisted with her."

Isla forced a smile. "That's what friends are for. When are you getting married?"

"You're having your baby in August, so we're getting married in September."

"You don't have to make your plans around me."

"I told you I would stay here and wait to make sure you're okay before I leave, and I meant it. That's what Benjamin would've wanted. Someone has to watch over you. And it wouldn't be fair to Sally to marry her now and have her forced to live in my parents' *haus* for that long. We will marry, spend one night at my parents' house and then we'll leave for Eggleton."

"You've got everything worked out."

"Sally and I talked it all out yesterday."

"And you're sure? It's not that I've talked you into it?"

"You opened my eyes to what a wonderful woman Sally truly is."

CHAPTER 19

And said, Verily I say unto you, Except ye be converted, and become as little children, ye shall not enter into the kingdom of heaven.
Matthew 18:3

THE NEXT MORNING, Isla sat down on her usual chair at the normal time and waited about ten minutes before James appeared. She could see from the way he was stooped over that he was upset.

He placed the two mugs down, placing the peppermint tea in front of her.

"I'm very sorry, James. I heard about Sally when I was at work yesterday."

He remained silent and took a sip of coffee. After a while, he said, "We had plans. We had our lives planned out, and now she's gone, disappeared without a word—run off with another man like I never meant a thing to her."

"I'm so sorry." She looked out across the fields sparkling from the sunlight shining its morning rays on the early morning dew. "I know how it feels to have your plans come crashing about your ears when you think you're going to marry someone." She leaned over and gave his arm a squeeze.

"I've made a fool of myself." He didn't look up. His eyes were on the floor of the porch.

"I don't think you have."

"Sally never cared about me. All along she was seeing the *Englischer*. I might have been just an excuse for her to leave the house when she wanted to meet him. She'd say she was meeting me, and then she met him instead."

"That hardly makes you a fool."

He shrugged. "It doesn't matter." He looked at her. "How was your day yesterday?"

"It was fine. Every day at work seems the same. My sales figures are good, which I'm pleased about — they won't get rid of me." She giggled. "Apart from me being paranoid about being fired, everything's okay."

"No more morning sickness?"

"I haven't had any since the visit to the doctor."

"That's good."

"Forget about Sally, James. I'll find you someone else. What about Jessica? She's very nice."

"I should've listened to my heart at the beginning. None of these women are suitable. It's a waste of time."

"Sometimes you have to get to know somebody first before you can *really* know them. You've barely spoken to Jessica at all. Only a little bit at my house when we had that dinner together that time."

"And what's Jessica going to think if I ask her out straight after the disaster I had with Sally?"

He had a point there. She wouldn't be flattered to think she was second choice. "Maybe just wait a while then, and get to know some of the single women here as friends."

He nodded and took a mouthful of coffee. "I'll concentrate on you," he said when he'd swallowed the coffee.

"Oh, no you won't. That means you're going to boss me about."

He laughed. "I'm not bossing you. It's just that sometimes you don't know what's good for you."

"Same thing, in my book." Isla looked over the fields, wondering how and why Sally suddenly left the community. Maybe James was right and Sally had been using him as an excuse to leave home and meet her mystery man these past weeks. *What a cruel thing to do,* she thought.

"Have you got things ready for the *boppli* yet?" he asked.

"My sisters and my mother are all knitting and sewing for the baby, so I don't have to do any of that. And that's good because by the time I get home from work, I'm too tired to do anything."

"What about a crib?"

"I forgot to tell you; Daniel and Peter have given me a crib from work as a present."

He raised his eyebrows. "You must be the favorite employee already."

"It probably doesn't hurt that I'm the boss' *schweschder*-in-law."

"Or it might be that Daniel sees you as more than an employee."

Isla looked away. She liked Daniel and she couldn't deny it, but she'd never marry again. It was probably the pregnancy hormones that fed her attraction to Daniel.

"What can I do for you, then? I can't buy you a crib, I can't sew or knit, so what is there left I can help you with?" James asked.

"If you're free today, you could drive me to my appointment at Carmen's."

She saw his face light up. "I'd be delighted to do that. You aren't working today?"

"*Nee*. I have the day off."

"What time is your appointment?"

"This morning at ten thirty."

"Fine. Then why don't I take you out for lunch afterward?"

Isla had planned to give her house a thorough cleaning and wash the linen that day, but she knew James needed a friend right now. "That'll be *wunderbaar*. I'll look forward to it."

He looked pleased.

CHAPTER 20

And the peace of God, which passeth all understanding,
shall keep your hearts and minds through Christ Jesus.
Philippians 4:7

RIGHT AFTER JAMES took the coffee cups back home, she hurried around the house doing as much as she could in the little time she had. She'd make the most of her time with James before he went back to Eggleton.

If Sally had led him on any longer, it could've been a disaster. What if they had gotten engaged and then she had disappeared? Them planning a life together, and then her running out on him, obviously that had been hard on him.

When she was waiting outside for James and he was nowhere to be seen, she wandered up to the barn and then she saw him hitching the buggy.

"I'm sorry, I got a bit caught up with Aunt Mary."

"Did she have you do something?"

"*Jah*. She had me write a letter back home because she has bad eyesight now."

"Oh, was it interesting?" she asked.

He chuckled. "Well, *jah*. She told her husband that she would be staying on a few weeks more. The only thing is that *Mamm* thinks she's going home any day."

"I'd stay right out of that one if I were you."

"That's exactly what I intend to do. I hope I'm not making you late."

"No, there's still plenty of time. I think it only takes twenty minutes to get there. Depending on how fast your horse is... we might have to gallop." She smiled.

"I can't gallop the horse too fast."

She raised her eyebrows.

"Joking again. Right?" he asked.

"Kind of."

"I'll get used to that sooner or later. I think."

"*Jah*, you should." She nodded.

Once he had the buggy properly hitched he led the horse away from the barn so she could get in. He held her by the arm and helped her up.

"*Denke,* but I can manage myself, you know."

"I like to help you," he said.

"Do you know where Carmen lives?"

"I sure do."

They made their way down the road in silence. The cold weather was nearly upon them and a frosty breeze swept over them. James reached behind him and then handed her a blanket.

"*Denke.*" She spread the blanket over her to keep warm.

He glanced at her. "Don't you have a shawl, or a coat?"

"I do somewhere, I think."

"You'll have to find out where, and use it."

"I will."

When they stopped outside Carmen's house, Isla said, "You can come in and wait in the living room. She's got a separate area where she takes her victims."

He laughed. "Okay. I'll come in."

Fifteen minutes later, Carmen told her that all looked normal, and then added, "I'm going to send you to the hospital for an ultrasound."

"Why? Do you think there's something wrong?"

"Nee, just a precaution that I have my patients do nowadays. You don't have to go, but I'm advising you to."

"Okay. I'll do whatever you say."

Carmen ripped off a piece of paper from a yellow pad. Call this number on the top, and make an appointment. When you go, take this with you," she said, tapping the sheet of paper.

"Okay."

"Stop looking so worried," Carmen said. "I have everyone do this. Some refuse. It's a personal choice."

"Nee, I'm not worried about that. I know it doesn't hurt or anything. I'm just nervous about the whole thing."

"You'll be fine. Women have been giving birth since the beginning of time. We'll talk more about the birthing process as the pregnancy progresses. When you call the hospital, it might take a week or so for the appointment."

"Okay, *denke.*"

"We're all done for today."

"Where shall I have the baby?" Isla asked.

"At home, or here if you prefer."

"I think I'll have the birth at home. I'm sure *Mamm* will come and stay with me for a few weeks."

"*Gut.* I'll want see you in another month, then, but call me if there's any concern."

Isla went to meet James in the next room.

"All good?" he asked.

She nodded. "I have to go to the hospital and have an ultrasound, but Carmen says that's just routine procedure."

Carmen walked out behind her and heard what she said to James. "*Jah*, it's all normal. You're perfectly healthy, Isla, and your baby seems fine. No cause for alarm."

"*Denke,* Carmen," James said before they left.

When they got back in the buggy, Isla asked. "Where are we going for lunch?"

"Ah, I have a special place lined up for us. I can't tell you, you'll just have to wait and see."

She hoped James wasn't going to take her to some fancy restaurant like he'd taken Sally. She wasn't up for anything grand or fancy, and besides, she wasn't eating much lately.

Twenty minutes later, he stopped the buggy by a river.

"I can't see any restaurants around here."

"Come along. You'll see one soon."

They walked a little distance and then she saw a take-out hamburger place. "Oh, wow!"

"You'll love their hamburgers, even if you don't normally like hamburgers."

 "I've never been here before."

"Haven't you? That's terrible."

 She looked at the menu and chose a hamburger with the works, and he had the same with a side of fries.

When the order was ready, he grabbed her arm. "Come on. We'll go and eat these by the river."

They found a wooden table with bench seats, and the sun had just poked through the clouds.

Then Isla noticed ducks on a nearby pond. "This is beautiful, James."

She glanced up at him to see that he was pleased.

He placed everything down on the table, opened the wrapping of her burger and then unwrapped his own.

She stared at the large burger. It certainly looked good, but it was far too big to wrap her mouth around. "I'm going to make such a mess of myself here."

"You'll have to open it and have half at a time. And take a bite of each half in turn."

He picked up paper napkins from underneath the fries, and showed them to her.

"Don't lose those. I think I'm going to need plenty of them," she said.

Isla sat eating in the filtered sunlight and feeling perfectly happy and content. *Gott* had provided her with a house, a good friend, an income, and a loving family. She would be grateful for every blessing.

When James had finished his food, and she couldn't eat anymore of hers, they walked along the river throwing the leftovers to the ducks.

"This has been a perfect day," she said.

"I'm glad. I've appreciated watching you enjoy yourself."

She giggled.

"You haven't had one worrying thought in the last two hours have you?"

Shaking her head, she admitted, *"Nee,* I haven't."

The next morning on the porch

"I think today is the day," James said.

"Today is the day of what?"

"I think today is the day you should tell my parents. I'll invite you to dinner and then you can tell them during or after dinner."

"Don't you still have visitors?"

"Only Aunt Mary, and there's no telling when she'll go. She goes to bed fairly early, so maybe you can tell them after she's gone to bed."

Isla bit her lip. She knew she'd have to tell them, and sooner rather than later, and then the next person on the list was the bishop. He liked to know what was going on in the community, and well before everyone else did..

"So, what do you say?"

"Okay. I'll come to dinner. *Denke*. Then they will know you knew before them. Will that be okay?"

"They already know we have coffee every morning, so I don't think they will have a problem. Or be surprised that you've told me."

Isla sighed. "You're really helping me through everything. My head is in such a muddle, I don't know whether I'm coming or going half the time. I just hope I'm making the right decisions about everything."

"You're doing fine."

CHAPTER 21

I am not ashamed: for I know whom I have believed,
and am persuaded that he is able to keep that
which I have committed unto him against that day.
2 Timothy 1:12

After work that day, Isla stopped by the markets to get some flowers for James' mother. She had been getting along more comfortably with his parents ever since the day she'd visited with his mother, and they had happily allowed her to leave a buggy in their barn and a horse in their paddock. As he was most afternoons, James was waiting to take care of the buggy and horse when she got home.

"Is it still alright with your *mudder* that I come for dinner?"

"Of course, that's not a worry. We have people stopping in for dinner all the time unexpectedly."

"She knows I'm coming, right?"

"Of course she knows you're coming. There's no need for you to be nervous, Isla."

She followed him around while he tended to the buggy. "I am nervous, though. What time should I come over?"

"Just come whenever you're ready."

"I'll wash up and then think what I'm going to say."

"There's no need to rehearse. Say whatever comes to your mind. You're not making up a big story about something. Just tell them straight out."

"I feel I have to break the news to them gently."

"I don't know if there is a way to do that. Please don't worry. I can guarantee it'll be fine."

He straightened up and looked at her and she took a step closer to him and looked up into his eyes. "Are you sure? Benjamin and I weren't married, don't forget."

"I'm certain. Now stop worrying and go and do what you have to do."

"Okay, I'm going." She walked to the house and then remembered the flowers she'd bought. She walked back.

"Did you forget something?" he asked.

"*Jah,* I got some flowers for your *mudder.*"

He chuckled.

"Don't you think that was a good idea?"

"*Jah,* my mother loves flowers. Relax. You're worrying too much."

She reached into the back, grabbed the flowers and hurried home.

Isla had a shower and changed into a freshly-laundered dress and apron wanting to look as good as she possibly could when she gave them the news. Before she left the house, she said a prayer that everything would go well, they wouldn't be mad at her for what had happened, and they'd be pleased they were getting an unexpected grandchild.

She felt a bit better after she had prayed, and then she took the flowers out of the vase and shook the water off the bottom of them before she wrapped them in dry paper. Then she made her way to the Millers' house.

After she had taken a deep breath, she knocked on the door. The door opened and James stood there.

"Come in."

Aunt Mary and James' father were sitting on the couch. As she greeted them, Mrs. Miller came into the room from the kitchen.

"Isla, I'm glad you could join us tonight for the evening meal."

"Thank you for having me. Can I help you in the kitchen?"

"No need, *denke*. It's already cooked. Everybody can make their way into the kitchen now."

Mr. Miller helped Aunt Mary to her feet. She seemed much older than Mrs. Miller and yet they were sisters. There must've been a huge age difference between them.

When Isla walked into the kitchen, she saw a feast. There was more food than she was used to having. There were all kinds of meats and roasted vegetables, salads, and sauerkraut.

"This looks amazing. You must've been cooking all day."

"It hardly took any time and Mary helped."

She was shown where to sit, and was grateful that James sat next to her.

The conversation at dinner was a little awkward, and James spoke mostly about his farming methods in Eggleton. Isla was certain he was talking about that just because no one else was talking.

After dessert, Mrs. Miller suggested they have coffee in the living room, and Isla helped her get it ready.

When they were all settled with coffee, James, who was sitting opposite, made a face. She knew he was urging her to tell them now.

She couldn't do it. She'd have to tell them another time. Once she caught James' eye she pressed her lips together and frowned with a tiny headshake, letting him know that tonight was not the right time.

"Isla has something she wants to tell everyone."

Her mouth fell open and she wanted to hit him, but there was no time. All eyes were on her.

"Is that right, Isla?" Mrs. Miller asked.

"Well, the thing is....I'm having James' baby."

Mr. and Mrs. Miller gasped and stared at James, while Aunt Mary said, "What? What was that?"

The way they stared wide-eyed at James made Isla realize what she'd said. "No, no! That's not what I meant! I'm sorry. I didn't mean to say James. I'm having *Benjamin's* baby."

"Whose *boppli* are you having?" Aunt Mary asked trying to follow the conversation.

"Benjamin's," James told his aunt.

"I don't quite know what to say," Mrs. Miller stared at Isla.

"You're pleased, *Mamm,* aren't you? We've lost Benjamin, but you'll have his *kin.*"

"That's right," Mary said nodding now able to hear.

"How long have you known?" Mr. Miller asked.

She shook her head. "I found out recently and I wanted to tell my parents and you before I said anything to the bishop."

James looked over toward Mary. "What do you think, Aunt Mary?"

"I think she should move into this house. Who's going to look after her and the *boppli?* I think I'll have to stay on longer so I can help."

"No need to put yourself out, Mary," Mr. Miller said.

"Would you like to move in here? We've got plenty of room," Mrs. Miller said.

"*Denke,* but I love my home and it reminds me of Benjamin."

When they'd gotten over the shock and had asked all their questions, Isla excused herself and James walked her home.

"Of all the times to get Benjamin's and my name mixed up."

Isla giggled. "You should've seen the look on their faces."

"I did."

"I saw the look of horror on their faces, and it took me awhile while to realize what I'd said; that they thought it was your baby."

He chuckled. "It would be nice if the *boppli* were mine. Oh, I didn't mean anything disrespectful towards you in saying that."

"I know. Don't worry, you can't offend me. And thank you for making me tell them. And being there when I did. I was so nervous. Even more nervous than when I went to the doctor."

"You'll be feeling much better once everyone knows."

"I hope so. I hope the bishop is okay with the news."

"You were out of the community, and now you're baptized. You were on *rumspringa* and then you returned. No one's ever shunned for that."

"I know. Keep reminding me. I'm just scared. What if that thinking applies to everyone but me?"

CHAPTER 22

Be careful for nothing;
but in every thing by prayer and supplication
with thanksgiving let your requests be made known unto God.
Philippians 4:6

NOW THAT BENJAMIN'S parents had been told about the baby, the next thing was to tell the bishop. For that, Isla enlisted the help of Liz.

"I'm nervous. I haven't been nervous like this for so long," Isla said to Liz on the way to the bishop's house. "Well, maybe telling the Millers... It's a good thing you're driving instead of me."

"Relax, Isla, everything will be okay."

"You don't think I'll be shunned or anything?"

"Nee, there's no need to worry."

"James is always telling me to relax, too."

"You should. What have you been doing lately? I've barely seen you."

"I had such a good day with James recently. He took me to have lunch and we had hamburgers and then we fed the ducks and walked beside the river. I don't remember when I last had such a good day."

"James?"

"Now don't look at me like that. He's just a friend and he's Benjamin's brother. You know he's been good to me, making sure I got that house and everything. I still feel a little bit guilty about that and I'm not sure if the rest of the Millers wanted me to have it, but James said Benjamin had left him in charge of his affairs, and that meant it was his decision to make."

"It was generous of him, but I also think he's in love with you."

Isla laughed. "Don't be ridiculous." Although she laughed, she knew deep down it was true. She saw it in his eyes, that he adored her. "He'll be leaving to go back to Eggleton soon. He's just staying until I have the baby."

"He's going to wait until your weakest point and propose to you. You'll have the baby blues and you'll be up to your ears in dirty diapers, you won't have slept for two weeks and he'll propose and you'll latch onto him because you're desperate for a good night's sleep."

Isla pulled a face at her sister. "Nothing you said makes sense. I don't know where you get your storytelling ability, but you could write a book with an imagination like that!"

Liz chuckled. "Why do you think he's staying around? He's staying until you realize you're in love with him. That's what he's hoping, anyway."

"Are you saying that once I have the baby, I'll fall in love with anyone?"

"Something happens to your brain after you have a baby. You'll see."

"Anyway, that's what you and the rest of my family are for. You'll all have to help out so I don't get to that point. Just like I helped you with your babies." Isla poked her finger into her sister's shoulder. "Don't you dare forget the way I helped you. Remember, I'd often come in the middle of the day on the week-ends and whenever I had days off, so you could get some sleep. I wasn't even back in the community then."

Liz giggled. "I didn't know there would be payback time."

"I'm calling you on it. There is. There will be."

"Of course, and we'll all help you. Ah, here we are now." Liz stopped her buggy at the side of the bishop's house and Isla got out first.

They'd already told Bishop John and Hilda they were coming, and the couple no doubt wondered why Isla had asked to speak with them without giving a reason.

When they were both seated with John and Hilda, Isla opened her mouth and spoke. "I came here tonight to let you know that I'm pregnant with Benjamin's child." She added that last part so there would be no confusion.

Hilda remained silent, and so did the bishop until he slowly nodded.

"Am I in trouble?" Isla asked. "I didn't find out until a few weeks ago and then I thought it was too early to tell people."

Liz said, "She's worried about being shunned."

"Your baptism and repentance of sins has washed you clean by the blood of the Lamb."

Isla felt the tension leave her body.

Hilda added, "It won't be easy for you without a husband. It might be a good idea to have a look around for someone to marry in a hurry. Every man should have a wife and every woman should have a husband. That way they'll be no temptation."

"That would be best," the bishop agreed.

"I can help find you a suitable husband," Hilda said.

"*Nee.* It's far too soon after Benjamin died. I just can't do that." She shook her head. "I can't even think of another man at the moment." Just to get them off the track, she said, "Maybe after awhile I might think about marrying."

Hilda narrowed her eyes. "You can't be selfish, you have to think of your child. It's not just your life any more. The best thing for your *boppli* would be for you to have a husband."

"I will help you find one, Isla," Liz said. Turning to face Hilda, she continued, "I'll find her someone suitable."

"*Denke,* Liz," the bishop said.

"Isla, I do have some people coming to dinner tomorrow," said Hilda. "I know it's short notice, but it wouldn't hurt for you to get to know people better. You've been away for so long."

"Okay. *Denke.* I'd like that very much."

"Be here at seven."

When Hilda asked them to stay for tea, Isla said she wasn't feeling well, and the sisters made a hasty retreat.

On the way home, Isla turned to Liz and said. "You didn't mean it, did you?"

"Finding you a husband?"

"*Jah.*"

"Well, I said it... So, now I have to do it."

"Are you serious?"

Liz pulled a face. "*Jah!* I'm not gonna lie to the bishop."

Isla groaned. "I just don't want the stress of it all. Why would I want to think about another man when Benjamin 's just gone and I loved him so much, and all I want is to concentrate on my baby?"

Liz stared at her. "You had to have known they would say you should get married, Isla."

"It didn't cross my mind. I was too worried about being shunned and all that."

Liz shook her head.

Isla pointed to the road ahead. "Keep your eyes on the road. I don't see why I can't be a single mother."

"The bishop probably doesn't want that trend to take off within the community."

"Why would it?"

"Girls might go on *rumspringa* and get pregnant, and think they can come back to the community as though nothing has happened."

"Wouldn't that be better than giving their babies away, or abortion?"

"You're being too argumentative, Isla. Of course that would be better than those choices. Just find yourself a nice man and get married. Why do you always have to be different from everyone else? You've been like that ever since you were born."

Isla sighed again. "I don't want to be different anymore." Isla looked out from the buggy into the darkness of the night. She had wanted to be different, and that's why she'd left the community. She hadn't wanted to live her life wearing the baggy Amish dresses and living in this slow-paced world. Then, after she and Benjamin had gotten together, the world of the Amish seemed a good place, no, the only place, to raise their children. If it hadn't been for Benjamin, she might never have come back. Now there was her child to think about.

"You've gone quiet now," Liz said.

"I'm thinking. I'm grateful that you drove me all this way out here. *Denke, Liz.*"

"You're welcome. I'm always here; don't forget that. You're not alone."

"I know."

After she had been taken home and Liz had gone, Isla looked out at the Millers' house and saw that James' bedroom had a soft light glowing from the window. James had told her that he had the bedroom that looked out over the road. She wished she could talk things over with him and tell him what the bishop said, but she'd have to wait until morning.

CHAPTER 23

Casting all your care upon him;
for he careth for you.
1 Peter 5:7

THAT NIGHT, Isla barely slept. Once again she had too much churning around in her mind. When it was morning, she washed up and changed into clean clothes before she went out on the porch to wait for James.

She smiled when she saw the familiar figure bringing two steaming mugs toward her house.

As he sat down, he asked, "Did you tell the bishop?"

"*Jah,* and he said I should marry someone quickly. Hilda wanted to find me a man and then Liz had to jump in and say she'd do it." Isla rolled her eyes, took a breath, and then she thanked him for the tea. "Hilda has invited me for the evening meal tonight. Are you going?"

"I haven't been asked yet."

"I wonder who's going to be there. She said I should get to know people better."

"Are you working today?"

"*Nee.* I have the day off." Before he could suggest that they do something, she quickly added, "I'm going through the whole house and giving it a good cleaning while I've still got the energy."

"Could you do with some help?"

She shook her head. "I think I need to be alone."

He smiled. "Just asking."

WHEN LSLA WAS WELCOMED into the bishop's *haus* that evening, she saw that Daniel was there with Bishop John and Hilda, and no one else. This had to be Hilda's doing; she wasn't content to let Liz find her a husband.

"Hello, Daniel, I didn't know you were you coming to dinner as well."

"I didn't know you were coming either."

Daniel had to know it was a set up.

"Can I help you with anything in the kitchen, Hilda?" Isla asked.

"Nee, that's all done."

Isla knew she was in for an awkward night. When they were alone in the living room, Daniel leaned in and whispered, "Don't they know we see each other all the time at work?"

Isla shrugged her shoulders. "I don't know. Sorry about this. It wasn't my idea."

"Don't worry about it. We'll have to suffer each other's company tonight the best we can. It would've been more enjoyable if it were just the two of us."

She stared at him, wondering what he meant.

"Well what do you think?"

"About what?"

"Come to dinner with me next week and it will just be you and me without people listening in on everything we say and trying to force us together."

"We can't do that."

He smiled. "And why not?"

"That will mean they would've won."

179

"Not if we keep quiet about it. We won't let anyone know."

"Not anybody?" Isla asked enjoying the fun.

"It'll get back to them if we tell anybody. What do you say? We won't make it a big deal. We'll have dinner one night after work."

That would mean that was one dinner she wouldn't have to cook. It was tempting. "I don't think—"

"Here they come. We'll talk later," Daniel whispered.

"Dinner's ready now," Hilda said.

Isla and Daniel stood, walked into the kitchen and sat down with Bishop John and Hilda.

The next morning, James asked Isla about her dinner with the bishop and his wife.

"Would you believe that they had Daniel there too? And nobody else. They were trying to pair me with Daniel. What do you think about that?" Isla had expected him to think it was odd for the bishop to go to those lengths.

"Good. If you're not going to marry me, you should marry someone like Daniel."

Isla frowned at him. "I don't have to marry anybody, and I wish people would stop trying to make me. I can't just forget about Benjamin. I'll never forget it, I mean *him,* as much as people want me to."

"I'm sorry. I didn't mean to make you upset. I won't say any more." He raised his hands up in a sign of surrender, which made Isla giggle.

"When we were alone last night, Daniel invited me to dinner."

"Then you should go."

"Do you think so?"

"If I were a woman I'd go out with him."

Isla giggled again.

"Why are you laughing?"

"Firstly, you'd make a dreadful woman."

"I said, 'If I were a woman...' I'm doing great! I created a source of amusement for you."

"You often do."

"Perhaps you should just drink your tea and be quiet."

Isla stared at her tea. "I didn't want peppermint this morning. I wanted nettle tea."

"I'm not a mind reader. Yesterday you wanted peppermint." He sprang to his feet. "I'll get you some."

"Don't you dare! Sit down."

He shook his head as he sat. "I guess I'll bring you nettle tomorrow morning."

"Denke."

CHAPTER 24

Follow peace with all men,
and holiness, without which no man shall see the Lord:
Hebrews 12:14

Several weeks later

OVER THE PAST WEEKS, Isla had deflected Daniel's offers for dinner on two occasions. On his third try, she had accepted. They'd agreed on dinner after work on a Thursday evening. Today was the day.

Isla's workday was drawing to a close and she'd been nervous all day about going out with Daniel. She was certain that it had been all the pressure on her to find a husband that made her accept his invitation, but she probably wasn't doing Daniel any favors by accepting his invitation. He was handsome and he was very nice, but he wasn't the man for her—no one was, except

Benjamin. On the other hand, there was the issue about her child growing up in the community and possibly being the only child she knew that didn't have both a mother and a father.

Isla decided not to close herself off from the idea, for her child's sake, but she wasn't going to rush into anything. There was no divorce in the Amish. If a married couple found that they were incompatible and couldn't live together, they were allowed to live separately and remain in the community, but neither was allowed to marry another.

When the rest of the staff had gone home, Isla had stayed behind to help Daniel with locking up.

"I haven't organized our night very well. I should've collected you from your *haus* and driven you home. Now we both have our buggies here."

"That's fine."

"The restaurant I booked is in walking distance, anyway."

"Good."

She knew James wouldn't be happy she was going to be driving home by herself late at night. Then again, nothing made James happy. He'd only be happy if she was resting all day, and letting him drive her everywhere, and that's not what she wanted. Isla loved her job; meeting the customers and helping them choose furniture.

After the short walk, he pointed to an Italian restaurant. "That's the one."

"It looks nice."

"The food's good."

They walked in, he gave his name, and they were shown to a table in the corner of the room. The lighting was intimate and soft classical music made the atmosphere more so. In the center of the table, a candle flickered.

When they were seated, Isla asked, "Did you ask for this table?"

"I asked for a private table."

"It's certainly private and very nice."

While they looked through the menus, Isla wondered whether Daniel might open up about his late wife.

After they ordered the main course, he told stories about his childhood and how he was the worst one in the family with woodwork. He told her how dreadful he was with tools, and that he couldn't hammer a nail straight, and the rest of his family had no idea why he was so bad.

"My *vadder* always told me 'measure twice and cut once,' but I was always too anxious to have the thing finished. In my youth, near enough was good enough. But for the rest of my family, everything had to be precise and exact."

"I know what you mean. There are some people who are detail oriented, and other people who just want to get the thing finished."

"And I'm one of those people who just want to get the thing finished." He chuckled and then took a mouthful of wine while

Isla took a sip of iced water. "What kind of person are you?" he asked.

"Well, if I've only got the choice of those two, I suppose I would be the last one as well. I like to get things done." She thought about James; how he was a detail person. He thought things through to the minutest detail and everything had to be exact and perfect. Maybe that was the problem he'd had in the past with women, he wanted them to be perfect.

"What are you thinking about?" he asked.

"I'm just wondering if there aren't more than those two types of people." That's all she could come up with quickly, rather than having to tell him she was thinking about James.

"I suppose there's a whole range of behaviors and types in between. Let's just talk about you and me since I have your undivided attention tonight."

"Okay," she said.

"What would you like to know about me?" he asked, catching her totally off guard.

"Oh. I know quite a bit about you. I know you have the furniture store with your younger brother, Peter. Come to think of it that's all I really know, except that you're a very good boss. Oh no, that sounds like I'm trying to get on your good side."

He laughed. "You already are. You're doing well at work. Anyway, I try to be a fair employer. Tell me, what are your thoughts on marriage?"

"Marriage is a very good thing."

"Does that mean you want to get married?" he asked.

"I'm in no rush if that's what you mean. You know that the bishop and his wife think I should be married and that's why they invited you for dinner at the same time as me. Liz thinks that the bishop doesn't want unmarried mothers to become a trend in the community."

"How could they?"

"Girls might go off on *rumspringa* and come back pregnant. I guess that's what they're thinking."

"I see."

"But, I have to think about my own life and do what's right for me."

"And surely for your *boppli?*" he asked.

"Naturally. I want to give my baby everything I can. All the security, happiness and all the love that I can."

"And you think you can do that alone?"

"I'm going to try."

He frowned. "I hope you keep an open mind about marriage."

"I do. I have an open mind."

After he took a mouthful of his Chicken Sorrento, he continued, "I've been alone for quite a few years since Celia died in childbirth. I suppose you heard?"

"I'm sorry. I did hear that. And I wanted to tell you how sorry I was, but I also didn't want to mention it. I heard you lost your baby at the same time?"

He nodded. "There were complications in childbirth. We knew beforehand that things weren't going to be easy and that's why she had the birth in the hospital rather than at home like she wanted. Even the high tech gadgets and knowledge couldn't save Celia from God calling her and our baby home to be with Him."

Isla felt herself tearing up, and willed herself not to cry.

"I'm sorry, I didn't mean to make you sad."

She shook her head. "How could you not? It's so sad." Tears streamed down her face. She picked up a napkin and dabbed at her eyes. "I'm sorry. I'm just so sad about your wife. And your *boppli.*"

He offered her a glass of wine.

She shook her head. "I can't."

"Sorry, I keep forgetting."

She took a sip of iced water, and then pushed her pasta and meat sauce around on her plate with her fork while he went on eating.

"Are you okay?" he asked after a few moments of silence.

"I'm fine. I just don't know how you'd ever get over such sorrow and tragedy."

"The pain lessens with time, and you start thinking about the good times. The first few years after she died, I thought marrying again would be a betrayal because I loved my wife so much. Now, years on, I know it wouldn't be a betrayal. Celia was a selfless woman; she would want me to be happy. If I love again, it doesn't mean that my love for Celia fades or has less meaning."

"If you ever marry again, won't you always be comparing your second wife to Celia?"

"*Nee.* That person won't be Celia. That person will be a different woman, and why compare someone with someone else?"

"I see. I never thought about it in that way before."

"Would Benjamin want you to be happy?"

"I guess so. It's not something we ever talked about. I guess because we were so young the subject didn't come up."

"You don't think about the future when you're young. You expect everything will turn out the way you plan."

"That's the hard part for me. I'm a planner and now here I am, and not one of my plans has worked out."

He laughed. "Doesn't the scripture say we don't know what tomorrow will bring?"

She smiled. "It sounds familiar. We're not really in control of our lives, are we?"

He shook his head. "It's a grand illusion to think so."

He was refreshingly open and honest, and his perspective on life had helped her enormously.

"Did you say something about dessert?" she asked.

"That's a good idea. And you're eating for two so don't hold back." Daniel caught the attention of the waiter for the dessert menus.

CHAPTER 25

And be not conformed to this world:
but be ye transformed by the renewing of your mind,
that ye may prove what is that good,
and acceptable, and perfect, will of God.
Romans 12:2

As Isla had hoped, in the last couple of weeks before the baby was due her mother came to stay with her. She had opted to have the birth in her own home, since the midwife was happy with the results of the ultrasound. *Dat* was staying with his youngest sister, Amelia.

Isla and her mother developed a daily routine. Their morning routine was that James still came for his mornings on the porch with Isla, while her mother had breakfast in the kitchen. Isla told her mother she could join them, but she said she didn't want to intrude.

One morning, after James left with the empty mugs, Isla went into the kitchen and spoke to her mother.

"You really can come outside with us, *Mamm*. James can bring out an extra chair from the kitchen."

Her mother was busy filling the sink with water, and she turned around to stare at Isla. "How old is James? Thirty-one?"

"A bit older, I think. What are you getting at?"

"He's a bit old for you."

"We've talked about this before. We're just friends. Anyway, age has nothing to do with anything."

"I like James," her mother said as she turned back to wash the breakfast dishes.

Isla pulled out a chair to sit down on and then, before she'd even sat down on it, the small twinges she had been feeling all morning suddenly got more intense. Lots more intense. "I think it's starting."

Her mother swung back around. "Are you sure? You've been saying that every day for the past week."

"This is different."

"I'll call Carmen from the Millers.'" Her mother shook the water from her hands and hurried out of the kitchen.

Not knowing what else to do, Isla paced up and down.

AT THREE THAT AFTERNOON, a baby girl was born to Isla.

With Isla during the birth, along with the midwife, were her sister, Liz and her mother.

Liz cradled the baby in her arms. "She's perfect, Isla." Isla watched as her sister picked up a tiny hand and studied the delicate fingers. "Complete with tiny fingernails."

"She's beautiful, Isla," her mother said.

Carmen took the baby from Liz and handed her to Isla, after her mother had helped the new mother to sit up. Isla looked into her baby's eyes. "She's looking right at me. She knows me."

"They can't see right away," her mother informed her, "but she would know your voice after hearing it for these many months."

"I say she can see me," Isla insisted which made Liz giggle.

Carmen set about cleaning the room, and then Liz stepped in to help her.

"Have you thought of a name yet?" her mother asked, knowing Isla had wanted to wait until the baby arrived before choosing the name.

"Her name is Hope. She's given me new hope for the future."

"That's a lovely name," Liz said.

"I suppose we'll get used to it," her mother mumbled.

Isla didn't care who else liked the name, or didn't. She stared into her baby's unusually dark blue eyes and wondered if they'd stay that color. Hope had a fine smattering of dark hair, and long fingers. Isla could not stop staring at her. "I have a *boppli*. I can hardly believe it." She drew Hope closer and kissed her softly on her forehead before she cuddled her closely to her heart.

"She's barely cried," her mother said.

"She might make up for that later," Carmen said.

After the cleaning was done, Liz said, "I'll let everybody know the good news."

"Tell *Dat* first, and Amelia, and don't forget to let the Millers know."

"That's the first place I'm heading because I'll need to use their phone."

Her mother called out to Liz before she got to the front door, "Tell James she won't be able to make it for their morning chat tomorrow."

"But I'll make it the morning after," Isla called after her sister, much to her mother's disapproval.

"When the *boppli's* young you have to sleep when she sleeps. You might miss out on some much needed sleep."

"I'll work around it. The mornings with James keep me sane."

As James was directed, he skipped one morning and came the next with two mugs, one of tea and one of coffee. Isla had had no visitors yet because her mother wasn't allowing any until the baby was a few days old.

Her mother looked out the window. "Here comes James."

Isla was dressed, but too tired to walk out to the porch. "Please have him come inside, *Mamm*. He can sit here with us."

She opened the door and James walked in.

"Can I see the *boppli?*" he asked Mrs. Zook who pointed to the crib next to Isla.

"How are you, Isla?" he said as he walked in.

"Wunderbaar."

He set the drinks on the coffee table and looked in the crib to see Hope sleeping soundly. "My, she's so small, and the nicest looking *boppli* I've seen by far."

Isla giggled. "You can hold her when she wakes."

"Nee, I'd be too scared."

"You'll be fine. Surely you've had practice with your brothers' babies? Sit down," she ordered him as he nodded to her question, and he sat on the couch opposite.

"I'm glad everything went okay," he said.

"It did."

"What's her name?"

"Hope. She's given me hope for the future."

He nodded and his lips turned upward at the corners. "I like it."

"So what's been happening in the world?" She reached for the tea and he jumped up and handed it to her and then sat back down.

"Everything is the same, nothing different."

She took a sip of nettle tea. "Are you still going back home? You've been here for a long time now. Do you think you'll just stay?"

"I'll be making arrangements to go back as soon as I know you're okay."

She nodded wanting to tell him she was okay, but at the same time, she didn't want him to go. The sounds of a buggy were heard outside.

Mrs. Zook came out of the kitchen. "It's Liz, Isla, and she's brought your *vadder.*"

James sprang to his feet. "I should get out of your way then."

"*Nee,* please stay. I have hardly seen you and I didn't see you at all yesterday."

He chuckled. "I'm not far away if you need anything. I'll be back again tomorrow morning, as long as that's okay." He walked over and had another look at the baby. "I'll see you later, little baby Hope." He smiled at Isla, and then picked up his coffee mug and walked to the door.

"*Denke* for the tea," she called after him.

Her mother rushed to the door after James left, and excitedly showed her husband in to greet their new grandchild.

CHAPTER 26

Trust in the LORD with all thine heart;
and lean not unto thine own understanding.
Proverbs 3:5

IT WAS a week later that Daniel visited. Daniel and Isla had seen each other regularly since their first dinner together. They weren't dating, she was careful to tell people. They were good friends. She showed Daniel the baby. Hope was asleep in the crib near the couch, the crib that Daniel and Peter had given her. "What do you think of her, Daniel?"

"So precious. You're blessed to have her."

Hope opened her eyes and looked right at him.

"Do you want to hold her?"

"I'd love to."

She lifted Hope from the crib and carefully handed her to Daniel. It was heartwarming to see her tiny baby in the arms of a large strong man.

Her mother walking toward the front door distracted Isla, and as she opened it, Isla realized there was another visitor. It was James, and her mother showed him in.

"James!"

He nodded hello to her and to Daniel. Isla could tell by the look on James' face he wasn't happy to see Daniel holding Hope before he'd held her.

"She's awake now, James, so you can hold her too."

"*Gut.* I've been looking forward to seeing her awake. Every time I've been here she's been fast asleep. That's why I thought I'd call in later in the day this time."

He walked closer and had a look at her as she lay in Daniel's arms. "Look at those eyes. What an unusual color."

"They say they might turn brown, but who knows?"

"Who would like a cup of hot tea?" Mrs. Zook asked.

"Not for me, Mrs. Zook," Daniel said.

"Me either, *denke*," James said.

"Here, have a hold," Daniel said to James.

"Are you sure?"

"Yeah."

"Mind her head," Isla cautioned as Daniel passed Hope to James.

"I have plenty of nieces and nephews," James reminded her. He held the baby in his arms, looking very comfortable, and slowly rocked her to and fro.

"I'll head off now," Daniel said. "I called in to see how you are and tell you we're all missing you at work."

"I'll be back in a couple of months, if you'll still need me."

"We will."

Daniel said goodbye to James and Mrs. Zook and made a hasty retreat out the door.

James sat down with Hope still in his arms. "I hope he didn't leave early on account of me."

"*Nee.* He stopped here on his way to run errands, and he has to get back to the store."

"I just stopped by to let you know I've made my arrangements to go home."

"I don't want you to go." Isla knew her mother was most likely listening in while she made herself busy in the kitchen, but she didn't care. It was true; she did not want him to leave. He was her best friend.

"It's time. I can see you're safe now and in good hands. I've made arrangements to go at the end of the week, on Friday."

Isla sighed and knew she had to be grateful that he'd stayed as long as he had. *"Denke* for staying so long."

"I've enjoyed getting to know you and meeting my niece. Why wouldn't I stay for that?"

Isla smiled at the way he was looking down at her daughter. Then Hope cried and Mrs. Zook came out of the kitchen.

"Hope is due for a feeding," Mrs. Zook told James.

James stood up. "I'll leave you to it."

"Denke, James. I'll take her." He handed Hope to Isla and before he left, Isla said, "I'll be waiting on the porch in the morning."

"I'll look forward to it." And then he left.

While Isla fed Hope, her mother sat beside her. "He's in love with you."

"James?"

Her mother nodded.

"Do you think so?"

"It's obvious, particularly if I noticed. I've never been quick to spot such things."

Isla wondered if she was in love with James. She certainly didn't want him to go, but was that love? If she had to choose Daniel or James there was no question in her mind that she'd choose James. He would stay, she knew, if she asked him, but then she'd need to make him a commitment. She knew she had a big decision to make, and she wasn't sure if she was ready to do that yet.

THE NEXT MORNING Isla waited on the porch while her baby slept inside. However, it wasn't James making his way to the house. She saw Aunt Mary coming across the lawn with something in her hand.

Instead of saying hello to Aunt Mary, the first thing she said was, "Where's James?"

She offered her an envelope. "He said to give you this. And then I'll be headed back to the house."

"*Denke* for bringing it."

Aunt Mary nodded, and turned around.

Isla opened the sealed envelope and pulled out a one-page letter. While Aunt Mary made her way back to the Miller house, Isla read.

In the letter, James explained that he was never good with saying goodbye. He gave his word he'd return before Hope's first birthday. The rest of the letter told her how much their friendship meant to him.

She ran into the house, calling for her mother.

"What's the matter?"

"He's gone, *Mamm,* he's gone." Isla thrust the letter into her mother's hand.

Her mother read the letter and looked at her daughter. "And you are in love with him, too."

Isla opened her mouth to speak and no words came out. All she knew was that her world was brighter with him in it. Without him, it would be like living in a world without sunshine or fresh air.

"Call him and tell him how you feel. He'll come back."

"Will he?"

"*Jah.*"

"I don't have his number."

"Get it from his parents. I'll watch Hope."

"It'll take him a good day or two to get home."

All Isla could do was wait for James to get home, and then call him.

TWO DAYS LATER, Isla called James only to find that the number was disconnected. All she had was his address and there was no choice but to write to him.

What would she say in the letter? Come back and be my friend? I don't want to move to Eggleton, away from my family? That was a conversation that would need to be had face-to-face and she'd missed that opportunity.

The truth was, she would move away for him even if it was to the remotest part of the country—as long as she'd be with him. She wrote and told him how much she missed him and urged him to come back for another visit; that was all she could do. As soon as she finished the letter, she sealed it and set it aside, ready to mail.

Then she realized that she'd have to stop spending time with Daniel, and she'd have to tell him so.

THREE AND A HALF WEEKS LATER, she got a letter back from James. The letter was not the one she'd hoped for. He hadn't got the point of what she'd said. He told her how much he'd enjoyed their mornings together and that he was getting back into the swing of things there.

The opportunity had passed her by and James could meet another woman and she would lose him.

FOUR MONTHS later at a Sunday meeting, Isla heard there were visitors from Eggleton. She made further inquiries as to who they were and was introduced to an older couple. They told her James was fine and they said nothing else about him. Isla invited them back to her place for supper along with some other people, in the hope that she'd hear some information about James. As many times as she brought up his name, she still didn't learn any more.

CHAPTER 27

But seek ye first the kingdom of God,
and his righteousness;
and all these things shall be added unto you.
Matthew 6:33

Some months later.

ON THE WAY home from her job at the furniture store, Isla collected ten-month-old Hope from her parents' house and headed home. When she turned into her driveway, she saw James sitting on her porch. She blinked and looked again—it was he, in the flesh, popping up from his chair.

She stopped right by the house and he walked over toward her.

Isla jumped down and ran to him. "James! What are you doing here? You didn't tell me you were coming." He looked taller and more handsome than she remembered and she wanted to throw her arms around him and never let him go.

He chuckled. "I wanted to surprise you."

"You certainly did that. You've been gone way too long."

"Where's Hope?"

"In the buggy."

He walked to the buggy and looked in at Hope. "Hello, Hope. I'm your *Onkel* James. I saw you once before when you were just a tiny *boppli*."

"Say hello, Hope," Isla told her. When Hope just stared at him with her striking green-brown hazel eyes, Isla said, "She only says *Mamm*."

He laughed. "I'll have her saying *Onkel* James before I leave."

"When are you leaving? You only just got here."

"Take Hope out and I'll unhitch the buggy and we can talk when I come back."

"Well, come back in half an hour, and that'll give me time to feed Hope."

"Okay."

Isla did as he suggested, lifting Hope out and carrying her toward their house. It was just like old times, having James take care of the horse and buggy for her. "That's your *Onkel* James," she told Hope as they both watched him take the buggy to the barn.

When he disappeared from sight, Isla took Hope into the kitchen and heated her dinner.

Once Hope had eaten, Isla put her down in her crib to sleep. With perfect timing, Hope was dozing off when Isla heard James walking up the porch steps. She closed Hope's door and went to meet James, just as a horrible thought occurred to her. What if he'd come back to tell her he was getting married?

As soon as they sat on the couch, Isla asked, "How are things back home?"

"Lonely without you."

She couldn't stop the smile that tugged at her lips.

"How's Daniel?" he asked.

"Daniel and I no longer see each other outside of work. Sally came back and got baptized, and now Daniel and Sally have been seeing a lot of one another."

His eyebrows pinched together. "That wasn't something I was expecting. I'm sorry to hear that—about you and Daniel, I mean."

Now she was confused. "Are you?"

"Daniel is a good man."

"A better man than you?"

He tipped his head to one side. "What's going on, Isla?"

She swallowed hard. Couldn't he just take the hint? "It was horrible that you left so suddenly without saying goodbye. As soon as you left, I called you and found the number was disconnected."

"That's right. They had to tear down the barn and when it was rebuilt, we were assigned a different phone number for some reason. I didn't think to give it to anybody. He looked directly at her. "What were you calling me for?"

She had to tell him outright. "To tell you that I have feelings for you, James."

"I have feelings for you, too."

Isla shook her head knowing from his expressionless face he still had no idea how she felt.

"Feelings… Do you mean more than friends?" he asked.

She nodded smiling trying to find the right words.

"Are you saying you'll marry me and move to Eggleton with me?"

"Jah."

He shook his head. "I'm sorry, Isla. That'll never work."

Her stomach knotted and a pain jabbed her heart. She'd left it too late.

She nodded, and didn't want to hear anymore. "I understand," she said as tears welled in her eyes.

"Aren't you going to ask me why it wouldn't work?"

"Nee, I can't hear it." The months without James had swept away any doubts about marrying him if God saw fit to give her another chance with him. She breathed deeply knowing God had a plan for her and Hope.

"You'll need to listen. The reason it wouldn't work is that I'm moving here." His face softened into a smile.

She put her hand over her mouth. "Are you serious?"

"I'm very serious."

"You pick this very moment to find a sense of humor?"

He laughed. "It was payback for making me wait so long."

"That's not fair! I didn't know how I felt." Peace filled her heart. He was back and back for good.

"You should've known right away that you were in love with me. Even I knew you were in love with me."

She sniffed back her tears. "Are you seriously moving here?"

He held out his hand, and she grabbed it with both of hers. "You'll marry me?" he asked.

"Jah, James, I will."

"Then I'll move here because that'll make you happy, which will make me happy. And I couldn't take you or Hope away from the rest of your family. Or my family, for that matter. It would break my parents' hearts if I took Hope away. We'll see the bishop today, before you can change your mind, and we'll make a date for the wedding."

Isla said, "You'll be making the bishop a very happy man."

"I'll be the very best husband you could ever have. You said you'd find me a wife, and you did. The best possible wife for me."

"I did, didn't I?" Isla said with a laugh. Her life had come together beautifully after leaving it in God's hands, without her having to plan every detail. God was the best planner, and she'd keep trusting Him.

James turned to look in her eyes. "I love you, Isla, with all my heart."

And Isla knew that it was true.

~

~

AMISH WIDOW'S STORY

EXPECTANT AMISH WIDOWS BOOK 14

CHAPTER 1

Levi King ran a hand through his dark hair and huffed in agitation as he stared at his older brother.

"I don't know what's going on with you," Andrew said. "She's been married to Abraham for going on five years now."

"I know that." Levi sat on a bale of hay and took off his hat while his brother sat down on a covered tin of horse food. "When Miriam told me Hannah was expecting, that brought it all back again—the fact that she's gone and I'm never going to be her husband."

Andrew shook his head. "I was worried about you when Hannah married Abraham, but I thought you'd get over it."

Levi nodded. He had thought he'd get over it, too.

"You're still a mess. And you know why?"

Here it comes! "Why?" Levi asked.

"You thought you could bury yourself in your business and your work while life continued on around you."

"Jah. That way I'm too busy to think about anything." Levi sat there in silence as he listened to his brother lecture him once more. This was just what he needed—some good common sense from his older brother.

Andrew breathed out heavily. "If you'd asked her out as soon as Matthew Miller ran off with that *Englisch* girl you'd probably be married to Hannah right now. I was sure Hannah always liked you."

"Hey, how is that helping me, saying things like that?"

"It's helping you because if you know where you went wrong you won't repeat the same mistake in your future."

Levi fiddled with his hat, spinning it in circles. "The moment is gone. This is a mistake that … It just became … all became real, you know? She'll have a family. Do you know how hard it's been to see her all the time, knowing she's married to someone else?"

"Levi! You can't have thoughts like that about another man's wife! It's wrong and you know it."

"I struggle with that. I know you're right. I'm doing my best."

"You need to get married and have your own *fraa* and *familye*. The sooner you marry, the sooner you'll forget the feelings you hold for Hannah."

"The woman I wanted to have that *familye* with..." he trailed off. "Never mind." Levi shook his head and looked down at the cement floor of the barn.

"Tricia and I have met a woman who's visiting here and we think you'll really like her. Her name is Lizzy Weaver. She's asked Tricia's help in finding a husband. Maybe that's the answer for you."

That meant his brother and sister-in-law had been discussing him and his reason for being miserable. He wasn't happy about that, but it was decent of them to try to help him. "There's a place in my heart and that place has been taken. It was her, or no one."

"Brother, you're on dangerous ground. It's one thing to be single and content with it. But you know what the word says about coveting another man's wife."

Levi rubbed his forehead. "I struggle and I admit that I struggle. I know it's wrong to have these feelings for her."

"All I ask is that you meet this woman."

He took his eyes off the floor and stared at Andrew. "For what purpose?"

"Don't you want your own *familye* — *kinner?*"

"You know how I love kids. It would be *wunderbaar* if you and Tricia could move back to Lancaster County."

Andrew shook his head. "I've got the farm and Tricia's got her *mudder* here."

Levi knew that Tricia's mother helped with their five young children.

Waving his hands in the air to make his point, Andrew continued, "You've got to face reality sometime. And I don't know why you didn't do it years ago, when she first married Abraham. You should've put her out of your mind back then."

"I did. I knew she was gone then, but finding out she's expecting has just reinforced that she and I will never happen. I guess it's my fault. I didn't let her know how I felt. I regret that now but I can't go back."

"Exactly! You have to move forward and if you don't want to be alone for the rest of your life, I suggest that you meet Lizzy. No pressure, just see what you think of her."

Slowly, Levi nodded. His brother had always given him good advice in the past. Maybe meeting this woman wouldn't be so bad.

"Good." Andrew finally smiled.

Levi knew he'd have to put Hannah out of his mind. "Will this woman leave here and come back with me if things work out well between us? I can't move here."

Andrew laughed. "That's a fast change in attitude."

"I'm being practical."

"She told us she'd move for love."

Levi nodded again. "Okay, I'll do what you suggest."

"You'll like her. She's very easy to get along with and easy on the eyes."

Deep in his heart Levi didn't know how he could ever have a relationship without comparing everything the woman said and did to Hannah. And that would be unfair to any woman.

"I'll have Tricia invite her for dinner tomorrow night." Andrew stood. "Now we've got some fencing to do down in the south paddock."

Levi blew out a deep breath, rose to his feet, ran a hand through his hair, and placed his hat back on his head. He was no stranger to hard work and he'd worked even harder these past years to take his mind off one special woman.

Andrew wagged a finger in his face. "No thinking about Hannah."

Levi sighed. "I'll do my best."

THE NEXT AFTERNOON when Levi and Andrew had finished working, they arrived back at the house to see a buggy.

"She's here now," Andrew said.

"Good. I'm happy to meet her," Levi said, surprising himself. He was looking forward to meeting someone who might give him a new beginning, a new start, and a new lease on life.

"That's the way," Andrew said, jumping down from the wagon. "Why don't you go inside and wash up and I'll finish up out here?"

Levi jumped down from the wagon. "Thanks, Brother."

Levi washed up in the mud-room at the back of the house. Tricia liked her house spotless and insisted the men change clothes and shoes, and wash up thoroughly, before they entered her pristine and spotless home. Even with five young children there was never a thing out of place. The young ones played on the floor on a large blanket and when they finished, all the toys went back into the box and the blanket was folded on top.

When Levi had washed and changed his clothes, he walked through the back door of the house. A few steps further and he saw two women sitting at the kitchen table drinking tea. One was his sister-in-law, Tricia, and the other woman was pretty with fair hair. When she turned her smiling face to him, he saw her eyes were light blue. His brother had been right, she was easy on the eyes.

Hannah was a tall slender woman with light brown hair that had some blonde streaks when she was in the sunlight, and her features were remarkable. He silently admonished himself when he found he'd already compared the two women before he'd even said hello. *This is a new start,* he reminded himself. He pushed Hannah out of his mind and stepped toward the woman who might possibly be his helpmeet.

Tricia sprang to her feet. "There you are. Levi, this is Lizzy Weaver."

Levi dipped his head, and smiled at the attractive young woman. "Hello, Lizzy, I'm pleased to meet you."

She stood and put out her hand to shake his. "Nice to meet you, Levi."

"Likewise," he said, feeling a little nervous and realizing he should have said something else.

"I've been hearing a lot about you," she said, fluttering her lashes.

He smiled. "Oh no, that's not good. Who was telling you about me?"

Lizzy giggled. "Don't worry, it was nothing bad. It was all good."

It pleased Levi to hear her laughter. He'd been living amidst a gloomy cloud for years, and a woman like her might be able to cause him to enjoy life again.

"Sit down, Levi, and I'll fix you a hot tea before dinner to warm you up." While Levi sat down at the table in the kitchen, Tricia continued, "Lizzy and I were having such a nice time talking together that the dinner is going to be a bit late, I'm afraid."

"It's my fault. Tricia says I talk too much." Lizzy giggled again.

"And you live nearby?" Levi asked her.

"I'm staying only a few miles away. I just moved here from Harts County."

"You're a long way from home."

"I'm staying with my *ant* and *onkel* for about six months, and then I might move on again."

Levi got the idea she might be traveling around to find a husband. Many of the young Amish did that when they were searching for a spouse — travel from community to community. That showed him that she was a woman of determination and strength. He liked that in a woman.

"And are you a farmer just like your *bruder,* Levi?" Lizzy asked.

"*Nee.* I have a business back home, just a small business." He liked the polite way she spoke and how she held his gaze.

"What kind of business?" she asked.

"I'm a saddler."

"You make saddles and reins, and things like that?"

"I do."

Tricia brought back a cup of tea to the table and placed it in front of Levi. "Lizzy does bookkeeping."

Lizzy nodded. "I do. I used to do the work for many businesses before I left home."

Levi thanked Tricia for the tea, and then asked Lizzy, "How do you occupy your days now that you're here?"

"I sew, and I help my aunt look after her *haus,* and then there's pie drives and sewing bees and quilting bees." She giggled. "I'm probably busier here than I was at home."

Levi found that he liked her company. She was pleasant, sociable, and if she was a bookkeeper that showed she was an industrious woman who had a level-head. She would make a good *fraa*. He wondered how she was with children.

"Where are the children?" Levi asked Tricia.

"The older ones are playing in the living room and the little ones, are asleep."

He stood up and looked around the corner into the living room and saw the children playing, and then he went back to the table. "I've never seen them playing so quietly."

"Lizzy has a way with children. She set Maizie, Lily, and David up with games, and then she put Milly and Stephen to sleep by singing to them."

Lizzy giggled. "I adore children."

Question answered, Levi thought. And the woman laughed a lot, and Levi knew he needed some different energy around him.

Once the dinner was ready, Levi watched as Lizzy organized David and Maizie on their small table and the younger two, Lily and Stephen in their highchairs, all while cradling Milly, the baby, in her arms.

That gave him a mental picture of what his life could be like with Lizzy looking after their *kinner*. He could come home to a cheerful house full of children and laughter, and with Lizzy as the one to raise his children, they would all be organized and well-behaved.

His brother had been right. He was glad he'd come to visit Tricia and Andrew. This vacation was solely so he could put Hannah out of his mind once and for all, and this was an excellent way to do it.

LATER THAT NIGHT, Andrew and Levi stayed up to talk after Lizzy had gone back to her aunt and uncle's house and Tricia and the children had gone to bed.

"I think I saw a little bit of a spark between the two of you," Andrew said.

"I did find her pleasant company, and I think she would make a *gut fraa*. She was excellent with the children."

"See, what did I tell you?"

Levi managed a laugh. "If it's all right with you and Tricia, I think I might stay on a little longer. I'd like to get to know Lizzy better before I go back home."

"Good! Stay as long as you like."

"*Denke*. I'll have to make a phone call and organize some of my workers to do extra shifts to cover me."

"Do whatever you need to do. This is important. These next few days could change your whole life for the better."

"Do you think so?" Levi hoped his brother was right.

Andrew nodded. "I do."

SO LEVI STAYED a few weeks longer, and every time he was in Lizzy's company he found himself happy and smiling. He wanted to hold onto that happiness.

Finally, Levi felt it was time. He had to make a decision. He would ask Lizzy to marry him, and he'd bring her back home. He'd inherited the family house as he'd told Lizzy, and had lived there by himself since his brother moved away and his sister had married. The house was large, too big for just him, but it would be perfect for a family.

On the day he chose to propose, he prepared a special day for the two of them. He planned a picnic by the water's edge where they could feed the ducks, leisurely eat and drink, and look into each other's eyes as they talked.

He collected Lizzy from her aunt and uncle's place. And as soon as she had sat in the seat beside him, she started talking and hadn't stopped. She looked beautiful as she sat next to him. The warm morning sun made the hair that framed her face that much lighter, and her eyes sparkled and danced with enthusiasm.

"You haven't said much today, Levi."

He glanced back at her. "I haven't had a chance to get a word in."

She giggled. "I'm sorry. I'm just excited for our day. It's nice to have a whole day together. I'm glad Andrew is giving you the day off."

"So am I. He needs my help, and I'm happy to give it to him while I'm here. I'll be gone soon."

"Don't say that. I'll miss you when you're gone. I'm so glad you came when you did. I was getting bored out of my mind. I know it's a big community here and everything, but there aren't many people my age. Not ones I feel that I fit in with, anyway."

He glanced over at her, pleased she was genuinely sad about him leaving. "You'll miss me?"

She slapped him playfully on his arm. "Of course, I'll miss you. Maybe I could visit you?"

"That might be a good idea."

Out of the corner of his eye, he could see her draw back. "Might be? I thought you'd be happy about me visiting you."

He glanced over at her again to see her disappointed expression. He didn't want to ruin his surprise. He planned to ask her over lunch while they were sharing the picnic, so he changed the subject as he fixed his eyes back onto the road ahead of him. "I like this time of year. Look how beautiful the sky is."

She folded her arms and slouched down in the seat. Seeing her body language he knew she wasn't happy and she wanted to be sure he knew it.

"I'm sure the sky is just the same as where you come from. Haven't we been enjoying each other's company, Levi?"

"*Jah,* I've had a lovely time with you. That's why I've taken this whole day to have the picnic with you."

"You don't have a special girl back home, do you?"

"If I did, I wouldn't dishonor her by spending time with you," Levi said.

"I'm sad because you'll be gone soon and I'll be stuck here in this place."

He was starting to see a different side of Lizzy, but he reminded himself no one was perfect and everybody had their off days. She might have had women's problems. He knew from what his brother said that there were certain days where he could say or do nothing right as far as Tricia was concerned. He had to give Lizzy the benefit of the doubt because she certainly hadn't been sulky or sullen before now.

"I've got a great day planned," he said.

"*Denke,* that's thoughtful of you, Levi," she said, sounding a little less sulky.

They stopped at the park by the water, and he was glad that there were no other people there; it was just the two of them. Tricia had been good enough to prepared him a lovely picnic basket with wine, cheese, fresh bread, and grapes. He hoped to woo Lizzy with lovely surroundings and good food, in the hopes that she would say yes to his marriage proposal.

He pulled the blanket and the picnic basket out of the back of the buggy. She plucked the blanket out of his arms and marched in front of him.

Jah, she was definitely having an off day.

She spread the blanket out over the grass under a tree by the waterside. And when he placed the basket down, she said, "Sit down."

He obeyed, and she took over spreading out the food, passing him a plate and a glass.

"How are you feeling today?" he asked.

"I was feeling fine before you said you were going home soon. Now I'm feeling pretty upset."

They were at the picnic spot, a beautiful spot by the water, just like he'd imagined he would be when he proposed to her, so what was he waiting for? He cleared his throat. "Lizzy, there's something I've been meaning to ask you."

She placed everything down and looked into his eyes. "*Jah*, Levi?"

"I know we've only known each other for a very short time ..." When he saw her eyes grow wide, he knew that she knew he was going to propose. He shook his head. "I'm a little nervous."

"Don't be. What were you saying?"

"Lizzy, I know we haven't known each other for very long, but I've seen the kind of person you are. You're kind and caring. I've seen your strengths and your great virtue and I was wondering if you'd do me the honor of marrying me?"

A smile quickly spread across Lizzy's face, and she jumped up and squealed.

Levi winced as her screams pierced through his head.

"Do you mean it?" she asked.

"Of course I do." He felt he should stand up since she was standing. When he was on his feet, he repeated his question, "Lizzy, would you be my wife and come back to Lancaster County with me?"

"*Jah,* oh, *jah.* Of course I will."

He was delighted with her response, and then didn't know what to do next. Should he kiss her on the cheek? Shaking her hand was certainly a little too formal under the circumstances. He leaned over and gave her little hug and a pat on the back. She stood on her tiptoes and planted a kiss on his cheek and then giggled again.

He chuckled, and they sat back down. Levi was relieved that it was behind him.

Lizzy grinned as she pulled out more food from the basket. "I'm so excited I'm getting married. I just can't wait until I tell everybody. Will we get married here or back where you live?"

Levi rubbed his chin. He hadn't quite figured out all the details. "Well, I'd like to get married back home."

"That's fine with me."

"Good. I'll speak to the bishop when I get back, and I'm sure he'll organize a place for you to stay when you get there."

She pouted. "Wouldn't I go back with you when you leave?"

"I would have to organize things for your stay first, and that will be the first thing I do when I get home."

"*Jah*, husband," she said with a giggle. "Now I'll have to do everything you say, since you are the man now in charge of me." She giggled and then poured two glasses of wine and handed him one.

Levi sincerely hoped he was doing the right thing, and if not, it was too late to back out now. He'd given his word and he'd been raised to know that a man's word was a man's bond.

CHAPTER 2

Back in Lancaster County in Hannah's house.

WHEN HANNAH WALKED into the kitchen in the morning, she saw her best friend, Miriam, busy making breakfast. She pulled out a chair and sat down. "*Denke* for staying here, I don't know what I would've done without you."

"You'll never have to be without me, we're just like sisters."

"These last few days have been the worst of my life. And then I'm faced with all of his clothes and all of his belongings. I'm going to have to figure out what to do with all of that, soon."

"I'll help you bundle them up when you're ready. Then we can send them to a charity."

"*Denke*. I'd appreciate that. Half of me wants to keep some things and then at other times I think I should get rid of every-thing. I just don't know what to do."

"You'll figure it out. There's no reason to be in a hurry, give yourself some time."

"I want to keep some things for the *boppli*. My *boppli* should have something from his or her *vadder*—some kind of keep-sake." Hannah sighed and rubbed her eyes. "Maybe his bible." Everything was overwhelming. There were so many things to do—so many decisions to make.

"Did you sleep last night?"

Hannah shook her head, knowing she needed to keep calm and relaxed for her baby's sake. She put her hand over the slight rise of her tummy. "This was the very worst time for Abraham to die. We were starting to get along better, you know? He was so happy about the *boppli*. He said he was starting to think he'd never be a *vadder*."

Miriam put a plate of eggs in front of her. "Eat up; you'll feel better with some food in your stomach."

"Why did it happen like this, Miriam?"

"It's not for us to ask why. *Gott* wanted him home. It was as though He reached down from the sky and plucked him up to take him back with Him. The last time I heard of someone being killed by lightning was when I was a little girl."

"It's so sad. My *boppli* will never know him. And he was never a *vadder* just like he thought—never really a *vadder* if he can't hold his *boppli*." A tear trickled down her face and she quickly wiped it away.

"Don't be sad. *Gott* wouldn't be putting you through this if you couldn't handle it."

"I can't. I can't." Now her tears flowed. She wiped them with the back of her hand.

Miriam leaned over and put her arms around her. "Oh no, I hope I'm not saying the wrong things."

"*Nee,* you're not." Hannah tapped her friend's hand. "I'll feel better once the funeral's over."

Abraham's body was in the living room already. The funeral director had brought the coffin there for the customary viewing. Only there could be no actual 'viewing,' given the state of the body.

"Will Levi make it back here for the funeral?" Hannah asked, hoping to have her good friend there beside her.

Miriam sat down. "I haven't been able to get in contact with him. I've called Tricia and Andrew loads of times, but there's been no answer. I've sent a letter, but it won't get there until tomorrow at the soonest."

Hannah shook her head. Miriam had already told her that her brother, Levi, had extended his stay in Ohio. She would get through the day much better if Levi was there. There was something about him that always made her feel calm.

"When will he be back?" Hannah asked.

"I can't say. All he said with was that he was staying there a little longer and he had to organize his workers here. I don't think he'll be away too long. He never likes to stay away from home."

"And the ladies are bringing all the food? I feel dreadful, not being able to do anything."

"In your condition, no one expects you to do anything. Just get through the day, that's all you have to do."

"Just don't leave my side today, Miriam. Everyone thinks I'm strong, but I'm not. I wish *Mamm* and *Dat* were still around. Nothing's been the same since they've been gone." It was times like these she wished she'd had siblings. She'd grown up playing with the next-door neighbor children, Miriam, and her two older brothers, Levi and Andrew. They were her family now that everybody close to her had died.

Hannah looked at the plate in front of her and pushed a fork into the fluffy scrambled egg, forcing herself to eat one mouthful after the other. She thanked God again that she hadn't had one sick day during her pregnancy; that had truly been a blessing. Because Hannah was only in the early months, not everyone knew her condition and she preferred to keep things that way for a while yet.

After breakfast, Hannah readied herself to receive the hundreds of guests that would flow through the house prior to making the trip to the cemetery.

Her head grew dazed as people and more people rolled up in their buggies and meandered through the house offering their condolences and saying goodbye to Abraham their friend, neighbor, and brother in the Lord. Nothing seemed real. To Hannah, it was almost as though she was watching someone else's life play out—this was someone else's funeral and not her husband's.

When the time came to move to the cemetery, four men picked up the coffin and loaded it onto the special long buggy that carried the Amish coffins. The buggy headed off, followed by a long procession with Hannah being first as she traveled with Miriam and Stephen. Hannah clutched at the black cape that she had wrapped tightly around her neck and shoulders.

When she had agreed to marry Abraham, she'd known how much older he was, and that one day she would possibly be a young widow but she had expected that to be a long way into the future. When she was in her forties or fifties, she'd thought, certainly not in her mid twenties and with a child, their first child, on the way.

As soon as Hannah stepped down from the buggy, a cold shaft of wind blew across her and she pulled her black over bonnet on more firmly and tied the strings tightly. The sky was filled with rounded gray clouds, not even a speck of blue finding it's way through the blanket of gray. It was an eerie day, she thought, a gloomy day, a perfect day for a funeral.

With Stephen and Miriam either side of her she made her way to the grave. The bishop's wife, Ruth, hurried over to her and Stephen stepped aside, moving behind his wife.

"How are you, Hannah?" Ruth asked.

"As well as I can be, *denke,* Ruth."

"Let Bishop Joseph and me know if you need anything, anything at all."

"*Denke,* I will. Everyone's been so nice and helpful already."

"I'm staying with her for a few days," Miriam said.

Ruth gave a kindly smile. "That's best. And you've been keeping well now that you're expecting?"

"Remarkably well. *Gott* has blessed me with good health."

"Good to hear."

They had been the first people to reach the grave and Hannah stood there looking at the coffin with Ruth on one side and Miriam on the other. For years she'd regretted her marriage to Abraham and had to seek God's guidance and grace. With news of the baby coming, Abraham had softened somehow. She had believed that once the baby was born her household would run smoother and Abraham would be a good father, and maybe a kinder husband.

It had been her parents who'd suggested that she marry Abraham, a good friend of theirs because, they had told her, he'd be a steadfast husband and a reliable provider. This suggestion had come at the lowest point of her life when the man she had been dating, Matthew Miller, left the community for an *Englisch* girl. She'd cried for two weeks after she'd found out about Matthew. Figuring she was doomed and all hope of marriage gone, her parents had offered her hope when they suggested she marry Abraham, who was looking for a wife.

Marriage to him hadn't been as easy as Hannah thought it would be. Hannah had thought that once she was married that would be the end of her worries and she'd have a life of bliss. How wrong she'd been. And all the hard work she had done on her marriage relationship was for nothing, now that he'd been called home. It seemed unfair, too, that he would not even see his child.

She was jolted out of her melancholy thoughts by a soft shower of rain. It was something that gave Hannah a bit of pleasure. She loved the rain, and she felt that *Gott* might have sent it at that moment to give her a little consolation.

The bishop cleared his throat. "Let us begin." Bishop Joseph talked about the cycle of life, and how death would come to each one, and the importance of staying on the narrow path until God called us home. After he finished speaking, Hezekiah Yoder stepped forward and sang a hymn. Then another man closed in prayer. When they were finished, the rain shower ceased, too.

All Hannah wanted to do now was go home and be by herself, but her house wouldn't be quiet until later on that night. First she had to get through the hundreds of guests who were coming for the post-funeral meal. Two of the ladies had stayed back at her house to prepare the food and lay it out.

"Come on. Let's get you home," Miriam said.

Hannah nodded and then looked around the crowd hoping Levi might have arrived, but he wasn't anywhere to be seen. "Still no word from Levi?"

Miriam shook her head. "I tried to call him just before we left your *haus*. I'll call him again when we get back there. That's all I can do."

"I know. *Denke.*"

CHAPTER 3

IT WAS over dinner on the night Levi had proposed to Lizzy, and Andrew thought he heard the phone ring.

"Is that the phone?" Andrew asked.

"*Jah*, it is. Leave it go, please," Tricia said. "We're having dinner and if it's important they'll call back."

Andrew jumped to his feet. "It could be an emergency." He headed out the door, leaving his brother, his wife and their guest, Lizzy.

"I'm so excited to be getting married," Lizzy said as she looked adoringly at Levi.

"*Jah* that is good news," Tricia said.

"And I've never been to Lancaster County before and that will be my new home."

Tricia nodded. "Good."

"I can't wait to have my own home. What's your home like, Levi?"

"It was our parents' house and now it's mine. It's quite big."

"Do you own it or does the bank?" Lizzy asked.

Levi was surprised she would ask such a question, but she had every right to know. Perhaps it might have been better to ask him that in private. "I do. Andrew has moved here and my *schweschder* and her husband have a *haus* and they didn't need that one, so now it's mine. It's the *haus* I grew up in, that we three grew up in."

"And does it have a large garden?"

"It had a lovely garden when *Mamm* was still alive, but I'm afraid it's been let go. And it had a wonderful area for growing vegetables."

"I can soon get it back to where it used to be. I will have lots to keep me busy."

Levi was delighted that she was so excited, and he was pleased that his home would soon go back to the standards that his mother had left it, with her lovely garden restored. And soon he'd be able to eat produce from their own garden.

When Andrew walked back into the room all eyes were on him.

"Who was it?" Tricia asked.

As soon as Levi saw his brother's face he knew it was bad news. "What's happened?" Levi asked.

"It's Abraham Fisher."

Levi sprang to his feet, pushing out the chair from underneath him and knocking it to the floor. "Is Hannah okay?"

"Hannah is fine. Abraham has been called home."

A stunned silence filled the room.

Lizzy began to wail and Levi frowned at her. "Did you know Abraham Fisher, Lizzy?"

She looked up at him with tears in her eyes. "No, I just cry whenever someone dies." She put both hands up to her face and sobbed.

Levi had to get out of the house and get some fresh air. "Sorry about the chair, Tricia," he mumbled when he picked it up before he dashed out into the night.

He had to get home to make sure Hannah was okay. She was alone and to have this happen when she was expecting... She would be distraught. He had to call her and speak with her. He dashed into the barn and picked up the phone.

A hand grabbed the phone from him. He turned and saw his brother.

"What are you doing, man?"

"I've got to make sure Hannah's okay."

"The funeral was today. The community would've rallied around her. There's nothing you can do and besides, Miriam is there. She's the one who called, and she's staying with Hannah for a few days."

Levi felt all strength leave his legs and he staggered to sit down on a nearby hay bale. He held his head in his hands. "I can't believe that this is happening. I should've been there at the funeral. She's my good friend, we've got this connection."

"You've got to forget her. She's having a child. Her husband's child."

"She needs me, Andrew."

Andrew pulled up another hay bale and sat in front of his brother. "You've got a lovely woman in there who you're about to marry. You're going to start a fresh new life together. If you and Hannah had been meant to be, things would've turned out differently."

"Maybe *Gott* is giving me another chance to be with Hannah. He's giving me a third chance because I ruined my first two. Hannah is free now with Abraham gone. I had two chances to be with her, and I hesitated on both of them. I'm not going to hesitate now. The last time I waited too long and the next thing I heard, she was getting married to Abraham. Don't you see, Andrew? *Gott* is giving me another chance. We're both free to marry each other. There's nothing blocking me or standing in my way."

"You're not thinking straight. What are you gonna do with that woman in there? Can you see how her face lights up when she talks about your lives together? She's excited about getting married."

"I see where you're coming from, but you've got to understand it's no good for Lizzy if I have feelings for another woman. I'd be doing her a disservice if I marry her knowing that my true love is free to marry again. Don't you see, she's free now—she's a free woman? I'm not going to lose this opportunity. I'm not!"

"Hannah is having another man's child. Do you really think you could feel the same and give that child the same love as you would give one of your own?"

"Of course! I could love any child that *Gott* gives me as though it was one of my own. I've got a lot of love to give." He put his hand over his heart. "I will marry Hannah and I will love that child as a special gift."

"I caution you, brother. You must listen to me because my years on you come with wisdom. And it's with this wisdom I tell you that I think God is showing you, with the timing of it all, that it wouldn't be the right decision. You've given your word that you will marry Lizzy. Doesn't your word mean anything to you?"

"My word is everything to me, but the stakes are high here. Lizzy can find someone else. She's young. I'll tell her what's happened."

"You're that confident that Hannah would marry you?"

"Well, I hope so."

243

"Hope? We can all hope anything we like. Hannah wouldn't be the same woman you knew years ago. She's been married for five years, and before that the pair of you weren't that close."

"That was my fault."

"Are you sure you haven't created a grand illusion that isn't based on truth? Hannah wouldn't have given you two thoughts in years."

Levi didn't like anything that his brother was saying and a huge knot formed in his stomach. "The last five years have been wretched for me knowing that Hannah was married to another man."

"You're being selfish. Life isn't about pleasing you, it's about pleasing others. The word says, in honor preferring one another."

"You're saying I should be unhappy and marry Lizzy?"

"If you stand by your word, God will bless your marriage to Lizzy. I can't see that God will bless you if you let that woman down. How do you think she will feel once you've told her you'll marry her and then you dump her and go off and marry someone else? You can't do it. Besides that, you don't even know if Hannah will ever return these feelings you have for her."

Levi thought for a moment. "I'd imagine Lizzy would feel pretty bad. I see what you mean. But it would be good for Hannah and the baby if I married her because then she would be so happy and I'd be happy. And the baby would have a *vadder*."

"At the expense of Lizzy's happiness?"

Levi hated hearing his brother's words, but he knew Andrew was right. The right thing to do was keep his word, marry Lizzy, and put her first rather than himself.

Andrew continued, "This life we have here is a vapor and will soon disappear, but what we do here determines where we will spend eternity."

"I think you're being a little dramatic, Andrew. *Gott* is not going to turn his back if I decide against marrying Lizzy."

"Maybe not. The decision is yours to make. I hope I've brought up some things for you to think about. I want you to weigh up everything before you make your next move."

"*Denke.* I'll think things through thoroughly before I do another thing. First, though, I need to make a call to Hannah and offer my condolences and tell her I'll be home soon."

Andrew nodded. "I'll go inside and tell the women you'll be back soon to finish the meal."

CHAPTER 4

JUST AS THE last buggy full of people headed down Hannah's driveway on the day of the funeral, she and Miriam heard the phone ringing from out in the barn.

"Could you get that, Miriam? I'm far too tired."

"Of course." Miriam hurried out of the house.

The phone had rung often over the last few days with people offering their sympathies and asking if Hannah needed anything done. Hannah also had a pile of correspondence to read and reply to.

When Miriam walked back into the living room, she was grinning from ear to ear.

"Good news?" Hannah asked.

"*Jah*, Levi is coming home. He said to tell you that he's sorry he missed the funeral and he's coming back as soon as he can." Miriam sat down on the couch next to her.

"That is good news. I'm looking forward to seeing him."

"You two always did have a special bond."

"*Jah*, we did."

Miriam said, "I always thought that the two of you might marry."

Hannah smiled. "At one point, so did I, but that was a long time ago. We were only teenagers and then we grew up. If only I hadn't gone on that buggy ride with Matthew ..."

"Now don't start thinking about things or people that will upset you."

"No, don't worry, all of that happened so long ago now that it doesn't upset me. Matthew wasn't the right man for me."

"*Gott* will find you the right man when you're ready to marry again. You're still young."

Hannah shook her head. "I can't think of that right now."

"Of course not. And neither should you think of anything but adjusting to life without Abraham and preparing to welcome your *boppli*. Everyone knows it's not easy for you."

Hannah shook her head. "It's not. It was such a shock. It would've been easier if he'd gradually grown ill and then got worse. He left the *haus* perfectly healthy and then I got the news that he was gone. It's just been a lot to take in. I just have so many questions and I don't think they'll ever be answered."

"Life's like that. We probably won't know everything until we're in *Gott's haus*. Perhaps then all our questions will be answered and we'll understand it all."

"*Denke* for staying here, but you should get home to Stephen. I'm okay here and the sooner I get used to being in the house by myself the better. I really needed you over these past days, Miriam, and I don't know what I would've done without you."

"Am I wearing out my welcome?"

Hannah smiled at her good friend. "You could never ever do that. I'll be okay from here on in."

"Are you sure?"

"*Jah,* and if I change my mind I'll come fetch you."

"You could come and stay at our place if that would help."

"This is still my home even though he isn't here anymore. And I'll have to make it a happy home for me and my *boppli*."

"You will. You'll make a *wunderbaar mudder*."

"*Denke*, and so will you one day."

"When the Lord wills it."

Miriam had been married for years and longed for a baby. It almost made Hannah feel guilty when she shared the news of her pregnancy with her friend. Although, Hannah also had waited a long time—five years—for her baby to come along.

"As soon as Levi comes home you'll both have to come for dinner," Miriam said.

"I'd like that," Hannah said.

"Not tomorrow night, but the night after. He'll be home by then."

"Really? That soon?"

Miriam nodded.

"I nearly forgot I've got... I've got an appointment with the midwife the day after tomorrow. She said with all the stress, I should make appointments more often."

"Then I should come with you."

"*Nee denke.* I need to get used to doing things on my own. It's not far and my horse needs the exercise."

CHAPTER 5

LEVI WALKED outside the barn to see Andrew waiting there for him.

"There, happy now you spoke with her?" Andrew asked.

"It wasn't her. I spoke to Miriam. Hannah wasn't in any fit state to answer the phone."

"She's grieving. That's only normal. It'll take her some time to adjust. Miriam will help her wherever she can. The two of them have always been close."

"It was the four of us who were close if I remember correctly. We were always in the fields together and playing in the barn if it was cold or raining."

Andrew laughed. "That's not quite how I remember it. I was older than the rest of you, and thought your games were silly."

Levi slapped his brother on the shoulder. "*Denke* for giving me guidance. You're still being bossy and telling me what to do even now at this age."

"It's a tough job but someone's gotta do it."

Levi chuckled. "I better get back in to see what my fiancée's doing."

"That's what I like to hear," Andrew said.

When they went back inside, Levi told them he was going home. He could see plainly that Lizzy wasn't happy that he was going to go home the very next day, and going without her.

"You two were gone for a long time," Lizzy said.

Levi looked at Andrew. "Didn't you tell them I was calling Hannah?"

"I did."

Levi said to Lizzy, "I called home to offer my condolences to Hannah."

Tricia said, "I will write to her. I say things much better when I write them down."

"I told Miriam I was coming home as soon as I could. I'll get on the bus tomorrow," Levi said.

"And me?" Lizzy asked even though Levi had said he'd send her a bus ticket when he'd gotten things ready for her.

"I need to find you a place to stay first."

"I think you should take me with you. It would be hard to explain to my *ant* and *onkel* that you proposed, and then left me here."

Levi tried to hide his embarrassment at having to have a conversation like this in front of his brother and his sister-in-law. He said in a quiet voice, "Do you want me to explain things to them for you?"

Her lips turned down at the corners. *"Nee!"*

"We have already spoken about this, Lizzy. There's no accommodation. I wouldn't know where you could stay."

"Well, what about your *schweschder*, Miriam?"

"My *bruder*-in-law is extending their *haus* and they're living amongst rubble at the moment. They don't have guest space. I couldn't allow you to stay there. As soon as I get back, I'll speak to the bishop and he'll arrange suitable accommodation for you."

"And at the same time you'll tell the bishop we're getting married and make a date for our wedding?"

"Jah, I'll tell him. It's a little early to make a date, isn't it? My good friend's husband has just died and I'd like to make certain she's okay before my mind is consumed with wedding plans." When he saw her pout, he added, "I'll also have to arrange further time off for a vacation for after our wedding."

"It sounds like it will be ages away."

He shook his head, wanting to see her smile again. "Not ages. I'll make a date for our wedding when I meet with the bishop."

That put a smile on Lizzy's face.

Levi hoped that his brother had given him the right advice. But then again, he knew that the right thing to do often seemed the hardest thing to do.

WHEN LEVI ARRIVED back home he visited his sister's house first, wanting to hear news of Hannah before he went to see her.

Miriam ran out to meet him and flung her arms around him as soon as he stepped down from the buggy.

"Levi, how have you been? You look well."

"The extended vacation did me good. But I don't think I picked a very good time to leave. I should've been here for Hannah."

"I don't know how many calls I made to Tricia and Andrew's *haus* and they all went unanswered except for that last one."

"At least I'm here now. How's Hannah doing?"

"She's coming for dinner tonight. I told her you'd be here."

That was the best news Levi had heard in ages. "She'll be here, tonight?"

"*Jah*." She pulled him into the house. "Stephen has come a long way with the renovations. You'll have to see everything. *Jah,* we've still only got one usable bedroom and one working bathroom, but everything's coming along."

"Good."

Levi couldn't bring himself to tell his sister that he was marrying a woman he'd only known for a few weeks. Now that he was home, the whole thing seemed ludicrous. The thought crossed his mind how easy it would be to end the relationship from afar, but his conscience wouldn't allow him to entertain that notion for too long. Lizzy now expected a husband, and rightly so because he'd given his word. His word had been given in haste, he now thought, but it still was his word.

"What time tonight?"

"Come at six or thereabouts."

"I can stop by Hannah's place and collect her on the way."

Miriam shook her head. "No need, Stephen's doing that."

"It's on the way. Tell Stephen I'll collect her."

"Are you sure?" Miriam asked.

"Positive. I'm looking forward to seeing her. I never should've gone away. I should've been here when all this happened to Abraham. I heard he was struck by lightning."

"That's right. He was burned to a crisp and barely recognizable. The coffin had to be closed."

"That's awful! And Hannah's health?"

"She's doing fine."

. . .

LEVI WAS DRIVING HOME from his sister's house when he saw a buggy at the side of the road. When he drew closer, he saw it was Hannah. His heart beat fast with excitement at seeing her again—the first time in many years they'd see each other as single people. Lizzy wasn't even in his mind at that moment.

He pulled his buggy off to the other side and secured his horse. "Hannah!" he ran across the road.

"Levi, you're back already."

She looked just as beautiful as ever, yet at the same time pale and vulnerable. *"Jah.* I'm so sorry to hear about Abraham."

She nodded. *"Denke."*

"I'm sorry I was away when it happen. I didn't hear about it until the day of his funeral." He looked at her horse. "What's happened here?"

"I think Blackie's lame. I didn't want to walk him too far if he was, so I was sitting here not knowing what to do."

"Have you just traveled a long distance?"

"Nee. I've just come back from Sally Lapp's *haus."*

Levi knew Sally Lapp was the midwife all the women in the community chose to have their babies with. "Oh. Is everything okay?"

Hannah nodded. "Everything's just fine."

"I'll take a look at Blackie. I'll unhitch him and walk him out and have you watch for a limp." Levi unhitched him and then walked him up the street. "How does he look?" he yelled back at Hannah.

"I think he looks okay. He seems to be favoring one of his legs, but I can't tell which one."

Levi turned around and led the horse back. "Could be a stone bruise or something. He doesn't seem too bad." He picked up one of Blackie's feet and used a stick to remove some mud so he could see better. "His shoes are nearly worn through. I'll follow you home and take his shoes off and then you'll need to call the blacksmith in a day or two."

"Okay, *denke.*"

When they got back to Hannah's house, he took a tool out of the back of his buggy and removed the horse's shoes while Hannah looked on. "Where are you keeping him?" he asked.

"I was keeping him in the main paddock, but I can put him in the stall in the stable for now. That's got the adjoining paddock where he goes in the colder months."

"It's best if he goes there. You go inside. I'll put down the bedding in his stall. That'll be better for his feet if he's got an injury. I'm no expert, but he doesn't look bad to me."

"*Denke,* Levi."

Levi led him into the stable and filled the stall with straw. With Hannah in no fit state to clean the stable, he'd offer to call there every second day. When he walked back to the house, Hannah was waiting for him with a mug of hot coffee.

"Denke. This is just what I need." He took a sip and she sat on the porch seat.

"Take a seat."

He sat next to her. "Hannah, I'm so sorry I wasn't here. I know I've already said that, but I want to be here for you."

"You're here now. And it was something that couldn't be helped. You weren't to know."

"How are you—really?"

SHE LOOKED into his dark eyes. And felt as though she were home. She should have been with this man at the beginning and they should've married each other. As they sat there on the overcast gray day, she was sure that he felt it too. It seemed like they were the only two people in the world. Taking a moment, she put everything into her memory like taking a snapshot so she could remember that moment forever.

"I'm as good as I can be," she finally said.

She heard him exhale before he took another mouthful of coffee.

"Denke for coming to my rescue just now."

"Always. I'll come back and clean out Blackie's stall for you tomorrow. And we'll see each other tonight at Miriam's. Are you still going?"

"*Jah.* I am."

"I'll collect you."

"I think Miriam arranged for Stephen to do that."

He laughed. "I told Miriam I'd do it, so Stephen has been canceled."

"Oh." Hannah gave a little laugh. "I feel it's just so odd that Abraham has gone. He was here one minute and in an instant he was gone. It's hard to take it all in. He wasn't even sick or anything."

Levi nodded. "It must've been a nasty shock. I'm here though. Anything you want or need, just ask me."

"*Denke,* Levi. I'm glad you turned up when you did. I might be still sitting on the side of the road not knowing what to do."

He chuckled. "You would've figured it out. You've always been independent."

She sensed things were a little off between them and wondered if it was coming from him or her.

"*Denke* for the coffee. Now I'd better get home and wash up for dinner. I'll be back soon." He rose to his feet, smiled at her and headed to his buggy.

CHAPTER 6

HANNAH WAS EXCITED about seeing Levi again so soon for dinner. She often wondered what it would be like to be a single available woman, and had regretted allowing her parents to push her into the marriage with Abraham. But back then she'd been immature, and had thought being married solved all problems.

It had been a struggle being married to Abraham, a daily struggle. He wasn't a happy man to be around and they never saw eye-to-eye on anything. But they had both made the most of things. She dared to think that this might be another chance, just maybe, another chance for Levi and herself. What if they married?

Levi had been single all this time and had never even dated a woman. Could he have been secretly in love with her this whole time? Now they could finally be together. She dared not think any more thoughts like that. It was far too soon after Abraham's death, but she couldn't help her mind running away with her. Maybe it was the pregnancy hormones that urged her to look for a man to care for her and her unborn child. In her mind, the only man who could do that for her was Levi.

Hannah wanted to have a proper marriage before she took her last breath on this earth. A proper marriage where she loved and adored her husband, rather than struggling every day to make something work that never should've been.

She placed a hand over her stomach. If she married Levi, her baby would have a wonderful father. She knew how Levi loved children and she was sure he would love the child as his very own. Excited to see Levi again, she put on her best Sunday clothes. The dress was dark green, and her white apron and cap were made from lightweight sheer fabric with a slight sheen on its surface.

Before she put her cap on, she brushed out her long hair. It had only been cut once when she'd managed to get thistles in it when she'd been playing in the fields as a child. The only way her mother could get them out was to cut her hair. Hannah smiled as she recalled how she'd cried at having short hair like a boy. She was around the age where girls start wearing caps, and was pleased when her mother made her one that very night. In the morning, she wore a cap and no one saw her dreadful chopped-off boyish hair.

She now braided her hair into several sections before pinning it on her head and placing her cap over the top.

A little before six she waited for Levi and soon she saw his buggy coming toward her.

Hannah closed the front door behind her and went out to meet him.

He jumped down from the buggy. "How's Blackie?"

"I haven't checked on him."

"I'll stop by tomorrow and take a look. We should get going to Miriam's *haus*."

"*Jah*. I suppose we should." When they got down to the end of the driveway, Hannah asked, "How was your visit with Andrew?"

"Good. It was great to see all my nieces and nephews again. They're growing up so fast and this was the first time I'd seen the *boppli*."

"It's a shame they live so far away."

"He had to go there, really, because Tricia lived there and she desperately wanted to stay near her mother."

That remark didn't go unnoticed by Hannah. Any other man could've said that Andrew would've found a wife closer to home, but Levi was a man who understood about love, she was sure of that.

Levi had never mentioned that she was pregnant, but she knew that Miriam would've told him because Miriam and Levi were very close.

WHEN HANNAH SAT down for dinner with her friends she felt a great sense of comfort and peace. Eventually, she would like to marry again, and what better husband for her and father for her child than Levi? The way he'd talked to her and looked at her, she thought he might still have feelings for her and was being respectful of her and waiting a proper amount of time after Abraham's death.

She couldn't let him know that she was open to a second marriage, not this close after her husband's death. A suitable time would have to pass so she wouldn't look like she was jumping from one husband to another. The last thing she wanted was to be the subject of gossip.

"Andrew said you have a surprise for us, Levi?" Miriam said.

The three of them at the table turned to look at Levi.

"I can't think what that could be." He leaned over and helped himself to more potato salad.

"It sounded important," Miriam said.

"*Nee,* he must be having a joke with you."

"You know how serious Andrew is? He doesn't joke about anything."

Hannah gave a little laugh. "He is rather serious."

"How are the renovations?" Levi asked Stephen. "They look like they're coming along quickly."

"They are. I'll show you after dinner. I've got my brothers coming to help me on the weekend and then we'll be just about done except for the roof."

"Sounds good."

Hannah worried about what the news could be. She feared that he might have plans of moving to Ohio. She couldn't bear to lose him. "You're not moving, are you, Levi?"

He smiled at Hannah. "*Nee,* I couldn't if I wanted to. I've got my *familye haus* here, and my sister and the business, and you to watch over."

Hannah smiled and looked down at her plate of food. She was happy that he was staying put.

"You've gotten so secretive in your old age, Levi," Miriam said.

"My life is an open book. I don't know what you're talking about."

"If Levi has something to tell us, he'll tell us when he is good and ready," Stephen said.

"*Denke,* Stephen. I knew you were a good match for my *schweschder.*"

"I can't win with the two of you. Speak up for me, Hannah," Miriam said.

"*Ach nee,* I'm keeping out of this one. I've learned long ago not to come between *bruder* and *schweschder.*"

When they finished the meal, Hannah stayed in the kitchen helping Miriam while the men went to the living room.

"He's got something on his mind, I can tell," Miriam whispered to Hannah.

Hannah wondered if it could be that he had her on his mind. That would be the best thing that she could hope for.

"What do you think it is?" Hannah whispered back.

"I don't know. But I'll find out soon. He's never been able to keep a secret."

Hannah winced. "I wouldn't say that."

"He can probably keep other people's secrets, but not his own."

"That might be right," Hannah said. When they had washed up the dishes and cleaned the kitchen, they brought coffee and cookies out to the men and sat down with them.

"I know I've said it before, Hannah, but I would've liked to have been there for the funeral. I picked a bad time to go away."

Hannah shrugged her shoulders. "I guess things turn out how they're meant to."

"You're like my *schweschder* and I feel I need to protect you, especially now that Abraham's gone."

"Miriam and I are here too," Stephen said.

"I'm very blessed to have you all." A tear trickled down her cheek. The reality was she was alone, and she didn't like that feeling.

Miriam moved closer, "Don't cry."

Hannah sniffed. "I'll be okay."

WHEN LEVI DROVE HER HOME, he stopped outside her door and then before she got out, he said, "I need to tell you something, Hannah."

Hannah smiled. Was he going to hint at the fact he had feelings for her? Anything other than a hint would be too much too soon.

"*Jah,* Levi?"

"When I went to visit Andrew, I met a young lady."

All Hannah's hopes fell away. He'd met a woman and they were getting married. What a fool she'd been. It served her right for thinking about a man so soon after her husband had died and while she was carrying her late husband's child. She wanted to block her ears and run away.

Levi continued, "I asked her to marry me."

"Oh." Hannah looked up into the night sky at the twinkling stars and then looked back at him. "She said yes?"

He nodded.

"I'm sorry, that was a silly thing to say. Of course she would've said yes."

"I wanted to tell you first. Andrew knows and my sister-in-law, but I wanted you to be the first to know here. Miriam and Stephen have no idea. I'll have to tell them soon."

He didn't like her at all—it had been her imagination. And why would he like her? She felt she'd aged fifteen years in that five years of marriage and it must've showed on her weary features. It was only natural he'd want to start his married life with a young woman—she *was* probably young and fresh-faced, a woman who was quick-witted and also smart. She was no match for a woman like that. "I'm pleased for you."

"*Denke*. It's probably about time. I'm not getting younger."

"None of us are. Where is she from?" Hannah asked.

"Harts County, but she was staying with some people close by Andrew's *haus*. She's coming here soon to stay. I guess I'll have to look into that tomorrow."

"Things are moving quickly."

"*Jah*, I think that's best."

"*Jah*. *Denke* for driving me home, Levi." She got out of the buggy. "Good night."

"Good night, Hannah. I'm glad you're okay."

Hannah continued into the house and closed the door behind her, listening all the while to the clip-clop, clip-clop of horse's hooves as Levi's buggy continued back to the road.

She held in her tears and lit the gas lantern beside her and then she walked over to the couch and collapsed onto it. Now she felt truly alone. More alone than she had ever felt in her life. Her spark of hope had been snuffed out like the last candle in the darkest night.

CHAPTER 7

HANNAH HAD CRIED herself to sleep right there on the couch. She couldn't bring herself to move into the bedroom. Climbing the stairs seemed way too much effort.

When she woke, she did her best to pull herself together for the sake of her baby. She washed her face and showered, and then she felt a little better. As she toasted some bread under the grill, she wondered what would become of her.

Her home was large and unencumbered, but she wouldn't be able to handle the land on her own. She'd have a talk with Stephen and Levi and see what they suggested she do. Abraham had left her with enough money so she wouldn't have to work for many years if she was careful, and that was before any money came in from farming. She thanked God that she had a solid roof over her head and money for her child and herself to live on. Things weren't that bad, she told herself.

She also had her friends, and soon she would be holding her sweet baby in her arms. Already she had so much love for the child that grew within her. Thinking of her baby brought a smile to her face. They would get through everything together.

Levi's news had left a hole in her heart, but Levi had never promised her anything. Not once had they ever expressed their feelings to one another although she knew in her heart that he had once loved her. But everyone changes with time and perhaps what had appealed to him about her in their youth was gone.

"But it just wasn't meant to be," she said out loud. Perhaps she could get a cat or two to keep her company. Abraham had never allowed cats around the place due to him being allergic. Hannah wondered if it wasn't that he just didn't like cats. Most people had cats in the barn to keep down the vermin. But a couple of house cats would be wonderful to keep her company in the coming days leading up to the birth.

She busied herself that day washing the curtains that hadn't been washed in many months. The busier she was, the less time she'd have to think about being alone. And when her baby arrived, she'd be plenty busy. By then Levi would be married and she'd be happy for him. He deserved happiness.

Just as she was sitting down for lunch, she heard a buggy. Immediately she hoped it was Levi coming to tell her that he'd changed his mind and he was no longer going to marry the young woman he'd met. Perhaps he was coming to tell her that he would marry her and take care of her and her baby. Then she remembered he'd said he'd stop by and check on Blackie.

She hurried to the window and looked out, and her heart sank through the floor when she saw Ruth, the bishop's wife heading to the house.

Hannah filled the teakettle with water and placed it on the stove, put her plate of food in the oven, and went to the door to meet her. All the while she was holding back the tears.

"How are you, Ruth?"

Ruth climbed down from the buggy. "I'm fine, *denke*, Hannah. I've come to see how you are."

"I suppose I'm doing as well as I can hope to be doing, under the circumstances."

Ruth nodded.

"Come in. I have the kettle on."

When they were sitting opposite each other, Ruth looked into Hannah's face. "Oh, Hannah, have you been crying?"

"I'm just so sad." The tears flowed, and she couldn't stop them.

Ruth patted her shoulder and moved her chair closer to Hannah's.

"I know it'll probably take you months to get over his death. Take comfort in knowing that he's in *Gott's haus*."

Hannah nodded. And felt bad for crying over Levi and never knowing how his arms would feel around her, never having him be the last person she spoke to at night before her head hit the pillow. Ruth would be horrified if she knew what was really

273

upsetting her. "I'm just a bad, bad sinner," Hannah blurted out as she cried some more.

"We have all sinned. Not one of us is perfect. You couldn't have done anything different. When *Gott* calls someone home, they go home. Abraham is happy and at peace."

Hannah nodded but inside, Ruth's words made her feel worse.

"I'm sorry I'm crying."

When the kettle whistled, Ruth said, "You stay sitting and I'll make the tea."

"*Denke.*"

"You must feel so lonely in this house by yourself now."

"I do, it's very lonely, and this place is so big for just me. I suppose in a few months I'll have my little *boppli*. And I've been thinking of getting some cats."

"What a lovely idea."

"*Jah.* I think so. It'll give me some company."

"Do you feel that's what you need?"

"I do. I feel empty inside and two little kittens will make me happy, I think. Two little tabbie cats maybe. I don't really mind what color."

"Well, then I have good news for you."

"You know where I can get two cats from?" People often had kittens and puppies to give away to good homes.

Ruth's lips smiled so widely that vertical wrinkles formed in her cheeks. "*Nee.* I have something better than that."

"A puppy?"

Ruth laughed. "I have a young lady who needs a place to stay, and since you're lonely, it will be perfect."

That was the worst thing Hannah could imagine. She shook her head. "I couldn't have anybody staying here. *Nee,* I couldn't."

"You said yourself just now that you're lonely."

Hannah had a sneaking suspicion who this woman might be, and it would be her worst nightmare-come-true to have the woman who was to marry Levi staying with her. "Who is this woman?"

"It's the young woman Levi is going to marry. He said you and Miriam are two of the few people who know."

Hannah stared at Ruth wondering if she should make a confession and then decided against it. But it just wouldn't be right, her harboring feelings for Levi and having his fiancée stay there at the house. "I don't think I could have a guest. Thanks all the same, Ruth, but it just wouldn't work out."

"You can help each other. She'll be company for you, and I've already told her all about you. She knows you're a good friend of Levi's and she said she would do everything here to help you. And she said you wouldn't have to lift a finger. She'd do all the cooking and all the cleaning, and everything else for you."

"Oh, she sounds very kind and generous, but ..."

"That's settled then." Ruth nodded her head.

"*Nee.* But, Ruth, I didn't say ..."

"What is it, Hannah?"

"I would have to think about this some more. I don't want anyone here."

"There's no time to think about it, Hannah. She arrives tomorrow."

Hannah gulped and felt like she was going to be sick.

"Tomorrow?"

"*Jah,* tomorrow."

"I'm sure there's somewhere else she could stay that would be better suited."

"There's nowhere else for her to stay. As I said, you can both help each other." Ruth's attention was taken to something behind Hannah. "Mind if I have a cookie?"

"Oh, I'm sorry. I'm being so careless and not looking after you properly."

"I'll get it.' Ruth stood up and reached for the cookie jar and offered one to Hannah.

Hannah shook her head. "*Nee denke.*" The last thing she felt like right now with her queasy stomach was a cookie.

All Hannah wanted to do was wallow in her self-pity. Being alone was the only thing she wanted now. Having Levi's fiancée in her house would be like having a thorn in her side, a stone in her shoe, more thistles in her hair.

"You'll see this is just what you need. Someone to look after you."

AFTER RUTH HAD her fill of cookies and tea she left Hannah alone. Hannah had only a few precious hours, and then the very woman who had taken her last hope would invade her space.

Hannah scolded herself. The woman that Levi chose would be a wonderful woman, and perhaps the two of them could become friends. Hannah cheered herself up with that thought.

It was half an hour later that Miriam visited her.

"I just had Ruth here," Hannah said as Miriam came into her house.

"Let me guess. She wanted Lizzy to stay here?"

"Is that her name? She never told me her name."

Miriam nodded. "Lizzy Weaver. So you know that he's getting married?"

"He told me when he brought me home last night." Hannah hoped Miriam wouldn't see that she'd been crying.

"Are you okay with having someone live here with you?"

"*Jah*, it'll be fun."

"I suppose it will be company for you," Miriam said.

"Ruth said that Lizzy has offered to do everything around the place." Hannah gave a little giggle.

"Well, that's just what you need. You need to sit back and relax for a while and think about your *boppli*."

Hannah put her hand on her swelling stomach.

"What did the midwife say? I'm sorry I didn't even think to ask you last night."

"Everything's fine. Everything's going perfectly well."

"I know you're sad right now, Hannah, but you do have a lot to be grateful for."

"I know I do. I was just thinking the very same thing this morning. Sometimes we don't appreciate what we have until we lose it."

Miriam nodded. "That's right."

Hannah bit her lip. She'd had so many losses in the past few years. Now, she had to be happy for Levi and Lizzy. "*Jah*, I'm looking forward to her coming to stay with me."

"Good."

"She could become a good friend for us," Hannah said, forcing a smile.

"We can always do with more of those."

"*Jah*, we can."

"You know she's coming tomorrow?" Miriam asked.

"Everything is happening so quickly."

Miriam said, "I think Levi was a bit surprised because he was arranging her ticket, and then he found out that she'd bought her own. I think he was expecting her to come in a week or two or maybe three, and she surprised him by coming early."

"A nice surprise, I'm sure."

"*Jah*." Miriam nodded and looked into the distance.

Miriam was still there when Levi came to check on Blackie, so Hannah couldn't talk to him alone. He cleaned out the stable for her and then told her to wait a few days before she called the blacksmith. Then he was gone, and minutes after, Miriam left too.

CHAPTER 8

The next day.

HANNAH HAD BEEN TOLD that Lizzy was arriving at two o'clock. She had already made up one of the rooms for her and had prepared a nice meal in case she was hungry from her travels. It was ten minutes after two when the bishop and his wife came up her driveway toward her house. Hannah had done well, she thought, telling herself repeatedly that having someone stay there would be a good thing for her.

Hannah waited at the door and soon Ruth and a young lady were walking toward her while the bishop pulled various sized suitcases out of the back of the buggy.

"Hi, Hannah, this is Lizzy Weaver. Lizzy, this is Hannah Fisher."

SAMANTHA PRICE

"Pleased to meet you, Hannah. And *denke* for having me to stay at your lovely home."

"You're quite welcome. It's just me in this big place. I'm glad for some company."

Lizzy giggled loudly and Hannah thought she was nervous. She was a very pretty woman just like Hannah had suspected. Her eyes were blue, her complexion creamy and her hair was a pale golden-blonde color.

Looking over at all the bags Lizzy had brought with her, Hannah said, "Oh, you did bring quite a lot with you."

"I've got more at home and I'll get everything after Levi and I are married."

"*Jah*, good idea. Well, come inside and let's have a cup of hot tea."

"We can't stay, Hannah, Joseph has someone coming to the house to see him."

"I understand. Stop by another time."

"*Jah*. I will visit you two and see how you're getting along."

"We'll get on fine," Lizzy said with another giggle, and this time it was more high-pitched than the last one.

"*Jah*, I'm sure we will. I'll show you to your room, Lizzy."

The bishop carried all of Lizzy's bags up the stairs and into her room, and after Bishop Joseph and Ruth left, the two women sat down for tea.

282

"I don't know why Levi couldn't have got me from the bus station. Do you know I had to get two buses and two taxis?"

"Well, it's quite a distance to come from Ohio."

"And that's exactly why Levi should've collected me rather than the bishop and his wife."

"I think it's because Levi's been away from his business for so long, and —"

"I'll soon find out. I'm seeing him tonight."

"Oh, is he coming here?"

Wrinkles formed in Lizzy's forehead. "Hasn't he arranged anything? I thought he'd want to see me on my first night here." Her lips turned down and she looked as though she was about to cry.

"I don't know. I haven't heard from him. Don't worry, I'm sure he'll stop by and say hello."

Lizzy sniffed and nodded. "I hope so, or this is not a very good start to the rest of our lives together."

"Don't worry, Levi is a very good man who'll do everything he can to keep you happy."

"I'm not happy now." She pouted, shaking her head rapidly.

"Cookie?" Hannah said, offering her the jar, and at a loss to know what to say or do.

"Denke." Lizzy nibbled on a cookie while her eyes glazed over.

"I've made us a chicken casserole. Would you like some now? Have you eaten?"

"I ate before. A little while ago."

"We'll leave the chicken casserole for dinner, in that case."

"I intend to make myself useful while I'm here. Just let me know of any jobs that need doing."

"Just do something when you see something that needs doing," Hannah said, not wanting to have to give the young woman instructions.

"I heard your husband died."

"*Jah,* it was sudden. The funeral was just days ago."

"He must've been a very good friend of Levi's because he was so upset when he heard."

"*Jah,* Levi is a dear friend, to both me and my late husband."

Hannah was sure Lizzy had some lovely qualities and Levi must've seen them in her. She was still looking for what he'd seen.

"Ruth says you're having a baby, but you don't look like you are."

"*Jah.* I'm only a few months along and not showing very much." Hannah looked down at her midsection.

"I hope Levi and I have many *kinner.*"

"That would be nice."

"But I suppose you'll only have one since your husband has died."

"Most likely, unless I marry again some day."

"*Jah,* many women marry a few years after their husband dies." Lizzy wriggled in her chair. "What are we going to do tomorrow? I'm guessing Levi will be working since he isn't even going to make the effort to come to see me today."

"I hadn't given it much thought. Did you bring any sewing with you?"

"I can't sew all day. Maybe we can go shopping, or out to the markets."

"We could've but my horse has gone lame. He's got a stone bruise, we think."

"Does that matter?"

"*Jah,* I can't take him anywhere. He needs to heal."

She pouted.

"I get quite a few visitors. Perhaps someone will visit us. Miriam will probably visit."

"*Jah.* I would like to meet her, but I imagined it would be Levi who introduced me to his *schweschder.* Can we call him?"

"I've got a phone in the barn. Feel free to use it anytime you like."

"Okay, I'll call him at work right now. He gave me the number."

Before Hannah could say anything, Lizzy jumped up and headed out to the barn. Hannah looked out the window at her striding purposefully toward the barn. That was one woman who knew what she wanted, and right now she wanted Levi's attention.

CHAPTER 9

HANNAH KEPT a watch on the barn and very soon Lizzy was marching back to the house.

When she came back into the kitchen, she told Hannah, "He said he can't stop by after work. I asked him to come for dinner, but he said he wouldn't impose on you."

"It wouldn't be imposing."

"That's what I told him. I thought I'd be spending more time with him when I got here." She slumped into a chair at the kitchen table.

Hannah sat beside her. "There's plenty of time; you've only just got here."

"I'm sorry, Hannah, you must think I'm awfully grumpy. I'm not like this normally. I'm just tired."

"That's understandable; you've had a long journey. I expect you'll feel much better after a good night's sleep."

"I don't know when I'm going to see him. He said he'd call and collect me on Saturday morning. But that's four days away. What am I going to do with all that time? The bishop's wife said I should help you around here." She swiveled her head around to look at the kitchen. "The place looks clean enough. I don't see the point of scrubbing things and scrubbing things, day after day. Once a week is enough."

"I do a little bit every day and that way, the cleaning doesn't get away from me. It's surprising how much dust accumulates on things if you leave it too long."

Lizzy shook her head. "The bishop also said I should look after you, but you look perfectly fine. You're pregnant, not sick. Are you sick?"

"I'm fine. Perfectly fine."

"*Jah*, you look fine. They were making out you're an invalid that I had to look after. I'm not good at looking after people who are sick."

"When you become a mother you'll have sick children. They catch colds and things. You'll have to look after them."

"That will be different. I'll have to do that. And they'll be mine."

"My husband has just died, so I think Ruth thinks I'll be distressed and things like that."

"Will you?"

"Yeah, I go through ups and downs sometimes."

From what Lizzy was saying, she hadn't been the one to volunteer her help after all.

"Oh, Hannah. Couldn't we do something tomorrow?"

"Miriam will probably stop by to meet you."

"*Jah*, I have to make a good impression on her because she's my future *schweschder*-in-law."

"She's lovely; you'll really like her."

"Levi didn't tell me much about his family."

"Didn't he?"

"*Nee*. Could I have another cup of tea?"

"Of course." Hannah got up and poured her another cup.

HANNAH WOKE THE NEXT MORNING, and headed down to make breakfast.

It was ten o'clock when she went back upstairs and peeped into Lizzy's room to see her fast asleep.

She slowly walked back down the stairs and when her foot hit the last step, she heard a buggy. Hannah hoped it was Miriam and when she opened the front door she saw that it was.

"I'm glad you came, since we can't go anywhere at the moment," Hannah said when Miriam came into the house.

"Blackie still lame?"

"Jah. He won't be going anywhere for a while, Levi said."

"I forgot about that. Good thing I stopped by." Looking around, Miriam asked, "Where's your visitor?"

Hannah leaned in and whispered, "Still asleep."

"Is she sick or something?"

"I think she's just tired from the long journey from Ohio."

Miriam nodded.

"I'll make you a cup of tea."

Miriam followed Hannah into the kitchen. Just as they each had a cup of tea in front of them a bright and breezy Lizzy rushed into the kitchen smiling. When she saw Miriam, her face fell.

"Oh, I thought the buggy was Levi's."

Miriam stood up. "Lizzy, pleased to meet you. I'm Levi's *schweschder,* Miriam."

Lizzy smiled and shook her hand. "Hello, Miriam."

"Sit down, Lizzy, I'll get you a cup of tea."

As Lizzy sat, she said, "It's late. I'm sorry I slept so long, Hannah, but we had no plans for the day."

"Miriam has come to visit us like I thought she might."

"Wonderful," Lizzy said in a less than enthusiastic tone.

After Hannah made the tea, she was about to sit down when Lizzy spoke. "I haven't had breakfast yet. Could you make me some eggs, Hannah? I'm starving."

"*Jah,* of course. Would you like anything, Miriam?"

"*Nee denke.* I just ate at home."

Hannah set about making Lizzy some eggs while she listened to Miriam and Lizzy's conversation.

"I'm so pleased to meet you, Miriam. I had hoped that Levi would be the one to introduce us."

"He had more time off than he expected to spend in Ohio, so he's got a lot to catch up with."

Lizzy screwed up her nose. "He told me he has workers who help him."

"He does, but the more things he can do himself the more money he makes, rather than paying the wages."

Lizzy sipped her tea. "He's coming to collect me on Saturday and then he'll show me his house where we'll live."

"Good. It's a nice house; it's the one we grew up in. And Hannah used to live right next door, and the four of us used to play together. We'd go fishing, swimming, play ball games. We had a lot of fun." Miriam turned around. "Would you like some help there, Hannah?"

"No, I'm nearly done."

"I don't like my eggs runny, Hannah."

"Lizzy, do you know Hannah is expecting?"

"*Jah,* I know that."

"It's not really my place to say anything and normally I wouldn't, but I hope you don't expect Hannah to cook for you every morning?"

"It's okay, Miriam," Hannah said slightly embarrassed.

Lizzy drew her eyebrows together and pouted. "Of course not. I'm here to help out. I'm sorry, Hannah. I just really wasn't thinking. I'll make all the breakfasts from now on."

"That's perfectly all right."

She put a plate of eggs and toast in front of Lizzy.

"I don't want us to get off on the wrong foot, Lizzy, but I'm just very protective of Hannah. Her husband has just died, and she's having a baby, so it's good that you're here to look after her."

"I thought I was here to ... no one told me that's why they made me stay here. I don't mind helping out a bit, but I can't do everything. Even at my relations' place in Ohio I wasn't expected to do everything. I don't think that's fair."

Hannah sat down at the table. "No one expects you to do everything, Lizzy. I think you've misunderstood what Miriam said."

Lizzy raised her eyebrows and picked up her knife and fork. "Anyway, Miriam, now that you're here with a buggy and a horse that isn't lame, why don't the three of us go somewhere? Maybe to the stores? I hate staying home all the day long."

Miriam jerked her head to look at the clock on the wall. "Oh, look at the time. I just remembered there's somewhere I've got to be. I'll see you two later." Miriam pushed her chair out and moved away from the table.

"I'll see you out," Hannah said.

As she walked out of the kitchen toward the front door, Miriam called out goodbye to Lizzy, who responded with something that sounded like a grunt.

Miriam and Hannah exchanged glances.

"I've started off on the wrong foot. I should've kept my mouth shut," Miriam whispered.

"Don't worry about it," Hannah said.

"Stop by on Saturday, since she'll be out with Levi."

Hannah nodded. "I will. Well, I'll see how my horse is. If he's completely recovered I'll stop by."

"If you don't show up I'll come here and bring something special for lunch."

"Sounds good."

Miriam hurried to her buggy and Hannah headed back into the kitchen to finish her tea.

As soon as Hannah sat down, Lizzy said, "She hates me."

"She doesn't. You just have to get used to her. She's very blunt and says exactly what she thinks."

"And she thinks I'm lazy, just because you made me breakfast this one time. I'm not lazy, I'm not."

"It's fine. Don't worry about it."

"Now what are we going to do today? With the whole day stretched before us. We could go to the markets."

"My horse is a little lame and I can't take him out yet. And he needs new shoes once his foot is better."

"Have you really only just got the one horse?"

"*Jah,* just the one."

Lizzy shook her head sending the strings of her prayer *kapp* fluttering about her shoulders. "I hate it when I have to stay home and do nothing."

"We could rearrange things in the barn. I've been meaning to do that for some time." She still had Abraham's things to sort through, but she guessed Lizzy definitely wouldn't want to do that. And she wasn't ready to face it yet, especially with unwilling help.

Lizzy nodded and still looked unhappy.

Wanting her guest to have a pleasant visit, she said, "We could stop by the neighbors, the Beattie's. They're lovely people."

Lizzy smiled. "That sounds better than working in the dirty barn all day."

Hannah resisted pointing out that her barn wasn't dirty and kept quiet. "I just need to do a few things around here first, and then we can visit them in a couple of hours. How does that sound?"

"*Denke,* Hannah. I appreciate that. And I'll wash my own dishes. How's that?"

Hannah gave a little giggle. "Okay."

"And then you can tell Miriam when you see her next that I'm not lazy."

"Okay. I'll do that." Hannah was pleased that Lizzy was trying hard, and reminded herself that everyone had flaws.

CHAPTER 10

THE BEATTIES' house was not far from Hannah's house, and Hannah pointed it out when she and Lizzy were at the front fence of the house paddock.

"Are you okay to walk that far, Hannah?" Lizzy asked sweetly.

"*Jah*. The midwife said it was good for me to do a little walking."

They walked through the tall grass of the paddocks until they were at the Beattie's property.

"Are they old?" Lizzy whispered.

"About in their fifties, I'd say. They have one grown up son and he's moved away."

Hannah walked up the stairs of the porch with Lizzy close behind her. The door opened before Hannah knocked.

Mrs. Beattie stood there smiling. "Hannah, I'm so pleased you've come. We were going to stop by and see you later today. We've got Joel coming back home to look after the farm."

"That's wonderful news. He's moving back to live here?"

"*Jah,* but we're giving him the *haus* and we're moving into the *grossdaddi haus.*" Mrs. Beattie's eyes traveled to Lizzy.

"I'm so sorry. Where are my manners? This is Lizzy. She's staying with me for a while—Lizzy Weaver."

"Nice to meet you, Lizzy."

"Nice to meet you too, Mrs. Beattie."

"I'm Linda and my husband is Luke. Come in and meet him, Lizzy." They both walked into the house and the ladies all went into the living room where Luke was reading one of the Amish newspapers. He stood to greet them.

After Lizzy was introduced to Luke Beattie, he said, "Sit down, sit down. Both you young ladies should come for dinner tonight. Joel will be here by then."

"We'd love to," Lizzy said, speaking for both of them without thinking to ask Hannah first.

"*Jah, denke.* How is Joel?" Hannah asked.

Linda explained, "Coming back here will be good for him. He was about to get married and it was eight weeks before the wedding and the young woman just up and left the community."

Lizzy gasped. "That's terrible. The poor man. He must be devastated."

"He is. That's why he said a new start would do him good."

Lizzy nodded. "*Jah,* everyone needs a new start once in a while. My parents died a year ago and I miss them dreadfully."

"Oh, I'm sorry, Lizzy. I didn't know," Hannah said.

Lizzy looked across at her. "You didn't ask me anything about my *familye.*"

Hannah hung her head while Luke and Linda offered Lizzy words of comfort.

After Lizzy thanked them for their kindness, she looked around. "Would you like some help around the place? I can see you've got boxes there, do you need them moved into the *grossdaddi haus?*"

"Oh, you're so kind, Lizzy. That would be lovely since Luke has a bad back and mine's not too good either."

Lizzy sprang to her feet. "I don't mind at all."

Hannah stood up too.

"You sit down, Hannah. You can't do anything in your condition," Linda said.

Hannah sat back down knowing Linda must've heard about her pregnancy. "I can do some small things."

"Nonsense."

"*Jah*, Linda and I will be just fine. Come along," Lizzy said. "You can show me where you'd like everything placed."

When they left Mr. Beattie chuckled. "It must be such a delight to have some company."

"*Jah*, it is. She only arrived yesterday and she's livened the place up already."

"Good."

Two hours later, they were walking back to Hannah's house.

"How did you like your outing?" Hannah asked Lizzy, half expecting her to

grumble and groan about lifting boxes.

"What a lovely couple. I'm so happy to be going back there for the evening meal."

"*Jah*, they've been my neighbors for many years, ever since I moved into the house as a newlywed."

"It must be hard for you, now that your husband's died and soon you'll have a *boppli* to raise all by yourself."

"*Jah*, the timing wasn't ideal, I can tell you that."

"Where is all your *familye?*"

"My parents died a couple of years ago, and I never had any siblings."

"Your parents died just like mine," Lizzy said.

"*Jah*." Hannah nodded.

"And that's why you're so close with Miriam, because she grew up right next door to you?"

"*Jah*, that's right."

"Well, you can tell her how I helped the Beatties just so she'll know I'm not lazy. I wouldn't want her to tell Levi I'm lazy."

"Okay."

"I didn't want to tell the Beatties I'm here to marry Levi. It's proper if everyone hears it from the bishop when our wedding announcement is published. What do you think?"

"It's up to both of you—you and Levi—to do whatever you think is best."

CHAPTER 11

RIGHT ON DUSK they were walking back to the Beattie's for dinner, and Lizzy looked over her shoulder back at Hannah's house. "Oh, what if Levi comes tonight to surprise me and we aren't home?"

"He would've said if he was coming. I don't think he'll do that."

"I hope not. It would be a shame to miss him."

When they knocked on the Beattie's door, Joel answered it. Joel was a little younger than Hannah and she guessed him to be around twenty two. In the three years he'd been gone, he'd become more stocky and muscular and Hannah thought he seemed taller.

He lunged forward and grabbed Hannah's hand. "Hannah, I'm so sorry. And I feel dreadful that I couldn't get back for Abraham's funeral."

"That's fine, I understand, and *denke,* Joel. I appreciate the sympathy."

When Hannah introduced Joel and Lizzy, she could tell by the sparkle in Lizzy's eyes that she was quite taken with him. The attraction seemed mutual.

The three of them sat on the couch and Joel explained that his parents would be out soon. Hannah guessed they might have been washing for dinner.

"It's lovely to meet you, Lizzy. And what brings you to this community?"

"The bishop and Ruth asked if I would look after Hannah, seeing her husband just died, and she's expecting a child."

"Hannah, I didn't know," Joel said. "That's such good news."

"It's only early days. Not many people know," Hannah said. "Your parents know, so I thought they might have mentioned it."

"No, they didn't. Don't worry, I'll keep it quiet." Joel looked back at Lizzy. "That's very kind of you, Lizzy, to stay with Hannah."

Lizzy smiled sweetly and gave a small giggle. "I'm sorry, Hannah. I hope I didn't give away any secrets. I didn't realize some people didn't know."

"Some do, some don't. News like this eventually gets around."

"And usually quite quickly," Joel said.

"And what do you do with your days, Lizzy, when you're not looking after Hannah?" Joel asked.

"I've just arrived here. I'd love to have a look around, but Hannah's horse is lame."

"Well, that's not, good. Would you allow me the honor of showing you around?" Joel asked with a smile.

This was the opportunity — the perfect opportunity for Lizzy to mention that she was engaged to marry Levi.

"*Jah,* I'd like that. But, I am busy on Saturday."

"Saturday's far away. I was thinking of perhaps tomorrow?" He looked at his mother and father who had just joined them, and they nodded in agreement.

"Perfect. I'd love that."

Hannah wasn't quite sure what was going on. It wasn't good for her to lead Joel on like that. Hannah wondered if she should mention the engagement, but it wasn't really her place. Lizzy was the one who should've mentioned it.

Throughout dinner, Lizzy was delightful. She listened politely, helped Linda serve and she even washed up afterward. Lizzy was the ideal dinner guest.

When Lizzy and Hannah were ready to go, Joel insisted he drive them home so they wouldn't walk through the fields in the darkness. When they arrived Hannah got out of the buggy, but Lizzy lingered there for a few extra minutes talking to Joel.

When she came into the house and Joel had driven away, Hannah was waiting for her.

Hannah didn't want to be put in a position to have to tell Lizzy what to do, but she couldn't believe the way she'd acted toward Joel. "What was all that about, Lizzy?"

"What do you mean?"

"I noticed you didn't mention to any of them that you're to marry Levi. And you should've seen that Joel was interested in you. It's a recipe for disaster. And accepting his invitation like that—"

"But am I, though? Am I going to marry Levi? Where is he? If he cared about me enough, he would've collected me from the bus stop. And he hasn't been here all day. So am I engaged? You tell me." Lizzy stood there staring at Hannah with her hands on her hips.

"His sister explained that he was busy with work. He sometimes works about sixteen hours a day. I hope the Beatties aren't going to get mad at me when they find out. They're probably hopeful that Joel has met a nice young single woman."

Lizzy crossed her arms in front of her chest. "Levi needs to put me as his first priority."

"He's seeing you on Saturday, he said."

"That's what he *said*. Anyway, Saturday's a long way away."

"What about Joel?"

"I like him."

"That was more than obvious. But how is he going to feel when he finds out about Levi?"

"I'm not married yet. Perhaps I might like Joel better."

"Lizzy, the reason you're here — the only reason you're here is to marry Joel — I mean, Levi."

Lizzy giggled in a high-pitched tone. "See what you just said?"

"I just got the names mixed up."

"Perhaps you know in your heart that Joel is a better match for me than Levi."

"But you've only just known Joel for a few hours," Hannah said.

"Time will tell." And with that, Lizzy turned away from Hannah and marched up the stairs.

Hannah walked over and slumped onto the couch. This was putting her in an awkward position and it added extra stress. What was she to do? Should she say something to someone, or keep her mouth shut? She didn't want to say something to Levi because of her feelings for him. And that was exactly why she couldn't mention anything. Hopefully, things would sort themselves out.

CHAPTER 12

THE NEXT MORNING, Hannah woke to the smell of baking. She pulled on her robe and slippers and when she walked into the kitchen she saw Lizzy taking cakes out of the oven.

"*Gut mayrie,* Hannah. I've baked some cakes. I hope you don't mind."

"I don't. They smell simply divine."

"I've made an orange cake for Luke and Linda and a chocolate cake for Joel. He told me yesterday over dinner that he loves chocolate."

"What about Levi?"

"Saturday is days away. I can make him something on Friday. You sit down, Hannah and I'll make you breakfast."

Hannah pulled out a chair and sat down while doing her best to ignore the mess that spread from one end of the kitchen to the other. It seemed every pot and pan and every cooking ingredient was out on display.

"Oh, Hannah. I've used all the eggs for the cakes."

"That's okay. I'll just have cereal this morning."

"Oh, I'm sorry, Hannah. I've used all the milk too. I used the last drop in my coffee."

Hannah laughed, seeing the funny side. "I'll find myself some leftovers. Don't worry."

"I've already eaten. I ate before I cooked."

"What did you find to eat?"

"I had scrambled eggs. You really should get some chickens and then you'd never run out of eggs or have to go to the store."

"Perhaps you're right."

"So, that's another buggy horse, and chickens."

"Jah, it's all on the list inside my head," Hannah said, staring at the cakes cooling on the racks. "I'll call Miriam and ask her to take me to the store to collect some groceries."

Lizzy sat down. "I'm exhausted after making all those cakes. Would you make me a cup of coffee?"

"Sure." Hannah made Lizzy a cup of coffee and sat down with her once she'd made herself a hot cup of tea—black, of course, she thought with a wry smile.

"What do you know about Joel?" Lizzy asked.

"Lizzy, you're going to have to tell him you're engaged as soon as he arrives. Otherwise, people will get hurt."

"Hannah, Joel's just a friend."

"That's not what you said last night. You need to tell him."

"You're not my *mudder,* Hannah."

"I know, because if you were my *dochder* you'd know that you shouldn't do something like this."

Lizzy's lips turned down at the corners. "I can't cancel him. That would be rude. Anyway, it's my life. Just remember that. I'm not even certain if I am still engaged to Levi. He could've changed his mind for all I know."

"How about you wait until you talk with him before you see Joel again?"

Lizzy stood up and took hold of her mug of coffee. "I'm going to drink this on the porch. I think you and I need some time without speaking."

Hannah watched with her mouth open while Lizzy walked out of the room. She could see there was no point saying anything to Lizzy. She would have to do what she'd decided the night before, which was to keep out of things entirely and hope things would work themselves out. This was a matter for prayer.

Hannah heated some leftovers that she found in the gas-powered fridge, and when she finished breakfast, she set about cleaning up the kitchen.

Once she had gone upstairs to change out of her dressing gown and into some clothes for the day, she heard Lizzy back in the kitchen.

Wanting to keep out of her way, Hannah spent the next few hours sewing in her bedroom. She looked out the window when she heard a buggy and saw Joel coming to the house. The next thing she heard was the front door close. Lizzy hadn't even said goodbye to her, and she had no idea when to expect her back.

When Hannah went downstairs and back into the kitchen, she was confronted with another mess to clean. Hannah sighed, pushed up her sleeves, and began putting things back into cupboards.

Hannah had just finished tidying the kitchen and was on her way to the barn to call Miriam when she saw a buggy heading to the house. She looked closely to see that it was Levi.

CHAPTER 13

Now Hannah was in the very worst position possible. All she could do was stand there and answer questions, and she knew he'd ask where Lizzy was.

"Hello, Hannah," he said when he jumped down from the buggy.

"Hello, Levi. I'm afraid you just missed Lizzy."

His dark eyebrows drew together into a frown. "That's too bad. I arranged to have the morning off to spend with her. I'll take another look at Blackie and clean the stable while I'm here. I didn't think to tell her because I thought she'd be here. Where is she?"

"Joel Beattie was kind enough to offer to show her around."

"Joel's back already?"

"*Jah*. Lizzy and I had dinner at the Beattie's last night."

Levi rubbed the side of his face. "I heard some weeks back that Joel was getting married."

"Not anymore. It didn't happen. Now he's back to take over their farm. I was just about to call Miriam to see if she could take me to the store."

Hannah hoped that Levi wouldn't see how nervous she was. He didn't look too worried about Lizzy and Joel being together.

"I've got some free time, I guess. I can take you as soon as I check on Blackie."

Hannah shook her head. "No, that's all right. I'm sure Miriam could take me."

"I'm here. Let me take you."

"I couldn't," she repeated.

"How about I take you to Miriam's *haus* then?"

"*Denke.* I'll accept that offer. I'll just get my cape and watch what you do with Blackie." Hannah walked into the house and pulled her black cape off the peg by the door. She left the door unlocked just in case Lizzy arrived home first.

Levi led the horse outside to a soft grassy spot. He bathed Blackie's legs with Epsom salts and warm water. "I don't know what this does, but my *vadder* used to do this to our horses."

Hannah watched for the next twenty minutes as he bathed Blackie's hooves and legs in the warm water and salts. Then he carefully towel dried the horse's legs and placed him back in the stable.

"Are you ready to go?"

"*Jah*, but are you?"

He looked down at his wet clothes. "I've got a spare set of clothes in the buggy. I'll get changed in the barn and meet you back at the buggy."

"Okay." Hannah headed across the yard and waited for him in the buggy.

When he got into the buggy, Levi was laughing.

"What's so funny?" she asked.

"Girls and shopping. You probably plan to make a day of it and that's why you don't want me to take you."

"It's not that so much. It's just that I don't want to take up your time."

Levi stared at her. "You're acting a little distant today, Hannah. Is everything okay?"

"Everything's fine."

"Should I be worried about Joel and Lizzy?"

"In what way?"

He hit his head. "I'm such a fool. They're both single people who barely know each other. Does Joel know Lizzy is engaged to me?"

She was caught out and couldn't lie. Lowering her head and looking away from him, she said, "Not as far as I know."

"Hannah, how could you have allowed this to happen?"

"Me?"

Levi blew out a deep breath and turned his horse around to head back down the driveway.

Hannah wondered if she should tell him that she told Lizzy to tell Joel she was engaged, but she decided against it because that might cause trouble for Lizzy.

"I'm not Lizzy's nursemaid. She's staying here at my *haus* and that's all. She's old enough to know right from wrong."

"I thought you and I were closer than that, Hannah."

Hannah knew he was angry and she couldn't blame him. "I think Lizzy feels like you're not making much of an effort and she was upset that you didn't collect her from the bus stop."

"Didn't you tell her I had arranged for other people to do all that because I was working?"

"*Jah,* I told her that."

He shook his head. After a tense journey, they arrived at Miriam's house.

"Thank you for driving me here, Levi."

"I'm sorry I took my temper out on you, Hannah. You don't deserve it. I just wish you would've said something to Joel and she wouldn't be out there with him right now."

"Maybe I should have. And now I'm sorry I didn't. It just kind of happened so fast."

Hannah walked to the house while Levi's buggy headed back to the road.

Miriam met Hannah at the door. "Come in. Was that Levi?"

"*Jah*." Hannah looked over her shoulder at his buggy, which was now a small speck on the road.

"I wonder why he didn't come in?"

Hannah shook her head. "He's upset with me."

Miriam smiled. "Upset with you? Come inside and tell me what you did."

"It was terrible, Miriam," Hannah said as she sat down. "We were asked to the Beattie's place for dinner because Joel came back. Joel and Lizzy hit it off immediately and now they're out together and he's showing her around the town."

"Are you serious?"

"I am." Hannah nodded. "And the other thing is that Lizzy hasn't told Joel she's engaged to Levi. I had a talk with her and told her that was the right thing to do."

"And what did she say?"

"She told me she wasn't sure if she was engaged to Levi because she hasn't seen him very much. Or, something like that. And then she got sulky with me and didn't even say goodbye when she left this morning. Of course, I couldn't tell Levi all of that, and now I'm sure Levi sees that it's all my fault." Hannah sighed. "I shouldn't be talking like this. I don't want to make trouble."

"That girl makes me so angry. She seems determined to get her own way with everything. She seems annoyed that Levi has to work all the time."

Hannah kept to herself how Lizzy had been acting in the house. That was information that Miriam could do without knowing, but as for the rest, Hannah felt much lighter having unburdened herself with what she had told Miriam.

"Anyway, enough about Lizzy. I came here to see if you would mind taking me to the store. I need some eggs and milk and a few other things."

"I've got a dozen eggs I can give you," Miriam said.

"Do you? That would be wonderful."

"I'm baking bread at the moment but we can go as soon as I get it out of the oven."

"*Denke.* I thought I could smell something nice."

"I don't know why Ruth thought to have that woman stay with you."

As Hannah followed Miriam into the kitchen she said, "It's certainly taken my mind off my own problems."

Miriam laughed. "That's something then. You'll have no time to think about yourself, but I do hope you'll get some rest while she's there."

"Me too. What is the date of the wedding?" Hannah pulled out a chair and sat down.

"No one's told me anything yet. I don't think a date's been set."

"Oh, I was hoping you might know something from Levi. Lizzy doesn't think a date's been arranged, either." Hannah sighed.

CHAPTER 14

L ATER THAT DAY when Hannah and Miriam were about to walk into the store, Hannah saw a buggy she was sure was Joel's.

"Look! I'm sure that's Joel's buggy. I wonder if they're having coffee in the shop there. Let's walk past and look in."

"Okay."

"You look in, Miriam, and see if you can see them, but don't appear to look too hard just in case they see you."

They walked by the window at a fast pace and when they were out of sight of the occupants of the coffee shop, Miriam said, "They were in there, and she was laughing."

"She's always laughing."

"I mean they looked close."

Hannah pressed her lips together, thinking how bad Levi would feel. "This isn't good. Do you think she'll end the engagement with Levi?" Hannah asked, now not wanting it to happen.

"I don't know, but I have to tell Levi about this right now."

"Nee don't. It will cause a lot of trouble."

"I have to, Hannah. He's my *bruder."*

Hannah shook her head hoping the backlash wouldn't come at her. Levi was already angry with her. "It could be innocent."

"They didn't look innocent, and you said she hasn't told him she's engaged."

"She might've by now."

Miriam glanced back at the coffee shop. "I can't imagine Joel knowing about her and Levi and still doing something like this, but I suppose we should give her the benefit of the doubt."

"I think we should," Hannah agreed.

"Let's just get what we came here for."

Hannah and Miriam headed into the supermarket.

When they were ready to leave, Miriam suddenly pulled Hannah back just as she was about to step out of the store. "Stop! There they are," Miriam said nodding her head toward them while she tugged Hannah's sleeve.

Hannah watched the couple walk to Joel's buggy. Lizzy looked happier than Hannah had seen her since she had arrived. Perhaps she was a better match for Joel.

Miriam said, "It sure doesn't look like she's told Joel anything."

"I'll ask her later when I see her at home." It was a conversation Hannah could do without.

"Joel wouldn't have taken her out for the day if he knew she was engaged. He just wouldn't."

"Just take me home will you, Miriam?"

"Sure."

They waited in the doorway of the store until Joel's buggy was out of sight before they left.

BACK AT HANNAH'S HOUSE, Miriam helped Hannah pack her groceries away. And then Miriam helped Hannah make a start on packing up Abraham's things, until Hannah suddenly felt overwhelmed. Miriam offered to do it all for her, but Hannah didn't want anything important tossed aside. Completing the task was put off to another day.

When Miriam left, Hannah pushed all her worries from her mind and settled down with pen and paper and a stack of letters to reply to. Abraham had so many relations—so many cousins. There were around twenty letters from people she didn't know, and around thirty other letters from people she knew, who had all been unable to attend the funeral.

Hannah decided to reread the letters so she could make a careful reply to each one and answer any questions that the senders might have asked. She pulled out the first letter and was halfway through reading it when she heard a buggy. Assuming it was Lizzy arriving home, she didn't get up to see who it was. When there was a knock on the door and there were no sounds of a buggy leaving, she knew it must've been someone other than Lizzy. She opened the door to see Levi standing there.

"Oh! Hello, Levi."

"I'm here to apologize to you, Hannah." He took off his hat and his gaze dropped to the ground. "I know you're not to blame and I took my anger and disappointment out on you."

"That's understandable. Apology accepted. I think you've already apologized to me, though."

She noticed he swallowed hard. "I've been so busy trying to get everything organized for Lizzy's visit that I'm afraid I have neglected her. Like you said."

Hannah was quick to point out that it wasn't she who had said that. She reminded him that she had merely been telling him how Lizzy had said she felt.

With the worst timing in the world, Joel's buggy approached the house.

"This is Joel and Lizzy now," Hannah said as they turned toward the approaching buggy.

Levi pushed his hat back on his head and walked away from the house a few steps. He stood there with his arms crossed over his chest.

Hannah leaned against the doorpost, waiting to see what would happen.

Lizzy got out of the buggy and started walking toward Levi as though nothing was wrong, but before she reached him, Levi marched right past her to Joel.

When Lizzy saw Hannah standing at the door she went over to her. "What is he saying to Joel?"

Hannah shook her head. "I don't know."

"He wasn't supposed to be coming here until Saturday. Why the sudden change of plan? You didn't say anything to him, did you?"

"*Nee*. He rearranged his day so he could see you, and when he got here you weren't here." She bit her lip and then turned and looked at the two men who were engrossed in conversation. "You might have a choice to make, Lizzy," Hannah said.

"What? Between those two?"

"*Jah*."

Lizzy looked back at Hannah. "I like both of them."

"It doesn't work like that. You can only have one."

Lizzy looked back at the men.

When Joel's buggy headed down the driveway, Lizzy walked over to Levi and Hannah slipped inside the house. She sat down again with her letters trying to keep out of things. But then she heard the raised voice.

"What did you say to him?" Lizzy hollered at Levi.

She didn't hear Levi's response, but then she heard Lizzy's loud voice again. "You don't care about me. We're through," Lizzy screamed and then she marched straight into Hannah's house, slammed the door behind her, and then marched up the stairs.

Hannah froze, not knowing what to do. She hadn't wanted Levi to get married, but now she felt dreadful about the whole thing. Should she console Levi or just leave him be? She walked over to the door and opened it to see Levi's buggy leaving the yard.

Hannah sat back down and resumed her letter writing, trying to put everything else out of her mind—she was glad to have the distraction. When Hannah had just finished her third letter, she heard thumping. When she turned her head, she saw Lizzy stomping down the stairs.

"I'm going for a walk, Hannah. What time is dinner?"

"Um, around six?"

"I'll be back before then and I'll even help you with it."

"*Denke.*" And then Lizzy was out the door before Hannah could ask where she was going, but she had a sneaking suspicion she was heading to the Beattie's *haus.*

A few minutes later, she was back.

"That was quick," Hannah said.

"I was going to find out from Joel what Levi said to him, but then I saw Levi's buggy at his *haus.* Now they'll both hate me.

They'll be talking about me right now." She ran up the stairs again before Hannah could say anything.

Hannah was just about to walk upstairs to see if she could comfort her, but she stopped herself. She'd allow Lizzy a few moments alone and then she'd see how she was. *On to the next letter,* she thought.

CHAPTER 15

IT was the worst idea possible that Lizzy was staying at Hannah's house. And he never should've asked her to marry him before he got to know her properly. Joel was shocked when Levi told him that he was engaged to Lizzy, and Joel had apologized to him and asked him to come back to the house to discuss things.

Levi had no idea what Joel wanted to discuss, but he was sure they could sort something out between them. What had happened was not right. The only thing he knew was that it had nothing to do with Hannah. He regretted the temper that sometimes overcame him out of nowhere. It was his major flaw.

If only he'd ignored Andrew telling him he needed a wife. Sure, he wanted a wife and a family, but what he didn't need were problems at this stage of his life. He knew now that he and Lizzy weren't suited, and if he were to ask Hannah to marry him anytime soon she would feel second best—second choice.

When he got out of the buggy, he walked over to Joel who was unhitching his horse from the buggy.

Joel straightened up. "As I said, Levi, she said nothing about being engaged to you."

"I believe it." Levi shook his head, feeling he'd been made a fool of, and it happened in front of Hannah. "I don't think Lizzy and I are suited. If we were, she wouldn't have accepted your invitation."

Joel shook his head. "I feel bad about this, Levi. Are you calling off the engagement?"

"I think I will have to have a talk with Lizzy and then we both have decisions to make."

Joel nodded. "I understand. I have to be honest with you, Levi, and tell you that if things don't work out between the two of you, I would like to see her again."

"Well, at least that would mean she hasn't come all this way for nothing."

"There would be no hard feelings?"

"If that's the outcome, then there'd be no hard feelings, but I do have to talk to Lizzy first."

"I understand."

"Anyway, Joel, it's good to see you home, my good friend"

"It's good to be back. I was meant to be getting married but that didn't work out and now my parents need me here, so here I am."

"I'll go back and talk to Lizzy now. There's no use allowing this to linger for a few days."

Joel nodded. "Understood. And I surely wouldn't have offered to show her around today if I had known you were engaged."

Levi nodded. "I know. I know."

The two men shook hands and then Levi headed back the short distance to Hannah's house.

He felt foolish that this was all playing out in front of Hannah, but there was nothing he could do about it now.

He knocked on Hannah's door and when she opened it she looked surprised to see him. "You're back."

"I am. I was wondering if I might speak to Lizzy?"

"Come in and take a seat in the living room. I'll tell her you're here."

"Okay, thanks." He settled himself down in the living room and looked at the pile of letters on the coffee table. Then he heard muffled voices above him, and Hannah came down the stairs alone.

"She'll be down in a minute," Hannah said.

"*Denke.*"

"Well, I've got some things I need to tend to in the barn, so I'll leave the two of you to it."

"Thanks again, Hannah." He was pleased that she would be well out of earshot when the conversation took place.

CHAPTER 16

HANNAH WALKED into the barn and reminded herself to get those two kittens she'd been thinking about.

When she was a young girl she'd had three cats, but they had lived mostly in the barn. It seemed odd now to go into a barn and not see a cat or maybe two stretched out fast asleep.

This wasn't exactly where she'd seen herself in her mid-twenties—a widow with a baby on the way.

She sat down on the chair by the phone, waiting for Levi to finish speaking with Lizzy. Levi was ending the relationship by his tone of voice and the expression on his face. She knew him well.

Hannah closed her eyes and wondered how things would be different if she had just said no when Matthew Miller had asked her on a buggy ride all those years ago. It seemed like a lifetime ago. She'd decided at the time she couldn't wait for Levi forever.

Life seemed so full of possibilities back then. Now, she knew how crucial it was to make the right decisions in one's youth.

She put her hand over her swollen belly. Why did life have to be so complicated sometimes? Things hadn't been straightforward for her in regard to relationships, and neither had they for Levi, it seemed.

Hannah stood up and peered through the partly open barn door and back toward the house. "I wonder if they've started talking yet?" She mumbled to herself. "Or, she could still be in the bedroom." Sitting back down she gave a deep sigh.

LEVI ROSE to his feet when he saw Lizzy walking down the stairs. His heart was flat when he saw her and he knew that if he were truly in love with her, or if they were meant to marry, he would've felt something inside. All he felt was confusion. He didn't know this woman at all, he realized, and neither could he work out what she'd been thinking to go off with Joel like she had today.

"You wanted to talk with me, Levi?"

"I do. Take a seat."

She sat opposite him. "If I'd known you were coming out today I wouldn't have gone with Joel."

"You went out with a single man and didn't tell him that you are engaged to me."

"No one knows we're engaged."

He couldn't work out what she was talking about. Was she trying to deflect what she'd done? "They do. The bishop and his wife, and so do all my *familye*."

"Does it really matter?" she asked.

"*Jah,* it does matter. Of course it matters."

"I don't want a husband who puts me last, Levi. And I think you're too involved in your work to have a *fraa*. A woman can't just live on cooking and cleaning and raising *kinner* alone. You've made me feel unwelcome. You hardly said two words to me on the phone when I called you."

"I was busy and had people all over the place, and orders to fill. I don't know what you think I'm supposed to do. If I'm going to be a good provider, I need to work."

"Perhaps I'd be better off with a farmer like Joel. He'd be close to the *haus* and he'd come home for the midday meal."

"Is that what you want?"

"*Jah.* That's exactly what I want. And I wish I'd never come here. You've made me feel so unwelcome." She blinked rapidly as though she was going to cry.

He stared at her and wondered why he'd listened to his brother. She had wanted to come early and that's why things weren't organized. "I was trying to fix things for you before you came here. If you had just waited a few weeks like I wanted, I would've had everything properly arranged by the time you got here."

"Are you making out it's my fault?"

He shook his head. "*Nee.* It's no one's fault. I'm just pointing out to you that I had no time to make you feel welcome and, had you waited, you would've felt welcome. I would've arranged somewhere for you to stay. I don't know that it's right for you to stay with Hannah after she's just lost her husband in such a tragic way."

"I don't want to fight with you, Levi. I don't like arguing."

"I don't want to argue either. It seems we are just two different people and we want two different things out of life. We're too dissimilar to be together."

"That's right. So this relationship is officially over."

He was relieved to hear it and glad she'd come to that conclusion rather than it be his decision, since she'd moved there for him. "*Jah,* if that's your decision it is over."

She bounded to her feet. "Well, goodbye." She marched back up the stairs while Levi watched open mouthed.

He blew out a deep breath. Now he had to go to the bishop and explain that the wedding was not going to take place. Hopefully, the bishop wouldn't ask too many probing questions on why the relationship hadn't worked. He did not want to bring Joel's name into it.

He walked into the barn to say goodbye to Hannah.

~

"ARE YOU HERE, HANNAH?"

Hannah stood. "*Jah,* I'm over here." She walked closer to the door. "Have you finished your talk?"

He shrugged. "We're finished talking, and you might as well know that the relationship is over."

"I'm sorry. That's too bad." She was genuinely sorry for him, although glad in another way because she didn't think they made a good pair.

"We weren't suited and it's better to find that out now, and not after we were married."

Hannah felt tears stinging behind her eyes and before she knew it the tears were flooding down her cheeks. It hurt her to think that Levi was sad.

"What's the matter?" he asked stepping closer.

"I don't know. It's just so sad. You thought you were getting married and now you aren't."

"Hey, stop crying. It happened to me not you."

She gave a little laugh and managed to make herself stop. "I've just had a lot of changes in my life and it's hard for me to get used to everything that's been going on."

"I know, I know. It must be hard for you, all of this… Abraham gone and having a *boppli* without a man by your side."

It was at that moment the realization hit Hannah that she was in this alone. Her husband had been snatched away from her and the only man she loved couldn't have loved her like she had thought if he was looking for love elsewhere. The tears came back.

"Sorry, Hannah. Was it something I said?"

Hannah shook her head and cried harder. Embarrassed to be crying in front of him, she placed both hands over her face and sobbed. Soon she felt arms around her and she hugged him back and cried into his shoulder as he patted her on the back in a comforting manner.

"Everything will be okay, Hannah. I'll see to it." He held her tight.

"Well, well. Isn't this a cozy scene?"

The two of them jumped apart and looked over to see Lizzy silhouetted in the doorway of the barn.

Lizzy said, "I can see now why you wanted me to tell him about Joel, Hannah. It was so you could have him all to yourself. I bet you couldn't wait for your husband to die so you could be with him."

"Lizzy!" Levi said.

Hannah took a step forward. "This isn't what it looks like. I was just upset and Levi was comforting me."

"Ever heard 'judge not lest ye be judged?' The two of you were quick about judging me over Joel and now I find you cozying up to each other." She put her hands on her hips and looked at Hannah. "You should be ashamed of yourself, Hannah. Your husband has only just been buried. And you, Levi, we've only just ended things between us. You both disgust me. I wonder what the bishop will say about the pair of you." She turned and stomped away.

Hannah wiped her eyes and giggled, seeing the funny side. But Levi wasn't laughing.

"I'm sorry," Hannah said. "Every time bad things happen I see the funny side of them."

Gradually, his face broke into a smile. "It is a little funny when you think about it."

"It is, isn't it?"

They both laughed and Hannah wiped the moisture left over from her tears, drying her cheeks. When they walked out of the barn, they saw Lizzy walking out of the house with one small bag tucked under her arm.

"Where are you going, Lizzy? It's nearly dinner time."

"I'm leaving. You were probably sweet on him all along," she said nodding to Levi.

"You've got this all wrong, Lizzy."

"We're only friends," Levi added. "Hannah and I have only ever been friends."

That was the last thing Hannah wanted to hear. Lizzy ignored both of them and kept walking.

"Where is she going?" Levi asked.

"My best guess is she's going next door to the Beatties. She got along with them really well."

"I should leave you in peace, Hannah."

"I'm sad that you're not getting married now. But as you said, this is good to find out before you married—that you're not suited."

"I know. I'm sorry this all happened at your *haus*. You don't need all this around you. You need to have peace around you. I hope she doesn't say anything to the bishop."

"I don't think she will, considering she'd have to tell him she neglected to tell Joel about your engagement when they went out this morning."

Levi smiled and nodded. "It was the quickest engagement ever."

"I don't think Lizzy will be back."

He gave her a nod. "I'll leave you in peace. Bye, Hannah."

"Goodbye, Levi."

When Hannah walked back into the house, she was secretly pleased she was by herself again.

CHAPTER 17

HANNAH HADN'T SEEN a single person all day and she had
no idea what was going on with Lizzy, but at least she'd had
time to answer all the letters of condolences for her husband's
death. She hadn't been able to get out of her mind how it felt to
have Levi's arms around her. Whenever she had a moment of
feeling alone, she would close her eyes and pretend she was
back in his warm embrace.

She happened to look out the kitchen window just in time to
see Miriam's buggy heading to the house, and she met her at
the door.

"It's nice to see you! Come in."

"You'll never guess what happened," Miriam said as she hurried
through the door.

"What? Do I have to sit down?"

Miriam giggled. "Probably."

When Hannah was seated in the living room, Miriam took a deep breath and began. "Joel and Lizzy are getting married."

Hannah slapped her hand over her mouth in shock. "*Nee!* I don't believe it. It's only been a day or two. They've only known each other two days."

"*Jah!*"

"How did that happen so fast?"

"I heard from Levi that she left your house and went to the Beatties.'"

"That's right. We guessed that she was heading to their *haus* right after she and Levi ended things. I can't believe the bishop has allowed this. He usually cautions young people who end one relationship to wait awhile before they start another."

Miriam shrugged.

"I can only imagine how poor Levi feels."

"Well, what happened was that the Beattie's moved back into the main *haus* from the *grossdaddi haus* so that Lizzy could stay with them, and Joel moved into the *grossdaddi haus* by himself."

"That's a big upheaval for them, since they'd only just moved in."

"I know."

"How is Levi?" Hannah asked.

"Worried about you more than anything. I told him I'd come to check on you."

"You're the first person I've seen today."

"Blackie's still lame?"

"Levi said he's coming back after work to check on him. Do you mind if you walk him up and down while I watch and see if he's still limping?"

"Okay, but let's have some hot tea first," Miriam said.

"Sounds like a good idea."

They both moved into the kitchen.

"I can't believe that she's getting married so quickly to Joel. Does Levi feel awful?"

"*Jah,* pretty much. I think he mostly feels a little foolish. Especially since it all happen in front of you."

"He shouldn't let that worry him."

"Well, it wasn't an ideal situation for him."

"It wouldn't be good for anybody. He brought her out here and then she's set to marry someone else in a matter of days."

Hannah didn't say so, but she was glad that she was by herself now and living in peace rather than having Lizzy stay with her. It was such a relief, and it made being alone peaceful rather than lonely.

"So, has Levi talked to the bishop? I guess he has."

"*Jah*. Levi went to the bishop's house last night. Joel went there after to tell him he wanted to marry Lizzy."

"Joel's a sensible man even though he's young. They must really have gotten along well together. I just can't see him rushing into anything," Hannah said. "Well, I couldn't until this happened."

"Unless he's on the rebound. He was about to get married to somebody else remember?"

"That's right."

Hannah thought back to her own rebound situation when she was so devastated about Matthew Miller it was easy to fall into the arms of Abraham. Especially when her parents were pushing him at her. "Rebounds are never good. We'll have to hope this one is the exception," Hannah said.

Miriam nodded while she filled up the teakettle with water.

"I wish this had never happened to Levi. He's such a good man and I hate to see him be disappointed like this," Hannah said.

"Disappointment is a part of life sometimes."

"You've got that right. It sure seems to be."

"We've each had our share," Miriam said.

Hannah knew that Miriam was talking about the fact that she still didn't have a child after many years of marriage. That was Miriam's disappointment. And Hannah's disappointment was that she never married Levi.

"It's all hard to believe somehow," Hannah said.

"I shouldn't say it, but I'm glad that things didn't work out with Levi and Lizzy. Is that awful?" Miriam asked.

"You're being honest."

"*Jah,* I think that you and Levi are far better suited."

Hannah giggled. "Don't be silly."

"I mean it."

"If Levi and I had been meant for each other we would've gotten together years ago."

"And perhaps you should've."

"Ah, but we didn't," Hannah said.

Miriam laughed. "We could go back and forth like this for hours. Who knows what the future holds?"

"I suppose only *Gott* knows and we just have to hope for the best."

"And pray," Miriam pointed out.

"*Jah,* and especially pray."

"How about I take you out for lunch? I think we could both do with some cheering up."

"And lunch will do that?" Hannah asked.

"Absolutely. Especially if it's followed by dessert."

Hannah laughed. "I like the sound of that. I've been very hungry lately."

"Good. I'll take the kettle off the stove and we'll make our escape."

Hannah stood up. "Let's do it. I'll let Blackie wait for Levi."

CHAPTER 18

HANNAH AND MIRIAM had a lovely day out together and Hannah tried her best to put all the problems behind her.

She walked into the house. It felt odd being in the house without Abraham, having never lived there without him. Hannah slumped down onto the couch, pleased that she wasn't hungry after such a big lunch. Since no one was staying with her, she could just have a piece of fruit or cheese or something for dinner if she felt hungry later.

It was silly to have those crazy thoughts about Levi that she'd had the last few days. God was surely showing her that it was a bad idea. It was God who had charge over the rest of her life, she told herself. What was most important was her child, and she was determined to give her child the very best life that she could.

She put her hand over her stomach and for the first time she thought she felt the baby move. Were those tiny flutters really her baby moving about? She stayed still and felt them again. It was the first sign of life, and her heart was filled with an extra surge of love.

"Hello, my *boppli*. I can't wait to hold you in my arms."

"Hello," a male voice called out, startling her.

She opened the door to see Levi and her heart beat faster. Was he there to tell her he'd always been in love with her and couldn't go on another day until he knew whether she felt the same? "Hello. I didn't hear your buggy."

"I'm here to check on Blackie."

"I put him back in the house paddock. I was going to move him back into the stable later."

"Okay. I'll get a lead." Levi headed to the barn.

Hannah walked out of the house, glad that he'd stopped by. As she watched him striding into the barn she imagined that they were married. They'd always gotten along so well and they understood each other completely.

Levi came out of the barn.

"I can see you need some new leathers."

"Do I?"

"You do. They're practically worn through."

"Thanks for letting me know."

Together they walked to get Blackie.

"As soon as Blackie is better, come into the store with him and I'll replace what needs to be replaced on his harness at no charge."

"Now, Levi, I can pay for it. I'm not destitute or anything. Abraham left me with —"

"It's my gift to you, not because I think you're destitute." He gave a little chuckle.

"Well, *denke*. That's very kind. I'm glad you spotted it because I wouldn't have noticed until something broke. Abraham used to look after all that kind of thing."

"You're welcome." He opened the gate and they both walked through. Blackie stopped eating grass and looked up at them, and started walking toward them.

"He looks alright to me."

"Yes, he does today."

Levi slipped the halter over his head and led him up the paddock for Hannah to watch.

"He seems fine," Hannah said. "I'll walk him now, and you see what you think."

Levi handed the lead to her and then she walked quickly up the paddock, breaking out into a little run.

"Don't exert yourself, Hannah."

"I won't."

"Yes, he looks fine." Levi walked over and picked up one of Blackie's legs to check his hoof. He worked his way around the horse until he had looked at each hoof. "I don't think there are any concerns. It's time to call the blacksmith about getting his new shoes put on. Best leave him a day or two after that before you drive him again, just to be safe. Do you have to go anywhere?"

"No, but I was thinking of going to go into the markets to see if they had any kittens for sale. Sometimes they do, and I was just going to go on the off chance."

"I can take you."

"I can't take up all your time."

"I've already organized people to look after the workshop today, thinking I'd be spending the time with someone else. I can't think of anything I'd rather do than have a look for a kitten with you."

"Kittens," Hannah corrected. "I'd like two."

"I'm ready when you are."

"*Denke,* Levi. I'm glad you came when you did."

After they put the horse back in his stall, they headed toward the markets.

On the way there, he asked, "Are these going to be house cats or barn cats?"

"House cats. I've always wanted to have cats, but Abraham was allergic."

They kept the conversation away from Joel and Lizzy, and as they drove Hannah pretended they were a married couple on their weekly visit to the markets.

Together they walked into the farmers market, and right under an awning at the front there was a young girl of around twelve sitting with a basket of kittens. The hand drawn sign said, "To give away, free to a good home."

Hannah was delighted and she looked at Levi. "*Denke* for bringing me here, this is perfect timing."

He chuckled. "Let's hope she has two left," he said.

They walked over and asked about the kittens.

"I had six. I wanted to keep them but my mother won't let me. We didn't mean for our cat to have these kittens. We took her to the vet to be fixed and he told us she was already having kittens."

"How many are in there?" Hannah asked, as the girl hadn't opened the basket yet.

"There are four left," she said. "You could have two each."

Levi chuckled. "You're a good salesperson."

The young girl smiled as she proudly opened the basket.

Hannah crouched down. "Oh look at them! They are so tiny. How old are they?"

"They're eight weeks old. Our cat had six kittens, and the other two were black, but I gave them away this morning."

Hannah looked up at Levi, "Which ones do you like? The tabbies or the calicos?" There were two of each.

"I don't know. I like them all the same. It's your decision."

"How many do you want?" The young girl asked.

"Two," Hannah and Levi answered at the same time.

"I think I like the two tabbies," Hannah said.

"Which ones are the boys and which ones the girls?" Levi asked.

The girl started picking the cats up and turning them upside down. "I can't tell. But calico cats are almost always females."

"I guess it doesn't matter. I'm not going to breed from them or anything. As soon as they're old enough I'll take them to the vet to get fixed."

"Don't leave it too long," the young girl said.

Hannah laughed. "I definitely won't!"

"The tabbies?" Levi asked.

Hannah nodded and looked back at the young girl. "Is it okay if I take the two tabbies?"

"Sure. You look like you would look after them."

"They'll have a very good home. You stay here," Levi said. "I'll see if I can get a cardboard box."

"You can get one at the food store," the young girl called after him.

When he was gone the young girl informed Hannah that the kittens hadn't had any of their shots yet.

Hannah assured her that she would take them to the vet and made sure they got everything they needed, and that made the young girl smile.

Soon they were heading back home and Hannah was delighted. She was holding the kittens on her knees in a cardboard box.

"You look pretty happy, Hannah. I haven't seen you like that in a while."

"I've wanted cats for such a long time."

"You should have whatever makes you happy."

"*Denke,* Levi. And what can we do to make you happy?"

"Spending time with you makes me happy, Hannah." He glanced over at her and she looked away feeling a little embarrassed. "I'm sorry. I shouldn't have said that."

"No, that's okay. I like spending time with you too."

He smiled. "Now, do you have everything you need for the cats?"

"I do. I've been thinking about them for awhile, so I've got everything ready. I've got old saucers that I've kept to use for food bowls and a large water bowl, cat trays and a large basket they can sleep in. I'll fill it with a warm blanket."

When the buggy stopped at the house, Hannah said, "Are you coming inside to watch the kittens?"

"Okay. I'll carry the box in for you."

As soon as Hannah let the kittens out in the living room, they sniffed around. "I think I'll leave them in the kitchen at first, so they get to know one space before they explore another."

"Good idea. And leave the box on its side for them to get into. They might like something familiar for a few days."

Soon the cats were hiding back in their box on the kitchen floor, curled up with a woolen blanket.

"They certainly like it in there. They prefer the box to the basket."

"They feel protected," Hannah said. "Would you like a hot tea, or anything?"

"*Nee, denke.* I should go. I had a nice time today."

"Me too."

He turned and walked out of the kitchen and she followed.

When he got to the door he turned around to face her. "I'll be back tomorrow to check on Blackie. Do you want me to call the blacksmith?"

"*Jah.* I'd appreciate that. Bye, Levi."

"Bye, Hannah."

Hannah closed the door and then moved to the living room to look out the window at him. She was a little disappointed that he didn't take their admissions of liking each other further, since it had taken a huge amount of courage for her to admit she liked him as well. Or, had he just meant he liked her as a friend?

CHAPTER 19

LEVI DROVE AWAY from the house glad that he had let Hannah know his true feelings toward her. But, had she taken that to mean that he liked her as merely a friend? It was too soon after Abraham's death to ask her on a date. Then again, he reminded himself he'd thought it too soon after Matthew Miller left the community to ask her out, and then the next thing he heard she was engaged to Abraham.

He pulled back on the reins and moved his buggy off the road. What if the same thing happened again? Just telling her that spending time with her made him happy wasn't expressing the true extent of the love that he held for her. He looked back over his shoulder at her house and wondered whether he should go back and tell her that he loved her.

"There's no one she'd marry," he said to himself. "Then again, I didn't imagine that she'd marry Abraham." Could he risk losing their friendship if he laid it on the line how he felt and she didn't feel the same? He decided that he couldn't tell her how he felt at this time. She was having a baby and her husband had only just died. At this time of her life what she needed more than anything was for him to be a friend.

Putting aside his desire to be with the woman he loved, he clicked his horse onward.

HANNAH WENT to bed that night pleased that she finally had her kittens. She'd played with them for hours before they'd worn themselves out. She'd made toys for them by tying pieces of rags on strings and pulling them along the floor while the kittens ran after them.

While Hannah tried to sleep, she tossed and turned, trying to push Levi out of her mind. If he loved her, he wouldn't have gotten engaged to Lizzy. That was a fact and she had to face it no matter how much she hoped it wasn't the case.

THE VERY NEXT day Levi looked at Blackie and said he was fine. He told her the blacksmith would be there in the afternoon. Levi then asked her, if the blacksmith said Blackie was okay to go the distance, to bring the buggy into the workshop soon to get new leathers.

· · ·

THE NEXT DAY, as she hitched Blackie to go to Levi's workshop, she realized how everything was so much easier with a man around. She had taken it for granted exactly how much Abraham had done around the place.

Just as she had taken hold of Blackie to back him into the harness, she caught sight of a familiar buggy coming to the house. It was either the bishop or Ruth. She patted Blackie on his neck. "Wait here, boy." She secured him and then walked away from the barn to meet the buggy.

When it drew closer she saw that it was Ruth, by herself.

"On your way out, are you, Hannah?"

"I was just going to Levi's workshop. He's going to replace some of the harness leathers for me. I don't have to be there at any particular time. Come inside and I'll fix us some tea."

"Are you certain?"

"*Jah,* of course. Come in."

Ruth followed Hannah inside and sat down at the kitchen table.

"How are you coping by yourself, Hannah?"

Hannah placed the kettle on the stove. "Very well. Everything's fine. I was just thinking this morning, though, how everything is easier with a man around."

"Perhaps you'll get married again."

"One day, maybe," Hannah said as she sat opposite Ruth.

"You're still young."

Hannah got up from the table. "I'll get us some cookies."

"*Denke.*"

"I do have a lot of help from Miriam and from Stephen. They're always watching over me."

"*Gut.*"

The kittens came out of their box.

"Oh, these are my kittens. I only just got them and I haven't named them yet." When Ruth didn't look too impressed to see the kittens, Hannah shut them in another room.

"It was a surprise about Lizzy and Joel," Ruth said.

"*Jah,* it was."

"I thought it would've been good that the two of you be here together until her wedding, but she said you didn't get along."

"*Jah,* that's true. We had a few tense moments. Excuse me, I'll just wash my hands before I fix the tea." Hannah slipped into the next room to wash her hands where she had a basin, soap, and a hand towel. She hoped to change the topic away from Lizzy, Levi and Joel.

When she walked back into the kitchen and started fixing the tea, Ruth said, "Next week there'll be a single man staying with us and I thought we might invite you for dinner while he's here."

Hannah stopped pouring the hot water. "Oh, no. I'm not ready for that kind of thing. Not yet."

Ruth giggled. "It doesn't hurt to ask. You just said yourself that things are easier with a man around."

Hannah continued making the tea and when she passed a cup to Ruth and sat down with one herself, she gave what Ruth had said a little more thought. "And where does this man live?"

"He's from Harts County."

"That's where Lizzy was from originally."

"*Jah,* I know." Ruth sipped her tea. "I didn't know whether to raise the subject of his visit with you. I hope I didn't upset you. Some people heal faster than others."

"Wouldn't people talk if I was suddenly keeping company with a man so soon?"

"Most likely." Ruth chuckled. "I wouldn't let what anyone says bother you. You wouldn't be doing anything wrong."

"I just want to do what's right. I've only just answered all the letters that people sent me. Most of them were from Abraham's relations. I mean, what would they think?"

"Hmm. You're giving this a lot of serious thought."

"Oh, well, not really."

Ruth leaned forward. "Have you been thinking about one man in particular?"

Hannah gulped. She couldn't lie and neither did she want to admit thinking about another man so soon after Abraham was gone. "I can't answer you, Ruth."

"That says a lot."

Hannah breathed out heavily.

"I shouldn't pry. Forget I said anything. You'll know when the time is right for you. Now, how's your *boppli?*"

"I've been seeing the midwife regularly. She said all is well."

"I'm glad to hear it."

An hour later, Ruth left and Hannah finished hitching the buggy and made her way to Levi's workshop.

When she got there she saw exactly how busy he was. He was on the phone when she arrived, and no sooner had he hung up then it rang again. She could see through to his workshop from the small office where she was, and there were two workers using various industrial sewing machines, and she guessed the other machines were to cut the leather.

He looked up from his desk, "I'm sorry, Hannah. The place has gone crazy today. I'll let the phone go to message and I'll take a look at the harness."

Once they were outside, he measured the harness and made some notes. "We've got all that you need in stock, I'm sure. Why don't you have a seat inside and I'll have this replaced for you in no time."

"Okay."

Soon Hannah was on her way home with a brand new harness. Levi had agreed to come to dinner that night as her way of saying a small thank you. On her way home, she stopped by Miriam and Stephen's house and invited them as well. Talk would surely get around if anyone found out that she and Levi had been having dinner alone at her house.

CHAPTER 20

IT WAS two months later and Hannah was at the wedding of Lizzy and Joel. Very few people in the community knew that Lizzy had originally come there to marry Levi. Hannah and Miriam had certainly told no one, and the bishop and his wife would not have liked things like that to get around.

Lizzy had only spoken to Hannah briefly at the Sunday meetings and their relationship was still strained, although both of them were making an effort. Hannah still had many bags of Lizzy's possessions in the spare room; Lizzy had never come back to collect them. Hannah never mentioned it, figuring Lizzy would be back sooner or later.

Levi was noticeably absent from the wedding and both Hannah and Miriam were concerned for him.

When the reception was over and they were having the meal after the wedding, Miriam said, "I don't blame him for not coming. If this had happened to me I wouldn't go to the wedding either."

"I guess I would feel the same way."

"It's ruined his confidence with women."

"Do you think he'll be alone forever?" Hannah asked.

"I hope not. I would like to have some nieces and nephews here, without having to travel to Ohio."

"You'll have your own soon," Hannah said hoping she wasn't bringing up a sore topic.

"I certainly hope so, but it's easier for me if I don't think about it."

"Of course. I'm sorry for bringing it up."

"Don't be. It's something I have to deal with."

"We can share my *boppli*," Hannah said.

Miriam laughed. "Don't you worry about that. I'll be a second *mudder* to your *boppli* whether you like it or not."

"My child will be very blessed to have you around."

"Your child might be the closest I get to having one of my own. And now I have to go and help the ladies in the kitchen."

"Okay, I'll just sit here and watch everyone enjoying themselves."

. . .

HANNAH HAD SLEPT IN, and now she hurried to get dressed when she knew that Levi would be there for his usual Saturday morning visit. On Saturday mornings, he came to see if she was okay and to do whatever jobs had surfaced during the week. This time there were no jobs for him to do but she would enjoy the morning cup of tea.

Hoping she had enough time, she had a quick shower. As soon as she turned the water off she heard a buggy. She dried herself off and pulled on her clean clothes and set a prayer *kapp* over her already pinned hair.

When he knocked on the door, she yelled out that she was coming. She walked down the stairs telling herself not to rush and she stepped carefully. Just as she was on the second-to-last step, the two cats rushed beneath her feet and she had to take a giant step to avoid them. She took a tumble and fell hard onto the floor.

Levi rushed through the door and saw her on the floor. "Hannah, what happened?"

"I tripped on the cats."

He knelt down and helped her move to sit on the bottom step. "Are you okay? Are you hurt anywhere?" He stood back up.

"I think I jarred my ankle or something."

"Wiggle your toes."

She looked down and was able to wiggle them.

"I think that means nothing's broken at least. You fell hard; I heard it from outside. I'm taking you to the hospital."

Hannah stood and held onto his shoulders for balance. "*Nee.* I'm fine. I just need to sit down for a while longer."

He helped her to the couch. "You sit down, and I'll call a taxi and take you to the hospital to get checked over."

"I'm sure that's not necessary."

"You can't be too careful."

While he was calling a taxi, Hannah put her hands over her face. If something happened to her baby she'd never forgive herself.

Minutes later, Levi came back into the room. "How are you feeling now?"

She wiped her eyes and then he saw that she was crying. Levi quickly sat beside her and put his arm around her. "Don't be upset."

"What about the *boppli?* What if—"

"Everything's going to be okay."

"You don't know that; you can't say for certain."

"Let us pray." He took hold of both her hands and prayed for the safety of her baby and for her health. When they opened their eyes, he said, "I don't think the taxi will be long. I told them to be quick because we have to take someone to the hospital."

"*Gut, denke.* Where are the cats?"

He smiled and said, "Don't worry about the cats."

"I think I managed to avoid them."

He shook his head.

"I was so careful going down the steps and at the last minute they ran underneath my feet."

"Well, that's what cats do."

When the taxi pulled up, he helped her to her feet, wrapped her in a shawl and helped her get in the backseat of the taxi. He went around and got in beside her.

On the way there, Hannah said, "I'm starting to worry about the baby. I haven't felt any movement or kicks since the fall."

When Levi didn't say anything encouraging, she felt quite worried.

"We just have to trust, Hannah," he finally said.

Hannah nodded and prayed the rest of the way.

Levi had called ahead and the hospital staff were expecting her. They were alarmed when he'd told them she was pregnant.

They arrived at the hospital and Hannah was whisked away, while they directed him to fill out paperwork.

When he was finished, he asked the receptionist where he should go. He was told she was having an ultrasound and was directed to the emergency department, where he sat and waited.

It was a chore for him to push negative thoughts out of his mind while he sat there. Half an hour later, a man in a white coat came into the room. He appeared to be a doctor. His eyes fixed upon Levi as he strode toward him.

"Are you Mr. Fisher?" For all intents and purposes, he was looking after her, so he'd taken on the role of husband. He nodded. "Have you been looking after my wife?"

CHAPTER 21

THE DOCTOR MET his eyes and then smiled. "Yes, and your wife and the baby are fine. You can go in and see her now."

Levi leaped up and shook the doctor's hand. "Thank you, Doctor, thank you."

Levi was shown into a room with three empty beds, and there was a nurse next to Hannah's bed writing something on her chart.

"Here's your husband now," the nurse said.

Levi walked over to Hannah and grabbed her hand.

"I'm all right, Levi and so is the baby."

He nodded, not trusting his voice for the moment.

When the nurse left, Hannah said, "Did you hear what the nurse said?"

He smiled, and nodded again as he let go of her hand.

Hannah said, "I'm sorry about that. They assume you're my husband because you brought me in."

"I'm not sorry." He shook his head and moved closer to her. "Hannah, I'd like to be your husband and I know the timing is wrong and if I waited for the right timing I might be waiting forever. Hannah, I would be the happiest man in the world if you say you'll marry me. If you say no, we'll forget what I just said." He gave a nervous laugh.

"You want to marry me?"

He picked up her hand. "I do."

"I can't believe it."

He looked away from her. "I'm sorry. Forget I said anything."

"I don't want to forget."

"Really? Wait... then you ..." When he saw her smiling face he knew she felt the same. "Years ago, I was just about to ask you on a buggy ride and I tried to pluck up the courage, and the next thing I knew I saw you with the Miller boy."

"I grew impatient while waiting for you. I should have told him no."

"You had feelings for me back then?" he asked.

"I did, but I was foolish and impatient. I should've waited."

He was pleased with how things were going, so he continued, "And then when Matthew left, you were so upset about him and I wanted your full attention so I waited again. And then..."

"And then I married Abraham."

"*Jah.* Hannah, I've loved you forever, and I had to try to forget about you."

"Shh. It doesn't matter now."

"*Jah,* it does. I need to confess some things to you. It was selfish of me that I fell to a new low when I heard you were having a baby. Please forgive me for my selfishness. I wasn't thinking of the joy that the child would bring you and Abraham. It somehow made you feel even further away from me. That's why I had to get away and I visited my brother. Andrew saw my pain and that's when he suggested I marry and invited Lizzy to the house. A day after I got engaged to Lizzy, I found out Abraham had died." He looked down and shook his head. "I was torn. I didn't want to be engaged to Lizzy, I admit that now. It seems the timing was wrong every step of the way."

"So you didn't know Abraham had died when you proposed to Lizzy?"

"That's right." He shook his head again. "I don't mean it to sound like I was ready to pounce on a man's wife as soon as he died."

"I know that's not what you're trying to do."

"Asking Lizzy to marry me made sense at the time. I have so many regrets. I could never shake you from my mind—never."

"I didn't know. I thought you weren't interested in me, and my parents were pushing me to marry Abraham and I thought why not? I was so low at that time, I thought marrying would make things all better."

He laughed. "So we've just admitted a few things to each other. Will you marry me, Hannah? It doesn't have to be right away, I can wait."

She looked into his eyes and put her hand over her tummy. "I come with a *boppli,* and two cats who run up walls and do crazy things and scratch the couches."

"And I come with myself and a business where I work a lot. Do you think we could make this work?"

She nodded. "I think so."

"Does that mean you're saying yes?"

"Jah."

He laughed. "I can't believe it's taken us all this time. We could've been together years ago."

"Jah, all this time to get it right."

He looked around and then said, "Are you ready to go home?"

"They want to check the baby again in another couple of hours. You can go and I'll get a taxi later."

He held her hand tighter. "I'm not leaving your side."

HANNAH WAS two months away from having the baby when she and Levi got married. From the wedding they were moving into Levi's home and they would begin their new life together there. Everyone in the community seemed pleased about it and there were no whispers circulating about it being too soon after Abraham's passing. Hannah's baby would have a father and the long-term bachelor, Levi, would be married.

The wedding took place at Miriam's newly renovated house. Hannah sat at the wedding table with Levi, finally feeling that her life made sense. Even though she'd made choices in the past that weren't right for her, in the end it had all worked out. She never thought for a moment that she would marry for the second time in her life when she'd been this young.

Levi put his head close to hers. "I never thought I could be so happy."

"I hope I'll keep making you happy."

He smiled. "You always have."

They'd talked about having many children and the life they'd share together.

In usual late pregnancy fashion, Hannah had to excuse herself to go to the restroom. On the way she was confronted with Lizzy.

"I knew you wanted him, Hannah."

"Well, you knew more than I did, then."

"Anyway, it worked out well for both of us. I'm married to Joel and I'm happy, and you look happy with Levi. Hannah, do you think we ever might be friends?"

"I'd like that." Hannah saw no reason why they couldn't be polite to one another and eventually they might even enjoy each other's company.

"Good. I'll make the effort to be friends with you. That will make Joel happy. And then we can have you and Levi to dinner."

"I look forward to it."

"Thank you, Hannah. I'm glad we had this talk."

"Me too." After they exchanged smiles Hannah continued to the ladies room.

After she came out from the bathroom, she poked her head in the kitchen to see ladies busily rushing about.

"Go back out and enjoy yourself, Hannah," Miriam had just come up behind her.

"I'm just having a peek to see what's happening."

"Come on." Miriam slipped her arm through hers and took her back out to the table where Levi was waiting. "There. Sit down with your husband, *schweschder*-in-law." Miriam gave a little laugh.

CHAPTER 22

IT WAS TWO MONTHS LATER, and Hannah was two days over her due date. Levi had taken time off from work so he could be there with her.

He made her breakfast and had her sit down on the couch while he brought it to her.

"I'm not an invalid, you know. I can still do things."

"You don't need to do anything, that's why I've taken time off."

Hannah didn't mention it to Levi, but all night she'd had slight twinges of tightening across the stomach but they weren't painful so she didn't mention it. "I think I should go to see the midwife today."

"*Nee,* she'll come to you. I'll call her." He took a swallow of coffee and placed his cup down. "Do you think the *boppli's* close?"

She hoped so, since she was past her due date. "I just want her to check me over. Maybe the bumpy buggy ride will bring on the labor. I've heard of that happening and I just want this baby out."

"I'm not going to argue with a woman's instinct. When do you want to go?"

"Soon."

Levi finished another mouthful of coffee. "I'll hitch the buggy and call her and tell her we're coming." He leaned over and kissed her on the forehead and walked out.

A minute after Levi was gone, she felt something that she had no doubt was a contraction. Things were getting painful and she was still in her nightgown. Wanting to get dressed, she stood up and then her water broke. Shocked, she stood there staring at her wet nightgown and the puddle of water on the floor.

This was happening, and happening in a few hours. Her long awaited baby would soon be in her arms. "Levi!"

He came running back. "What is it?"

"My water just broke."

A look of fear washed over his face. "I'll call her back."

Hannah didn't know what to do until the midwife got there, but she remembered that walking around brought labor on quicker. She'd waited nine months for this baby and didn't want to wait any longer than she had to. She paced up and down until Levi came running back into the house.

"How are you feeling?"

"I don't know."

"I'll get you a dry nightgown." He ran up the stairs, taking them two at a time. When he got back he said, "You should come upstairs now if you want to give birth in the bedroom."

She shook her head. "I don't know what I want." Hannah changed gowns, and kept pacing up and down until the midwife arrived.

THREE HOURS LATER, Hannah was propped up in bed and holding her baby in her arms while Levi, Miriam, and the midwife looked on.

"We have a *dochder*. Levi, we have a *dochder*."

Levi wiped the tears from his eyes. "It's unbelievable."

"Do you want to hold her?"

"Of course." He leaned down and carefully took the bundle into his arms. He looked down at the tiny pink face with the perfect features. "She's even got small eyelashes and everything. She's *wunderbaar*."

"Have you chosen a name yet?" Miriam asked.

"We always said if it turned out to be a girl, we'd call her April because she was to be born in April."

"Only just a day later and we would've had to call her May," Levi pointed out with a laugh.

"April is a beautiful name," Miriam said. "I'm sure Tricia and Andrew will visit soon to see her."

Levi said, "I was disappointed that they couldn't make it to the wedding." He looked at Miriam. "Here, Auntie, have a hold."

Her face lighted up as she took the baby and held her close against her.

HANNAH LOOKED at each person in the room and was grateful. She thanked God that her life was turned around. It had taken her and Levi a long time to be married to each other and they'd made many mistakes in between times, but now they were together and deliciously happy. Things could've turned out very differently. She reminded herself not to push April into a relationship when she got older, and she determined to allow her to follow her heart. And she'd warn April that the decisions she made in her youth were vital to the happiness of the rest of her life—no one had thought to tell Hannah that.

WHEN LEVI and Hannah were alone that night, Hannah said, "I hope I'll be a good *mudder*."

"You'll be the best." Levi peeped in at baby April who was in their room in her crib.

"Levi, we very nearly didn't marry at all."

He sat on the bed next to her. "I know. We have to be grateful that everything turned out well for us."

"I am, but I feel bad that Abraham had to die for us to be together."

He picked up her hand and held it. "Shh. Don't think of things like that. You made him happy in his last years, that's what you should focus on. We live in the present, we learn from the past, and we must be mindful of the future."

"I hope I made him happy. Anyway, when did you get so wise?"

He laughed. "As soon as April came into the world, so about six hours ago. I'm a *daed* now. I have to be wise." He leaned over and kissed Hannah on her forehead. "I'll feed the cats and then I'll come to bed. Do you need anything from downstairs?"

"Nee."

When he walked out of the room Hannah wondered if it was possible that her future could be better. Levi had brought so much happiness into her life, and now there was April. She had a proper family and there was no effort that had to be applied to her marriage—it was effortless to get along with Levi. She closed her eyes and thanked God for finally bringing Levi to her.

TWO YEARS ON, Hannah and Levi were expecting their second child while Miriam and Stephen were delighted to finally be expecting their first. Miriam and Hannah were pleased their children would be the same ages to play together just as they'd done as children.

WHAT BECAME OF LIZZY? Lizzy had found it hard to get along with everyone in the community in Lancaster County, and had talked Joel and his parents into moving to Harts County. In her letters to Hannah, Lizzy said they were all much happier there. Hannah hoped so.

AMISH WIDOW'S DECISION

EXPECTANT AMISH WIDOWS BOOK 15

CHAPTER 1

FAYE KIRKDALE WAS CLEANING her kitchen while awaiting the arrival of her husband. His evening meal was in the oven keeping warm. Hank always arrived home too late for Faye to wait and eat with him. When she heard the familiar hoofbeats, she poured a glass of his favorite cider and placed it on the table. Faye kept his meal in the oven, knowing it would take him a while to unhitch the buggy and rub down the horse. She sat on the couch and resumed her knitting, waiting for the familiar stomping footfalls up the porch stairs that led to the front door.

After she'd knitted a few rows, she thought it strange that he was still outside. She opened the front door and saw the horse and buggy, not even unhitched.

"Hank!" When there was no reply, she yelled in a louder voice, but still she was met with silence except for the horse snorting in agitation.

She lit one of the gas lanterns and hurried out to see what was happening. Before she reached the horse and buggy, she saw that the horse had his neck up straight and his reins weren't tied to anything. When she got closer, the horse backed away from her, but she managed to lift the lantern high enough to see her husband slumped over in the buggy.

She yelled at Hank, but he didn't move. When she tried to reach for the horse, he reared up and trotted away. All she could do was wait until the horse stopped and then she slowly walked over to him, speaking soft words so he would stay put. There was an eerie feeling about all of this.

"Everything's all right." She continued speaking in a calming voice as she carefully reached over and grabbed the reins and then tied them to a nearby fence post so the horse wouldn't take off again. The horse had been upset by something. Then she stepped over to the buggy and looked at her husband, and gasped when she saw that his white shirt was soaked in blood. She looked closer in case she was wrong. Yes, it was blood. She called out his name. "Hank!" No response. With the lantern in one hand, she felt for a pulse with the other but there was none. "Hank!" she screamed again.

It sank in that he was dead. Her first thought was to call the bishop. She ran into the barn and placed the lantern by her feet. With trembling hands, she picked up the receiver and dialed the bishop's number. She was relieved that she could remember it right now, even though she knew it by heart.

Bishop Luke answered the phone. "Hank's dead!" she screamed into the phone. Then she broke down and sobbed and could barely speak.

"Faye? What's happened?"

She managed to stop crying enough to speak. "He's in the buggy—dead. There's blood all over."

"I'm coming immediately, Faye. Don't do anything. I'll be there soon."

"He came home in the buggy and didn't get out. I went out to see where he was and he's in the buggy covered in blood. He's dead!" Tears rolled down her face.

"Faye, listen to me carefully. Are you alone?"

"*Jah.*"

"Go back into the *haus* and lock the doors. I'll call 911 and then I'll come there. Until then, don't answer the door to anyone unless it's the police or the paramedics."

"Okay."

"Lock yourself in. Do it now."

Without saying anything further, she hung up the receiver, picked up the lantern, and ran into the house. Once she was inside, she obeyed the bishop's words. She made sure the front door was bolted, then she locked the back door, and then she ran around locking all of the windows.

Once she had done that, she looked out the window at the buggy standing still in the darkness. Had someone killed her husband or had some medical problem caused him to bleed so much? She touched her dress and felt it was wet. When she looked down, she saw she was covered in blood. Knowing that the bishop and the paramedics were on the way, she hurried to the mudroom at the back of the house and stripped off her clothes. She washed her hands, then wrapped herself in a towel and hurried upstairs to find clean clothes.

As she grabbed the first dress she came to, a chill shuddered through her body. What if Hank had been murdered right outside her house? What if the murderer had slipped into the house while she'd been on the phone? Or had Hank been murdered elsewhere, and then the horse found its way home?

She made her way back downstairs and sat on the couch. Within minutes, she heard wailing sirens. Jumping to her feet and looking out the window, she saw two police cars and an ambulance pulling into the yard. She opened the door and stepped out of the house.

The paramedics made their way to the buggy with two policemen, and two more policemen walked toward her. "Are you Mrs. Kirkdale?"

"I am." She wiped tears from her eyes. "I found my husband in the buggy. He was dead. He's covered in blood. He was supposed to come in for his dinner." She gasped; she'd forgotten that the dinner was still in the oven. Without saying anything, she turned and rushed to turn off the oven. The two uniformed policemen followed her inside. "I forgot that I hadn't turned off the oven. You see, I was keeping his dinner warm."

"I'm Officer Bryant and this is Officer Carmody."

"I'm Mrs. Kirkdale. Oh, you already know that."

"Yes, we got a call from your bishop. Is he here?"

"No, the only person here is me. And my husband." Just as she was finished saying that, they heard hoofbeats heading toward the house. "That will be the bishop now."

She walked back out of the kitchen to greet the bishop and saw that his wife, Abigail, was there too.

Abigail ran to Faye and put her arms around her. "Oh, you poor thing."

The officers introduced themselves to the bishop and his wife.

"It was horrible." Faye looked back at the police officers who were behind her. "How did he die?"

Rather than answer her question, Officer Bryant said, "We'll soon know. Let's just sit down somewhere and you can tell us exactly what happened."

Tears flooded down her cheeks again. She covered her face with her hands. "I can't say anything at the moment."

"Do you mean you want a lawyer?" Officer Carmody asked.

"I don't want anything at the moment, except to find out what happened to my husband." Suddenly the yard was awash with light. Three battery-operated lights had been erected in her yard. "Was he stabbed? Is that why there was so much blood?"

"We'll talk to the team in a minute."

Her attention was drawn to flashes of light near the buggy. "Are they taking photos?"

"It looks like the buggy is being considered a crime scene," the bishop said to Faye. He asked Officer Carmody, "Is it all right if I look after the horse? He looks like he's been badly spooked, and he might be injured, too."

"Not right now. Maybe in half an hour or so," Officer Carmody said.

The bishop looked a little shocked at the seeming disregard for the animal's well-being, but nodded in agreement.

"Let's sit down."

When they sat down with Officer Bryant, Officer Carmody said, "Mind if I take a look around your house?"

"Yes, yes, do it if you want."

She slumped back into the couch with Abigail on one side of her and the bishop on the other.

"What happened?" asked Officer Bryant. "When did he arrive home?"

"He came home but he didn't come inside. After a while, I went to see what was wrong. I called out to him and there was no answer. I took a light out to check on things, and then I saw him covered in blood and slumped over, almost like he was asleep. I felt for a pulse and couldn't find it. Then I called Bishop Luke."

"And I called 911, and then my wife and I came here," the bishop told him.

Officer Bryant shook his head at the bishop, telling him to keep quiet.

"Can I get you something, Faye?" Abigail asked.

She shook her head. "The only thing I want right now is some answers. Why did this happen?"

Officer Carmody came out of the mudroom with her bloodied clothes hanging from a stick. "Do these look familiar, Mrs. Kirkdale?"

"Yes, I just changed out of them, just now."

"You admit they're your clothes?"

"Yes."

He glanced at them and then looked back at her. "They're covered in blood."

"That's why I changed out of them."

"We're going to need you to come down to the station for questioning," Officer Carmody said.

"Right now?"

"Yes."

She nodded.

"We'll come with you," Abigail said.

"There's no need for that," Officer Bryant said. "We can drive her home when we're finished. It might take some time."

"I'll be fine," Faye said to them. "You go home. I'll call you later."

CHAPTER 2

JUST AFTER THE bishop and his wife left, Faye was waiting to leave the house for the police station when a different uniformed officer knocked on the door. One of the officers went to the door, and Faye heard the new man say that a paramedic wanted to take a look at her.

The officer turned around. "Mrs. Kirdale ..."

She bounded to her feet, thinking to correct his mispronunciation of her name, and then everything faded into darkness. When she opened her eyes, she was on the floor and someone in white was leaning over her.

"Can you hear me, Mrs. Kirkdale?"

She didn't have the strength to answer. She looked around and realized she must have fainted.

"I can hear you," she whispered weakly.

The paramedic helped her to a seated position. "Easy does it." He took her blood pressure with a portable machine.

"Did I faint?"

"Yes, but it's only normal with the nasty shock you've had." He looked around him and then handed her a couple of loose pills, and said in a low voice, "These will help you sleep."

There was no prescription or anything. She wondered if he was supposed to be handing out sleeping pills like that. "Thank you."

He gave her a reassuring smile. "Physically you're okay. You should go to your local doctor tomorrow. You might need something to get you through the next few days."

She had no intention of going to the doctor. In her mind, going to a doctor was a last resort, and she'd only fainted. "Thanks. I'm okay. The only thing wrong with me is a bee allergy, but ..."

"You have an EpiPen?"

"Yes, somewhere."

"Good." He nodded.

"I never had a phone before and when I nearly died the bishop urged me to get a phone on. Now I'm married the first emergency was for my husband and not for me."

"You'll be okay." He gave her a reassuring smile and she felt embarrassed for rambling about herself when her husband was dead.

· · ·

AT THE POLICE STATION, Faye gave permission for them to fingerprint her, and then they took her fingerprints as well as photographs of her hands and of both sides of her face. After they were through, they took her into an interview room. There she waited for someone else to interview her.

Faye shivered, and wondered why she was being treated like a criminal. Her husband was dead. She was tired, yet she didn't want to sleep. She was hungry, but didn't want to eat. Faye didn't know what she wanted to do with herself. Closing her eyes in the cold, sterile environment of the room, she asked God why He had taken Hank away from her. Was it because she had prayed once or twice to be set free from the marriage? If that was it, she took it all back. It wasn't the greatest marriage, being wife to the cold and indifferent Hank, but she never wanted him dead. She'd grown used to the life she had and it had brought with it the comfort of routine. Now what would become of her brothers, who relied on Hank's business for employment?

Her parents were the ones who'd wanted her to marry Hank. It hadn't mattered that she didn't love him, not to her parents at least. Their sole reason for her marrying him was to give her younger brothers secure employment.

Long ago, Faye's parents had made a plan, and that plan was that her father would build up a business big enough for their four sons to take over. When her father's legs were crushed in a buggy accident, her parents' plans were crushed right along with them. They then hatched another plan for their sons which involved their oldest child, Faye, marrying the much older

Hank. So far, that plan had worked perfectly from her parents' perspective, and each of Faye's brothers had been employed by Hank. No plan had been made for Hank's sudden death. Or had it? She remembered her mother, some time back, asking Hank to make a will. The will left everything to Faye and the children they would have.

Faye jumped when the door was swung open and a tall, broad-shouldered detective walked into the room. He wore a dark suit that didn't fit him very well at the shoulders, and the top three buttons of his shirt were undone, giving him the more casual appearance of someone who didn't particularly like wearing a suit.

When he smiled at her, she immediately relaxed. "Hello, Mrs. Kirkdale. I'm Detective Jed Hervey."

"Hello, Detective. Just call me Faye."

He nodded. "I'm sorry about your husband."

Faye dabbed at the corners of her eyes with a tissue. Her eyes stung because she'd wiped them so much. "Thank you. How did he die?"

"The coroner's trying to ascertain that right now. All we know is that he was stabbed."

Faye sighed. That meant it wasn't a medical condition; someone had taken his life from him.

"Do you have any idea who would want your husband dead?"

"He had no enemies. Everyone liked him. At least, I don't know anyone who didn't. Not enough to kill him, anyway." She shook her head. "Who would do such a thing?"

"Officer Carmody found your clothes in your house, all covered in blood, and one of the officers found a large knife covered in blood by your house."

"I don't know anything about a knife. I told the officers that I changed my clothes because they had blood on them from when I tried to check my husband's pulse." Then Faye remembered something. "I have a knife missing. I used it to cut meat. It was a carving knife with a distinct curved handle. The handle was made from a pale colored wood and it was heavily grained. I looked for it this afternoon when I started fixing dinner, and it wasn't there."

"Wait here a moment." He left and then came back with a cell phone. He showed her a picture on it.

"That's my knife!" It had blood on it, as he'd said.

"That could possibly be the murder weapon."

The detective sat back down then, and clicked on the end of a pen. "What can you tell me about your relationship with your husband?"

"We've been married for four years."

He jotted something down and then looked up at her. "Happily?"

"Adequately." She couldn't lie and say they were happily married. Hank might've been happy, she didn't know, but she wasn't that happy.

He pulled a face. "Adequately?"

She nodded. "I had no cause for complaint."

"How old was your husband?"

"Forty-six."

"And you?"

"Twenty-six."

"That's quite an age difference."

She nodded. "It is. It was."

"And I understand he was a wealthy man and owned a large door-manufacturing business?"

She nodded. "He had a good business. Doors—wooden doors. Sliding doors, French doors, entry doors. They're good quality. Everyone loves them."

"And what will happen to that business now that he's dead? Did your husband have a will?"

"Yes. Everything was left to me and our children. If we had any, that is, but we never did. I can't believe he was stabbed. Who would do that?"

"I can tell you from experience that when someone has been stabbed so many times, there's an emotional element involved.

Someone was very upset with him and that's why I asked if he had any enemies."

"You didn't ask if he had enemies. You asked did I know anyone who'd want him dead."

"Did he have any enemies?"

"I can't think of anybody who would be that upset with him."

"What about you?"

She gasped. "You don't think I did this, do you?"

He looked down at the notepaper on the desk and then looked back up at her. "Your dress and apron were covered in blood. The murder occurred on your property, and then there's the knife." He raised his eyebrows as though he was waiting for her to blurt out her confession.

"How do you know he was murdered on my property? It could've happened somewhere—anywhere—on the way home and the horse found his way home."

"You want us to believe that your horse found his way home just like some kind of Lassie?"

"I have no idea what or who a Lassie is, but horses find their way home all the time. When they throw their rider, they find their way home. When a buggy driver falls asleep, they pull the buggy home. Don't you know anything about horses, Detective?"

He leaned back and folded his arms across his chest. "The forensic team will be able to ascertain whether it happened on your property or along the route from his place of business to your house. Now tell me, Mrs. Kirkdale, do you have any reason to want your husband dead?"

"No! Of course not!" She was getting frustrated by answering the same question over and over.

"If you tell us now, things will go easier for you. Did he beat you, and you got angry with him?"

She shook her head. "No, never."

"Was he verbally, emotionally, or physically abusive to you?"

"Never. Not once. He was a good man."

"I know the Amish way of life can be a harsh one. I also know the only way out of marriage, since you folk don't believe in divorce, is death. Did you want out of the marriage?" The officer's brown eyes bored through hers.

She would've loved to have gotten out of the marriage. "I thought about it at times, but that would never happen. Marriage is for life and I knew that when I married him. I didn't kill him. It never entered my head. I could never harm anyone."

"Maybe you got tired of being dominated by a man and wanted your freedom back, and the only way out for an Amish woman is if her husband dies, isn't that right?"

He was repeating himself but she wasn't going to antagonize him by pointing that out. "If you mean the only way she can be free to marry again is if her husband dies, then that is correct. We Amish do allow a husband and wife to live separately if they cannot be compatible in the same house, but there is no divorce."

"Do you want to marry someone else?"

"No! I didn't kill him. I would never kill him. And I don't want to marry someone else."

"You have blood on your hands, literally, and you had blood all over your clothes. He was stabbed viciously and repeatedly and I'm afraid you are our only suspect."

"You'd better find another one soon, because I didn't do it. You should try to find out who did this so it doesn't happen to someone else."

"Would you like to talk to a lawyer?"

"I don't have one. They asked me that before, a couple of times, and I said no. I have nothing to hide because I didn't do it. You're wasting your time with these questions."

"You could find a lawyer. Was it self-defense?"

She pushed out her chair and stood up. "No. Am I free to go?"

"Don't get upset. We're only asking questions that we need to ask."

"I understand, but am I free to go?"

"Yes, but we'll want to talk to you again."

"Where is my husband now?"

"An autopsy is being performed as we speak."

"Where?"

"At the hospital."

"I'd like to see him."

He shook his head. "I'm afraid that's not possible right now. We'll let you know when he's ready to be collected by a funeral director."

She'd already given them the number of her phone in the barn, and the bishop's number.

"We'll be in touch." He reached into his pocket and pulled out a card. "If you remember anything else, or can think of anyone who might have had reason to cause him harm, please call me."

She took the card from him. "Thank you."

"I'll have someone take you home. We'll have officers patrolling your home for the next few days and nights, so don't be nervous."

Faye nodded. "Thank you."

All the way home in the police car, Faye wondered who would have wanted to kill Hank. She couldn't think of a single person.

When she arrived home, it was in the early hours of the morning and all she wanted to do was have a warm shower and wash all the wickedness and murkiness away. It felt like she was living a bad dream. She didn't want to be alone, yet neither did she want anyone near her.

The hot water jets pounded over her body and she untied her hair and let it fall down around her. Since her hair had never been cut, it reached way past her thighs, all the way to her knees. Normally she didn't wash it at night because of the length of time it took to dry. Right now, she didn't care if she caught a chill from damp hair.

For the next few hours she tossed and turned, and when it was light, she heard someone knocking on the door. She hoped it wasn't the police coming to arrest her for her husband's murder.

"Coming!" she yelled out. She quickly changed into a clean dress, wound her still damp hair in a towel, and opened the door. She was relieved to see Rain, her good friend, standing there.

"Oh Faye! I heard what happened from Bishop Luke."

Faye took hold of Rain's hand and pulled her inside the house. "I'm so glad to see you. It was dreadful." She told Rain everything that had happened.

Rain gasped. "And they think you did it?"

"*Jah!* I think so. I couldn't tell them a name of someone who might have wanted him dead, and they wanted me to tell them. There's no one. They asked me if Hank abused me. They think I did it in self-defense. They kept asking if I needed a lawyer."

"You look dreadful."

"I haven't had any sleep."

"Go upstairs now and get some sleep. I'll keep everyone away from you until you wake up."

"It's no use. If you've heard, everybody will hear and they'll be stopping by to see how I am."

"I'll keep them away. I'll tell them to call back another day."

"Would you?"

Rain nodded. *"Jah."*

"Denke. I haven't even told my parents or Hank's parents."

"The bishop said he'd do that. What you need now is some sleep."

"I'll try, but I don't know if I'll be able."

"Did they have a doctor look at you?" Rain asked.

"One of the paramedics examined me and gave me a couple of pills to help me sleep if I needed them."

"Did you take them?"

"Nee."

"You should take them, because if you don't sleep you might get into a bad pattern of not sleeping. Believe me, there's nothing worse."

"I can think of a few things. Like finding your husband dead, covered in blood in a buggy."

"I know. It must've been awful."

Tears fell down Faye's face once more.

"Try not to cry."

"I have to get it out. I can't bottle things up."

Rain nodded. "Cry after you've had a good sleep. Take the pills."

"I don't like taking things, and I don't know exactly what these pills are."

"It's not every day something like this happens, so I think you need a little bit of help to relax. Don't feel bad about it."

"I'll see how it goes. I don't know why I resist things like that. I might take them."

Rain smiled. "Now upstairs with you and get into bed. Would you like a cup of tea, or something?"

"Maybe a cup of hot tea will help me sleep. I don't know if I'll ever be able to sleep again."

Faye tossed and turned, and finally managed to get a little sleep. When she woke, the sun was high in the sky.

CHAPTER 3

I T   W A S the morning of the day before the funeral and Rain came to the house. She told Faye it might help her feel better if they went out somewhere rather than Faye staying in the house all day.

The police were no further ahead with their investigations. All Faye was told was that her husband had been stabbed eight times, and so far they'd been unable to ascertain the location where the stabbing had taken place. All they knew from the blood evidence was that it had happened inside the buggy. The police had taken possession of the buggy as evidence, and Faye was glad she and Hank had a spare and three buggy horses. She was relieved that the horse Hank had been driving that awful evening was doing okay, having recovered from its fright once it had been returned to its stall after a soothing rubdown by Bishop Luke.

Just as Rain and Faye were about to walk into the markets, Rain stopped abruptly. *"Ach, nee!* I've left my money in the buggy. You wait here, I won't be a moment."

As Faye waited for Rain to return, she admired the flowers at the entrance. She was careful not to get too close. Where there were flowers there was pollen and where there was pollen there were bees. With her bee-sting allergy, she had to keep away from flowers as much as she could, but she loved to see all the beautiful colors. Faye jumped when someone touched her on the arm. She turned to see Hillary Bauer.

"Hillary?" she said in surprise. She hadn't seen Hillary for years. Faye knew that Hank had once dated Hillary, and then their relationship had ended abruptly. Hillary had been furious about it. She had left the community immediately and married an *Englischer.* Rumor had it that the marriage hadn't lasted long, and then she married another *Englisch* man.

"Yes, it's me," Hillary said with a quick laugh, and then her face turned serious. "I heard about Hank, and I just wanted to say I'm very sorry for your loss."

"Thank you." Faye wasn't sure what to think about Hillary, with what she remembered from the past.

"It must've been horribly shocking to find him like you did."

"It was. It was a dreadful shock." Where was Rain? She looked over at the parked buggy and saw Rain inside moving about as though she couldn't find the bag that held her money. Rain had said she was going to protect her from everyone. Faye looked back at Hillary. "How did you hear about …?"

"It was in the newspapers."

"Oh. I didn't know. I haven't left the house until now." Except for necessities, neither had she left the bedroom, or more accurately, the bed, but she didn't tell Hillary that.

"Do they know who did it?" Hillary asked.

"No, they don't. Are you living in these parts? I thought you moved away."

"I moved away when I married my first husband, and after he died I moved back here."

"Oh, your husband died?" Faye had heard she was twice divorced.

"Yes, my first husband died, and I remarried after I moved back to this area. So, I know what it's like to lose a husband. Anyway, I just wanted to tell you that I'm sorry. Hank was a good man."

"*Jah*, he was."

"I must go."

She watched Hillary hurry away. The woman still had a mad gleam in her eye. A day after Hank had broken off their relationship, his barn had been set on fire, and he only just managed to get his horses out in time. Hank had always blamed Hillary for the fire and maybe he'd been right. Could Hillary have harbored anger for so long that it built up to the point where she wanted Hank dead? It didn't seem likely, since so much time had passed and the woman had married—twice.

"Sorry I was so long finding my bag," Rain said as she returned. "Who was that you were talking to?"

"That was Hillary Bauer."

Rain looked over at the figure in the distance. "I haven't seen her for years and years."

"She said her first husband died and now she's married again."

"I always wondered what happened to her."

Faye kept to herself that Hank had suspected Hillary of setting his barn on fire. "Let's get what we came here to get."

Rain stared at her. "Did she upset you?"

"*Nee,* I'm okay. She just brought back some memories."

"Of when she was in love with Hank?"

Faye nodded. "Something like that, *jah,* but that was a long time ago. Way before I married Hank."

"She always was a strange woman. Everyone wondered why he ended things with her so suddenly. I was only young back then, but my *mudder* liked to know everything that was happening and I found out too."

Faye walked into the farmers market wishing she'd stayed at home. Sooner or later, though, she'd have to go back out in public and today was as good a day as any. *Might as well get the first time over with,* she thought, *and then it'll be easier next time.*

"We'll hurry to get the food we need for tomorrow and then we'll leave," said Rain.

Faye nodded, glad that her friend was helping her with the food after the funeral the next day. Normally, the two of them made a day of it at the markets while Rain's children were at school. They'd linger, looking at all sorts of things, and then they'd stay for a cup of something and a bite to eat at their favorite café. But today wasn't normal.

CHAPTER 4

THE NEXT DAY at the viewing, Faye gazed at her late husband's lifeless body as he lay in the coffin in her living room. The funeral director had delivered his body to her house at daybreak. It was customary at an Amish funeral that the body be viewed at home before being driven to the graveyard in the specially designed buggy. Faye stared at her husband. He looked like he was asleep. The only difference was his face had taken on a paler gray tone.

There had never been any affection between them—well, not much. There had been respect, and no unkindness. It had been a marriage of convenience, in the sense that it was convenient for the rest of Faye's family and Hank, but inconvenient for her.

Faye stood back a little and greeted all the mourners as they poured in through her front door.

When Faye had a space between the visitors, Rain hurried toward her. "Hank's *bruder* is here."

"You mean half-*bruder*," Faye corrected her. Hank had two brothers, but they were both half-brothers to him, and oddly, to one another. Faye had always had a crush on John, one of Hank's half-brothers. He was closer to her in age than Hank, but he was still much older. She'd grown up hoping to marry him, but he left the community in his late teenage years. Her crush on John was something she had never shared with anyone, not even Rain.

"Half-*bruder*, full-*bruder*, what difference does it make?"

"It makes quite a difference to the *mudders*." Faye looked over the crowd. "Where is he?"

"Over near the door."

Faye wondered if Rain was talking about John, or the younger one, Silas. They stood on tiptoes and looked over the crowd, and then Faye saw him. It was John. She hadn't seen him for years. He looked a lot like Hank except he was better looking, and he didn't have Hank's grim, expressionless face. He was just as tall as Hank was with the same broad shoulders. John's coloring was dark and his face was pleasant with even features.

"John's a lot younger than Hank, isn't he?"

"*Jah*. When Hank's *mudder* died of pneumonia, his father married John's mother and then she tragically died in childbirth, and then later his father married Mary Anne, wife number three, and then they had Silas. That's why there's such an age gap between Hank and John and a smaller one between John and Silas." Of course, Rain knew all of this since Hank's family was in the same community and Hank's brothers had grown up with them, but it quieted Faye's nerves to talk.

Faye dug Rain in the ribs. "There's Silas now."

Silas had walked in behind John. Then came Silas' mother and then Faye's father-in-law. Mary Anne had raised Silas' older half-brothers as if they were her own. Hank stayed on in the community whereas John and Silas left the community as soon as they were old enough.

"When was the last time you saw John and Silas?" Rain asked.

"I haven't seen them since the wedding."

"Since your wedding?"

Faye nodded. "*Jah.* Hank didn't get along with them."

"Why not?"

"Who knows?" Faye shrugged her shoulders. "He didn't get along with anyone much."

Rain giggled. "You shouldn't say that, Faye."

"But it is the truth. He only got along with people he wanted to get along with. Only when it suited his purpose. And they'd both left the community."

"*Ach nee!*" Rain whispered. "Here comes your *mudder.* I'm going."

Faye's mother and Rain didn't get along, and Faye was certain that was because her mother didn't approve of anybody she liked.

Her mother arrived by her side, but not before frowning in disapproval at Rain's hasty getaway. "There's a big turnout today. Your husband was a very popular and influential man."

Faye turned around to look at the coffin. "And yet here he lies dead, and he had the same ending as everybody else. What became of all his hard work and the late nights when he missed dinner with me? None of that saved him from what happened."

Her mother opened her mouth in disgust. "That's a dreadful thing to say. He was a hard-worker and that's a good thing."

"*Nee,* it's not. He could've come home at a regular time and he never did. He hardly talked to me unless it was telling me what he needed me to do." She wanted her mother to hear loud and clear that she hadn't gotten over being forced into the marriage.

Her mother's lips pressed together.

Couldn't her mother just admit she'd made a mistake? Faye added, "I didn't ask much. I just wanted to be loved and looked after. He never told me he loved me and that's because he probably didn't."

Her mother leaned forward. "Don't let the police hear you say that."

"They can think what they want. I don't care. I just wanted a good marriage."

"And you had one. Not all men tell their wives they love them. What do words matter?"

"They matter to me."

"Well, did you bother to tell him that you loved him?"

She stared at her mother. She couldn't say right there at the funeral that she had never really loved him, but her mother should've known that. Why didn't she ever listen? It had never been a real marriage. The two of them had coexisted under the one roof, shared the same bed, and that was it. Instead of answering her mother's question, she referred back to her mother's previous comment. "Where did all the wealth and popularity get him?"

"I didn't say anything about wealth or money."

"He had a lot of money." And then it struck her fully that all of his money was now hers. As well as the business he'd built.

Her mother tipped back her head and spoke down her nose at her. "Speaking of wealth. I've arranged a family meeting for next week and we'll see which of your brothers is going to take over the company."

Faye narrowed her eyes. "What company?" Faye knew very well what company—her company, and her mother shouldn't have any say in the business she knew nothing about.

"Hank's company. It's now yours and one of your brothers will have to take over."

417

"*Nee,* they won't." Her mother had bullied her into the marriage and Faye wasn't going to let her bully her into giving up control of the company. Her company.

Her mother looked at her in surprise, her blue-green eyes bulging. "Are you going to employee someone to run the company?"

"You mean employ?"

Her mother frowned. "Don't take that tone with me. I know nothing of business matters. You know what I meant. Someone has to run the company now that Hank has gone."

"I'll do it."

Her mother's mouth fell open in shock. "What do you know about running a company? You can barely run your household. If Hank didn't meet your expectations, I'm sure that likewise, you didn't meet his. *Gott* knows I tried to teach you all I knew, but you never listened properly."

She ignored her mother's mean comments. "I overheard a lot of Hank's conversations to his suppliers and such, and I'll be able to do it."

Her mother stepped closer and put a hand on her shoulder. "You're not thinking straight in this time of grief. You'll soon get that silly notion out of your head. Women just don't do things like that."

"Things like what?"

"Run businesses."

"Mother, that is nonsense. Abigail Gingerich has a very successful quilt store and employs six people."

"That's different. Hank employed nearly fifty."

"Forty-nine, and it's not different at all. Hank's business is larger, but it's the same principle."

"It's not the same, because Abigail's only got women working for her. You can't be in charge of men; it's absurd. A woman can't be in charge and above a man. You can't be a boss over your brothers. You're a woman."

Just when Faye was about to reply to her mother, they were interrupted by people who approached Faye to offer their condolences. Her mother stayed close by.

After the people moved on, Faye said to her mother, "Hank left the business to me. He left everything to me, and that means I have the say of what goes on in the business. And if any of the men aren't performing properly, I have a right to fire them, including my brothers."

Her mother gasped. "Don't you dare." She shook her finger at her, as though Faye were a misbehaving little child.

Embarrassed by her mother, Faye looked around, hoping no one was looking at them. When she didn't see anyone watching them, she turned back to her mother and desperately tried to get her point across. "This is my husband's funeral. Please don't speak to me in that way at this time. I'm a grieving widow."

Her mother lowered her voice. "You're probably happy he's gone. Now that he's gone, you're free to marry again. You never wanted to marry him in the first place."

"I won't lie. I didn't. You know you forced me into it. It was a huge mistake that I listened to you."

"I didn't force you into it. I just made you see common sense. With your *vadder's* failing health, he had to close his business. It was his dream that all his *kinner* work in the business that he built up, and you know that."

"Correction—you mean all of his sons, not all of his *kinner,* because I was never included."

"Women get married, they don't have to go out to work." Her mother held up a hand. "Don't tell me about all the women you know who have jobs. I don't want to hear it. Be at that family meeting on Tuesday night, and we together as a family will decide who's going to take over Hank's company. I think it should be Jacob since he's the oldest, but we'll just have to see. Maybe the task is too large for Jacob. Simon has more confidence and is better with people. Hank was good with people."

Faye scoffed.

Her mother gave her a steely gaze, daring her to utter a word. Out of respect for her late husband, Faye kept quiet. She had no intention of allowing any of her brothers to take over the company. None of them was cut out for it. She'd learn what to do and run the business herself.

As for ever marrying again, now that she'd already been married, she didn't know that she wanted any part of it. She was certainly not looking to marry again any time soon, as her mother had suggested.

As more people arrived, Faye's mother stood next to her greeting people as they came past the coffin. As much as she could, Faye put on a brave face. It wasn't easy being a widow at such a young age. It would've been easier if Hank had been sick and had slowly deteriorated. Then it wouldn't have been such a shock. The suddenness coupled with the fact that he'd been murdered was a double blow.

A little later, when Faye was by herself, Boris Lineberger walked over to her. He was one of the handful of *Englischers* at the funeral. He and Hank had worked together in the past and then he'd become a friendly business rival.

"I'm sorry about what happened to your husband."

She gave a little nod. "So am I."

He raised his eyebrows just slightly, seeming to be surprised by her response. It was hard to know what to say to people sometimes.

"I have some things I want to discuss with you, but right now is neither the time nor the place."

"What kind of things?"

"Business kind of things."

"Oh."

"I know where you live. I'll stop by your house to see you on Monday next week if that's all right."

"I won't be home. I'll be at work."

"Hank's work?"

"*Jah.*"

"Very well, that's where I'll find you."

She nodded. "Okay."

He tipped his head and walked away. She immediately knew that he wanted to take back some of the contracts that Hank had won from him. Maybe he figured the company might be dissolved with Hank's passing, and his firm would be able to benefit.

CHAPTER 5

WHEN ALL THE guests had gone home after the meal, Faye tried her best to relax. This had been a big day. First the mourners viewed the body at the house, followed by the trip to the cemetery, and then after the burial, people returned to the house for the meal.

At least she'd had a day free of police. From the day Hank had died until today, the day of the funeral, the police had been at the house every single day.

The day after Hank's death, Faye had allowed them to do a full search of the house and property. The police made her nervous, particularly Detective Hervey, who made her feel uncomfortable, almost guilty. She was certain he thought she'd done it and was looking for evidence so he could accuse her of murder. He even seemed annoyed that she'd admitted the knife they'd found was hers, but then she hadn't confessed.

After four nights without Hank, Faye was finally coming to terms with being on her own. Because Hank had worked such long hours, loneliness was a familiar friend. And with that absence of Hank from the home, she'd even become adept at doing odd jobs and maintenance work around the house, tasks that a man would've normally done. She sat down on the couch, glad that everybody had left and she was finally alone.

She'd never been in love, and she was sure most people had never been truly in love. In a general sense, she had an idea what love was, and before she married she used to long to be in love. That had made things worse when her mother told her she should marry Hank for the sake of her brothers. Faye had wanted to do the right thing to keep everybody happy. Hank had been a good provider, and apart from spending too little time with her, he hadn't been a bad husband. If he'd shown her the attention he should've, Faye might have been able to open her heart to him.

Faye kicked off her shoes and then swung her legs up onto the couch. When she was settled and comfortable, she ripped off her prayer *kapp* and tossed it onto the opposite couch. What was God's plan in taking Hank away so young? He was too young to die, and she was too young to be a widow.

THAT NIGHT, Faye was unable to sleep, but that didn't stop her from arriving early at work the next day. She had often helped her late husband with filing and general office work when the bookkeeper was on vacation. She overheard and discussed business with various people and figured she knew the workings of the company well enough to make a start of running it. The very thought of the meeting that night with her parents unsettled her, so she pushed it out of her mind the best she could.

After a briefing with Ronald, the office manager, Faye sat behind her husband's desk and leafed through the papers that he'd been going through on the last day he'd been there. She'd given instructions that no one touch anything in his office. Unfortunately, that didn't apply to the police. They had wanted to look through his office and Faye had given the okay. They informed her afterwards that they hadn't taken anything with them.

Spread over the top of his desk were orders that had to be processed and things that needed to be done, but there was nothing out of the ordinary. She was hoping to find a clue to who might have murdered him, but if the police hadn't found anything she didn't like her chances.

Two hours later, when she was deep in thought and up to her neck sorting out invoices and bills, she heard someone clear his throat. She looked up and in the office doorway was Hank's brother, John.

"John! I wasn't expecting to see you here today."

He slowly sauntered into her office. "We need to talk." He pulled out the chair and sat down opposite her. "I've come to offer you … relief."

"You're going to help me with this paperwork?" she joked, holding up a handful of papers.

"No. I've come to take this place off your hands."

She studied his face for a hint of a smile, then quickly realized he was serious. "What, the business?"

He smiled and nodded.

"That's simply out of the question."

The smile left his face. "I am Hank's brother and he would've wanted me to take over from him."

"You might've been his brother, but you barely spent any time together these past years so I hardly believe you could know that."

"I grew up with him. I reckon I knew him better than anybody."

"I don't think so. You didn't visit once in all the time Hank and I were married."

He leaned forward. "That's only because I wasn't invited."

"Do you see my point? If you had been closer with Hank, or had stayed in the community, he would've invited you. Anyway, I'll be running the company from now on, since Hank left it to me."

John laughed. "Women don't know how to run companies."

"Many women run companies."

"Not of this size."

"Even larger than this."

"*Englischers* maybe, but not Amish women. It's not your place."

"It's the principle of the thing that matters, and it doesn't matter if the company is large or small. If Hank had wanted you to run it, he would've left it to you. I can run a company just as well as a man."

"What does your bishop say about that?"

"The bishop will be fine with it. As long as the company doesn't employ over one hundred people." Faye vaguely remembered the bishop cautioning her husband that his business not get too big. If the business grew to the stage where it employed over one hundred people, he would've had to cut back somewhere, or maybe even divide the business somehow.

"Now that I'm here, you don't have to worry about any of that. I'll make sure you're looked after financially. With me running it, there's no limit to how big it'll grow. We can franchise it."

It wasn't herself she was worried about. She was worried about her duty to her brothers. Purely out of interest, she asked him, "What makes you more capable than one of my brothers?"

"From what I know of them, they're too young and have no experience. I've already franchised a coffee shop and sold it off. I'm looking to do something like that again." He looked around. "This business would be a perfect model."

"There's no use talking about it because it won't happen." Then a thought occurred to her. She should invite him to dinner that night to do battle with her mother. And then her mother might see sense in leaving her to run the company rather than Hank's brother. At the very worst, nothing would be resolved and no decisions would be made. "Actually, why don't you come to dinner at my *mudder's* place tonight?"

"That's very kind of you. I'm not sure that I should accept, though."

"Do you still live nearby?"

"Not far away. Nothing's that far when you have the advantage of owning a car. I didn't mean to sound ungracious just now. I'd be delighted to accept your offer as long as it's okay with your folks."

"*Jah.* You're Hank's *bruder.* It'll be fine." He looked so grateful to be invited that Faye almost felt bad for setting him up for an argument with her mother. Her mother was like an angry mother bear who would fiercely protect the business that kept her sons in employment.

"Faye, I'm not coming here to take away your company or take anything from you. I want to buy the company from you. I'm here to give, not take."

Faye shook her head. "*Denke,* I appreciate that, but it's not for sale."

"You haven't heard my offer."

She shook her head. "It won't matter."

"And what do your parents think about that?"

She had to tell him the truth even though her instinct was to keep him in the dark. "My parents want one of my brothers to be in charge."

He pressed his lips together, and his brow furrowed. "What does any of them know about management?"

"What do you know about it?"

He scoffed. "I've had vast experience. I just told you that."

"And nothing's going to stop you from doing the same thing as what you mentioned, but not with this company. Hank left it to me."

"Are you sure about that?"

"*Jah*, I'm sure." She noticed him smiling smugly. "What makes you ask that?"

"It seems odd that he would leave it to you."

"I was his wife."

"I'm just saying I think it's odd. Anyway, I'm prepared to buy you out, or come to some arrangement. Possibly a share of the profits when I grow the company. We could sell it off when it's built up and none of your family would have to work again—if all goes to plan."

"What would my brothers do if they didn't work? I've never heard of such a thing."

"I'll explain it all to them."

She sighed. "You can make a few suggestions tonight. You can be involved in a family discussion, since you're part of Hank's family—his earthly family at least."

"*Denke*, once again. I hope *they* can see sense."

She looked down at the papers on Hank's desk. It would take her hours to go through them. "I don't mean to be rude, but I've got a lot of work to get through. I'll see you tonight." Normally she wouldn't speak like that to anyone, but she considered that he had been impolite, the way he'd just barged in expecting to take over the company.

He leaned over and looked at the paperwork. "What are you doing? Maybe I can help you with it."

She snatched the paperwork away from him. "It's nothing I can't sort out for myself. Thanks all the same." She took a piece of paper from the side of her desk and grabbed a pen. "I'll write down my parents' address for you."

"Have they moved?"

"No."

"I remember where they live. I grew up in the community, remember?"

She nodded. "Vaguely."

"What time shall I be there?"

"Seven."

He stood up. "I hope your parents will see sense. I'm a sales-man, I'll bring them 'round to my way of thinking."

Faye hoped she was doing the right thing by inviting him. Either way, she had to do something with her time. Running the company was a challenge, and she liked the idea of seeing what she was capable of. However, it would be nice to have some support and if her family didn't support her, who would?

Faye called her parents' phone in their barn. After trying three times, her mother finally answered. She told her to expect one more for dinner that night. It gave Faye a small sense of satisfaction that having Hank's brother there would send her mother into a flap.

CHAPTER 6

AFTER A DAY SPENT GETTING some of the paperwork sorted out, Faye left work and headed to her parents' house.

When she approached the house, she could tell by the absence of a car that their visitor hadn't arrived. Perhaps he'd thought better of doing battle with her mother. Faye giggled to herself. Yet, he wouldn't know what her mother was really like.

She secured her horse and walked into the house knowing all of her four brothers would have arrived home before her. Since none of her brothers were married, they all still lived at home.

Her mother pulled her aside as soon as she walked in the door. "Faye, what do you mean by inviting John Kirkdale? I was too shocked to ask this morning when you told me."

"He was interested to know what would become of the business, so I thought he should be here tonight."

Her mother frowned at her. "Why does he have any interest in it?"

"Because Hank was his *bruder* and besides that, he wants to take it over and do some franchising thing."

Her mother's face twisted into a scowl. "He what?"

"Wants to buy it, or run it—something like that. 'Sort something out,' I believe that's what he said. He might even think that Hank left it to him." Faye shrugged.

"Nee. Hank assured me he left it to you and your *kinner.* Since you never gave him any *kinner,* it's just yours now."

"We'll just have to see what John says tonight." Her mother had said that last part as though she believed Faye had deliberately withheld children from Hank.

"I still don't know why you invited him here. The boys would have an uncertain future if he took it over."

"Not if they do a good job."

"Faye! Are you saying you want him to take over?"

"Why don't we wait and hash this out when he gets here?"

Her mother shook her head. "Come and help me in the kitchen. I never could work out what went on in your head, and you haven't gotten any better as you've aged."

Faye followed her into the kitchen. "You make me sound like I'm ninety-five or something."

"I meant grown up. You know what I meant, but you'll never agree with me, will you?"

"I will when you're right."

Her mother shook her head again. "I just don't know who you took after. No one in the family is like you."

"Maybe I'm adopted."

"*Nee,* I can tell you that you definitely weren't. You caused me twenty-eight hours of excruciating pain when you were being born. You just didn't want to come out."

Faye had heard that many times. She was sure it was a gross exaggeration. "It can't have been that bad, *Mamm.*"

"You wait and see."

"I'll never know because I'll never be pregnant because I'll never marry again." One thing she'd desperately wanted was a child. A child might finally have brought Hank and her together and they would've all been a family. Hank might've even come home from work earlier—early enough to have dinner with them.

Her mother turned to her with a wry smile turning the corners of her lips upward. "How do you know you're not pregnant already?"

Faye gulped. "I couldn't possibly be."

"Everything is possible. I had a dream you were pregnant."

"*Nee.* It's not possible."

"*Jah,* it is. Unless you and Hank didn't …"

"*Mamm!* I'll not discuss those things with you. Never say anything like that again to me, please." Faye covered her ears to drown out her mother's cackles.

When her mother finally stopped laughing, she said, "We're both women and it's only us in the kitchen. I'm sure you talk to your friends about things like that."

"I never do. That would be weird. Weirder still talking about things like that with you. Let's talk about something else, okay?"

"We can talk about why you invited Hank's half-*bruder* to dinner. It's worse that he's an *Englischer* too."

"I already told you that, and anyway, he's family."

"You told me Hank hardly ever saw either *bruder,* and you said they never visited you even."

"He's still family, though. Once family always family, I guess."

"I suppose so. We can't make a habit of entertaining him, though." Her mother wrapped her hands in tea towels, leaned down, opened the oven, and pulled out the roast.

"That smells amazing, *Mamm.*"

She placed it on the wooden chopping block. "*Jah,* it does. You can't really go wrong with a roast. I suppose you found that out. Is that why you cooked Hank a lot of them?"

"They were his favorites."

"Hmm, I wonder why that was?"

Again, Faye ignored her mother's barbed comment. "What do you want me to do?"

"You can make the gravy using the pan juices. You always make it very well—without lumps. At least that's one thing I was able to teach you. It's a pity you can't have a meal out of gravy and nothing else. It's got so much flavor when it's made well."

"*Jah,* I do know how to make it without lumps." Faye scooted her mother out of the way and took over the gravy making duties.

When they heard a car, her mother hurried out of the kitchen while Faye was stuck stirring the gravy over the stove. *I should've seen that coming,* Faye thought. Her mother had arranged for her to be busy so *Mamm* could talk to Hank's brother first. Her mother and father would be nice enough to John, but he certainly would not be leaving the house thinking he would be running the company, or that he would have a chance to buy it. Her mother was a very stubborn woman, and since his accident, *Dat* went along with everything his wife said.

Faye finished the gravy-making as quickly as she could, not caring whether the gravy had lumps in it or not. In her mind, it was more important to get out to the living room and hear what was being said. She placed the pan of gravy on a section of the stovetop where it would keep warm and then she hurried past the already set dinner table to see what was taking place.

When she saw John being greeted by her brothers, she leaned against the doorway of the kitchen and admired how handsome he was.

When he looked up and saw her, he flashed her a smile. "Hi, Faye."

"Hello, John. I'm glad you could make it."

"I told you I'd be here. And thanks again for the kind invitation."

"We're very happy to have you here," Mrs. King told him. She looked up at Faye. "Are we all good in the kitchen?"

"*Jah*, all done."

"Shall we eat?" Faye's mother said, looking first at John, and then everyone else.

"I'm ready," Faye's father said.

"Me too," one of her brothers said, and then all the men joined in, agreeing that they were ready to eat.

There was always plenty of food at Faye's parents' house. Her brothers had hearty appetites, and she figured that John would be just the same.

Halfway through dinner, Jacob, the eldest brother, asked, "When are we going to start talking about the business?"

John looked directly at Faye.

"*Jah*," Faye's mother said. "John, you wouldn't believe it but Faye thinks she should run the company."

All of her brothers laughed, and Faye's father cast his gaze downward and shook his head as though he felt sorry for Faye for being so ridiculous. Faye kept quiet to hear what John would say.

John took a deep breath. "That's not right. A woman can't do something like that and be in charge of men."

"Quite right," her mother agreed.

"That's why I'm sure you'll see that I'm the best choice to take over the company. I've had three successful businesses of my own and I've franchised the last one and sold it for a small fortune. I'm even willing to take the company off your hands." The last part of what he said was directed to Faye's father, the head of the King household.

Faye could keep quiet no longer. "I don't know what you're looking at my *vadder* for, John. I think everyone's forgetting that the company's mine, and not anybody else's. It's got nothing to do with anyone else."

Silence swept over the table, and everybody looked at Faye. She didn't usually talk out like that, but she'd had enough. "I'm going to run this company, and nothing anyone will say or do can stop me. I was often with Hank when he was making important business decisions, and I got a pretty good idea of the direction to take the company."

John burst out laughing as if she had told a joke. "Direction?"

"Faye, don't you think you should give this some thought?" Jacob asked.

"I have thought about it. I've thought about what a good job I'd do in running the company. We, I mean I, employ a lot of people and that's a lot of responsibility, and I'm not taking that responsibility lightly. I know it's something I can do and I'll do it to the best of my ability."

"I think Faye would be good at it," Timothy, the youngest son, said.

"You're no expert," one of his older brothers told him.

"I'm entitled to my own opinion," Timothy said.

Their mother frowned at Timothy. "*Jah,* you can have your opinion, Timothy, but since you are too young to have any experience in these matters, perhaps you should keep your opinion to yourself and not try to enter into adult conversations."

"I am an adult, *Mamm.*"

"Just finish off your carrots."

Now she was trying to embarrass Timothy into silence.

"I don't like carrots."

"Carrots are good for you. Just eat them and do so with a closed mouth."

John turned to Faye, saying, "I'm sure there are other things you can do with your time, Faye, like find a hobby. I'm sure there are many groups in the community you can join. Aren't there sewing or knitting circles? Aren't there things like that in the community?"

"*Jah,* similar groups. I can still do things like that if I choose to."

"Women just aren't cut out for business," John said, sounding a little frustrated.

"That's just ridiculous!" Faye knew she had to sound firm.

"Faye!" her father said.

Faye didn't like upsetting her father. She was used to upsetting her mother because her mother was constantly confrontational. Her father, on the other hand, was normally quiet and very mild tempered. "I'm sorry, *Dat*."

"John is right."

John smiled when he saw he had Mr. King on his side. "How about this—I run the company for six months, and then we take it from there?"

Faye's parents looked at one another as though they were considering John's idea.

Faye knew she was outnumbered. Since she'd inherited the company, nothing would happen without her final decision, but she still wanted her family to feel involved. "Why don't I give that some thought?"

"That's the girl," her father said.

Her mother seemed pleased with the way things were turning out. "I'm glad you're starting to see sense."

"I thought you wanted me to run the company, *Mamm*," Jacob said.

"Maybe when you're older."

"But that's not what you said before Faye and John got here," Jacob persisted.

Her mother set her eyes on Faye, and said, "It's important that the company does well, and John has a lot of experience."

"I do, Faye," John said, staring her down.

When she had invited John, she never thought for a moment she'd be so ganged up on. Her idea had been they'd fight amongst each other. Timothy was the only one who believed in her. "As I said, I'll think about it."

Her mother leaned over and patted her hand. "I know you'll make the right decision."

"Pray about it," her father said.

"I will. I definitely will."

"Isn't anyone concerned about who killed Hank?" Timothy asked. "Aren't we overlooking that?"

Everyone remained silent. It was too painful for Faye to comment on. She still hadn't gotten over seeing him slumped in the buggy the way he had been.

Eventually, her father said, *"Gott* will judge whoever killed him."

"What if ..."

"Enough said, Timothy." *Mamm* scowled at him.

When dinner was over and the men moved to the living room, Faye helped clear the dishes from the table. As she was placing a pile of dishes into the sink, she felt herself fading and lowered herself to the floor.

"What's wrong, Faye?" she heard her mother say as if from a distance but she couldn't even answer.

When the feeling passed, she looked up at her mother.

"You're as white as a sheet. What's wrong with you?"

"There's nothing wrong. My husband has just died, that's why I'm like this."

"I'm going to take you to the doctor tomorrow."

"There's no need for that. I'm okay. The paramedics checked me out the other night, the night Hank died."

"I'm going to take you to the doctor, and that's that. You're not yourself. Take my hand." Her mother helped Faye to her feet. "Sit down at the table. Now about the doctor ..."

"If that will keep you happy, I'll go tomorrow."

"*Nee*, that won't keep me happy because I don't think you'll go unless I take you. I'm going to call and make an appointment and I'll drive you there myself just to make sure you go."

Faye nodded. "All right. But I'll call and make an appointment to go there after work tomorrow."

"*Nee*, I'll call and make the appointment. On second thought, you can stop by and collect me and I'll go with you."

Since her mother was using her 'no-nonsense' tone, Faye didn't even bother arguing. "Okay, *Mamm*. You make the appointment, then call the office and tell me what time you've made it. I'll stop by and collect you."

"That's the girl."

Faye sighed. "But don't make it too early or I won't go. I've got so much to do. I'm sure I'll be fine. I just need a good sleep. A good nine hours would make me feel normal again."

Her mother nodded. "We'll soon see."

"Don't mention that I'm going to the doctor to John or *Dat* or anyone. I don't want anyone to worry."

"I have to tell your *vadder*."

"Okay, but no one else."

Her mother nodded. "I'll take *kaffe* out to them and I won't mention a thing."

"And please don't talk any more about the business while John's here. Enough's been said."

"All right. I can see it upsets you. You sit there and don't move."

"I can't sit here when John's out there. It'd be rude."

"I'll get one of your *bruders* to take you home."

"*Mamm,* I'm okay," she said firmly. "I'll sit here for a minute and then I'll join them in the living room."

"You don't have to bite my head off." Her mother picked up the teakettle and filled it with water.

Somehow her mother always got the last word.

· · ·

ON THE WAY home in the darkness, Faye was more than a little nervous, hoping she wouldn't meet the same fate as her husband. From what the detective had said, Hank was murdered by somebody who wanted him dead; the killer knew him. It wasn't some random killing. She didn't know if that was better or worse.

All Faye could think of was Timothy's question over dinner. Who killed her husband?

CHAPTER 7

THE NEXT MORNING AT WORK, she looked up from behind her desk to see Mr. Lineberger walking into her office.

"Oh, this is a surprise."

"I mentioned at the funeral I'd stop by and see you."

"*Jah,* you did. Please take a seat." When he'd sat down in front of her, she swallowed hard. "What can I help you with?" She hardly needed to ask; she had a pretty good idea what his visit was about. Another person was going to try to take the company away from her.

"I'm here to help you with something. I'm here to make you an offer for the company. I assume it's now yours?"

"That's right, it is." At least there was someone who didn't have a hard time accepting that.

"Well, then I'm here to make you an offer."

447

"Thank you very much, but it's not for sale."

"I know you've got family working here. I'll keep all the same employees if that's what you're worried about. Well, I'll try to keep them employed as far as I can, but with merging my business with Hank's there's bound to be some layoffs."

"How can I be any clearer? Nothing is for sale."

He reached into his pocket and pulled out a business card. "My number's here in case you change your mind. It's a good idea that you sell, for everybody's sake."

She looked at the dark blue card with its white writing, and then looked up at him. "What do you mean?"

"Let's just say that selling to me might just be the safest for all concerned." His words had taken on a sinister tone.

"'Safest'?"

He nodded.

"I'm not sure I understand what you're saying."

"Hank ran this business and he ran it well. If someone's in charge who doesn't know what they're doing then things can head south pretty quickly. For instance, what do you know about health and safety requirements?"

She knew he meant for the factory where the workers used cutting and grinding equipment. "Nothing, but I'm sure there are rules and guidelines I can study up on. I'm used to working by the rules."

He shook his head. "It's not like baking a cake."

She rolled her eyes and didn't care that he saw her doing so. He was just the same as everyone else. All she wanted to do was be a success and run the company well. That'd show all of them.

He bounded to his feet. "I'll be in touch. Don't hesitate to call me if you change your mind."

"I won't." She stayed seated while he walked out of her office. When he was out of sight, she stood and hurried to the door of her office to make sure he walked directly out of her building, and to her relief he did so. She didn't want any competitors snooping about.

When she sat back down, she couldn't stop her mind from racing, trying to figure out who had killed Hank. Was it John, since he was so keen all of a sudden to step into his estranged brother's shoes? Or was it the jilted woman who'd wanted to marry Hank all those years ago? Or maybe it was Boris Lineberger since he was in direct opposition to Hank. Hank had mentioned Lineberger's name to her and she knew he was in competition with Hank, and Hank consistently won contracts over him. With Hank out of the way, maybe Lineberger figured he'd be able to build his company further.

She jumped when the phone rang. It was her mother telling her what time she'd made the doctor's appointment.

AFTER FAYE HAD EXPLAINED to her doctor what had happened and described her fainting spells, he suggested taking blood and urine samples, which they did onsite. Once she'd done that, they had her wait back in the waiting room with her mother. Twenty minutes later, she was called back into the doctor's office and she sat down in front of him.

"Mrs. Kirkdale, I'm delighted to tell you that you're pregnant."

She sat there as the words sank in. How could she be pregnant when Hank was dead?

Yes, it was possible, but in all four years of their marriage she'd never gotten pregnant and this was the worst timing ever. She'd wanted a child while Hank was alive. There was so much she wanted to do now, and how could she do that and raise a child at the same time? "Are you sure you didn't get my sample mixed up with someone else's?"

He smiled at her. "I'm quite sure. I know this is probably a mixed blessing to you after your husband's just passed."

"That explains why I've been feeling faint."

"That will most likely pass as your pregnancy progresses. I'll recommend you an iron tonic."

"Iron?"

"It'll take a few days for the other tests to come back, but I'm certain they'll confirm you're low in iron which explains the dizzy spells. You have to build yourself up and eat properly for the baby's sake."

Baby? She was going to have a real live baby. "It doesn't seem real."

"It *is* real."

Her thoughts turned to her mother in the next room. She could not let her know. If her mother knew she was pregnant, she would be even more overbearing, and she'd insist on someone else taking over the company immediately. If John found out, he would be just as forceful in trying to take it over. "Thank you, Dr. Long. Now I know what's wrong with me."

He smiled at her. "Pregnancy isn't an illness."

"No, it's not. I would like to keep it secret for a bit, though. Thank you." She stood up.

"I haven't finished yet." When she sat back down, he said, "I wouldn't be doing my job if I don't ask you if you've got an OBGYN."

"Everyone in the community uses the same two midwives."

"Home birth?"

"Yes. We have our babies at home. Not all of us, but most of us. Is there anything else wrong with me or am I just low in iron?"

"The tests will be back in a few days. If everything's okay, we should be able to let you know over the phone. Or, you might have to be called back in. We'll see. Call us in three days."

"I'll call first, then, before I make another appointment."

"Very good." He ripped off a piece of paper and handed it to her. "That's the tonic I suggest you take."

She took it from him and folded it in two. "Thank you; I'll get it."

"I hope you rethink having a home birth."

"Women have been giving birth that way for thousands of years. It's normal. As you just said, pregnancy is not an illness."

"Giving birth can bring with it complications. I'd like you to have an ultrasound at the very least. They're routinely done at around six to eight weeks of pregnancy."

"I don't know … how far along I am."

He took some time to work things out with her. Then he filled out a form. "Take this to the hospital. I've written the address on the top of the form. Call them first and make an appointment for two weeks' time."

"Okay. I might do that."

"Please do. It'll give you peace of mind. You and me both."

"Thank you, doctor." She walked out of his office. After she had paid the receptionist, she turned around to face her mother.

"All okay?" her mother asked, searching her face.

She nodded and together they walked out into the street. "I just have to get an iron tonic. That's why I've been dizzy."

"That explains why you're so pale, too."

"I'll get it tomorrow."

"*Nee.* We'll go to the pharmacy right now."

There was no use arguing with her mother. After their visit to the nearest pharmacy, Faye took her mother home. Needing to tell someone her news, she went straight to Rain's house.

Rain would be the only person she would trust with the news. When she arrived, Rain was in the middle of cooking dinner for her family—her husband and their five children. The oldest two girls were helping in the kitchen, so Faye had to whisper.

"I've got surprising news."

"What?"

"I've just come back from the doctor and I'm pregnant."

Her friend's eyes bugged out. "Faye, that's wonderful news!"

"Is it? I'm not so sure."

"This is what you've wanted for years."

"It's just that it's come at the very worst time. How am I going to raise a child by myself? I could, but I don't see how I can do that and run Hank's company successfully."

"You won't be by yourself. You'll have the whole community there to help you, and you'll have me."

Faye smiled and nodded. "*Denke,* I can always rely on you with everything."

"I'm so excited."

Faye smiled at her best friend's excitement and wished that she felt half the joy that her friend felt. "I'm not telling anyone just yet. You're the only one. It's like I had my life sorted out and I was going in one direction and just when I got comfortable, things changed, and then I changed my plans and after I just changed my plans, they changed again."

"Maybe you should just plan things less. One thing you know for certain is that the *boppli* will be coming in—how many months?" She looked over at her daughters. "Set the table now please, girls."

"The end of February. That's when the doctor worked out my baby will be born. It'll be cold," Faye said.

"Not too cold."

"It would be easier to have the baby in summer."

"It doesn't matter. Babies are born at all times of the year. Stop worrying about everything."

"It's become a habit, I'm afraid. And we still don't know who killed Hank and that's on my mind every day. I'm worried the police will arrest me. You know they think I did it?"

"Of course they don't."

"I think they do. They asked me why I changed my clothes and they put my clothes into a plastic bag and when I asked where my clothes were, they said they were 'in evidence.' Can you believe it? Evidence!"

"That's probably just the routine they have to do. Eliminate suspects, so they can find the real person who killed him."

"In my head, I know it's good about the *boppli,* but in my heart, I can't be happy until everything's resolved. I need to find out who killed him. The police said it must have been someone he knew." She bit her lip. "I can't have this hanging over my head. I'm scared all the time that I'm going to be next. Now I have to take care of my *boppli* and I don't want anything else bad to happen."

"We're finished, *Mamm,*" Rain's oldest daughter said.

"Okay, *denke.* Go and play and I'll call you when I'm ready to serve the meal."

The two girls ran out of the kitchen.

"Let's sit for a moment," Rain said.

When they were both sitting at the table, Faye said, "I'm sorry for coming over right at dinner time, but I've got no one else I can talk to. I can't tell anyone what's going on."

"That's fine. We can eat a little later than normal. Anyway, Ben's not even home yet."

Faye nodded.

"Now back to what we were talking about before. If it's someone Hank knew, it could be someone you know."

Faye bit her lip again. "I didn't think of that. Do you really think so?"

"I do. Perhaps I know him too."

"Will you help me? If we can put our heads together we could find out who killed him and then, once that's out of the way, I can feel safe again and enjoy my *boppli*."

"Okay, I'll help."

"Denke. I've thought about it a lot."

"Tell me. Do you have some ideas?"

"Do you remember Hillary—"

"Jah, I do," Rain interrupted. "She was furious that Hank ended their relationship. She was always strange. She was a lot younger than Hank, too."

"Everyone was younger than Hank. Anyway, you're right, she was upset when Hank ended the relationship, I remember that."

"Me too. Do you think she burned down his barn?"

Faye shrugged. "Hank was convinced it could've only been her. The fire investigator said it was deliberately lit. But then there's John to consider. Why would he turn up suddenly and want to take over the business? I thought that was weird."

"Hmm, that's two. Anyone else?"

"Jah, Lineberger."

"The *Englischer* who was at Hank's funeral?"

"Jah, him. He wants to take over. He wants to buy the company. And I said no, and he wasn't too happy about it."

"That's three suspects. You know, this might be dangerous, trying to find out who killed him."

"I didn't think of that. Don't help me. Forget I said anything."

"There's no harm in us just asking around and making a few inquiries, is there?" Rain asked.

"I guess not."

Rain smiled. "Then that's what we'll do."

"I don't want to put you in harm's way."

"If it gets dangerous, we'll stop."

Faye nodded. "That sounds good. I'm too tired to think tonight. Let's both think of a plan of what to do and meet again in a day or two."

"Okay."

CHAPTER 8

AFTER ANOTHER GRUELLING day of trying to learn where the business was at, Faye had just sat down to her dinner at home when she heard a car pull up in her driveway. Being hungry, she popped a large bite of chicken into her mouth and hurried over to look through the kitchen window. Detective Hervey was just getting out of the car, and another man was getting out of the passenger seat. By the look of the other man, he too was a detective.

She hoped they weren't there to arrest her. Maybe they thought she did it because of the bloody clothes that she'd taken off and left in the mudroom.

She opened the door when they knocked. "Hello, Mrs. Kirkdale, we're sorry for this late hour. We called earlier, but you weren't here," Hervey said. "This is Detective Wilson."

She nodded hello. "I was at the office."

"And we didn't want to disturb you there," the detective added.

"Thank you; I appreciate that. Come in." She stepped aside to let them in. "Have a seat in the living room." When they'd sat down, she asked, "Have you found out who killed Hank?"

"No, but we've been looking into some things that have provided a few names. Does the name Hillary Bauer mean anything to you?"

"Yes, I know Hillary. Hillary and Hank were together for a short time."

"The reason we ask is that over a ten-year period, your husband filed a few complaints against her."

"Did he? He never told me that."

"One was to do with a barn fire."

"That's right. He told me he thought she might have done that when he ended their relationship. And after that she was following him everywhere and sending him threatening letters. He didn't say he'd made official complaints, though."

"Then there was another serious incident a couple of years after the barn fire."

"Really?"

"Someone had attempted to burn down his barn again; they had doused it with gasoline. He walked in and caught someone fleeing the scene before they could do the job properly. Your husband claimed he suspected it was Hillary again."

"I had no idea." She jumped up when she heard a buggy approaching the house. "There's a buggy. I have no idea who that could be at this hour."

The detectives rose to their feet. "There are some more questions we need to ask, but perhaps you could come into the station tomorrow?"

"I could do that. What time? Can I do that at around five, after I finish work?"

Detective Hervey said, "How about you come in before work?"

"The quicker we move on things, the better," said Wilson.

"Okay. I'll be there around eight. Will you be there that early?"

"Yes. That's not early for me. I work all hours on a murder case."

Faye was pleased he was working so hard. "Thank you."

He gave her a smile, and somehow that gave her hope. Faye opened the door for the detectives to leave. They walked down the porch steps and headed to their car. Mrs. King gave the detectives a nod as she rushed past to her daughter.

"*Mamm,* what are you doing here?"

"I've come to see how you are."

"I'm fine."

"Have you eaten?"

"I was just in the middle of eating when the detectives arrived."

Her mother elbowed her out of the way and pushed her way inside. When she got to the kitchen, she looked down at Faye's dinner of chicken and vegetables. "Is this all you're having?"

"I already had some of it before the detectives got here."

"That's not enough."

"It's enough for me. Who's cooking for the boys?"

"They're looking after themselves tonight. I'm here to help you."

While Faye's mother fussed around in the kitchen, Faye sat down and finished her meal, all the while wondering if the police thought Hillary had some involvement in her husband's murder. They had to have, otherwise, why would they ask about her?

When Faye had finished eating, her mother pushed her out of the kitchen and into the living room, saying she'd make her a cup of tea.

How could she get rid of her mother? Then she heard an excited-sounding scream coming from the kitchen. *What in the world?* she thought as she jumped up and ran in to see her mother holding up one of the baby jackets out of her secret stash of baby clothes she'd knitted over the years.

"You're pregnant and you didn't tell me?"

She plucked the pale-yellow jacket out of her mother's fingers. "These are clothes that I knitted just to keep myself busy." She didn't want to tell her they had been knitted in the desperate hope of becoming pregnant.

"You are pregnant and you found out at the doctor's. You were quiet all the way home. Plus, I had that dream."

Faye opened her mouth to speak, but the words wouldn't come out. Her mother had to find out sooner or later. Finally, she said, "Okay, *jah*, it's true, but I don't want anybody else to know just yet. It's too soon and I don't want a fuss made."

"When did you find out?"

"You were right. At the doctor's."

Her mother screamed again and pulled her into her arms for a bear hug. "Oh, I'm so excited! The first of my *grosskinner!*"

Faye gasped for air. "Enough, *Mamm,* I can't breathe." After a few breaths, she said, "Remember, I don't want anybody else to know yet—no one, *Mamm.*"

When her mother finally left a few hours later, Faye wondered how many people her mother would tell. *Mamm* was never good at keeping secrets. It would only be a matter of time now before everybody in the community found out.

AFTER A FAIR NIGHT'S SLEEP, Faye went to the police station to see Detective Hervey.

"Thank you for coming in."

"Well, you asked me. Or rather, you told me to come. I didn't think I had a choice."

He looked at her strangely and she knew she'd been too rude. "I'm sorry we didn't get to finish what we were saying last night. My mother never stops by so late at night."

"I need to confirm with you who the beneficiaries of your husband's will are."

"He left everything to me."

"Everything?"

Faye nodded.

"What we didn't get a chance to tell you last night was that Hillary Bauer wasn't the only person your husband had filed complaints about."

Faye looked at him in surprise. "I don't know what you mean."

"Are you familiar with a man with the last name of Lineberger?"

"Yes, I know him. Hank had known him for a long time. They used to work together and they were friends."

"Yes, we're aware of a long association your husband had with Lineberger. Lineberger had been in and out of prison during the last few years on various charges. One time for forging checks and the other on embezzlement charges."

An image of Lineberger came into her head. He had certainly seemed like an honest man. "I had no idea. I just thought he was a businessman." He hadn't mentioned any violent charges, she noted.

"A very busy and industrious one it seems."

"He was at Hank's funeral, and he stopped in at the office and said he wanted to buy the company."

"I think what he's trying to do is get the company into his name somehow without paying for it. I wouldn't have any dealings with him if I were you."

"I won't. Thanks for warning me." It made her think about John's offer. She was sure John wouldn't try to swindle her and he'd be aware of sketchy business dealings and people who were out to defraud.

The detective leaned back in his chair. "Mrs. Kirkdale, you're a small fish swimming in a sea of sharks."

A shiver traveled up her spine. Although she had never been in love with Hank, she'd felt much safer when he'd been around. Learning that she was carrying a child and was now responsible for another life made her feel vulnerable. "That's kind of what I feel like. I feel like everyone's trying to keep me from taking charge of my company."

He suddenly lurched forward. "Someone else besides Lineberger?"

"Oh, it's nothing drastic. It's just that my mother wants my brothers to be involved with the business and she wants me to stay home and do nothing. She doesn't think a woman should run the company."

"Is there anyone else who's offered to buy you out?"

"Only Hank's brother."

"John Kirkdale?"

Her heart sank. She was just starting to trust John, and it scared her that the detective knew of him. Was he, too, a criminal? "Yes, John. Do you know him?"

"Only because we questioned Hank's entire family after Hank's murder."

Relief washed over her. "Of course."

"And what was your response when your brother-in-law asked to buy you out?"

"The same response as I gave to Lineberger—the company is not for sale."

WHEN MID-MORNING CAME, the last person Faye expected to see walking into her office was Rain.

"Hi! What are you doing here?"

Rain lingered by the door, and then she stepped into the office. "I thought about what we said about doing a little investigating."

Faye raised her eyebrows. "Sit down."

Rain sat opposite Faye with Hank's large desk in between them. "I figured we could start off with Hillary. So I found out where she works."

"Before you tell me that, I need to let you know I had a visit from the detective last night and right away he mentioned

Hillary." Faye told her some of what the detective had said, and then asked, "Where does she work?"

"She works at a restaurant in town and I found out she starts her shift today at three. I thought we could accidentally bump into her at the parking lot before she gets to work."

"And do what?"

"I'm not sure. We could see what she has to say. See if she looks guilty."

"She didn't look guilty when I ran into her at the farmers market. But she still has that weird look to her eyes."

"We have to try something." Rain tapped her fingertips on the wooden desk. "Should we say something about Hank's barn fire, then?"

"*Nee*. I think that would be a bad idea. It was so long ago. *Denke* for finding out where she works, though. I should be able to slip away just before three today."

"*Gut*."

"What about your *kinner* getting home from school?"

"The older ones can be in charge. I told them I might be late getting home."

Faye remembered looking after her four younger brothers when they came home from school. Her mother was often out visiting or had long days at quilting bees and wasn't there when they arrived home. In larger families, the older siblings helped look after the younger; that was just the way it worked in an Amish family.

Rain said, "I'll get back here around two thirty then, and we can go together."

Faye nodded. "*Denke,* Rain. The police had more to say when they came to my *haus* last night. And this morning when I met with them at the station."

"What else did they say?"

"I forgot to tell you they asked me again if I could think of anybody else, besides Hillary, who might have killed Hank. I didn't want to name the people we discussed, but they knew about Lineberger and they had spoken with John already."

"Why didn't you want to name them?"

"Because not all of them are guilty. Maybe one of them is, and maybe not, but if the police ask them anything, they'll all suspect that I think they did it."

"I see what you mean. That would be awkward. Anyway, I'll see you back here this afternoon?"

"Jah."

LATER THAT DAY, Rain pulled up her buggy near the parking lot of the restaurant where Hillary worked, and both of them stepped out.

"What time is it now?" asked Rain as she secured the horse.

"It's a quarter before three."

"I wonder what time she arrives."

"How did you find out what time she starts today?"

"It wasn't easy. I found out from Elizabeth Yoder that she works here. Then I called the restaurant yesterday afternoon, pretended I was a customer who liked her service, and asked what time Hillary was working today."

"Ah, very clever."

"*Denke*. I thought so too. They had no problem telling me what time."

Faye shifted her weight from foot to foot. "What are we going to do? Are we going to just walk up and down the parking lot, or what? I don't want it to look like we're waiting for her."

"I found out from Elizabeth that Hillary drives a blue and white car, so as soon as we see that color car approaching the lot, we'll start walking up this way." Rain pointed up the street. "And then we'll act surprised to see her, and we'll call out."

Faye nodded. "Okay, but you'll have to take the lead in the conversation. I've got no idea what to say. And no running back to the buggy this time. I'm not comfortable doing this on my own."

"Okay. Leave it to me."

They were only at the lot for five minutes when an old blue and white car chugged into the parking lot.

"That must be her. Let's go." Rain pulled on Faye's sleeve and they started walking. Then they saw Hillary get out of the car and their eyes met hers.

Faye watched a man get out of the driver's seat after Hillary had gotten out of the passenger seat. The man was strangely familiar. She'd seen him before, but where? She couldn't remember.

Hillary waved, then said something to the man who walked away without looking up at them. Then Hillary called out, "Hello."

They walked over to her. "Hello, Hillary."

"What are you two doing around here?"

"We're just out doing a bit of shopping. What about you?"

"I work in that restaurant just there."

Faye turned to where Hillary pointed. "It looks nice."

"Actually, we've just finished shopping. We were shopping for tiny clothes because Faye's pregnant."

Faye couldn't hold in a large gasp. Rain knew not to tell anyone. Let alone the woman who had almost certainly burned down her baby's father's barn.

Hillary glared at Faye. "Is that true?"

"*Jah*, it is. Although, it's too early to tell people at the moment."

Rain's fingertips flew to her mouth. "Oh, sorry Faye. I forgot! I shouldn't have said anything."

"That's okay," Faye said, hoping her friend had just blurted out that information out of nervousness.

"Well, that is a surprise. You're not even showing at all."

"It's only in the early days."

"Yes, she's not due until February," Rain commented.

"And the baby is Hank's?" Hillary inquired through gritted teeth.

"Of course," Faye said. "I only found out just days after he left."

"You mean, after he died."

"He left to go home to be with *Gott*—that is what I meant."

Hillary continued to glare at Faye. "No matter how the Amish sugar-coat death, dead is just plain old dead."

"Either way, he's not here," Faye said. Not wanting Hillary to be envious of her, she added, "I'll have to raise the baby alone."

"At least you've got something and you won't be alone. I'll have to go right now or I'll be late for work." She stomped away, and said over her shoulder, "Congratulations."

"Thank you," Faye called back. Then Faye looked at Rain and they both grimaced before they headed back to Rain's buggy. Hillary had been much nicer, Faye thought, when she'd bumped into her the day before the funeral. "Why did you have to tell her I'm pregnant?"

"It's the truth."

Faye stopped in her tracks. "Wait a minute. Did you plan this all along? Did you deliberately goad her by telling her I was pregnant with Hank's child to see what she'd say in anger?"

"*Nee,* of course not. I don't know why I said it. I'm sorry."

"That's okay. But we didn't really find out anything."

Rain started walking again and put her arm through Faye's. "We found out that she's still in love with Hank and always has been, and thus she's envious of you."

"But that doesn't mean she hated him and wanted to kill him."

"Maybe, and maybe not. They say there's a fine line between love and hate."

"I better get back to work. I can do another hour's worth before it's going-home time."

Rain drove Faye back to work.

CHAPTER 9

TWO NIGHTS LATER, Faye arrived home worried. How was she going to learn to run such a large business? Ronald, the office manager, was a good help, as were the other office staff, and none of them seemed put off by her being a woman, but she was worried Ronald would soon lose respect for her since she had come into this with no idea what she was doing. She was a fast learner, but there was a lot to learn.

With her baby coming, she didn't even know if she could keep up with the stress of working in Hank's business. Why was she struggling so hard? What would it matter if someone else took over the place? Maybe John was the best person to do that. She went into the kitchen to heat up some leftovers and suddenly she saw two bees at the window. Not believing her eyes, she took a closer look to see if they weren't large flies. No. They were definitely bees!

When one took flight, and flew directly for her, she screamed and ran out of the room. She knew she could die if she got stung, so she ran upstairs and shut herself in her bedroom. And then realized she'd left her EpiPen downstairs. It was times like these it would've come in handy to have a man in the house, or a cell phone. A man could get rid of the bees. It wasn't easy being single. Reminding herself she'd be both mother and father for her baby, she knew she'd have to practice being brave and doing everything herself. She'd been given a fanny pack to keep the EpiPen in and had done that for a while. Now she knew she'd have to wear it all the time. And she'd talk to her bishop about getting a cell phone, so she could call 911 if anything happened. Every second counted.

She opened a closet and pulled on one of Hank's suit coats. It covered her entire upper body once she turned the collar up, and the sleeves hung low and covered her hands. Seeing a towel over the chair, she grabbed it and covered half her face with it so only her eyes were peeping out. And then she pulled on a pair of Hank's trousers. They were far too big, so she tied them at the waist with her dressing gown cord, and then rolled up the legs so she could walk.

The bees couldn't sting her with all her body covered. With nearly every inch of her body covered in fabric, she trudged downstairs, summoning courage to get the bees out of the house. When she walked into the kitchen, a shiver traveled up her spine when she saw they'd left the window.

An idea occurred to her. If bees were the same as flies and mosquitoes, they'd travel to the light. She lit a lantern, opened the front door, and placed the lantern on the porch. Back in the kitchen, she took out a large flat kitchen spatula to swat them if they came near her. Then she saw they were back by the window. With a firm hold of the spatula, she pushed at them with the end of it to encourage them outside. One of them darted at her again, and she screamed and ran outside. As she ran down the porch steps covered in Hank's large suit and with the towel around her head, she was relieved to see a car.

Then she worried that the person in the car was Hank's murderer. Which was worse, facing the murderer or facing the chance of being stung by the bees?

She was relieved to see John jump out of the car. He took one look at her and burst out laughing. "What on earth have you got on?"

Pointing the spatula toward the house, she said, "Bees."

He took a step forward, frowning. "What?"

She yanked the towel down to uncover her mouth. "Bees in the *haus.*"

Then his face straightened and his eyes went wide. "Stay back." He headed into the house.

Everyone in the community had heard about her near death from a bee sting. The bishop had announced to everyone the importance of her staying away from bees, and if she was stung she was to be rushed to the nearest hospital. She was relieved that John remembered.

He came out a moment later. "Where did you see them? And how many?"

"In the kitchen. There were two." As he headed back in, she yelled after him, "Near the window."

He was gone for a couple of minutes and then he came back outside. "I opened the window and they flew out."

"The both of them?"

"Yes."

She sighed with relief. "Thank you, thank you so much."

"You're allergic, aren't you?"

"Yes, I am." Tears rolled down her face. Everything was overwhelming. She was suddenly alone in the world, trying to run a business she knew nothing about, and now the surprise pregnancy. How was she expected to do it all? She dropped the spatula she'd been clutching and covered her face with her hands. She didn't want to cry in front of her brother-in-law, but she couldn't help it.

He stepped closer. "It's okay, they're gone. Come inside." He put his arm around her shoulder and walked her inside. When he'd sat her on the couch, he asked, "Have you had something to eat?"

She shook her head. "I was going to heat up some leftovers."

"Sit down, I'll do that for you. Are they in the fridge?"

She nodded. "I've got no idea how the bees got into the *haus*. It's been closed up all day."

"Shall I go around and check all your doors and windows?"

"Yes please." While the food was heating, he checked the doors and windows.

She suddenly grew nervous. What if he was the killer and he'd come back to kill her? But why would he get rid of the bees if he was trying to kill her?

Faye closed her eyes and prayed. If it was God's will that she go to meet Him now, that she go home, then so be it. Right at that moment, she didn't care what happened to her, but now she had her unborn baby to care for. She put her life and the life of her baby in God's hands.

He walked back into the kitchen. "There's nothing open. But we need to see about getting screens on all of your windows, and probably on your doors. The bees must've come in when you opened the door this morning."

"But there's nothing with flowers around the house, I make sure of that. There's nothing to attract them. There aren't even any weeds. Hank and I kept all the weeds and everything down because of the allergy."

"How did you first know that you're allergic?"

"It wasn't my first bee sting. I'd been stung by bees before and it hurt but that was it. It was the third time, and I broke out into hives and then started to have trouble breathing. There was a doctor in the park who recognized the reaction. He and his wife rushed me to the hospital, and Jacob had to run home and tell my parents I'd been taken to the hospital."

"What happened at the hospital?"

"They told me later my blood pressure was dropping, and my heart rate was spiking. They say you'll never have a bad reaction on the first bee sting. Something to do with the body creating antibodies, and my body has too many and overreacts to the bee venom. I have to carry an EpiPen with me everywhere I go. They told me my next bee sting could kill me."

"That's dreadful."

"How did you know I needed you just now?"

He chuckled. "I felt dreadful about how I pressured you earlier. I stopped by to tell you that I'm sorry. It wasn't my intention to upset you." He cleared his throat. "I also heard today that I'm going to be an uncle."

"How did you hear? I only told a couple of people and I asked them to keep silent."

He shook his head. "It seems everyone knows. And my parents will find out sooner or later."

She'd have to tell Hank's parents. She wasn't looking forward to that and for some reason it hadn't occurred to her to tell them until John had just mentioned it. Of course, they'd want to know because her child would be their grandchild. "I'll tell them soon. I guess I'd better do that right away if the word is out."

He nodded. "When I heard the news, it made me realize something."

"What's that?"

"I've been chasing money and that's not really important. What's important is family. I left the community at a young age wanting to make something of myself. I had a yearning, a deep yearning that I had to be successful. Today, I had an epiphany. You make something of yourself the moment you let go of needing to make something of yourself." He shook his head. "Everything that I thought was important isn't."

"And how did you realize this?"

"When I heard the news that my brother—my late brother—was having a child. I realized that's what I want. I'm going to change my life and come back to the community."

It pleased Faye to hear the news. "That's a big decision."

"Well, I need to make big changes. I've never been scared of facing challenges. I made myself a new life once before, and I can do it again."

She realized that she was hoping he was going to propose to her. She had always been able to sense something between them. Perhaps she would've married him if her mother hadn't forced her to marry his older brother. Maybe the next thing was he'd ask her to marry him. Her baby would have a father, and how perfect would that be that her baby's stepfather would also be his or her uncle? There would be such a bond.

"And you know what else, Faye?"

"What?" Her heart thumped in anticipation of a proposal. Of course, he'd have to take the instructions and be baptized before they married.

"I think I've burned your food." He jumped up and raced to turn off the oven.

She sniffed the air. And then she laughed at herself for getting carried away. "I think you have, but we can't open the windows or those bees will fly back in."

"I won't open the oven door either, or smoke will fill the room. I'll take you out for pizza."

She looked down at herself in Hank's old clothes and with the towel still draped about her neck. "Looking like this?"

He chuckled. "Why don't I bring a couple of takeout pizzas back? It won't take long."

"Thank you, I'd like that."

"I'll be less than half an hour."

When he drove off, she headed to the shower. The least she could do was make herself look presentable for her dinner guest. She was pleased he was coming back to the community. Even though he hadn't asked her to marry him and probably had no intention of doing so, at least her child would have an uncle on his father's side who was in the community.

THE NEXT DAY was the day to call the doctor for her blood test results. When they wouldn't give her the results over the phone, Faye started to worry. What if she had something seriously wrong with her? She was far too young to die. There were things she wanted to do and experience in her life, and besides that, she didn't want to have an illness where she would linger and be a burden to others. She made an appointment for that very day.

Her mother had forgotten she had other tests results coming in. She'd been too busy being delighted about becoming a grandmother. Faye's baby would be her mother's first grandchild.

After waiting three quarters of an hour in the waiting room, the doctor gave her the all clear. Faye was more than relieved, and on the way home she stopped by Rain's house to tell her about the altercation with the bees.

"DON'T YOU SEE, FAYE?" Rain asked, as they sat drinking hot tea in the kitchen. "The bees were placed in your house by Hillary."

"How?"

"I don't know. She probably had one of those insect catchers that children have, or she could have caught them in a jar. Did you lock your door?"

"I lock it when I'm inside, but I don't always lock it when I'm out. Do you really think she did that?"

"*Jah,* she was angry that you're pregnant. That's what she wanted—to be married to Hank and have his *kinner.*"

Faye slowly nodded. "She killed Hank in a rage, and then she tried to kill me?"

Rain nodded.

"Why not stab me, too?"

"The police are already on her trail. That's what you said, and she wouldn't want to give them more reason to think she did it. You should tell the police about it."

"Do you think so?"

"I do. I'll come with you. You should go there now."

"It's late. The detective's probably not working at this time."

Rain bounded to her feet. "Let's call him from the barn."

Faye called the detective and made an appointment to see him that night, and then told Rain she'd go by herself.

With her pregnancy, Faye was growing increasingly tired. It was either from that, or from working every day trying to fill Hank's shoes. Or maybe a good bit of both.

SHE WAS SHOWN into the detective's office when she arrived at the station.

He looked up when she walked in. He stood up and reached out his hand. When she shook it, he said, "What can I do for you?"

"Firstly, are you any further ahead in your investigations?"

He shook his head. "I'm afraid not. Please take a seat."

She sat down. "When I got home yesterday afternoon, there were two bees in the house." After she took a deep breath to settle her nerves, she looked up at his blank face. "I'm deathly allergic to them and everyone who was in the community when I was around fifteen knows that I nearly died when I was stung by a bee. I came way too close, and the doctor said the next sting could kill me."

"I'm sorry, but I don't know where you're going with this."

"A friend of mine thought that someone might have done that deliberately."

"Put bees in your house to bite you?"

"Sting."

"What? Oh. Pardon me, to sting you?"

Faye nodded. "It might sound silly. I suppose it does, but I told my friend what happened and she was insistent that I tell you."

"Who knows about your allergy?"

"Everyone who was in the community when I was fifteen and was old enough at the time to remember it."

"That would include Hank's half-brothers?"

"Yes, it would, and it would include Hillary Bauer."

"I see where you're going with this. You think Hillary put bees in your house?"

"Possibly."

"Why would she wish you harm? Your husband's gone so it wouldn't be to get back at him."

Faye took a deep breath. "I just found out that I'm expecting and I don't think Hillary's happy about it."

"How did she find out?"

"My friend and I bumped into her and somehow my friend blurted it out."

He clicked on the end of his pen. "What's the name of this friend of yours?"

"Her name is Rain Hersler."

He jotted the name down and then looked up at her. "Tell me what happened yesterday from the time you arrived home."

She told him everything that had happened, including how John arrived unexpectedly and saved the day.

"He arrived just in time to eradicate the bees?"

"The bees weren't harmed. He opened the window and they flew out."

"Interesting." He jotted a few more things down. "You should really have window screens, with that allergy." Then he looked up at her and smiled. "Congratulations, by the way."

"Oh." She giggled. "Thank you. It was a surprise."

"Has John been stopping by regularly?"

"*Nee,* he never stops by, but I was sure pleased to see him."

"Hmm. And how long has Rain Hersler been your friend?"

"For as long as I can remember. Why?"

"I'm just getting a broad picture."

"Rain wouldn't have anything to do with Hank's murder."

He put his writing pad down and looked across at her. "Have you seen any more of Lineberger?"

"I haven't."

"What about John's brother?"

"Silas?" she said in a startled tone.

"Yes."

"No, I haven't seen him since the funeral. Do you suspect him?"

"We've had to talk with everyone who was close to Hank. Starting with close friends and family. Although, we haven't found it easy to get information from those in your Amish community."

"Oh, I'm sorry." He never answered her question directly and she wondered why. She made a mental note to tell Rain about that. "I'm not sure whether I should've told you about the bees or not. I don't want to waste your time."

"You're not wasting my time. We need to explore all avenues; we never know which piece of information will turn out to be important."

"That's good. I'm glad."

AFTER A PARTICULARLY GRUELLING episode with Ronald, the office manager, Faye was nearly in tears. It was so hard juggling so many things, from the staff to overseeing orders and the quotes, plus a dozen other jobs. She closed her office door, picked up the phone, and called the phone in Rain's barn, hoping she'd be close by to answer it.

"Hello?"

"Rain!"

"Hi, Faye. Is everything okay?"

Faye sniffed back tears. She felt guilty for not being deliriously happy about the baby, and guilty for not having been in love with Hank. "I don't know if this is what I want anymore—to run this business."

"This is what you wanted before, so don't let a *boppli* change your plans."

"But it does."

"Don't make any decisions until you feel better. Why don't I move in with you for a couple of days?"

"*Denke,* but *nee,* it's okay. I'll get over it. I'm just so tired. How am I going to do everything?"

"You'll take the *boppli* to work with you, or you'll get a nanny to work a few hours a day."

"I don't know."

Rain gave an exasperated sigh. "Well, just give your business over to John to run, then."

"I might have to. I don't want to, although I don't see any other way around things right now."

"Something's got to give and you don't want it to be your health, or your *boppli's* health."

CHAPTER 10

WHEN FAYE GOT to work a gruelling week and a half later, she was expecting another typical day. Mid-morning was when she checked the calendar and realized what day it was. It was the day she was supposed to have her ultrasound. She'd been so busy trying to keep her head above water in the office, she'd forgotten completely.

She had to be there at eleven o'clock. She found Ronald and told him she would be going out for a while. There was just enough time to get there by taxi.

When she walked into the hospital, she had no idea where to go. As she was looking around, she saw Hillary and a man who was with her. The same man who had been with her in that blue and white car outside the restaurant. They got into an elevator and the door closed.

She hurried to the elevator and watched the red digital numbers. It stopped at floor two. She pressed the button and the elevator returned and the doors opened. They'd definitely gone to level two. She stepped into the lift and read the directory. Floor two was the oncology department. She was pretty sure that was for the cancer patients.

Did either the man or Hillary have cancer? Which one? She pressed the button to floor two after she got in the lift, and the doors closed. When the elevator doors opened, she was faced with a blank wall; she could either go left or right. She chose right and walked a little way, and then to her left was a large room. She saw that it was the chemotherapy treatment room. She had an uncle who'd had cancer and she had gone with him to some of his treatments to keep him company. She had a quick look into the room and then ducked back around when she saw a nurse setting Hillary up for treatment while the man leafed through a magazine. She ducked back so no one could see her.

"Can I help you there?" She turned around to see a man wearing blue scrubs. He was either a nurse or some kind of orderly.

"Yes, I'm lost. I've come here to have an ultrasound."

"You'll need to go to the floor below, level one."

"Thank you." She smiled at the man and hurried back to the elevator.

. . .

SHE FOUND her way to the place she was supposed to be and minutes later cold gel was moved across her abdomen, and she was having an ultrasound performed.

"CAN you tell whether it's a boy or girl yet?"

"Not at this early stage. Maybe in the next ultrasound."

"I'll only be having this one ultrasound, if everything's okay. I don't think I'd want to know anyway."

"Your baby looks just fine, Mrs. Kirkdale. You'll get the official report from your doctor."

Faye was relieved and a tear trickled down her face. "Thank you."

Rather than heading back to work, she stopped at Rain's house to tell her what she had seen on the second floor of the hospital.

"ARE YOU SURE?"

"I am. It was a chemo treatment room. I've been in one before. It was a different hospital but I know what they look like."

"So, Hillary has cancer?"

"Yes, and who was that man with her?"

"That's obviously her new husband."

"I guess that makes sense. I just wish I knew where I've seen him before. Can you go back to Elizabeth and find out everything you can about Hillary and her husband?"

"She's going to wonder why I'm asking her all these questions."

"I don't care. I don't care if it looks suspicious; make up a reason if you like. And remember to tell me every little thing she says."

"Okay, I'll go now before the children get home from school."

"Thanks."

When Faye arrived back at work, Silas was sitting in her office behind her desk going through paperwork.

"Silas."

He slowly looked up at her. "Faye, nice of you to show up for work."

She walked towards him. "I've been here every day. I had an urgent appointment to get to." Feeling she needed to explain her absence, she said, "For my baby."

"Yes, I heard about that. That's why I'm here. You're going to need help and I'm here to give it to you."

"Help?"

"I'll give you two choices. We go fifty-fifty. You give me fifty percent and I'll run the company and you'll get half the profits. Option two is that I'll buy you out."

"I told John and I'll tell you, the company is not for sale."

"I was hoping you would say that. I can always take it from you and then you won't get a cent."

She stood there staring at Silas, wondering whether he had killed his half-brother. Hank must have been killed for money, she figured, and specifically for his company. The murderer had to be someone who wanted it, and she was standing in the murderer's way.

All of Hank's family would've thought the business should go to one of Hank's brothers on his passing. But surely the killer would've found that out beforehand.

"You're in my seat," she said, standing her ground.

"Did you hear what I just said?"

"How do you think you're going to take the company from me?"

"Declare you incompetent. That'd be easy, and perhaps you are even insane if you think you can run a company like this with no experience. Anyway, you won't get a cent from my brother's estate when they prove that you killed him."

Her mouth fell open at his words. "How dare you say a thing like that to me? You probably did it, and you're upset that Hank didn't leave the company to you and John."

"If you cooperate with me, I'll help you with the police."

"I don't need help with the police and I don't need help with the business." That wasn't completely true; she probably needed help with both, but not from him.

Now Silas was on the top of her suspect list. She wondered what the police had found out about Silas. "Who let you in here?"

"I just walked in."

"Does Ronald know you're here?"

"I sent him off on an errand."

"What?"

He nodded.

"You've got no right to order my staff about."

"They need and want to follow a man, not a woman, and especially not an Amish woman."

"Leave now, or I'll call the police and have them drag you out."

He raised his arms. "I'm sorry, I think we got off on the wrong foot. Let's start again."

"Let's not. Get out!"

Without taking his eyes off her, he slowly rose to his feet. The cold, cruel look in his eyes turned her insides to stone. She did her best not to let it show how much he scared her.

"I'll give you a day or two to think things over and then you'll say what I say make sense. None of the staff wants you here," he continued. "Except your useless brothers."

By this time, he was halfway across her office floor. "Get out!" she yelled.

He slowly walked out the door without looking back. When she had watched him all the way out of the building, she sat down on the chair behind her desk, relieved that he was gone. And then his words came into her mind. What if it was true that none of the staff wanted her there? Who would want to follow a boss who didn't know what they were doing? The thought occurred to her that maybe John had sent Silas to be horrible and that way John's offer would seem that much more attractive. Were Hank's two half-brothers in this together?

She hoped that John was for her and not against her, as she was starting to develop feelings for him. But were they real feelings or were they feelings born out of her vulnerability, since she was suddenly alone and pregnant? Did she see John as an answer to her problems, a substitute for Hank?

All she knew was that she couldn't rest until she found out who had killed Hank. Until the police found out who did it, she would be unable to trust anybody. She felt like she was on a fast-moving conveyor belt taking her from one disaster to another. She closed her eyes and took a couple of deep breaths and then she picked up the phone and called Detective Hervey to report what had happened and to see if there had been any new developments.

CHAPTER 11

THE DETECTIVE WAS OUT, so she left a message for him to call back. Just as she was about to go through the next stack of paperwork, an image of Hillary's man came into her head. Aha! She remembered where she had seen him before. A couple of years ago, he had knocked on her door asking questions about Hank, saying he was looking for a man who was adopted into the Amish. She gave him the address of Hank's parents. A couple of days later she had a conversation with Hank's stepmother who hadn't been too pleased to get a visit from this man asking her questions surrounding Hank's background.

Was Hank adopted? And could his birth family have anything to do with his murder?

Just when she was leaving work for the day, she got a call from Rain. "Hello, Rain. Did you talk with Elizabeth?"

"I did, and I found out a lot. I described the man who was with Hillary, and Elizabeth said that that's her husband. And the restaurant where Hillary works—she owns it, that one and several other restaurants. She's a very wealthy woman. The husband who died owned a string of restaurants and she inherited them."

"Really? That is interesting. If they're rich, why were they driving that old beat up car?"

"Elizabeth said they collect rare vintage cars. That must've been one of them."

"Oh." Faye didn't know one old car from another and neither did Rain. "Anything else?"

"Isn't that enough?" Rain asked.

"*Jah,* it's quite a lot. *Denke* for finding that out. Does Elizabeth know that Hillary's sick?"

"She didn't mention it, so I didn't bring it up."

"That's best." Faye told her friend about Silas' visit and him turning nasty. Then she told Rain of her theory about Silas and John being in it together.

"Have you told the police any of this?" Rain asked.

"*Nee.* I called the detective earlier and left a message for him to call me back. But I worry that it's just a whole jumble of things and nothing concrete. Silas and Hillary might have nothing to do with Hank's murder. What if the police were wrong and it was just a random killing?"

"I don't know, but that's for the police to figure out."

JUST WHEN FAYE had gotten into her house, John arrived and knocked on her door.

"John, come in."

Am I letting a killer into the house? She decided not to mention Silas' visit and see if John mentioned it.

"How have you been?"

"Fine."

"Have you eaten?"

"I'm just making myself some dinner. You can join me."

"No, I won't keep you long. I just wanted to tell you that I've spoken to the bishop. I'm tying up a few loose ends over the next few days and I'll be back into the community next week. I'm taking the instructions and being baptized. I'll be a fully-fledged member of the Amish community before you know it."

Now all suspicion of him went out the window. He was really doing this, not just talking about it. "Really?"

He nodded.

"That makes me so happy."

He chuckled. "Me too. It hasn't been an easy decision and I know there will be hardships along the way and big adjustments to make, but I know I'm doing this for the right reasons—"

"What reasons?"

She wondered if she was one of those reasons—that's what she hoped.

"I want to live the best I can, for myself, for others, and for God. I figure that is more reasonable service, since God gave me this life. There's so much suffering and so much pain everywhere I look. It'll be hard for me to give some things up, but I'll be gaining so much more. I want a family and I couldn't imagine having a family in the world and raising children in a society that's collapsing. I want to raise my children within the structure of the community."

She nodded.

He continued, "And to think your child will be my children's cousin. That's a good start."

She forced a smile, but inside she was crushed. He wasn't seeing her as a potential wife at all. At least now she knew for certain. "It looks like you'll have a busy few days ahead of you."

"You've got no idea. I hardly know where to start."

They stared into each other's eyes for a moment, before he said, "I'll let you get back to your dinner." He turned around and walked out the door.

She took a couple of steps and put a hand on the front door.

He turned around. "Please let me know if you want anything, or if I can do anything for you."

"*Denke,* I will."

She watched while he got in his car and drove away.

IT WAS at the Sunday meeting that Faye came face-to-face with Hank's stepmother. Faye took the opportunity to ask her about the visit from that man, Hillary's husband.

"Do you remember a few years ago a man came to your door asking about Hank and adoption?"

She raised her head. "I do. The man that you sent there. Did you think Hank was adopted, or something?"

"*Nee,* I never had cause to think that at all. The man came asking me questions about Hank and whether he was adopted, and I said to my knowledge he wasn't. Then he asked for your address and I saw no harm in giving it to him."

"He wasn't adopted," she snapped.

"I didn't say he was, but do you remember anything about the man, anything at all?"

"No. Like what?"

Faye shook her head. "I don't know. I thought about it the other day, that's all. It was odd that someone would come around asking questions like that."

"I suppose he was just a man searching for his family."

"Did he say it was for his family?" Faye asked.

"From what I recall, he said he was searching for his wife's brother and that he'd been adopted into an Amish family."

"That's interesting."

If that man had been telling her the truth, that meant that Hillary had an adopted brother within the Amish. Did that mean Hillary was adopted as well? Who would she ask? Hillary's parents had long since died.

Faye rushed across the yard intending to report her findings to Rain, but before she got there, John signalled to her.

Then he walked toward her.

"Hi, John. How did you enjoy your first meeting back?"

"*Wunderbaar.*" He chuckled.

"I'm glad."

"I'll have to get used to speaking Pennsylvania Dutch again."

"That won't be too hard since you were raised speaking it."

"I guess. Where are you hurrying off to?"

"Oh, just to talk to Rain."

"You and Rain were always so close."

"She's been my best friend as long as I can remember. I only have brothers, so she's like a sister to me."

"Really?"

She studied his face. The way he said it was as though it wasn't a good idea to be Rain's friend. "Why do you say it like that?"

"Oh, nothing."

"Do you know something I don't know?"

"About Rain?"

She nodded.

"I've just always thought it's best to have a lot of friends rather than just one friend. If one friend disappoints you, it doesn't matter so much because you have so many others. But if you only have one friend and she disappoints you then you have no one." His eyes bored through hers as if he was giving her a hint about something and didn't want to say something negative about Rain.

Now she felt like she couldn't trust anybody. "Silas came to see me at the office the other day."

"Did he?"

"Did you know he was coming to see me?"

"I haven't talked to Silas since Hank's funeral."

"He wasn't very nice. He seemed to be threatening me or something."

John frowned. "What did he want?"

"He wanted me to give him half of the business, and he'd run it and he said we'd split the earnings."

A wave of fury covered John's face.

"Then he wanted … I don't know. It's just everyone has so many demands on me lately I just don't know whether I'm coming or going." She rubbed her eyes, realizing she was close to tears.

He put a hand on her arm. "Sit down, Faye. You've had far too much pressure on you." He led her over to a chair. "Can I get you something to eat?"

She nodded and looked back at the large table of food and all the people who were helping themselves. She had no energy to get any food for herself. "If you could just get me a little something I would appreciate it."

"Stay here, I'll be back."

She thought how good it would be to have him for a husband, so he could look after her.

On her way home, her horse pulled the buggy through the streets while Faye thought of the empty home that awaited her. Sunday was one day when Hank had been there.

There was never much traffic on a Sunday when she drove the buggy home from the meetings and Faye was surprised to hear cars zooming behind her. She glanced over her shoulder and saw two black cars. One overtook her and was so close that her horse jumped to one side, causing the buggy to lurch too. The next car accelerated and clipped the back of the buggy. That's when she knew these cars were only out to harass her. Then the car honked the horn and clipped the buggy again. She pulled the buggy over off the road and the car zoomed off. She tried to see who was driving but the windows were darkened.

Her horse's neck was held up and his ears were turned back. She waited a while until both she and her horse were calm. Making sure there were no cars around, she got down to inspect the buggy, the horse, and the harness. When she saw everything was okay, she patted the horse and spoke to him in soothing tones in an effort to calm him. The black cars had meant to frighten her and they'd done just that.

When she climbed back into the buggy, Lineberger came to mind. He'd threatened her. Maybe it was he who'd sent the people in that car to give her a warning.

As soon as Faye turned the horse out into the paddock, she picked up the phone in the barn to call the detective. What was he doing about finding Hank's killer? Not much, it seemed. She'd been living in fear since he'd been killed and she couldn't take it anymore. Each day she drove home half expecting that someone might jump into her buggy and stab her. Either that or in fear she'd arrive home to a house full of bees.

She called the detective's cell phone. When he answered, he sounded like he'd been having a nap.

"Hello, Detective, it's Faye Kirkdale."

"What can I do for you?"

"You can find my husband's killer," she snapped. "Now someone's trying to kill me. I was harassed by two black cars. One just missed me and the other hit me from behind deliberately—twice. I'm sure it was something to do with Lineberger, that man who's trying to buy me out. He said something about me being foolish and I might be in danger if I didn't take his offer."

"Are you injured?"

"No."

"Did you get the plate numbers?"

"I didn't even think of that." Faye felt stupid for not doing something so simple. "Anyway, what have you been doing about finding who murdered Hank?"

"We've been working on it and following up leads."

Faye gave an exasperated sigh. "It's not good enough. I live every day wondering if I'll be next. I'm having a baby soon and I'm worried about my child's safety. I want you to find the killer before I give birth."

"I had forgotten you were expecting."

"Well, I am."

"We're doing all we can. Do you have any new information?"

At the risk of sounding silly, she also told him about Silas' visit to the office and about Hillary's illness and Hillary's husband's visit to her some time ago inquiring about whether Hank might have been adopted.

"Leave it with me," was all that he said.

"I've been leaving it with you for too long." She slammed the phone down, and then picked it up and called a taxi. She opened the phonebook and found the address of Hillary's restaurant, and then she found Hillary's home address. She'd try her home first and then confront her about this adoption business and find out what was really going on. Tomorrow, she'd work out what was going on with Silas.

She arrived at Hillary's house and knocked on her door. She listened to heavy footsteps as they approached the door.

"Oh. Hello. I hope I've got the right place. I'm looking for Hillary Bauer. I suppose she has a different last name now."

"That's my wife."

"Is she home?"

"She's at one of our restaurants."

Before she could stop herself, she said, "Isn't she sick?"

"Yes, but she won't stop working until she drops. That's just who she is." He studied her. "Have we met before?"

"I don't know."

"Hillary knew you when she was Amish?"

"That's right."

"She should be home any minute. Come in and wait for her."

"Thanks." When he stepped back, Faye walked in.

He showed her to the living room and sat with her.

"I remember now. We have met before," Faye said. "You came to my door asking questions about my husband."

"You're the lady whose husband was just murdered?"

"Yes."

"I'm so sorry. Hillary told me about it. She knew him quite well."

"I know."

"The reason I was asking questions was that when Hillary found out about her illness, she wanted to leave half of everything to the older brother her parents had adopted out the year before she was born. I did some research and found out it was Hank. I'm sorry if you didn't know that, but he was the right age, and the only man in the community born in that month."

Faye realized that if it was true, it explained Hank and Hillary's sudden break up. Maybe Hillary didn't know that Hank was really her brother—he found out somehow and that's when the break up occurred. It seemed Hillary didn't find out until years later. "It must've been an awful shock for them."

"That's right, they had been dating. She told me that, but she had no idea. Now she knows why he ended their relationship. He must've found out."

Faye was right and Hillary must've been heartbroken and that drove her to set fire to his barn. Then Faye thought more about the likelihood that Hank had been adopted. His parents hadn't been married that long before he arrived. "I doubt you've got the right man. Hank can't have been adopted."

"He was."

She shook her head. "I can't see how it makes sense."

"I met with his stepmother, and she pretended she didn't know anything about it, but I found proof."

"What proof?"

"It's in the garage. Would you like to see it?"

"Yes." She followed him in, figuring she'd see perhaps a letter, or some kind of document.

When they were both in the garage, he pointed to a plastic carton. "Over there."

As she started walking toward it, she realized she'd seen him somewhere else too. He was the paramedic—the one who'd given her those pills the night her husband died. She whipped around to face him.

He had his two fists up and in between them was a cord. She tried to duck away, but he managed to slip it around her neck. He was pulling it tight—strangling her. *He's Hank's killer and tried to kill me that night.* She realized the tablets he'd given her weren't sleeping tablets; they were some kind of poison. It would've looked like she killed Hank and then poisoned herself. A nearly perfect crime, but she hadn't taken those pills.

She couldn't let him get away with it.

An image of her baby came into her mind and she knew she had to fight for her baby. Her hands went to her throat in an effort to loosen the cord. When that didn't work, she tossed and turned, trying to hit him or elbow him but she couldn't get at him. Her vision started going black and sparkly at the edges. Everything faded. In the distance, she thought she heard the siren of a police car, but it was going to be too late.

WHEN SHE OPENED HER EYES, she saw she was in bed surrounded by white. A familiar face appeared from out of nowhere and looked down at her. Was it Hank? Was she dead? A second later, she knew it was John and she knew she was alive. Her fingers went to her aching throat. It felt like it was on fire. She realized her neck was loosely wrapped in something cooling, and that seemed to be helping.

"Don't try to speak," he said.

She closed her eyes and the scene played out before her. Hillary's husband had tried to kill her. The pieces of the puzzle fell into place. Hank's murderer wasn't Silas, or John, or even Hillary. It was Hillary's husband.

Hillary was wealthy and searching for her brother. It seemed her husband didn't want to share her wealth with anyone else, so he had to murder Hank before Hillary died. Then when Faye hadn't died from those pills, he tried to kill her with bees in case Hillary's will wasn't changed before she died from the cancer. Bees would have looked like an accident, she figured.

Then he laid low for a while before his next attempt on her life, and she had obligingly stepped right into his lair.

When she opened her eyes again, she saw Detective Hervey standing next to John. She told them about the pills and the paramedic.

"We have him in custody. We'll need you to testify about what he did to you."

She nodded as best she could. "My baby?" she asked in a croaky voice, reaching down to her belly.

"The baby's fine and the doctor said you are, too. They did an ultrasound to be sure. You just need to rest," John's deep voice reassured her.

The detective confirmed everything she'd already figured out. Except for the fact that Hank wasn't Hillary's adopted brother. "We did some checking and there was a baby boy adopted by an Amish family. He was born in the same year and month as your husband, but he died at two years of age from a fever."

"Oh, that's so sad," she whispered.

"Hillary's a very sick woman—terminally ill."

"I know." Then she heard a squeal. She looked over to see her mother hurrying toward her.

The detective stepped back. "Her husband also admitted to taking a knife from your house to kill your husband with. And we found those pills you told us about. If you'd taken them, you wouldn't have lasted the night. They were cyanide—a deadly poison."

A chill ran down her spine that someone—a killer—had been in her house and she'd never known. If she'd taken those sleeping pills, she would've died and her unborn child would've died along with her.

"I'll stop by again tomorrow, Mrs. Kirkdale."

"Thank you," John said to him.

"What happened, Faye?" Her mother scurried over to her.

John told her mother everything.

"Oh, you poor thing, Faye." Her mother leaned over and smoothed back her hair just as she used to do when she was a small child.

Faye closed her eyes.

"I'll go now," John said.

Faye raised her arm. *"Nee,* please stay."

"I'll stay as long as you want."

"Can I have water?"

He poured a glass of water and helped her sit up. After a couple of sips, she asked, "How did the police find me?"

"Hervey figured it out from what you told him. He went to your house and when you weren't there he knew you'd gone to confront Hillary and her husband. You shouldn't have gone there alone."

She nodded. She knew that now.

"You could've been killed."

"My *boppli* and I are safe."

"Your *vadder* is worried and waiting by the phone in the barn. I'll call him and tell him you're all right."

"*Jah*, I'm okay."

Her mother used the phone in the room to call her husband, and while she was busy, Faye turned to John. "How did you get here?"

"I had just arrived at your house when the detective pulled up. He told me where he thought you were and I went in the car with him."

If only her mother wasn't there, this would be a perfect time for him to ask her to marry him. Then her life would be complete.

Her mother placed the receiver down and stood between the two of them. "When will you be coming home?"

"I don't know."

"She'll be here overnight," John said, "and the doctor said she shouldn't speak too much."

"You'll have to come back and live with us, Faye."

"*Nee*. I've got my own home. The danger's gone."

"You always were a stubborn girl."

"Don't speak so much, Faye," John told her.

She closed her eyes, in no mood to listen to her mother's reprimands.

"Well, if you're not going to talk to me, I might as well go," her mother said.

"Jah, she'll be okay. I'll wait with her until she goes to sleep."

"Denke, John. I do have the boys at home."

"She'll be fine," John said.

Faye's mother leaned over and kissed her on the cheek. "Bye, for now. Call and let me know when they let you leave."

"Jah, Mamm," Faye whispered. She watched her mother walk out the door, glad that she'd come, and now relieved that she had gone.

"The doctor said you'll be hoarse for a while, but the baby's just fine, so don't worry.," John said.

"That's all that matters."

"Is your throat sore?"

She nodded. "Hurts bad when I swallow."

"Try not to talk. *Gott* spared you. The doctor said a moment later and you would've died. I'll sit here with you for a while."

She nodded.

"Do you want me to wait until you fall asleep before I go?"

She nodded again and silently thanked God.

"It's nearly midnight. The nurses should be back to check on you soon."

She closed her eyes and hoped she'd feel better in the morning and then her life would get back to normal. Perhaps not normal, but at least she'd be free from the fear of being killed, since they'd arrested Hank's murderer.

WHEN SHE OPENED her eyes the next morning, the first thing she saw was John beside her, asleep in the chair. His head was leaning too far over to one side and Faye hoped he wouldn't wake with an ache in his neck. She pushed herself into a seated position and helped herself to water. It still hurt when she swallowed.

He woke up and smiled at her. "Good morning."

"Hello."

She couldn't believe that she had once suspected him of murdering Hank.

"How are you feeling?"

"I've been better."

He chuckled and then rubbed his neck.

"*Denke* for staying here."

"I had nothing better to do, since you won't let me near Hank's business."

"I might need some help. A little bit."

"I'll give you all the help you want. Now don't talk."

When a man in a white coat walked in the door, John said, "Here's your doctor. I'll wait outside."

He examined the wound around her throat and looked at her chart. "You'll be sore for a while, but you're all right to go home. I'll give you a script for some anti-inflammatory painkillers that are safe to use during pregnancy, and if anything changes for the worse I want you to go to your own doctor."

"I can go home?" she whispered.

"Yes. They've told you that your baby is unharmed?"

She nodded, a tear in her eye.

The doctor gently patted her hand and then left, and John came back into the room.

"I can go home."

"Good. I'll drive you."

"Can you call Rain and tell her ...?"

"*Jah,* I will. I'll do that now."

JOHN DROVE her home and walked her inside.

516

"Faye, you're going to need someone to look after you."

Of course she would, and he was just the man to do it. She smiled at him, waiting for his marriage proposal.

"Can you stay with someone? Perhaps you could stay with your *mudder* for just a while. You look so pale."

Her heart sank. He meant look after her in the short term. "I'll feel much better here in my own home."

"Then I'll have no choice but to check on you every day. Please don't tell me you're going to work."

"I've been thinking about that. Perhaps I could use a little help."

"Really?"

She nodded.

"At last you see sense."

"I said 'a little.' I'll still be in charge, since it's my company."

He chuckled. "Now, what can I do for you before I go?"

Faye didn't want him to go at all. "I've got hardly any food in the house. Can I give you a grocery list and you take it to Rain?"

"I'll do it. I'll get it now."

"I can't—"

He held his hand up to shush her. "You can't talk, remember?"

She nodded. "Okay."

"Shh."

She giggled. And stopped short, because that hurt, too.

When she had written out the list, she handed it to him.

"Denke. It's times like these I miss my car. I could've zipped down and zipped back with the shopping. Now it's going to take half a day." He looked back at her and smiled. "I'll enjoy the ride with the fresh air in my face."

She nodded so she wouldn't get into trouble for speaking. When he left, she walked into the kitchen and took out the baby clothes from their hiding place. She looked at each piece in turn, imagining what her baby would look like. They hadn't said if this ultrasound had showed the baby's sex, and she didn't want to know.

BEFORE JOHN CAME BACK with her groceries, Rain arrived. Faye was pleased to see her friend, but had hoped to have more alone time with John.

Rain rushed in to see her and Faye told her, in as few words as possible, everything that had happened. Just like Faye had thought, Rain was still there when John came back with the food. Then he left soon after.

CHAPTER 12

FOR THE NEXT SEVERAL WEEKS, Faye kept her distance from John as far as she could except at work. The John at work was all business and there was no conversation that was of a personal nature. She was having a baby and he was being integrated into the Amish. The day of his baptism, she thought she should say something. She was now at a point where everyone knew of her pregnancy as she was so large she couldn't conceal it.

"Hey, John."

"Hello, Faye. How have you been?"

"Good."

"Good."

It was an awkward start.

"I've been worried about you," he said. "I haven't been near you because I wanted to give you space."

"I figured that. I've been doing the same for you."

"Oh. Well, that's good."

"Good all 'round then." She smiled at their funny talk about nothing in particular.

"Have you thought about what's going to happen with work when you have the *boppli?*"

"I'll bring the *boppli* to work with me."

He frowned. "Is that being practical?"

"What do you suggest?"

"I suggest that I do more and you do less. I'll run every big decision past you. I know you don't want to give up control."

"I guess I could take a back seat for a few months, but I'd need to know everything that's happening."

"That seems like it would be best for you and everyone."

"We should talk more about that tomorrow," Faye said, not wanting to talk about business on a Sunday.

He nodded and she walked away. At least her mother had stepped back from trying to force her to have one of her brothers run the company, now that John was on the scene. Now Faye knew that John was interested in the business and not her. He'd had plenty of opportunity to express himself before now. If he hadn't proposed to her by now, he likely never would. There were so many single young women in the community and they outnumbered the men. He'd most likely choose one of them to settle down with. Seeing him at work every day while he was married to someone else would be hard.

A thought occurred to her. Perhaps he thought it was too soon after Hank's death. If she shared with him that she'd been forced into the marriage, maybe that would make a difference. That is, if he liked her in that way at all.

She glanced back at him and saw two young women approach him. Then she looked down at herself with a wry smile. Not many men would think of courting a widow who was heavy with child.

Then a funny thing happened. He looked around as though he was looking for someone, and when their eyes met, he smiled at her as though he'd been caught out. He was looking for her to see where she'd gone. At that moment, she knew for certain that he liked her. But if that was so, why wasn't he doing anything about it?

For the next several weeks, Faye had no choice but to exercise patience, which wasn't easy for her. Patience awaiting the arrival of her baby and patience waiting for John to propose, or at the very least suggest they do something together outside of work.

With Rain's help and her mother's help, Faye had everything ready for the baby's arrival. As each day got closer to her due date, Faye got increasingly sadder that her baby wouldn't know its father and that Hank wouldn't ever hold his baby.

As Faye sat behind her desk in her office, her mind drifted to how her life might be different if Hank was still alive. Now, Hillary's husband awaited trial, and Hillary was pondering returning to the community for her remaining months. So much had changed in the past year, Faye mused, and now her life was completely different. Silas had moved away, which Faye was pleased about, and Faye had grown closer with Hank's step-mother.

Her baby was due any day now and Faye had to wonder why she was hanging on to Hank's business. John had offered to run it, so why didn't she let him? Perhaps it was because she didn't like to be told she couldn't do something. She'd proven she could run the company adequately, with help, yes, but still she ran it. Could it have been pride that made her insist on doing everything herself? She placed her hand over her stomach when she felt a kick, and knew the most important thing was her baby, more important than anything.

In that moment, she decided she would step back and allow others to do things. John could take on the top management position. He was doing most of the work anyway and she always turned to him now before making decisions.

"Good morning."

She looked up to see John. "Hello. I need to talk to you about something."

"Good. Me too. You go first."

He sat in front of her and she had a horrible thought. What if he was leaving? What if he was getting married to someone else?

"You go first," she said, holding her breath.

"*Nee*, you."

"You're not telling me you're leaving, are you?"

"Never. Okay, I'll go first." He looked around, then he jumped up and closed the door. "I've been doing a lot of thinking and praying."

"About what?"

"About you and your *boppli.*"

"Oh."

"I want your *boppli* to have a *vadder*, and someone needs to look after you. I was wondering if you might consider marrying me?"

She smiled. It was what she'd wanted for so long, but not quite the way she wanted it said. He mentioned nothing of his feelings for her. "Out of duty?"

"*Nee.*"

"You're doing me a favor?"

He gulped. "I would like us to marry. I would like very much to be married to you."

She wanted him to say he loved her, but what if he didn't feel that love? If she ever were to marry again, there would have to be love on both sides. "I will only marry again for love."

He looked down. "Oh, I'm sorry. I thought …"

"Thought what?"

"I didn't think, I hoped … I hoped you might feel something for me."

"I do, I do."

He looked up at her. "You feel something?"

Now she could see in his hopeful eyes that he loved her. "I do."

"Like?" He was smiling now.

"I do like you and perhaps a little more."

He rubbed his chin. "You love me?"

"I can't say that until …"

He walked around to her side of the desk. "Until what?"

She shook her head and a large lump formed in her throat. She couldn't speak.

"Faye, I've been so frightened to say how I feel about you. I want to be in your life, and I thought if I told you how I really feel, you'd reject me and feel awkward around me." He took a large breath and kneeled down in front of her. "I still want to be in your life as your friend if you reject me. I need to tell you that

I love you and want more than anything for you to be my *fraa*. I want to be *vadder* to your child, not just *onkel.*"

She needed to make sense of it all and wondered if he'd loved her years ago before he left the community. "When did you start feeling this way?"

"When I came back and saw you after Hank died, I knew I should've never left in the first place. I had a burning desire to make something of myself back then and didn't know what love was. I liked you back when I was a teenager, but never showed it. I thought nothing of love or how rare it was. Now that I have a chance with you, I don't want to let you go. Unless you don't feel the same. If you don't, I'll still be the best *onkel* your *boppli* will ever have."

Faye giggled. Today was possibly the best day of her life. "I have so many brothers, my *boppli* will have no shortage of *onkels*. What my *boppli* needs is a *vadder*."

He smiled. "And what do you need, or what do you want?"

"You."

"Really?" He took hold of her hand.

She held onto his hand, squeezing tight. Tears rolled down her cheeks as she nodded.

He leaned forward and with his free hand he wiped her tears away. "Will you marry me, Faye?"

"*Jah*, I will."

He kissed her on her forehead. *"Denke."*

A stabbing pain thrashed across Faye's lower abdomen. "Oh! The *boppli's* coming."

"Now?"

"Soon. I need to call the midwife."

"I'll do that for you and then drive you home."

As he fussed about looking for the midwife's number, Faye smiled. She had someone she loved to look after her and her baby, someone to love them.

EIGHTEEN HOURS LATER, Faye held her baby in her arms. Rain, Faye's mother, and the midwife gathered around as Faye looked down at the baby girl. Faye had already told them the news about marrying John.

"What will you call her?" her mother asked.

"I don't know yet."

"Are you really marrying John?"

"Jah, I am."

"We'll get everything cleaned up so he can come in and see you," Rain said.

The midwife added, "The poor man must be exhausted after waiting downstairs all this time."

Faye thought that a weird thing to say. After all, she had been the one having all the agony and doing almost all of the work.

"When John comes in, can everyone leave us alone?"

Everyone agreed and minutes later, John walked into the room. "How are you?"

"Fine. Look at our little girl."

He stepped forward slowly. The baby opened her eyes. "Look at her. She's so beautiful." Tears filled his eyes.

"She is." Faye kissed her on the top of her bald head. "I can't believe she's finally here." She looked up at him. "Don't change your mind."

He chuckled. "I won't. I feel like I'm the most blessed man in the world. I'm back where I belong and I've got something I've always wanted, a wife and a child. We'll marry as soon as we can. When I leave here, I'll go to the bishop and make all the arrangements."

"Okay."

"Can I get you anything?"

She shook her head. "Everything I ever wanted is right here in this room."

He leaned forward and kissed her cheek. "I love you, Faye, and I love our child."

Faye knew he was going to treat her daughter as his very own. "Here, hold her. You pick a name for her."

"Me?" He carefully took the baby from Faye and cradled her in his arms.

She smiled at the sight. *"Jah,* you decide on her name. I'll have to like it, though."

"Of course. How about Faith? Faith in *Gott* brought me back to you and got me through hard times."

"I love it. Faith Kirkdale."

TWO MONTHS LATER, Faye and John married and moved into a new house so they could start afresh. Throughout the first year of their married life, Faye was involved in the business, but as their family grew over the next five years with two more children, a boy and then another girl, Faye was more content to stay at home.

John came home every night in time to have dinner with them, and even after years of marriage he never stopped being attentive and loving. John was the husband that Faye had always hoped for and she thanked *Gott* every day.

Thank you for reading this Volume 5 Omnibus of the Expectant Amish Widows series.

For a downloadable/printable Series Reading Order of all Samantha Price's books, scan below or head to: SamanthaPriceAuthor.com

THE NEXT OMNIBUS

The next Omnibus set is Volume 6 which contains:

Book 16 Amish Widow's Trust

Book 17 The Amish Potato Farmer's Widow

ABOUT SAMANTHA PRICE

Samantha Price is a USA Today bestselling and Kindle All Stars author of Amish romance books and cozy mysteries. She was raised Brethren and has a deep affinity for the Amish way of life, which she has explored extensively with over a decade of research.
She is mother to two pampered rescue cats, and a very spoiled staffy with separation issues.

Samantha Price
www.SamanthaPriceAuthor.com

Made in the USA
Middletown, DE
28 June 2024

56537694R00319